The Baltimore Chronicles Saga

The Baltimore Chronicles Saga

Treasure Hernandez

www.urbanbooks.net

Urban Books, LLC
97 N18th Street
Wyandanch, NY 11798

ISBN 13: 978-1-60162-564-9
ISBN 10: 1-60162-564-2

First Printing October 2013
Printed in the United States of America

10 9 8 7 6 5 4 3 2 1

This is a work of fiction. Any references or similarities to actual events, real people, living or dead, or to real locales are intended to give the novel a sense of reality. Any similarity in other names, characters, places, and incidents is entirely coincidental.

Distributed by Kensington Publishing Corp.
Submit Wholesale Orders to:
Kensington Publishing Corp.
C/O Penguin Group (USA) Inc.
Attention: Order Processing
405 Murray Hill Parkway
East Rutherford, NJ 07073-2316
Phone: 1-800-526-0275
Fax: 1-800-227-9604

Baltimore Chronicles

Volume 1

Treasure Hernandez

Chapter 1

The Take Down

Detective Derek Fuller splashed water on his face, took a deep breath, and looked up at himself in the small, dull mirror that hung in the men's bathroom inside the station house. He noticed the bags that were starting to form under his eyes, but he knew those came with the territory. Fighting against the Maryland drug trade was not an easy win. Shaking off his jitters, Derek stared at himself. He thought that despite those bags, his smooth cinnamon-colored skin and chestnut brown eyes still made him a fine-ass dude.

Refocusing, Derek spoke to himself. "Let's get it, niggah. This ain't no time to have second thoughts." He checked his gear, shifted his bulletproof vest, and shrugged into his raid jacket. It was six o'clock in the morning, and he had to get into the right state of mind for the task at hand. Walking back out into the squad room, he put on his game face.

"I hope everybody is ready for Scar. Let's fuckin' roll and take this nigga out. This mufucka only thinks he's the leader of the bitch-ass Dirty Money Crew," Derek announced to the four officers who comprised his unit. They all stood at attention and started gathering their battle gear.

"Yo, Fuller, can I bring this baby with me?" Officer Rodriguez asked, picking up the brand new MP-5 they had just acquired. The big weapon looked out of place in the petite woman's hands. To the average eye, she would appear weak and out of her element, but Fuller had come up in the academy with Rodriguez and knew never to underestimate her. She had the gumption that most men never mustered, and she was an asset to his team. He trusted Rodriguez with his life, and in the game they played, that meant a lot. She never hesitated to pull a trigger, and if he was the first man through the door, she was always right behind him.

"Damn straight," Derek replied, flashing his perfect smile and leading his unit out the door.

Derek felt powerful in his new position as a lead detective with the Baltimore Narcotics Unit of the Maryland State Police. Living and working in the roughest part of Baltimore, Derek had put in work, moving up from a car-chasing, ticket-giving state trooper to a narcotics street officer, and now leader of his own narcotics interdiction unit. Derek's unit was charged with taking down the so-called Dirty Money Crew and their notorious leader, Stephon "Scar" Johnson.

Everyone in the Baltimore area knew about Scar and his powerful drug ring. He ran cocaine up and down the interstate with ease. On top of that, he was a jack of all trades. He had his hand in everything from extortion and illegal gambling to prostitution. If there was money to be made in the underworld of B-more, then Scar was getting it. Scar had been reigning terror on the streets for years now. He was considered the Rayful Edmond of Baltimore; only difference was he didn't get caught. He deemed himself untouchable and moved like a ghost through the streets, getting money but going unseen most of the time. Rumor had it that on his climb to the top, Scar had taken out ten police officers and two government officials; but with no proof and witnesses who always turned up dead or missing, it had been an almost impossible undertaking for the over-matched and undermanned state troopers to touch Scar.

That did not stop Derek's unit from pursuing Scar. Derek was aware of what he needed to do to prove himself to his bosses and the crime syndicates in the streets. His success as a detective depended on the attention he would receive for taking Scar down.

As Derek and his unit arrived at their destination in the worst hood in Baltimore, Derek shook his head and smiled. It was just like the confidential informant had told the unit; Scar was making a very rare early morning creep appearance at one of his most lucrative trap houses. When Derek noticed Scar's tricked-out black Escalade, complete with its candy paint job, parked on the side of the trap house, Derek felt his dick jump in his pants. He was that excited by this opportunity to shine.

"Here we fuckin' go!" Derek mumbled under his breath, geeking himself up for the task at hand. His heart was beating so fast that it threatened to jump out of his chest. He turned to Cassell and asked, "You got the warrant?"

"Signed, sealed, and delivered," Cassell replied, revealing an edge of the warrant from out of his breast pocket.

Some would say he was being overcautious with the warrant, but Derek wasn't about to make the same mistake twice. A few years back, due to his recklessness, he had busted a local drug dealer without a warrant. Needless to say, the drug dealer was set free. That incident didn't help his reputation within the police force, and he had worked hard to gain back respect.

Satisfied that everything was in order just how he'd planned it, Derek was ready for the raid. Yanking his Glock out of his hip holster, Derek barely put his vehicle in park before he swung the door open and jumped out. He waved his hands over his head, placed his fingers up to his lips, and made a fist, signaling his unit to get into their rehearsed raid positions.

They all silently exited their black Impalas. Ducking low, they fell in line one behind the other and stacked on the door. Derek was first in the stack; he would announce their arrival. The ram holder stood on the opposite side of the door, and the rest of the unit knew their roles in bringing up the back of the stack. Derek raised his right hand and silently counted down. Three, two, one.

At that, the ram holder sent the heavy duty metal crashing into the shabby plywood door. The wood splintered open with one hit. Inside, bodies began scrambling in all directions.

"Police! Police! Put ya fuckin' hands up now!" Derek screamed, waving his weapon back and forth, pointing it at all of Scar's scrambling workers for emphasis. All of the members of the unit trampled inside, grabbing whomever they could and tossing them to the ground.

Derek continued into the house with his gun drawn, keeping his back close to the walls. He had his eye on the prize, and he was not going to stop until he had it in custody. Derek came to a closed door at the back of the house. With his gun trained on the door, he kicked it open.

"Damn, man, put the gun down. You ain't gotta go all hard and shit," Scar said calmly as he exhaled a cigar smoke ring in front of him, poisoning the air surrounding him.

Derek shook his head. He needed this take down to be as dramatic as possible, and Scar's laid-back attitude wasn't helping.

"Put your fucking hands up, mu'fucka!" Derek screamed, pointing his gun right at Scar's head. "Now! Show me your hands!"

"A'ight, a'ight. Calm down, cowboy," Scar said, smirking and stubbing out his cigar on the table he sat behind.

Derek was getting more pissed by the minute. He didn't want to look like a punk in front of his unit, while Scar was looking cool, calm, and collected.

"They pay you to act all extra?" Scar asked, still smiling.

"Let's go! Stand the fuck up, niggah!" Derek barked again.

"I got one better for you. I will put my hands out so you can cuff me." Scar chuckled, his smile causing his severely disfigured charcoal-colored face to contort into a monstrous mug. Pushing away from the table, Scar lifted his six foot three inch gorilla frame up from the chair. Laughing like he had heard a joke, Scar turned around and assumed the handcuffing position.

"Cuff this son of a bitch!" Derek spat as one of his officers moved in swiftly to lock the cuffs on Scar's thick wrists.

"Son of a bitch? Ain't that the pot calling the kettle black?" Scar replied, still laughing.

Derek grabbed the cuffs roughly, making sure they were clamped extra tight so the metal would cut into Scar's skin and shut him up. That would teach him not to play games. There were just some things that shouldn't be said in front of the members of the unit. No need to arouse anyone's suspicions.

Derek led Scar out of the house, and just like he had planned, the media trucks and cameras were right on time to get coverage of the raid.

"Detective Fuller, how did you do this so smoothly when no other law enforcement units could take down the notorious Stephon 'Scar' Johnson?" a female reporter yelled out as Derek rushed passed her with Scar in tow.

"It was all in a day's work," Derek wolfed out as he pushed Scar's head down into the back of the police car.

Derek looked and felt like a hero. He had taken down the big, bad drug kingpin. He could not contain his proud smile. He was the man.

Derek and his unit pulled into the prisoner drop-off area in the back of the station house and unloaded Scar and some of his crew.

"Ay, man, when all the pomp and circumstance is done, maybe we can break bread, you know, have a drink and shit," Scar said, smiling at Derek mischievously.

"Nah, buddy. You'll be breaking bread with your fellow inmates soon enough," Derek said smoothly, slapping five with some of his unit members and walking away, leaving Scar to be processed.

Derek continued to crack jokes with his unit as they proceeded to the front of the station house. Pushing open the door, they were surprised by the way they were greeted. It was like the other officers and staff at the station house had planned a surprise party. They all stopped to turn and see the unit enter, and they were cheering and whistling loudly.

Derek could not contain his pride. He loved the attention, especially when he noticed Chief William Scott standing in front of the uproarious crowd. The chief stepped forward, placing his hands up to quiet the cheers so he could speak. He loved to hear himself speak.

"Here they are, the untouchable Baltimore Narcotics Unit. They have done in one day what every other law enforcement agency in Maryland and the feds have tried to do for years. Led by one of the finest detectives in state trooper history, Derek Fuller," Chief Scott announced, placing one hand on Derek's shoulder and grabbing his other hand for a firm handshake. The crowd of state troopers and administrative staff erupted in cheers again.

Derek bowed his head slightly, trying to act modest, but he loved the attention. He basked in it. It was what he had waited so long for, to be considered great.

He returned the chief's handshake. "I couldn't have done it without the best unit around—Rodriguez, Bolden, Archie, and Cassell. Thank you all for being brave soldiers. This take down was only possible because of the hard work of every member of my team. We have all dedicated countless man hours in the pursuit of justice, and now today is our day," Derek said for good measure. In his head, he was thinking it was all him. Little did they know that he could have singlehandedly taken Scar down, but that was a secret he would have to keep.

"Come down to my office, Detective Fuller. I want to speak to you," Chief Scott leaned into Derek's ear and whispered as the crowd began to break up and surround the other unit members.

Derek's heart jumped in his chest. Everyone knew that it was hard for a black man to get ahead in the Maryland State Police. The fact that this white chief, who was known to be a redneck, wanted to speak to him alone made Derek feel important. It was all working out exactly as he had envisioned it.

He followed the chief downstairs to his office, where Chief Scott offered Derek a seat on his famed leather couch—another rare occurrence. Usually an invitation to Chief Scott's office was only for troopers to get an ass-chewing or disciplinary action taken against them. Derek knew this time would be different.

Chief Scott slid his fat stomach behind his desk, put a finger full of chewing tobacco into his cheek, and looked at Derek seriously. "Detective Fuller. I don't call many people to my office for compliments, but what you did today was beyond remarkable. Taking down one of the biggest bastard drug lords the state of Maryland has ever seen was more than a simple task. Those fucking DEA federal bastards couldn't do it this long with all their corrupt agents and payoffs. You have exceeded any expectations I had ever dreamed of for your unit, and for that, I commend you."

Derek leaned back and smiled. "Thank you, sir."

"Detective Fuller, I truly think you have what it takes to be higher up in the department one day . . . maybe even sit at this desk as chief," Chief Scott said seriously, spitting his gooey, chewed-up tobacco into a can on his desk.

Derek was glowing from the accolades he was receiving. “Well, Chief, I appreciate the compliment. I just want to work hard and continue to make you and the department proud. It took months of surveillance and lots of footwork on the streets,” he said, continuing the act he’d been performing all day, “but at the end of the day, that bastard Scar Johnson deserved to go down. I’m just glad it’s over.” Derek stood up from the couch. “Now, after I finish the paperwork, I’m going home to my family, who I have neglected for the last six months. I’m sure my wife will be happy to see me,” Derek said. Just thinking about his beautiful woman made him smile again.

“I’ve seen your wife. I would be on my way home too,” Chief Scott commented with a smile, sending Derek on his way.

Derek turned his key in the door to his modest single-family home, and he could already smell the aroma of his dinner wafting through the house. He loved his wife so much. She was a triple threat—a good mother, a working professional, and a damned good wife. “Hello?” Derek called out and then waited.

“Daddy! Daddy!” he heard his kids screaming as they ran toward him at top speed. They were not used to him being home at night. Most of the time, he would come in after a long stakeout and they would already be asleep, so his presence was a welcome surprise.

“Ay, baby girl and my big man,” Derek sang, picking up his two-year-old daughter and rubbing his six-year-old son’s head.

“We saw you on the news today!” his son announced proudly, holding onto his father like he never wanted him to leave again.

With kids hanging onto him, Derek moved slowly toward the kitchen, where he knew Tiphani waited for him. Just like he expected, his sexy wife stood by the stove with her back turned, her long jet-black hair lying on her back and her apple bottom looking perfect in her fitted jeans.

Derek put his daughter down and grabbed his wife around her waist from the back. He inhaled the scent of her strawberry shampoo and tucked her hair behind her ear so he could kiss the smooth skin of her neck.

She smiled. “Hey, hey . . . you have to wait for all of that,” she sang, putting her stirring spoon down and turning to greet her heroic husband properly.

“Well, hurry up and feed these rugrats so I won’t have to wait too long,” Derek whispered in her ear. He could feel his nature rising. After almost ten years of marriage, he was still attracted to his wife like they had just begun dating. He never grew tired or bored with her, and it was a plus that she kept herself looking right with regular manicures, pedicures, and facials. In his line of work, divorce was rampant, but Derek and Tiphani had stood the test of time. Derek was grateful to have a partner who understood that sometimes his work had to come first, and he gave her the same respect.

After dinner, Derek tucked the kids into bed while Tiphani cleaned up the dishes. As soon as the little ones drifted off, Derek sneaked back downstairs and watched his wife’s sexy frame move around the kitchen. Derek was in awe of her beautiful, flawless caramel skin, her almond-shaped eyes, and beautiful hourglass figure.

He rushed into the kitchen and grabbed her roughly, lifting her off her feet.

“Wait, silly. Let’s go upstairs,” she said with a giggle.

“I can’t wait anymore. Seeing your ass in them jeans got me on rock!” Derek exclaimed, fumbling with the button on her jeans. She acquiesced, throwing her hands around his neck. Derek hoisted her onto their granite countertop and yanked off her jeans, pulling her black lace thong off with them. He inhaled, excited by the sight of her beautifully trimmed triangle. “Fuck . . . you look so damn good!

“I missed you, baby,” he huffed, barely able to contain himself.

Tiphani licked her fingers seductively and rubbed her clitoris, causing it to swell slightly. Derek had finally got his own pants off. His medium-sized member stood at full attention. He was a firm believer that it wasn’t the size that mattered; it was what you did with what you had that made all the difference. Derek began licking the inside of her thighs.

"Ahh," Tiphani grunted, throwing her head back. Derek teased around her thighs until she put her hand on his head and forced it between her legs. He stuck his tongue out and licked her clit softly. Tiphani slid her hot box toward his tongue in ecstasy. "I want you," she whispered.

At that, Derek lifted his head, grabbed his dick, and drove it into his wife's soaking wet opening with full force.

She let out a short gasp as Derek dug further into her flesh.

Tiphani dug her nails into his shoulders. He began to pump harder.

Suddenly, something happened. Derek recoiled slightly. Tiphani closed her legs around his back, trying to keep him inside her. She was hoping that it didn't happen again.

"Urgghhh!" Derek growled, collapsing.

Tiphani slouched her shoulders and lowered her head.

He had finished less than two minutes after he had started.

"Fuck!" he cursed himself, his cheeks flaming over with embarrassment. "I'm so sorry, baby. I was just so excited to feel you," Derek said, making excuses for his shortcomings.

"I know you were just excited. That shit was still good, baby," Tiphani consoled as she hugged him.

"Did you at least cum?" Derek asked.

Is he fuckin' kidding me with that question? Tiphani screamed silently in her head. "Hell yeah, baby. You know I cum as soon as you touch me," she lied as she hugged him and hid her face. Derek continued to apologize, and she continued to console him.

This shit is so out of control right now! Tiphani thought as she rolled her eyes behind Derek's back. It wasn't like he came fast and stayed hard where he could please her too.

After his nut, he was a goner, leaving her unsatisfied and royally pissed the fuck off.

Derek didn't know if she was telling the truth, but he did know that his premature ejaculation was starting to become a problem.

Chapter 2

Tables Turned

It had been three months since the raid, and the day had finally come. Security was tight as Derek walked up to the courthouse. He could hardly make it to the steps because there were so many reporters and spectators outside. Scar's impending trial had been in the news for weeks. There had even been a countdown of sorts. The media had dubbed it the Trial of the Year. When some of the media hounds noticed Derek, they almost trampled each other to be the first to get a statement from him.

"Detective Fuller, are you nervous to face the notorious Scar Johnson?" a reporter called out, shoving a microphone into Derek's face.

"Are you kidding me with that question? If I wasn't nervous to bring him down in his own hood, why would I be nervous about facing him in a court of law?" Derek replied, giving the reporter a bit of heat. After he set the media straight, Derek smoothed the front of his Brooks Brothers suit and continued his stride up the courthouse steps.

It was no better inside the courtroom. There were throngs of cameras and reporters lined up around the back and sides. Derek sat on the bench directly behind the prosecutor's table and looked around. He could feel more than one pair of icy eyes on him. There were numerous members of Scar's crew peppered throughout the courtroom crowd, and they weren't hiding their glares. Derek didn't care because it just added to the drama of the scene and made him look better.

Derek turned around just in time to see the court officers leading Scar to the defendant's table. Scar had a huge smile plastered on his face, and he stared directly at Derek.

Knowing that all eyes would be on him, Derek frowned at Scar and shook his head. "Ain't this a bitch?" Derek mumbled when he noticed that Scar donned an expensive Armani suit, complete with a tailor-made French cuff shirt with diamond cuff links, and to top it off, what looked to be an authentic Cuban cigar sticking out of the breast pocket of his suit jacket.

Scar looked down at his suit and back over at Derek. Speaking with his eyes and facial expression, Scar was letting Derek know that he was still the man, regardless of the bust.

"All rise. The honorable Judge Irvin Klein presiding in the matter of the State of Maryland versus Stephon Johnson," the court officer called out. Everyone in the courtroom stood.

Derek broke his gaze on Scar, turned around, and stood as the judge slid into his seat on the bench.

With a bang of his gavel, the judge started the highly anticipated court proceedings. An eerie hush fell over the courtroom, and all eyes were front and center.

"Is the state ready to present its case? If so, prosecutor Fuller, you may begin," Judge Klein stated.

On cue, the prosecutor, who Derek thought was the most beautiful, sexy caramel specimen of a woman he had ever laid eyes on, stood up to start. *My wife is not only beautiful, she is on point. She got this shit,* Derek thought to himself, smiling proudly. She moved her sexy frame from behind the table and opened her mouth, but before she could speak, Scar's defense lawyer, a shark named Larry Tillman, jumped to his feet.

"Your Honor, I would like to move to have this case dismissed immediately," Mr. Tillman announced.

Everyone in the courtroom was looking at him like he was crazy. Not only was he interrupting the prosecutor, he was stepping on the toes of one of the most hard-ass judges in the Maryland court system. Hushed murmurs passed amongst the onlookers.

"Mr. Tillman, you will speak when spoken to," Judge Klein said.

"Your Honor, with all due respect, I am requesting to approach the bench," Mr. Tillman said.

Prosecutor Fuller looked around, confused. She was seething mad. This wasn't supposed to be happening. She ran her hands over her skirt and cocked her head to the side in an attempt to compose herself.

"Your Honor, please tell me you will not allow the defense to turn this trial into a sideshow," she said through clenched teeth.

"Approach!" the judge yelled.

Derek looked around and saw that Scar was smiling from ear to ear. The members of the media were going crazy, writing and recording.

The two attorneys approached the bench. The judge leaned in and spoke to them, while everyone else seemed to be holding their breath, waiting to see what would happen next.

Finally, the judge spoke somberly. "Mr. Tillman, you may proceed with your argument for dismissal," the judge said.

"I would be glad to," Tillman replied, smiling like a Cheshire cat.

"Your Honor, with all due respect, I am asking that the state's case against my client, Stephon Johnson, be dismissed, and that the evidence obtained be deemed inadmissible, as it was obtained with an illegal warrant. My client was arrested inside the house at the address 245 Covington Lane. The warrant used to illegally search my client's property was granted for the address 254 Covington Lane—a completely different, and might I add, nonexistent address. Therefore, it was obtained through an illegal search and seizure, which you and I both know was a direct and despicable violation of my client's rights.

"The state and their rogue cowboy troopers showed no writ of probable cause to enter my client's property and seize property or persons contained therein. This case was a prime example of the Maryland State Police's constant attempt at racial profiling and prejudice against young men like my client. I move to have this case dismissed without prejudice and expunged from my client's record," Mr. Tillman argued.

Tiphani Fuller looked back at her husband, contorting her face with anger. *He told me it would all be good. This better not come back to haunt my career*, she thought.

Loud gasps and murmurs erupted in the courtroom as Scar's attorney laid out his argument. Derek gripped the bottom of the wooden bench so hard that his knuckles turned white. He knew Scar would be released, but his lawyer was supposed to let the trial go on for a while first, to help Derek score a few more points with the chief. Making himself, his wife, and the department look bad had never been part of the plan. This was supposed to be a win-win for everyone, but Tillman was flipping the script.

Chief Scott and the entire unit sat in the back of the courtroom. They were up in arms as they heard the defense basically make them look like racist assholes. Scar just sat there with a smug look on his face, knowing he was about to be set free.

"Order! Order!" Judge Klein screamed out, banging his gavel over and over. Finally, things quieted down in the courtroom. "In light of this new and unsettling revelation and the fact that the court records reflect the address on the warrant is in fact the wrong one, I have no choice but to honor the U.S. Constitution, in accordance with the fourth amendment, which provides citizens the right to be free from illegal search and seizure. I hereby dismiss the State's case against defendant Stephon Johnson on the grounds that the State's evidence is inadmissible in the nature it was obtained," Judge Klein said regretfully, slamming his gavel and rushing up from the bench.

The courtroom erupted into pandemonium. Reporters scrambled to get the best shots of Derek and Scar. Tiphani threw her papers on the desk and stood up, enraged. The narcotics unit members and Scar's henchmen began exchanging harsh words, and the court officers were overwhelmed with trying to bring order in the courthouse.

Derek hung his head in shame. His wife shot him evil looks. This was no longer part of the act. She had put her ass on the line for this case, and she was truly pissed off now.

Chief Scott rushed over to him and grabbed him by the arm. "I need to talk to you, Detective Fuller . . . now!" he growled, pulling Derek into the hallway by his arm. "For Christ's sake, Fuller, what the fuck were you thinking? Something as simple as the right address on a fucking warrant!" Chief Scott said in a harsh whisper.

"I told Cassell two forty-five. I even wrote it down for him. I can't help it if he's dyslexic and can't write the right number!" Derek lied. The truth was he didn't write it down, and Cassell had written the address correctly. Derek just went back and reversed the numbers. He had failed to factor Scar's pain-in-the-ass lawyer into the equation, and now things had blown up in his face.

"Chief, I can fix this," Derek started.

"You let the department down. You better come up with some good shit to redeem yourself, Fuller," Chief Scott said.

Just then a huge, uproarious crowd began moving toward them. It was like the scene around a hot celebrity surrounded by fans.

Derek and the chief looked on and saw Scar in the middle of the crowd. He could not contain the still-smug smile that spread across his face as he rolled his unlit Cuban cigar between his fingers. As the crowd, complete with media cameras and Scar's henchmen, approached Derek, Scar stopped.

"If it ain't the fuckin' man without a plan," Scar said sarcastically to Derek, winking.

That was it.

"Fuck you!" Derek screamed, lunging at Scar. He instinctively reached to his waistband for his weapon, but felt nothing there. When he entered the courthouse, he'd had to check in his gun.

"You lucky bastard," Derek grumbled as Chief Scott blocked him. This take down was supposed to make Derek look good, and now Scar was standing here in front of all the cameras, rubbing shit in Derek's face. This was not the way things were supposed to go down, and if Derek didn't know better, he'd say that Scar was enjoying this a little too much.

Scar's crew had gotten ready for battle, stepping in front of Scar, ready to take on Derek. Chief Scott continued to struggle to restrain Derek.

"Fuller! This bastard is not fucking worth it," the chief said, dragging a raging Derek down the opposite end of the courthouse hallway. Scar popped his collar and stepped across the courthouse threshold into freedom.

The show looked good, and everyone was completely fooled, except one lone person, who sat in the back of the courtroom and witnessed the whole circus act. From the moment they saw Scar's lawyer argue the fourth amendment and the little wink that Scar gave detective Fuller after the trial, the observer knew something was not right. It was now time to find out exactly what was going on.

Chapter 3

Things Are Not Always What They Seem

Scar's custom built mansion sat on almost twenty acres in an affluent Baltimore suburb. The circular driveway was filled with every luxury car on the market. There was no mistaking his wealth because he flaunted it relentlessly. Music could be heard blaring from beyond the huge wrought-iron gates. Scar wanted to celebrate every day for the same amount of time he was locked up awaiting trial. This was just day one of his planned festivities.

Inside of his twenty thousand square foot home, Scar sat on his custom-made throne in his very own champagne room. He watched as two beautiful, exotic model-type chicks performed a striptease in front of him and his newest recruits—Trail, Sticks, and Flip. Scar was in the process of grooming the three young heads to be as deadly as he was at their age. He trained his little henchmen much like dogfighters trained their pit bulls to become deadly killers, with harsh treatment and just enough food—or in the young heads' case, money—to keep them loyal to him. They were the next generation of his Dirty Money Crew.

Scar sat surrounded by bottles of Moët and Cristal and stacks of money. He was definitely back at his best. He held his customary Cuban between his pointer and middle fingers and laughed. "Yo, the black bitch got a donkey ass. I would murder that pussy," Scar said as he tossed hundred dollar bills at the women's naked bodies.

"Niggah, you ain't never lied," Trail replied, touching his crotch for emphasis.

Scar took a bottle of Moët Rose to the head. He was feeling good. As Scar drank, there was a knock at the door.

Scar slammed his drink on the table and furrowed his brow. “Yo, who the fuck is that breaking up my private party? Niggas know I don’t like to be disturbed when I’m in my champagne room,” Scar complained.

“A’ight, I’ma take care of that,” Sticks replied, pulling his .357 Magnum from his waistband and heading toward the door.

Trail and Flip also pulled their weapons. Sticks pulled back the door to reveal the unlucky bastard who decided to encroach on their good time. Everybody aimed their weapons at the culprit guilty of breaking up Scar’s private party. “I fuckin’ surrender, damn!” the man at the door said, throwing his hands in the air.

“Nigga, you must got a death wish!” Sticks said, lowering his gun when he recognized who was at the door. Everyone else followed suit, and Scar immediately lightened his mood too.

“It’s all good. This here the only nigga I would let slide for fucking up my moment,” Scar announced at the sight of the man. Scar smiled wide. It did his heart good to see the dude.

“Damn, nigga, you gonna have your dudes put me on ice and shit,” Derek said, laughing and walking over to Scar to give him a pound and a chest bump.

“Yo, nigga. Detective fucking Fuller. I gotta tell you what; your ass deserve a fuckin’ Academy Award for all that acting you did during that fuckin’ bust and at the courthouse. Your ass was better than Will Smith and shit,” Scar said, chuckling at his own joke. “That fucking arrest was very believable. You said all the shit those fuckin’ pigs be saying: ‘Shut the fuck up! Stand the fuck up!’ Then at the courthouse you acted like you was really gonna kick my ass and shit. Talking all that blah, blah . . . I would hire you to be in my movies any day, nigga,” Scar continued, cracking up.

“Was I good or what?” Derek asked as he got comfortable. He picked up Scar’s bottle of Moët and took a swig, knowing in his head that not all of his anger was an act. Some of that shit was real, but he wasn’t going to let Scar know he was pissed that the lawyer ended the trial so fast.

The Dirty Money Crew was kind of taken aback at how easygoing Scar was around Derek.

"The whole 'son of a bitch' thing had me rolling too. I was thinking, shit, if I'm a son of a bitch, you a straight son of a bitch too, since we from the same bitch," Scar continued, laughing hard at his own jokes.

"You owe me for them days up in the clink. I'ma have to take some dough off the top," Scar said jokingly. He really looked at his time before the trial as a small sacrifice for a bigger payoff later.

"Don't play! I'm the one who should get extra pay for letting you fuck up my good name. I had to look big-time stupid and embarrassed for fuckin' up the warrant and shit. I don't even know how they fuckin' believed a debonair, sharp-ass niggah like me would fuck up a warrant. But that was some genius shit you came up with, my man, changing the numbers around. It's also a good thing I got my wifey on lock so I could convince her to go through with it," Derek said.

This wasn't the first time Derek had botched a drug bust, so he had to come up with a good plan for how to do it again. This time had to be different from last time, even though last time was a true fuck-up. He had legitimately forgotten to get a warrant a few years back while busting Scar's rival, a drug dealer named Malek. Scar had wanted his competition stomped and destroyed, and Fuller and his crew were more than willing to oblige in order to keep their share of the drug profits padding their pockets. Only problem was that in their eagerness to take Malek out, they forgot to follow the rules. So, Malek lived to sling another day, and Derek and his crew looked like chumps. That's the problem with working on that side of the law: those fucking rules get in the way.

"Yo, I'ma bounce." Derek didn't want to take a chance on anyone seeing him there. Scar wanted to meet in a few days at their normal spot, a small Italian restaurant in Bowie, a suburb of Baltimore, but Derek just couldn't wait. He knew coming to Scar's house this soon after the trial was risky, but not seeing his brother since the bust had Derek missing him big time.

"We make a good fucking team, bro. You keep the law up off me, I keep your pockets laced; you use me to look like a hero cop, I use you to buy myself a lot of time before any other five-O even thinks twice about busting up on me, for fear that my high-paid lawyer will make them look like shit. Nigga, it all worked out," Scar explained, extending his hand to offer Derek one of his prized Cuban cigars.

Derek took the little gift and nodded in agreement at what Scar was saying. He understood the being made to look like shit part, but that was the one thing that Derek had a hard time accepting. He had to admit that the money he made from helping Scar evade the law was more than he could ever dream of seeing from his state salary. But sometimes living a double life took its toll on him mentally, especially because of his special connection to Scar.

"Flip, give this man what he came for," Scar instructed, waving his hand like Flip was his servant.

"You wanna get up on that donkey ass right there before you go home?" Scar asked Derek, gesturing toward the strippers.

"Nah, I got a beauty at home. She's all I need," Derek said, thinking about his wife.

Scar smiled wide, almost smirking. He could never understand how a man could love one woman to the extent that Derek loved his wife. Scar thought Derek almost seemed like a punk for her.

"I hear that, nigga. That got to be some goodass shit if you gon' pass up that J-Lo ass right there. By the way, tell my sister-in-law I said hello," Scar commented with that smirk appearing on his face again.

Before Derek could respond, Flip returned and reluctantly handed Derek a black duffel bag filled with cash. It was the profit from their last cocaine flip. When Scar had told his young soldiers they had to give up their last flip, they weren't too happy. Flip was the most upset. Scar had decided to give Derek the entire profit. The crew thought it was like a slap in the face, since they were the ones on the front line putting in the work. They didn't think that Derek's help was anywhere near as important to the operation as their grinding. But none of them dared to question Scar. Not right now anyway.

Flip gave up what he thought of as his loot, but he filed it in his mental Rolodex. He had a plan.

Derek took a quick look inside the bag and looked back at Scar a bit confused. It was more than he had ever seen in his dealings with Scar. A line of sweat broke out on Derek's forehead as his mind raced with ideas on how he would "wash" all that money to make it look legit before he could spend it.

"Yeah, I thought you deserved a little extra. I mean, we are brothers, right?" Scar said seriously.

"Yeah, blood of my blood, flesh of my flesh, nigga for life," Derek said in an almost inaudible whisper. Seeing all that money gave Derek an uneasy feeling, almost as if he was getting in too deep. He wasn't about to go back on his promise to his mother now, though, so he put that uneasy feeling right out of his mind.

"That's what I'm saying, nigga. We blood for life, so when I can look out, I will. That bond is important," Scar commented.

Derek nodded. He was feeling a strong sense of love and allegiance. He never wanted to be separated from his brother again. Derek closed the bag, gave his brother a hug, and headed home to his wife.

Once he was outside of Scar's doors, Derek slid behind the steering wheel of his car, and with his heart racing, he checked the bag of money again. He rested his head on the headrest and thought about what he had done and had been doing for the past two years. He felt so caught in the middle sometimes. Derek loved his brother, but he knew this shit was all going to come to an end one day; however, right now he didn't see a way out.

Brother or not, Derek knew Scar was dangerous. When he had been reunited with his brother, Derek was so excited to find him after their tragic childhood separation that he overlooked Scar's life of crime. It wasn't long before he had been drawn into a web of lies and deceit. He felt an overwhelming need to stay connected and bonded to Scar, the only piece of his mother and his true identity that he had left. He had made his mother a promise that he would take care of his little brother—no matter what. Derek was determined to keep that promise. He felt it would keep his mother's memory alive in his heart and mind. Derek closed his eyes, and just like always, the memories flooded back.

In a car across the street from Scar's house, the observer from the courtroom had watched Detective Fuller enter the house and come out with a duffel bag. The person immediately picked up a cell phone and started taking pictures. After the trial, or rather the theatrical event at the courthouse, the lone spectator decided to take a trip to Scar's house and see what was going on. Little did they know that Detective Fuller would be there, entering the house of his enemy so soon after the trial. Even more interesting to the person was the detective leaving with the duffel bag.

Derek pulled away from the house, and his new shadow put down the cell phone and prepared to follow. Before they could pull away from the curb, a dark blue Chevy Impala pulled up. The Shadow stayed put so as not to draw any attention. Keeping as still possible, the observer watched as a tall black man with salt-and-pepper hair stepped out of the Chevy.

"That dude look familiar. Where do I know him from? Better take some pictures to document this shit for later perusal," the Shadow said, picking up the phone and snapping a few pictures as the familiar-looking dude walked into Scar's house. This shit was definitely getting interesting.

Chapter 4

The Past Dictates the Future

"Mommy! Ahhhh!" Derek screamed, his small, cherubic face turning almost burgundy as he jumped up and down in sheer terror. His brother stood next to him and peed on himself as he watched too.

"I told you before, bitch, you don't play with my fuckin' money!" a strange man screamed as he dragged their mother by her hair. The man was so big and his skin was so black that he looked to Derek like a giant monster.

As the boys screamed, the man hoisted their mother in the air by her throat. Derek felt vomit creep up his throat and his bowels threatened to release from the fear he felt. His mother clawed at the man's hands in a futile attempt to loosen his grip so she could breathe.

"Get off my mommy!" Stephon screamed, the scar he was born with dragging the side of his mouth down, causing his words to slur. Derek grabbed onto his little brother's shirt and pulled him back. He couldn't risk this monster harming his brother too.

"Please don't hurt my babies," their mother rasped, begging the man for mercy.

"Bitch, you should have thought about that before you decided to cross me," the giant said, hoisting her up and throwing her up against the wall. She hit the wall with a thud and slid down, her body going limp like a rag doll. She continued to scream and beg for her life as the man pounded on her.

He let his fist land at will, each punch harder than the one before. "You like to smoke crack? You like to steal from people, bitch?" the man growled as he lifted her weak body so he could get to her face easier. With the force of a Mack truck, he back-handed her, and one of her teeth shot from her mouth. Blood covered her face and the floor around her. “Now, I expect to get my money by tomorrow, or you and these bastard trick babies of yours gonna be dead,” the man said, spewing a wad of spit on her crumpled form.

Five-year-old Derek and his four-year-old brother Stephon cowered in a corner. Derek, being a year older, tried to shield his brother from harm as usual. Although he was only five, Derek often acted as if he were ten or eleven. On the nights his mother disappeared or stayed holed up in her bedroom with different men, Derek would pour cereal or make a sandwich out of whatever was there for him and his little brother. He would make sure his brother washed his face and brushed his teeth before they went to bed.

Derek always protected Stephon, who his mother had nicknamed Scar because of his misshapen head and the scar that dragged down one side of his face, making his head resemble a boulder. “Scar, Scar . . . Scar head baby,” she would sing to her youngest son. She would call Derek her “baby genius” and tell him he was destined for greatness.

People often thought the brothers were fraternal twins because they were the same size. Although Scar was a year younger, he was always just as big as his older brother.

When he was sure the giant was gone, Derek got up and went to his mother’s side. “Mommy?” he whined, nudging her frantically. When she didn’t respond, he thought she was dead for sure. “Mommy!” he called out again, with urgency rippling through his words.

Finally, his mother shifted, winced in pain, moaned, and turned over. Struggling to get up and barely able to speak through her swollen lips, she rushed her boys to put on their coats. Afraid and visibly shaken, Derek followed his mother’s instructions and helped Scar into his coat and put on his own. Their mother rushed them out of the apartment, looking around nervously the entire time.

Once they were outside, their battered mother let motherly instinct take over. She ignored the massive pains ripping through her entire body as she walked at a feverish pace to get her children far away from the potential danger.

Derek could keep up, but Scar had a hard time, and he gasped for breath because he had to jog just to keep in step. After walking for what seemed like an eternity, the trio finally came to a middle class white neighborhood.

"Go in there and y'all stand right by that green dumpster. Don't move until I come back. You hear me, Derek?" his mother said, her words garbled and her face becoming more swollen by the minute.

"When you coming back?" Derek asked, shivering anxiously.

"Take care of your brother, okay? He is special, and don't you let nobody bother him about his face. You hear me?" she said, ignoring his question as her body quaked with sobs.

"When you coming back?" Derek asked her again, an ominous feeling taking over.

"Just take care of your brother," his mother said, shoving them along.

As they started ambling forward slowly toward the dumpster, their mother turned and limped away as fast as she could. Her heart was breaking as she walked farther and farther away from her children. She knew eventually somebody would find them and take care of them. If she kept them, she feared, her addiction would eventually get them killed.

Scar began crying out, "Mommy! Mommy! Don't leave us."

"Shhh. Mommy is coming back. I'm gonna take care of you until she comes back," Derek consoled, squeezing his brother's hand tightly.

Derek took his brother and stood right where his mother had instructed him. They stood at the dumpster until the sun came up. Their legs throbbed and Scar whined and cried in between nodding from sleep deprivation. Derek refused to sit down or allow Scar to sit down. His mother had told him to stand there, and he would not let her down. Several people passed them and stared, but no one said anything to them. It was the trash truck driver who came to empty the dumpster who finally asked Derek why they were there.

"My mommy said she is coming back for us," Derek said. After waiting with Derek and Scar for three hours, the trash man finally called the authorities.

Derek never saw his mother again. When the child protective service workers and the police showed up, Derek still refused to move. They had to finally, forcefully remove him from the dumpster.

"No! I'm waiting for my mommy! No!" Derek screamed and kicked. It was to no avail. Derek and Scar were whisked away to the hospital for a medical clearance and then off to foster care.

The boys remained in foster care for more than a year, but with the mandatory expiration on parental rights, after eighteen months they were put up for adoption. Every Wednesday, Derek and Scar went to the agency along with about twenty-five other kids, to be on display for prospective parents. Derek would always hold Scar's hand and tell people that they were not being separated and if they wanted him, they would have to take Scar too. With one look at Scar's disfigured face, the potential parents always turned away and found other kids to adopt.

Derek's plan had worked for weeks, and each week, Derek and Scar would go together back to the foster home. After a few weeks of this flat out rejection, the social workers couldn't figure out why at least one of the boys could not attract an adoptive family. The workers finally started sitting close to Derek and Scar. When the workers got wind of what Derek was doing, the next Wednesday, they put Derek and Scar in separate rooms. Derek was picked immediately. He was seven, with the cutest dimples and the prettiest smile. Scar, on the other hand, had been overlooked again and again.

The day Derek's new family—a father who was a cop and a mother who was a teacher—came to pick him up, he refused to leave without his brother. He fought and cursed and even locked himself inside the bathroom. The social workers lied to Derek in order to coax him out of the bathroom so his new parents could grab him and get him home. "Your brother will be coming along soon. Go ahead. You will see him again," she said.

Not fully believing her, but also not wanting to do anything that would possibly delay his brother's departure, Derek reluctantly went. He wouldn't see his brother until almost fifteen years later, when they had both landed opposite sides of the law.

In Derek's new adoptive home, everything seemed to be perfect. His father fought crime and his mother taught him everything there was to know in any book imaginable. They were a real family. They ate dinner together and had fun movie nights on Fridays, his father's day off. Derek lived like a kid that had been born with a silver spoon in his mouth. He wore the finest clothes, had every toy before it even became popular with other kids, and most of all, he had a real family life—with both parents. But despite how it seemed from the outside, everything wasn't as peachy as it seemed.

Derek's father worked the midnight shift, and when he left home at ten o'clock after tucking his son in and kissing his wife, things would take a dark turn in the house. Derek's adoptive mother would creep into his bedroom at night and wake him up. She would shake him awake and stand over him wearing a see-through nightgown. Longing for her husband's touch and affection, Ms. Fuller was lonely and desperate. She would climb into bed with her adopted son and stroke his hair. Then she would tell Derek that she loved him more than anything in the world.

She knew the one thing that was most important to Derek, and she used it against him. Mrs. Fuller told him that if he wanted to see his brother again, he would have to touch her, and she would help him find his brother.

Most of the time, Derek felt disgusting and dirty, but he so longed for his brother that he ignored it and did what he was told. Sometimes he wanted to vomit. But things changed, and he felt differently as the years went by. His body would betray him and he started to experience sensations that he did not quite understand. Derek tried to fight the "good feeling" that he started to get as he got older, but soon realized that the faster he got to that feeling the better, because his nightmare would then be over. Derek would ejaculate after a few minutes so he wouldn't feel so guilty. It was ingrained in him as a coping mechanism; cum quickly and it will be over, he used to tell himself. It had become a way of life for him.

Derek had everything any child could want: toys, a private school education, and church every Sunday. Even with everything, he endured torture for years. The only thing Derek wanted was to see his biological mother and brother again.

On the other hand, still in the hood of Baltimore, Scar remained in the foster care system. After years of teasing and beatings at the hands of other kids in group home after group home, Scar grew angry inside. On most days he felt ruthless, and often had visions of killing the social workers and the other kids with his bare hands. It wasn't long before Scar was on edge.

"Hey, elephant man," a boy had called out to Scar, throwing a ping pong ball from the day room, hitting Scar in the head. Scar bit down into his cheek and ignored his tormentor. "You so ugly we could probably win a world war just by showing your face to the enemies," the boy continued, garnering laughs from the other kids sitting around. "Look at that scar and those saggy lips. I bet your mother must have fucked a gorilla to get something as ugly as you," the boy said, letting out a shrill, grating laugh.

That was it. Scar's ear seemed clogged, and the room started spinning around him. He snapped. He never tolerated anyone talking about his mother or his brother. "Arrrggh!" Scar screamed out, suddenly lunging at the boy. Scar gripped a pocket knife he had stolen from the local sporting goods store.

The boy's eyes popped open in shock. He had not expected the "ugly monster kid" to ever fight back. The boy backed up from Scar's contact. He was holding his throat and gagging. Screams erupted in the room, and some of the other kids ran out into the hallway to get help. Scar had buried the pocket knife deep into the boy's neck, hitting his jugular vein.

Scar stumbled backward at the sight of his deed. Thick burgundy blood—arterial blood—spewed from the boy's neck like a fountain. With every pump of his heart, the boy lost what looked like a half pint of blood.

Before any of the group home administrators could help, the boy had bled to death within minutes, right at Scar's feet. Although he was scared to death, something inside of Scar felt powerful, almost invincible. He had learned how to silence his tormentor. He was never going to let anyone disrespect him again.

The group home security tackled Scar to the floor and held him there until the police arrived. After the incident, Scar spent two months in a mental institution. When the psychiatrist cleared him, Scar was placed in a juvenile detention center, where he stayed until he was eighteen years old.

The detention center was where Scar learned all of his criminal ways. When he was released onto the streets of Baltimore, instead of being rehabilitated, Scar had become a ruthless dude with a nothing-to-lose attitude.

Derek went away to college, and only returned to his adoptive home when his father was laid to rest after a long battle with cancer. He felt he needed to pay his respects. He didn't hold a grudge against his adoptive father for the abuses that happened. After all, he never told his father about any of it, so how could Derek expect him to do anything about it?

When the funeral was over, Derek told his adoptive mother that she would never see him again. He had never forgiven her for years of sexual abuse. In fact, it had followed him like a looming nightmare. Derek had always felt like he had no control over his own body or his own sexuality. When he began having sex for pleasure with girls his age, his body would betray him. His mind would overpower his physical will not to ejaculate quickly.

Derek immediately moved back to Baltimore. Maybe, just maybe, he thought, he would run into his real mother or his brother. After a year of looking for corporate jobs, Derek joined the Maryland State Police.

After a while, Derek gave up the active search to find his mother and brother again. He didn't know the first place to look. Checking the foster care system had turned up nothing on Scar. The records were sealed on kids who aged out of foster care anyway. Then one day, as a highway patrol trooper, Derek walked into the squad room of the narcotics unit to get a white powder test done on a substance he had seized during a car stop, and right on the wall was a huge wanted poster with his brother's face and name plastered on it. It read: STEPHON "SCAR" JOHNSON, REWARD $10,000.

Derek stared at the picture for what felt like ten minutes. He was so overcome with emotion; he didn't know whether to laugh, cry, scream hallelujah, or kiss the poster.

When it had finally sunken in that the man in the picture was really Scar, Derek's little Scar head brother, Derek got so nauseated and weak he almost threw up.

"What's the matter, Fuller? You look like you saw a ghost in that mu'fucka Scar Johnson," one of his colleagues asked.

"Nah, nah. Just looking around," Derek said, quickly pulling himself together before anyone caught on to his interest in Scar.

After seeing that picture, Derek was hopeful again, and he set out to find his brother. It had never occurred to him before that he could use his police resources to try to find his brother and mother.

When he pulled Scar's criminal history, he learned just what his brother had been doing since he last saw him at five years old. Scar had a rap sheet as long as a city block.

Derek learned that Scar had become the founder of the notorious Dirty Money Crew, a crew of killers that had murdered their way to the top of the Maryland drug trade.

Derek was on the other side of the law, but the fact still remained that Scar was his blood, and he had been determined to find him one day. Derek worked hard to prove himself as the best trooper on the streets just so he could get enough clout in the department to put in his application to join the drug team. He was a man on a mission.

After six months, Derek made the narcotics force. He had officially become a jump out boy. Every time Derek went on a jump out operation to pick up the hand-to-hand street pharmacists, he was hopeful he would run into Scar or get some information on him. Finally, Derek and his team jumped out on a set of corner boys, and it just so happened that the little dudes they picked up were down with the Dirty Money Crew. They were low men on Scar's payroll.

It didn't take long for Derek to get one of them alone and promise him freedom if he told him where to find Scar. At first, the little soldier was living by the street creed: No Snitching! But the longer the boy sat in a cell, unable to use the bathroom, get anything to eat, and with no phone calls, he finally gave in and provided Derek with the information he needed.

Derek sat outside of all of Scar's trap houses for weeks, but Scar never showed up. Being out there undetected, Derek had figured out every drop off and pick up time. He had numbered Scar's workers, and used logic to figure out the one who must have been a higher-up, which meant he was probably closest to Scar. Derek noticed that the dude was the one that was the most consistent player at all of the trap houses, and he never stuck around long. Derek reasoned he was the lieutenant in charge of bringing the reup and picking up the profits. Finally, Derek decided to tail him. Sure enough, one night Derek followed the dude right to his leader.

Derek's heart thumped wildly when he covertly peeked out of his windshield and saw Scar in the flesh. It was his long lost brother. Derek could recognize that scarred face and huge head anywhere. There he was, his little brother all grown up and the leader of a crime syndicate. It made Derek proud and sad all at the same time.

He sat there and wondered what their lives would have been like had their mother not abandoned them that fateful night. His best guess was that the big-ass man that had beaten his mother unmercifully had probably returned and killed her. When Derek was a teenager, he had convinced himself that she was probably better off dead than running the streets chasing crack.

Derek watched Scar that first night and didn't reveal himself, although he wanted to rush out of the car and embrace his brother with a big hug and a sincere apology.

Derek didn't know how his brother would react to him, or if Scar would even remember him.

Conflicted, Derek went home to Tiphani, who was then his girlfriend, and confided in her his secret: he was a cop and his brother was a wanted criminal. Tiphani told Derek she wanted him to do whatever would make him happy.

For two days, Derek changed his car and disguise and watched his brother. Finally, he felt he had grown the balls to reveal himself to his brother.

Derek walked up to Katrina's, the bar and lounge that Scar owned and had named after their mother. It also housed Scar's office in a secret room in the back. Derek was stopped at the door and asked what his business was, since it was a bit early for patrons.

"I just wanna get a drink, man. Long fuckin' day," Derek said to the goons protecting the front door.

The front door man surveyed Derek, wondering if this square could be a cop or a fed.

Since he was dressed like a typical street dude, Derek was allowed entry. He ordered a few drinks and built up his courage. "He's your little brother, li'l Scar head," Derek whispered to himself.

With his liquid courage flowing, he walked to the back of the lounge. Derek encountered a tall, muscular dude, yet another layer of security.

"Yo, man, I need to see Scar," Derek said to the dude, trying to sound as street as he could. Derek had lost that edge a long time ago, so it was a stretch for him.

"Who the fuck are you, niggah?" the goon asked, trying to intimidate Derek with his snarl.

"Tell Scar I got information on his family," Derek said. The goon crinkled his face in confusion. Everybody on the street knew that Scar always proclaimed he was born from the concrete. "No mother, no father, no family. Just a pure bred street niggah," was what he proclaimed. "Nah, Scar ain't got no family," the goon told Derek.

"Everybody got family. Now, tell him I got information on his family," Derek said forcefully, not backing down.

Scar's security guard reluctantly went behind the secret door, which was obscured with police grade double-sided glass. Two minutes later, the man returned and asked Derek a question.

"Scar wants to know, if you got information on his family, where was his mother's birthmark?"

Derek swallowed hard because his mother's face came flooding back to his mind's eye. He could see her brown sugar–colored skin and straight white teeth so clearly smiling at him. Those memories were from a time when things were so good for them. In reality, the last time he'd laid eyes on his mother, she was a gaunt skeleton with missing teeth and riddled with bruises.

Shaking his head, Derek got it together. "It . . . it was a heart-shaped, cherry-colored mark on her left cheek, and she used to call it 'a mother's love' and tell us she got it from our kisses," Derek said, barely able to get the words out.

The man was really confused when Derek said "our kisses." He looked at Derek intensely then disappeared, armed with the answer. Within minutes, the man returned and Derek was allowed to follow him back to the secret office.

When Derek stepped into the room, it was like time stood still. Scar was sitting behind a huge mahogany desk like the CEO of a legitimate company. Scar's face looked much improved. His scar actually made him look dangerous, instead of ugly and deformed like it did when he was a kid. Who would've thought an ugly birth defect could benefit him? It was as if his deformity had dictated what he was to become.

Derek was at a loss for words. He stared at Scar, thinking his eyes were deceiving him. Derek's legs were weak and threatened to fail him.

"Ain't this a bitch! My little big brother," Scar said, standing up and stepping from behind the desk.

Derek was still speechless. Like the first time he saw the wanted poster, Derek didn't know what to do—cry, scream, or say he was sorry.

"I know the cat ain't got your tongue, nigga. You ain't happy to see your little brother after a hundred years and shit?" Scar said, grabbing Derek for a manly hug.

"I'm just so fuckin' happy to see you, man," Derek finally managed to say. "I'm so sorry I couldn't keep my promise. I was a kid. They snatched me away from you. I had promised Mommy . . ." Derek rambled, shaking all over.

"C'mon, man. I don't hold you responsible for nothin'. Them white people ain't care nothing about two black little niggas tryin'a keep whatever piece of family they had together. I ain't never blame you, my nig. Besides, if shit didn't happen the way it did, I wouldn't be the king that I am today," Scar assured, offering his dumbfounded brother a seat.

"I told Mommy I would always take care of you. I'm back, and I will keep that promise," Derek assured his brother. And he didn't lie. Although he had pledged allegiance to uphold the law of the state of Maryland, his allegiance to his family was stronger. Derek had another chance to keep his promise to his mother, and he vowed he would forever be his brother's keeper—that is, if his brother wanted to be kept.

From that day forward, Derek helped Scar stay above the law. He made sure Scar was always one step ahead of the jump out boys and the Narcotics Unit. But when the heat got turned up on Derek to make some big busts, he spoke with Scar and they agreed to put on their little show. Scar agreed to take a fall to help his brother look good in the eyes of the department and the public. It had all worked out—or so they hoped.

Chapter 5

A Tangled Web We Weave

Derek had daydreamed about his childhood and his reunion with Scar all the way home. He looked at the bag of dirty money he held and asked himself if it was worth it. It gave him an ill feeling in the pit of his stomach. That was a lot of fucking money, and the old street credo—more money, more problems—was about to ring true for Derek Fuller.

Shaking his head to clear out the cobwebs of the past, Derek pulled into his driveway. Thoughts of his wife and her warm hugs, kisses, and hot sex motivated him to snap the fuck out of it.

Derek crept into his house. He knew Tiphani would be in the bed, and he wanted to make everything up to her—the court thing, his recent shortcomings in the bedroom, and some of the lies he told her about where he got some of his extra money from.

Derek slowly pushed open the French doors to their bedroom. Tiphani was already asleep. He went into their walk-in closet and put his loot in the wall safe. He took off his weapon and all of his clothes.

Derek planned to wake his wife with a stiff dick and a good pussy pounding. At least he hoped that he could keep it together long enough. He got himself mentally ready. This time, he wasn't going to let himself cum too fast. He told himself he would fight the urge to ejaculate as long as he could stand it—at least until she came first. Derek stroked himself to get ready. He let a glob of spit fall into his hand, and rubbed it up and down on his dick.

"Mmm," he moaned as his manhood came to life in his hand. When he was satisfied that he was hard enough to rock his wife's world, Derek went over to the bed.

Sliding onto the bed behind Tiphani, Derek noticed that all his sexy-ass wife was wearing was a short lace camisole, no panties. Derek smiled. *She knew I was coming home to freak her*. Derek slid one of his knees between his wife's legs from behind to make room for him to get to her goods. "Mmmm," she moaned, acting like he was disturbing her sleep.

Derek wanted to laugh. He knew she was only playing hard to get. He never knew why women did that, acting like they were asleep when they knew damn well they wanted to jump up and ride the dick.

When Derek wedged his way between her legs and had them wide enough, he slid up behind her, licked his fingers, and searched blindly under the covers for her opening. When Derek touched her, she was already wet.

"You been waiting for me, huh?" Derek whispered, even more excited now.

At that, Tiphani knew the gig was up, and she turned over, smiling. Derek climbed on top of her and took a mouthful of her left breast into his mouth. Sucking roughly at first, than softening up, Derek pleasured her. She grew even more excited, letting small gasps escape her lips.

Derek was ready, mentally and physically. He reached down and grabbed his dick. It was time. He was determined to fuck his wife like she needed to be fucked.

Derek rammed his dick into her. "Urghh," he grunted when he felt Tiphani's warm, wet flesh around his meat.

"Ohhh," she cooed, wrapping her legs around his waist and pushing back at him.

Derek lifted his ass and came back down into the soft wetness. He grunted with labored breaths. He was excited now. The smell of sex, the sounds his wife made, the tingling he felt in his loins; it all came rushing back to his mind again. These were the same things he had experienced when he was too young to understand it.

Derek tried to hurriedly push the images of his adoptive mother's face out of his mind. But the images of her face, contorted with prohibited pleasure, kept flashing in his head.

"Yes, fuck me," Tiphani whispered.

That was enough. They were the exact words that wretched woman had said to him when he was eleven and twelve and thirteen. "Ahhhhh!" Derek screamed out as he fought a losing battle with his mind. His body involuntarily bucked and jerked against Tiphani's, and she was left disappointed.

She knew right away that Derek had ejaculated prematurely again. Tiphani looked at the clock when they'd started, and it had read 11:43. She looked at it now, and it read 11:53.

Ten fuckin' minutes, and subtract about eight for the tittie sucking and pussy touching, Tiphani thought. She rolled her eyes.

Derek lay on top of her, trying to get his dick hard again. "I'm so sorry, baby," he apologized as usual.

"Just get my toys. I need to cum," Tiphani said flatly, annoyed.

Derek felt like shit, but he jumped up and got his wife's vibrating dildo from her treasure box. He turned on the little device, wishing he could make her cum like the little plastic toy did.

Tiphani climaxed from her toy. It wasn't the same as the orgasms she had from a real flesh and blood dick, but she had to settle.

Tiphani turned over and gave Derek her back. She lay awake for the next two hours. She didn't know how much longer she could take it. It was fine when they first got together; it was easier to handle, and Tiphani was more willing to overlook certain "short-cummings," so to speak. She thought it would get better, but this shit was getting ridiculous. So, she lay there holding out hope that someday soon there would be a light at the end of the whack-dick tunnel.

The next morning, Derek was up extra early. Still feeling guilty, he busied himself with making Tiphani and the kids a huge breakfast of grits, bacon, sausage, eggs, and biscuits.

Tiphani had not said many words to him since the night before. After the whole embarrassing court episode, she planned to take a few days off, and didn't feel like getting out of bed. She felt that no amount of money was worth the embarrassment she had received at the hands of Scar's lawyer.

Trying to make it up to her, Derek brought Tiphani's breakfast to her. "I'm going to take the kids to school for you. You can stay in bed all day if you want," Derek said, trying anything to get her to smile so he would know she wasn't still mad.

"Thanks," she said dryly.

"I love you, Tiphani. It's going to get better," Derek said, not even sure himself. He kissed her on the forehead then turned and left.

She lay back down and pulled the comforter over her head. He had never told her about his molestation as a child. His pride wouldn't allow it. The same with his thoughts on Viagra: *Don't need no pill to make my dick hard,* he thought. Because of his silence on the subject, Tiphani did not understand the mental effects that sex had on him.

Tiphani didn't know how long she would be able to take this bullshit. She was at a real crossroads in her marriage.

If she had known the true reason behind her husband's sexual failure, she would have been much more supportive, but she didn't. All she knew was that her clit throbbed all day, every day, and she needed good dick in her life.

"C'mon, you two. It's time for school," Derek said, rallying his kids and ushering them out the door.

Derek pulled out of his driveway, oblivious to the eyes that followed his every move.

As soon as she heard the car pull out of the driveway, Tiphani threw the comforter back and jumped out of the bed. She was free from that limp-dicked excuse of a husband, and now able to take care of her needs. She walked into her bathroom and turned on the shower.

Stepping inside, she let the water cascade down her sculpted, muscular body. Tiphani placed her hands on the beautifully tiled shower walls as she took the massaging showerhead down from the holder and placed the pulsing head up against her clit. Throwing her head back, she rotated the showerhead up and down against her swollen clit until she came.

It's a damn shame the showerhead can make me cum, but my husband can't, she thought to herself.

When she was done, she lathered her body, cleaned up, and turned off the water. Suddenly, she heard a noise coming from downstairs. Stopping in her tracks, Tiphani listened intently. She didn't hear anything else.

"Maybe I'm losing it," she whispered, turning back toward the sink. She reached down to turn on the faucet and Clang! The bathroom door flew open.

Tiphani screamed. She had no place to run. She was trapped in the bathroom. Her eyes popped open in sheer terror, and a second scream got caught in her throat as someone grabbed her forcefully from behind, placing a huge hand over her mouth.

"Mmmmm!" she tried to scream as she struggled to see her attacker. The apparent assailant ripped her towel off of her and pushed her up against the sink in a doggie style position.

She moaned, barely able to breathe. The next thing she felt was a sharp pain stabbing through her vagina as the stranger forcefully penetrated her from behind. He drove his dick into her with brute force, and then removed his hand from her mouth.

"Oh shit!" Tiphani moaned in sudden ecstasy.

"You like when I fuck you rough?" he growled, banging up against her over and over again.

"Oh, Scar, you fuck me so good," Tiphani huffed out as she gripped the sides of the sink. She didn't have to look at his face; she immediately recognized the feeling of his dick.

Scar pumped her from behind like he wanted to send her through the vanity mirror that hung over the sink. Tiphani loved every minute of it. She inched up onto her tiptoes so Scar could get a better angle into her soaking wet pussy.

Scar was able to sex her without coming in two minutes, and that's all that mattered to Tiphani. She was a fucking woman with needs, she reasoned, justifying her betrayal each time.

Their affair had happened so suddenly. Once she had gotten a taste of Scar's dick, she was hooked. Tiphani had to admit that Derek was the more attractive brother, but what Scar lacked in looks, he damned sure made up for in bedroom skills and dick size.

Scar pulled his dick out of her sloppy hot box and turned her around. He buried his head in her chest and licked and sucked her nipples like a baby trying to get milk.

"Oh yeah," she groaned.

Scar lifted his head to look into her beautiful face. He felt powerful. Lifting her small frame, he cupped her ass and placed her legs around him. He positioned her onto his dick and pulled her ass into him so he could bury his dick deep into her sloppy wet pussy while he carried her.

Bouncing her up and down on his thick pole, Scar fucked Tiphani all the way to the bed she shared with Derek.

Tiphani was so hot and horny she forced her tongue into Scar's deformed lips and licked his tongue. She closed her eyes tight and relished the feeling of all ten inches of his swollen manhood filling the void her husband never could.

Placing her on the bed, Scar put his knees on the bed for leverage and proceeded to drive his pole in and out of her dripping wet hot box with forceful, even pumps. Her pussy made loud slurping noises. "Ah, ah, ah, ah," Tiphani called out, loud enough to wake up the neighborhood. That dick hurt so good, and she was in her glory.

"You . . . like . . . fuckin' . . . ya . . . brother . . . in . . . law?" Scar pumped into her with each word, his muscular legs and ass flexing as he used all of his strength to dig her back out.

Derek had gotten all the way to the kids' school before he realized he had rushed out and left his service weapon at home in his safe. That wasn't like him at all. He had been so preoccupied trying to make things up to Tiphani. "How the fuck did I leave Bessy at home?" he asked himself out loud as he made a U-turn and headed back home.

Derek didn't bother to pull into the driveway; he just pulled in front of the house and figured he'd run right inside. Twisting the lock and entering the house, Derek heard his wife's voice in a high-pitched tone, like she was in distress.

What the fuck? He furrowed his brows and listened. The sound was coming from the direction of their bedroom. Derek started rushing toward the stairs, but quickly realized it wasn't a distress call his wife was making. He had definitely heard those sounds before when he was with her.

He stopped in his tracks and listened for a long minute that seemed like an eternity. Flexing his jaw with each moan and grunt, Derek balled his fists so tight his fingernails dug half-moon-shaped craters into his palms. His heart was pounding wildly, but he seemed to be rooted to that spot. He was in shock, and his heart thundered so hard it felt as if it would rupture.

Derek did not move until he heard his wife say the words, "Scar, fuck me! Fuck me, Scar!" Spurred into action by her words, Derek bolted up the remainder of the stairs as if someone had strapped a rocket to his ass. He kicked open his bedroom doors so hard one of the doors flew off the hinges.

"Oh shit!" Scar yelled out, jumping out of Tiphani's pussy with one hop.

Tiphani fell off the bed and scrambled around on the floor, searching in vain to find something to cover herself. "Derek, wait!" she screamed, but it was too late.

Derek bulldozed into Scar with full force. Scar was caught off guard and naked, so he couldn't really defend himself properly. "Arrrggggghhh!" Derek growled out, swinging wild punches into his brother's face and body. Scar tried to gain some leverage, but Derek was a man possessed.

"You dirty mu'fucka! You traitor!" Derek screamed, landing more punches to Scar's face.

Finally, Scar had his bearings. He bucked Derek off of him and put Derek in a headlock. Scar landed some punches to the top of Derek's head.

Struggling to free himself, Derek thought back to his police academy training techniques. With his heavy work boots, he stepped on Scar's bare feet with all his might.

"Ahhh!" Scar shrieked, loosening his grip on his brother's neck.

"I'm gonna fuckin' kill both of you stinkin' mu'fuckas!" Derek bellowed, his voice a thunderbolt of anger.

"Derek, please! Let me explain!" Tiphani cried, trying to calm her husband.

"Explain! Bitch, what is there to explain?" he screamed. In all of his fury, Derek swung around and slapped Tiphani so hard she flew almost clear across the room. Blood squirted from her nose and busted lip.

"No!" she screamed, holding her face. She knew she was fighting a losing battle trying to convince her husband to calm down. She balled up into a fetal position, afraid that if she moved or said anything, her husband might beat her to death.

Derek rushed toward his closet to retrieve his weapon.

"I will kill you, mu'fucka! I'm gonna kill you!!" Derek screamed out, talking to his brother and meaning every word he said.

Scar had gathered his shit and was heading down the stairs. He wasn't one to run from anyone, but he had literally been caught slipping, butt-ass naked with his gun in the car. He had been in such a rush to bang up in Derek's wife that he left his fucking gat in the car. Scar was kicking himself for being so stupid. He knew he had to get the fuck out of dodge before his brother's temper got out of control.

Derek couldn't get his weapon out of his lock box fast enough. By the time he picked up his Glock, Scar was out the door and gone.

"You fuckin' bitch! You want to fuck a criminal? My brother? Well, I hope the mu'fucka takes care of you after I'm finished destroying him!" Derek barked, standing over his wife with his gun drawn. He was so angry he knew he could shoot her right there.

Derek blinked his eyes rapidly, trying to wipe the images of killing Tiphani out of his mind. He cocked his gun and pointed it directly at her head. He wanted to shoot her; he wanted to end her life and his pain and hurt.

Finally deciding that she wasn't worth it, Derek told himself he would get them both back in a different way. He would make them suffer slowly, while he took their lives apart piece by piece. Stopping himself before he did something stupid, he moved away from Tiphani and rushed out of his home in a fury.

"Fuck being my brother's keeper. This is gonna be some Cain and Abel shit. Scar, you done fucked up now," Derek gritted out loud, like his words would somehow telepathically reach his traitorous brother's ears.

Derek stormed into the station house, pushing past all of his colleagues. Everyone was still talking about the whole warrant dustup with Scar going free, but Derek didn't even care that they were whispering about him.

"Rodriguez, Bolden, Archie, Cassell, integ room now!" Derek screamed.

All of the members of his unit looked up. They were shocked at his outburst, and they looked around like they thought he was crazy. They knew he would be mad about what happened in the courtroom, but they had never seen him this worked up before.

Apprehensively, they all filed into the small interrogation room. It was soundproof, and no one else in the station house would be able to hear what Derek had to say. He looked like a man undone. His hands were shaking, and he paced up and down the small room like he was unable to sit or stand still. He was sweating from head to toe. His dress shirt was soaked under the arms.

The entire unit looked quizzically at the scratches and red welts on his face. "Fuller, you okay?" Rodriguez asked, her face crumpled with confusion.

"Yeah, but I thought shit through, and I can't just let that fuckin' Johnson get away like that." Derek huffed out his words, barely able to catch his breath.

"I was thinking the same shit. I still don't understand how that shit went down like it did," Bolden commented, twisting his lips to the side like he was a little suspicious. In fact, all of the members of the unit were suspicious. They had all been known to take some cash from the criminals from time to time. There were plenty of times that the unit would get together in that same room and split their profit. This wasn't the first time a criminal had gone free on their watch, but it was the first time a criminal went free and they didn't see any payoff come their way.

"I want all the stops pulled out to bring this ugly mu'fucka down!" Derek screamed, slamming his flat palms on the table until they burned. He couldn't control himself; his anger was apparent.

"But what happened all of a sudden? Why the urgency today?" Cassell asked, still confused by his leader's behavior and a little pissed that he got blamed for the mix-up on the warrant. He could have sworn he wrote the address that Fuller told him.

"Were you in court yesterday? Don't ask stupid fucking questions. Just do as I say and fucking trust me for once! I want all his files pulled. I want the cold cases of the two government officials Scar Johnson allegedly put the hit on pulled and reviewed. I want y'all to scour the streets to find informants, snitches, bitches . . . whatever. I want this mu'fucka down on an airtight case.

"Two of you need to go visit that fucking lawyer too. Rough his ass up and give his ass something to mull over before he thinks about representing a walking dead man again," Derek spat. His eyes were bulged out, and the vein in his neck thumped so wildly his subordinates could see it with their naked eyes. He was talking some crazy shit to them. He wanted them to rough up a fucking defense attorney? They were all uncomfortable now. Something wasn't right and they knew it.

"We have twenty-four hours, and I want that bastard behind bars on a charge that will take care of him for life. Either that or he needs to die," Derek said with conviction before turning around and storming out of the room.

The rest of his unit looked at each other, still taken aback.

They began filing out of the room, afraid to say anything. Apparently the unit was to set out on a new mission to bring down Scar Johnson . . . like it or not.

Chapter 6

Revenge Is a Dish Best Served Cold

Scar paced back and forth in his office. He couldn't think straight. The scenario with Derek had his mind going a mile a minute. Scar's conscience was weighing heavily on him. How could he be so foul, so fucked up toward his own flesh and blood over a bitch? Scar wished he could take it back. He was immediately sorry when his brother rushed in on him and Tiphani, but it was too late then. He knew no apology could erase the image of him screwing Tiphani from his brother's mind.

Scar had never even experienced remorse in his life. He had murdered people, assaulted women, had niggahs tortured, and never lost a wink of sleep. But he actually, for the first time, felt real fucked up inside about how he had hurt his brother. Not only was Derek his brother, but Derek had come back for him, had searched for him for all those years, something that Scar couldn't say he had done. Derek also kept the law off of him for all these years. Now he wasn't so sure his brother was going to play that game. Scar needed to fix this situation fast. If not, he wouldn't just lose a brother, he could lose his whole empire.

The first time he had slept with Tiphani, it was supposed to be a one-time thing. Derek had been so excited to introduce them; his baby brother and the love of his life is how Derek had characterized them. Scar had told Derek he didn't want to meet his wife because he knew she was a prosecutor and he didn't want any parts of her. Derek convinced Scar that she would be cool, and insisted they meet. He wouldn't take no for an answer. Derek wanted his baby brother to know the love of his life, especially since they had been reunited and promised never to be separated again. That promise was all a memory now. A woman had shattered the brothers' vow.

As Scar thought back, he decided it was all Tiphani's fault. That bitch! She had come on to him after only meeting him twice. She had cried to him about Derek's sexual problems. At first, Scar thought it was amusing, his big brother not being able to hold it down in the bedroom; but then he realized Tiphani wanted him to take care of her in a way Derek couldn't. She was like a fiend . . . some kind of nympho. Scar fell into her trap, and he had to admit that her beautiful face and body had not been easy to turn away. On top of that, her pussy shot was intoxicating. The best he'd ever had.

"Everybody get the fuck outta my office!" Scar barked, sending his little flunkies scrambling to get out of his way. They all fled his office in a hurry without looking back. They had noticed that his mood had been very dark for the past two days, and usually that meant somebody's head would roll.

Scar didn't really want to be alone, but he couldn't risk his workers catching on to his pity party. He also didn't want them to hear him leave yet another message on Derek's voice mail, begging for a call back. His mind was swarming with thoughts, especially thoughts of how he was going to fix shit between him and his brother before shit got out of hand.

Scar picked up his cell and dialed his brother's number again. "Yo, D, man, I'm fuckin' sick over this shit, man. I was dead-ass wrong, man. Blood is thicker than water, man. You can't pick her over me. We need to talk. There is too much shit at stake . . . for both of us. Call me, man," Scar said in a gruff voice, trying not to sound too much like he was begging, but also letting his brother know he was sorry for what he'd done.

Scar disconnected the call and continued pacing the floor. Finally his phone rang. His heart jumped. He looked at the screen and slouched his shoulders in disappointment—it wasn't his brother. Scar didn't recognize the number.

"Yo," he said into the receiver, trying to mask his disappointment.

"Watch ya' back, nigga. There's a bounty on ya' ugly-ass head," a deep voice said into the receiver.

He didn't recognize the voice. "Fuck you, pussy! Bring it!" Scar barked in response. It was his first instinct to lash out and show he wasn't scared. He knew it had to be Derek or someone connected to him. Scar figured no other niggah in the Baltimore area would have the fucking balls to call his phone and threaten him.

Although he didn't want to, Scar had already begun to mentally prepare himself for his brother's wrath. Now he knew he would physically have to prepare as well. Scar didn't want it to come down to war with his own blood, but he had also learned from years of hustling that there were three things in the street that niggas spilled blood over: money, bitches, and reputations.

The anonymous caller hung up the phone, pleased with the outcome. Scar acted exactly as expected, trying to act tough, but the caller could hear a little worry and confusion in Scar's voice.

The events the caller had witnessed in the few days of trailing Scar were quite interesting. First there were all of the people going in to Scar's mansion and coming out with duffel bags, and then the scene at Detective Fuller's house. The caller didn't know whose house Scar was entering that day, but it all became clear when he saw Detective Fuller enter the house and then, a few minutes later, Scar come running out in his underwear. *Holy shit!* The observer had thought. Scar is fucking Detective Fuller's wife!

Continuing to shadow Scar, the caller came up with the plan. After seeing the scandal at the courthouse and Fuller coming out of Scar's place with the duffel bag, it was obvious that Scar and Fuller were somehow connected. It was just a matter of finding out how. After witnessing their fight at Fuller's house, it was obvious both were vulnerable and probably not on the best of terms. It was the perfect time to stir up some shit. Somehow, the caller needed to get this war started sooner rather than later. There couldn't be a better and easier way to turn these two against each other than to have one fucking the other's wife.

I couldn't have scripted this shit any better, the caller thought just before implementing phase one of the plan.

"Pa-lease, Derek, think about this," Tiphani begged through a face full of tears. Her face was still bruised and swollen from the backhand she took from Derek. She was grabbing Derek's arms, trying in vain to block his exit from their walk-in closet. "I will get help. I promise. I'm sorry," she pleaded.

"Tiphani, move the fuck out of my way before shit gets ugly. I feel like breaking your fucking jaw right now. I'm getting my shit and I'm out of here," Derek said, yanking his arm from her grasp. "Expect to hear from my lawyer about divorce and custody, you fuckin' whore," Derek spat evilly, his words hitting her like a whip.

She doubled over with sobs wracking her body. Tiphani felt like the rug had been pulled out from under her perfect little life. She had a handsome husband, two beautiful kids, and a little something on the side to keep her satisfied. She had her cake and was eating it too. To Tiphani, it couldn't have been any more perfect.

Derek looked down at her in disgust as he stormed out of the closet and out of their bedroom. He had vowed never to return. This shit was killing him inside. Tiphani was the first woman he had ever allowed himself to really love and trust. Yes, he could admit that he had his problems sexually, but they had taken vows for better or for worse. For her to fuck his brother was the equivalent of stabbing him in the heart and twisting the knife. In Derek's eyes, there was nothing worse she could have done.

Derek dragged his bags and stopped at his kids' rooms. He kissed his sleeping children. He would let the judge set visitation for them. Derek fought back tears and exited his home for the last time.

The pain and humiliation were so great that Derek was planning to transfer to another division after he brought Scar to his knees. He needed to get as far away as possible from the mess that his life was turning into.

Throwing his stuff into the backseat, he climbed into his car. Once inside, he slammed his fist on the steering wheel repeatedly. "Scar, you are as good as fuckin' done. I will destroy you just like you have destroyed me," Derek said through clenched teeth.

Finally, the tears dropped. Realizing he had broken down, Derek wiped his face roughly, clearing the tears before anyone could see him crying like a bitch.

He picked up his phone and called Rodriguez. He and Rodriguez had the closest relationship out of any of the members of Derek's unit. Derek figured he'd lay low with Rodriguez until he was done reigning terror on Scar.

With a new fervor for revenge, Derek screeched away from the curb outside of his former home.

That night, Derek sat at a local watering hole with his unit. He downed at least seven tumblers of Hennessy and a bunch of shots of Patrón—so many that they'd all stopped counting. Derek had intended to drink his hurt away, but as always, the alcohol seemed to make shit worse. Derek was blitzed, and he started shouting out all of his business to anyone who would listen.

"I gave that bitch my life. She fucked around on me," he slurred. "Do you know she wanted me to fuck her six times a day? She was probably fuckin' one of you guys. I wouldn't put it past her," he continued, sounding like a drunken sailor. "Who was it? You, Cassell? Huh? Did you fuck my wife? Or . . . or maybe it was Archie! Yeah, fuckin' pretty Puerto Rican bastard, it was you!" Derek stammered, pointing a wavering finger at his subordinates.

"C'mon, Fuller. I know you're hurt, but don't tell your business in here," Rodriguez told him, realizing her boss was fucked up and talking out his ass.

Derek became incensed and continued shouting. "Don't tell me what to do! You mu'fuckas need to get to work! I want that fucking Scar Johnson killed! Fuck him! Fuck sending him to jail; I got a bullet with his fucking name on it!" Derek belted out, slurring all of his words.

"Shhhh. Fuller, are you fuckin' crazy? You don't know who's in here that got connections to that dude," Cassell said, looking at his other unit members for an explanation. "This fucking dude is out of control. We better get him out of here before he gets us all killed," Cassell commented, sliding off of his barstool and pulling out his phone to make a call.

They couldn't figure out what the hell Derek's wife fucking around on him had to do with his case against Scar Johnson. They were already working hard to put shit into place to try once again to bring Scar down, but Derek's outburst just seemed random and sudden. They all exchanged confused and telling glances, finally deciding that their leader was just distraught over his wife's infidelity and that work was getting to him. They figured once he slept off his drinks he would be fine.

"C'mon, Derek. You've had enough for one night," Rodriguez said. She threw Derek's arm around her shoulder as Cassell, Archie, and Bolden helped Rodriguez steady Derek and get him into her car.

"I want immediate reports on the Johnson case tomorrow." Derek garbled his words and hiccupped at the same time.

"Yeah, Fuller. We'll brief you when you can understand English," Cassell joked.

"That's good. That's good," Derek said, his words even more garbled and jumbled than before. Derek stretched out in the back of Rodriguez's car and slept all the way to her house.

His outburst in the bar had definitely been overheard and immediately relayed back to the interested parties. The streets were always talking, and this incident was no different. Derek was oblivious that his battle cries had definitely been heard.

Scar flexed his jaw when he received more than one hood news report that a cop had been in a public bar screaming out instructions to destroy and even kill him. The one report that pissed him off the most was the phone call from the same niggah that called anonymously to warn him to watch his back. This mu'fucka was starting to get on Scar's nerves. That was the first report he received, and it seemed to Scar like it was given to him right after the cop had said it. Scar immediately knew the cop was Derek. Scar was tired of trying to cop a plea to his brother and play nice. There were but so many white flags Scar was willing to raise. A truce was obviously not what his brother was looking for.

"If this mu'fucka was fuckin' his own wife right, I wouldn't have to. I bet he don't know his bitch is begging me to come over to the house he pays mortgage for and fuck her right now. At first I felt bad, but you know what? The pussy ain't half bad. I'm taking the gloves off on his ass," Scar announced to his little trio of killers—Trail, Flip, and Sticks—the Dirty Money Crew.

They all snickered, thinking about Scar fucking his own brother's wife. They knew he was a foul, ruthless-ass nigga, but damn.

"I still don't know why you gave that lame all that money that time," Flip said, trying to act like he was joking, but finally letting his real feelings come to the surface about Scar giving Derek their entire cocaine flip.

Scar turned on Flip like Dr. Jekyll and Mr. Hyde. "What the fuck did you say?" Scar asked, his eyes going low and filling with malice.

"I'm just saying . . . it was . . . it was our dough," Flip stuttered, realizing he had gotten too loose with his lips.

The look on Scar's face made Flip's heart speed up like galloping horses at the Kentucky Derby. He knew he had fucked up.

"Is this nigga questioning my authority?" Scar asked the rest of the crew rhetorically. Scar had a crazy look in his eyes. He had been looking that way for days now.

Sticks and Trail both shook their heads, not saying a word. They didn't want any part of what was to come.

"Yo, Scar, man . . . I was just commenting about that lame," Flip said, pleading with his eyes and trying to clean up the shit he had obviously stepped knee deep into. He tried to make light of the situation by putting a half smile on his face. That just made Scar even angrier.

"Fuck you smiling about, niggah? You think this shit here a joke?" Scar asked, moving in on the boy like an eagle getting ready to pick up a mouse.

"Give me your pistol, li'l nigga," Scar instructed calmly.

"C'mon, man . . ." Flip began, his teeth chattering.

"I said give me your fucking gun, nigga! Fuck is going on around this bitch? Now I gotta say shit twice," Scar boomed, rushing into Flip's personal space.

Flip leaned back to get his face away from Scar's hideous grill. Flip dug in his waistband and reluctantly handed Scar his gun. Scar cocked the 9 mm Glock and put it up to the young boy's head.

"Yo, Scar, man . . . I'm sorry. I will never question your authority again, man," Flip begged, tears welling up at the base of his eyes.

"You are a real bitch. You like to complain like a fuckin' woman? I'ma treat you like a bitch, too," Scar said, feeling more evil by the minute. This was just what Scar wanted. He had been looking for a way to release some of the pent-up stress he had been harboring over the situation with his brother.

Trail and Sticks were like statues, stiff and rigid. They were scared to even blink. Scar was unpredictable and they knew it. There was no way they were going to risk doing anything that would catch them the same wrath that was being brought down on Flip.

"Strip, mu'fucka!" Scar screamed. Flip furrowed his brows in confusion and didn't move. "You speak English, bitch? I said take off all of your clothes! Now! I fuckin' bought everything you got on! I am the one who provides for you like a mama and a daddy, and you wanna complain about a few dollars? Take off everything right fuckin' now!" Scar screamed, holding the gun on Flip menacingly.

Flip slowly obeyed Scar's wish. He removed his fitted cap, his Coogi leather jacket, his jeans, and his Timbs. When he was finished, he sheepishly stood in his wife beater and boxers.

"Nah nigga, I bought ya drawers and all that shit! I want you naked as a newborn baby," Scar demanded.

Flip flexed his jaw and swallowed hard. He had to make a decision. Would he test Scar? Was Scar testing him to see how much of a man Flip was? In the end, he figured he didn't want to take a chance. He did as he was told to save his own life. He got butt-ass naked.

Scar let out a shrill laugh at the sight of Flip's skinny body. "Look, everybody! This chicken-chest nigga thought he had the balls to question me—the king! But that's all he got is balls . . . little-ass meatballs. His dick look like a Vienna sausage!" Scar yelled out, laughing at the same time.

Humiliating Flip was making Scar feel more powerful by the minute.

Sticks and Trail were so terrified they wouldn't dare turn their eyes away, since Scar had told them to look. Flip just stood there humiliated, trying to use his hands to cover himself.

"Take this niggah up outta here," Scar said calmly, waving his hand and dismissing Flip like a discarded piece of trash. He never had any intention of killing the boy; he just wanted to show him who was boss.

Sticks and Trail walked over to Flip, but they didn't really want to touch him. Flip's eyes were popped open in confusion. He was still not sure if Scar was done with his game, or if he could relax. The only thing Flip knew was that he wasn't about to leave naked, so he bent down to pick up his boxers.

Bang! A shot rang out and everyone jumped. Flip let out an ear-shattering scream. He fell to the floor, holding his mangled hand, while Scar started laughing again like a maniac. The young boys were shaking all over.

"I said you had to leave, but not with the shit I bought," Scar explained.

Flip pulled himself up, holding his wound. His face was contorted with pain. Now Flip was unable to control the tears as the pain ripped through the bones in his fingers. Scar had shot him in the hand when he tried to touch the clothes. He was gritting his teeth and squeezing his hand, trying to stop the bleeding. Flip wanted to curse the shit out of Scar, but he knew that if he said one thing to Scar, it would probably be his last. His shit was aching so bad Flip was sure he'd lose all of his fingers.

Sticks and Trail, not wanting to be the next victims, hurriedly escorted a naked and injured Flip out onto the street. Flip had no way to get home, no money, no car keys. All of the cars the three of them drove were on loan from Scar. He basically owned them and controlled their every move. He gave them just enough material things to keep them dependent on him. Basically, Flip was fucked. He walked slowly out the door, the pain causing his body to go into shock.

People on the street stared at a bleeding and naked Flip. In his mind, Flip vowed revenge. "This mu'fucka thinks he's God . . . you fuckin' wait," he cried and mumbled as he walked along, naked as a jaybird, trying to figure out how the fuck he would get home.

Derek had made his third appearance in family court against his wife. The first two times were just to establish what they would be fighting each other for, and for each of them to hire the highest profile lawyers they could find. Today was different. Derek definitely had a strategy.

This time, the gloves had definitely come off in family court in front of the presiding judge and both of their lawyers. Derek had spilled his wife's business about her affair and her constant need for sex to the judge and any other people who had decided to come to their custody hearing. This was definitely making Tiphani livid, since a lot of people in the courtroom were her colleagues. She tried hard to hold onto her composure and some sliver of her dignity while her husband aired her dirty laundry.

Derek had described her constant need for sex, and how he had walked in on her having sex right in their own home where they were raising their children. Tiphani had kept her head held high while her husband degraded her in public, but it wasn't easy. She wanted to run away and bury her head in the sand.

The only detail Derek left out was that the person Tiphani was caught with was Scar Johnson. He knew that it wouldn't be good for either of them to be associated with the most notorious gangster in Maryland. But if he could have somehow mentioned it without getting himself connected, you know damn well Derek would have sold that bitch out in a heartbeat.

At the end of the hearing, the judge entered a temporary order giving Derek and Tiphani shared custody until a home study could be done. This meant that a child welfare investigator would be coming to dig through Tiphani's life, asking her all types of personal questions and questioning whether she was a fit parent.

Derek had definitely not heard the last from her. She was now hell bent on getting her husband back for this. There wasn't much she could say in the courtroom. If she brought up any of the dirt she knew about Derek, she would easily have been implicated in all of his dirty-ass dealings as well. The one thing she could not afford was to be associated with Scar Johnson in any way.

She stormed from the courtroom and immediately dialed Scar's phone number. Normally, she would have been more cautious when contacting Scar, for fear that his phone was being traced, but at that moment, Tiphani was so angry she wasn't thinking straight.

When he picked up, she couldn't hold back her anger. "I need to see you right away. This bastard needs to be stopped," Tiphani gritted out.

"Meet me at our usual spot tomorrow," Scar said and hung up immediately. He, too, was paranoid about his conversations being taped.

Derek left court feeling vindicated. He was going to pull out all of the stops to make Tiphani and Scar suffer. Derek called his team and asked if everything was in place for later. Derek got the answer he was looking for and smiled.

Later that night, Scar sat in his office feeding money stacks into his money machine. It was the only thing that made him feel better lately. Suddenly, he heard someone running outside the door to his office. Scar pulled his gun out and got ready.

"Yo, boss! We gotta get the fuck outta here! I just got word that all the spots in the east are getting hit right now! My phone is blowing up. All ten spots. Niggas said it's the DES, DEA, FBI, ICE—all those fuckin' pigs!" Scar's lieutenant reported, so out of breath he could barely get the words out.

Scar jumped up from his seat. He had to get the fuck out of his spot because he could not be sure if this was a coincidence or if Derek would be sending the feds to get his ass at his secret spot. Derek knew about Scar's secret spot, so it seemed logical that they would be coming.

Scar started stuffing his stacks of money into bags. He grabbed his weapon and raced out through the secret tunnel underneath Katrina's. As soon as he made it into his truck, he heard. "Police!

Freeze! Police!"

The police had busted into his spot from every direction. Scar's other workers were being taken down. There was no time to think about them now. Scar and his right hand man pulled out through the back road. They had just missed the raid by the skin of their asses.

Scar's chest heaved in and out. He wanted to fuck something up. He started banging on the dashboard. He banged until his hands hurt. "I'm gonna murder his whole fuckin' department! They wanna fuck with Scar Johnson? This fuckin' government is responsible for all the foul shit that ever happened to me in my life! I am the fuckin' King of Baltimore! Those mu'fuckin' boys in blue about to be singing the Maryland blues!" Scar screamed at the top of his lungs, his ugly scarred face twisted into a hideous mug.

Back at the station house, Derek smiled and did a little dance as he got word that all of the raids on Scar's spots were successful. His unit had reported back to him that they were almost positive that out of the sixty corner boys and trap house bodies they had arrested, somebody would be willing to roll on Scar in a court of law for their own freedom.

Derek was overjoyed. This time there would be no mishap with the warrant. He couldn't contain his joy as he slapped five with his unit and excitedly asked for details.

Derek could just picture how crazy Scar must have been going right then.

When his unit turned into the station house, Derek held a final outbrief with them and got all of the information he needed.

"That was a good fucking job today. I appreciate all of your hard work," Derek commended them.

"I'm going the hell home. This has been two weeks of long-ass days and nights and fuckin' crazy hours. I'll be back in the morning," Cassell announced, stretching his arms for emphasis.

"Yeah, me too," Bolden said, agreeing, standing up to follow Cassell out the door.

"Okay. Go home, recharge, and I will see you guys back here tomorrow," Derek said.

Derek, Archie, and Rodriquez were staying a bit longer to firm up some paperwork. They all watched the two officers leave the station house, happy to be going home to their families.

"What are you two going to do?" Derek asked Rodriguez and Archie. He wanted to go get drunk as hell—his new way to ease his pain.

"I'm about to get in my ride," Rodriguez started, but before the rest of her words could leave her mouth, Boom!

Derek and Archie jumped and ducked their heads down. The officers all looked at each other, puzzled. Rodriguez almost choked on her words. The noise, which sounded like an explosion, was coming from outside.

All three officers rushed to the station house doors. They first noticed Bolden's car on fire. "Oh, shit!" Rodriguez screamed. Just as they began scrambling outside to try to get Bolden out of the burning car—Boom! Boom!—two more explosions sounded, stopping them in their tracks.

"It's Chief Scott's and Cassell's!" Archie screamed, shielding his eyes from the bright light of the massive fires as he stumbled backward away from the danger.

"Oh shit!" Rodriguez screamed again, falling to her knees. Derek stood rooted to the ground with his mouth hanging open in shock.

"Go get the extinguishers!" Derek screamed, finally snapping into action. Derek didn't know what to do. He soon realized that a fire extinguisher wouldn't do anything for those firebombs.

"Get some fucking help! Call the bomb squad!" he screamed again, his voice as high-pitched as a woman's. Everyone inside the station house began scrambling. The cars had been rigged to blow up. Derek knew damn sure that he, Rodriguez, and Archie couldn't get into their rides, or no one else inside the station house, for that matter.

Derek stood frozen, staring at the flames. He knew right away why this was happening. While everything around him seemed to move in slow motion, he realized that if his brother could retaliate this fast and right under the nose of a whole police station, he was in a war with his brother that would only end with one of them dead.

Chapter 7

Nothing Is Fair in Love and War

"He's trying to take my kids away from me and destroy my career," Tiphani cried, her tears falling on Scar's thick, muscular shoulders. "I'll do anything to keep my kids. I can't let him do this to me. He has to be stopped," she cried even harder.

"I'm not gonna let him ruin you. I'll ruin him first. Matter of fact, we can ruin his ass together," Scar said, stroking her long hair.

Scar was playing his part. He figured enlisting Derek's wife onto his team to help get revenge was a good strategy. Scar knew that after Derek's last hit on him and his return hit, shit was going to get even more dangerous if he didn't come up with a plan. Tiphani played right into his hand. Scar knew she was the type of bitch that worried about what people thought of her. She had come from nothing, and being a lawyer made her feel like someone, so having her husband threaten her career and everything she worked hard for would cause her to do anything.

"I still care about him. I mean, he is my husband, but I needed sex. I can't live without it, and he . . . he just couldn't do for me what you could do for me," she continued, more tears flowing.

She was also using a strategy. Tiphani couldn't risk Derek revealing the name of the person she'd had an affair with. If anyone knew she slept with Scar, she would most definitely lose her law license, and her face would be plastered on every newspaper. She could see the headlines now: prosecutor sleeps with notorious drug dealer—she was on the case.

"Look, I think I'm in love with you, baby. All we gotta do is stick together. This nigga is as good as done," Scar said, putting on his Academy Award–worthy sad face.

He wiped the tears from her cheeks. He knew just how to seal their deal. “Let me find out you a little nymphomaniac and you need a piece of the Scar,” he whispered. Scar rolled over and thrust his tongue into her mouth deeply.

Tiphani opened her lips and welcomed his tongue into her mouth. She immediately felt herself heating up down below, and thoughts of her husband destroying her started to fade.

Scar wedged his way between her legs as he continued to kiss her. He could feel a slick sheen of her body’s natural moisture on the inside of her thighs. Scar grabbed his coveted manhood and drove it roughly into her slippery hole.

Tiphani almost choked, it felt so good. A gasp got caught in her throat. “Oh, Scar,” she was finally able to manage.

“Do . . . you . . . believe . . . in . . . me?” Scar grunted out as he banged into her flesh with no mercy.

Tiphani’s eyes popped open. Scar had never been this rough with her.

“Yes!” she screamed, grabbing onto the bed sheets in an effort to keep him from banging her through the wall.

All of a sudden Scar stopped, grabbed her roughly and flipping her over onto her stomach. “I control everything and everybody,” Scar growled, grabbing a handful of her hair.

Tiphani tried to scramble away, but Scar’s grip was too powerful. He snatched her back under him, parted her ass cheeks, let a glob of spit fall from his mouth onto her ass, and mounted her roughly from behind.

“Agggghh!” Tiphani screamed out in a soprano that was a mixture of pleasure and pain.

Scar loved to hear her scream as he drove all ten inches of himself into her asshole. That had sealed their agreement to work together to get Derek out of their way.

Derek attended Chief Scott’s memorial service first, then Cassell’s. He looked around at both services and saw some of Scar’s henchmen peppered throughout the crowd of mourners. He exchanged menacing glares with them to let them know he knew they were there, and that he wasn’t scared of their punk asses. Derek knew shit was real in the field, though.

He was thinking night and day about his next strategy. He wanted to hit Scar where it hurt, but he knew that would take some time to put together. His unit had been put on modified duties because of the mental anguish they'd suffered from Cassell's death, and from just knowing that someone was trying to blow all of them up. Derek knew he couldn't take too long to hit Scar back or else he'd strike first.

"Detective Fuller, I'm Chief Hill. Newly assigned to Division One," a tall black man with salt-and-pepper hair said, extending his hand to Derek.

Derek lifted his head and furrowed his eyebrows. He was a little taken aback. There wasn't any talk about a newly appointed chief, and he definitely never expected a black man. Derek silently extended his hand.

"I hear that this hit on Scott and your officer might have something to do with some dealings you've had with Scar Johnson," the chief said suspiciously, wasting no time letting Derek know he was being watched.

"I don't have any dealing with Scar Johnson. I have spent my entire time in narcotics trying to bring Scar Johnson down," Derek said indignantly. The lie slipped from his mouth so fast and with so much ease he almost believed it himself.

Derek acted offended by the chief's accusatory tone, but all the while his heart was thundering in his chest. He didn't know how much this new chief knew, and that bugged Derek.

"Well, all I'm going to say is tread lightly and get your shit together. There will be no more officers killed on my watch because of what you either did or didn't do," Chief Hill grit
out, giving Derek an icy look that spoke volumes.

Derek wiped sweat from his head and stormed
fuck is he coming up in here, trying to te
didn't do? Fuck him too, Derek thou
badly he had to put them into his pock

Even though he might not have war
shaken from the conversation. The p
had to take Scar down before anyone

his narcotics unit was into. His uneasy feeling from before was starting to creep back into his thoughts.

Rodriguez walked over to Derek. "What was that all about?"

"Nothing. New chief introducing himself. Wants me to turn the heat up on the Scar Johnson case," Derek lied, pulling himself together.

"Really? He wanted to fuckin' talk about work at a time like this? Fucking asshole," Rodriguez said, looking over at the new chief and shaking her head.

"Yeah. Seems like an asshole already," Derek said in a low voice, hoping he had convinced Rodriguez to stay on his side and help him get back to work against Scar.

After the service and burial, Derek left the cemetery alone—or so he thought. Derek was so caught up with everything going on and trying to figure out what the new chief was talking about that he didn't notice the person trailing him throughout the service and then to the bar after the burial.

Seeing the old dude with salt-and-pepper hair talking to Derek was a surprise to the observer. *It was the same old guy that had been in front of Scar's mansion. That old dude is the chief. I knew I recognized his ass from somewhere. Niggah be a cop! This is going to play out nicely. Scar, the chief, and Detective Fuller are all in it together. Time to play these fools like marionettes.* The Shadow couldn't have been any happier.

It had been an emotional and fucked up couple of days, and returning to Rodriguez's house, all Derek wanted to do was get some much needed rest. When he walked in, Rodriguez was waiting for him.

"This was left here for you," Rodriguez said, tossing a manila nvelope to Derek.

What's this?" Derek asked angrily.

n't know. Someone rang my doorbell and left it."

as it?

w. They were walking away by the time I got to the

the back of her. I'm assuming it was your wife."

Rodriguez was happy to let Fuller stay at her house, but she wasn't happy that his crazy wife was leaving envelopes on her doorstep, or, for that matter, that she knew Derek was staying there. If Fuller wasn't still married to the tramp, Rodriguez would have run after her and beat that bitch to a pulp.

"Fuck that bitch!" Derek spat, grabbing the envelope and tearing it open.

Rodriguez looked on curiously, wanting to see what was in the envelope. While she waited for Derek to arrive, she had started to open it, but although the curiosity was killing her, she decided against it.

Derek almost fainted when he pulled out the contents of the envelope. He looked up at Rodriguez with wide eyes. "What is it, Derek?" Rodriguez asked, walking toward him.

Trembling all over, Derek placed the contents up against his chest to hide it. "It's nothing. This bitch thought sending me naked pictures of herself was going to get me back," Derek fabricated on the spot, thinking quick on his feet.

His heart was beating like crazy. His stomach muscles were tightend, and he felt like he'd shit on himself.

Speechless, Rodriguez looked at Derek curiously to gauge his reaction. To her, his wife had been a fool to cheat on him. Rodriguez had always been attracted to Fuller, ever since she had first met him, but knowing that he was married stopped her from expressing her interest.

"But doesn't she think that it's too little too late for all of that?" Rodriguez commented. She walked up behind him and put her hands on his tense shoulders as she began to rub them softly.

At first Derek was taken by surprise, but then he began to relax. Her hands felt good. A woman's touch felt good. He felt wanted.

"I mean, she didn't appreciate you when she had you," Rodriguez flirted. Her hands moved from his shoulders to his neck, and she reached up and rubbed his head. Rodriguez's heart raced as her pussy grew moist. She could feel her clit begging to be touched, and she felt the rise and fall of Derek's labored breathing.

"I'd appreciate you, Fuller," she whispered. She turned him around and looked up at him while her hands roamed his chest, now underneath his shirt.

He looked at her lustfully. Her Hispanic roots gave her a goddess-type body, and her long hair was down around her face. She only wore it that way in the comfort of her home, but it was a welcomed change from her usual sleek ponytail. She looked sexy, and for the first time, he remembered that Rodriguez was more than a cop. She was a woman.

"I've wanted you for a long time, Derek," she admitted, lust lacing her words. She reached up and pulled his face toward hers and put her tongue in his mouth.

He sucked it hungrily, kissing her deeply as he palmed her luscious ass and hips. His dick instantly rocked, and Rodriguez could feel it pressing against her flat stomach.

"I love you, Derek. I've watched and loved you for a while now," she admitted. "My pussy is so wet right now," she moaned as he ripped her blouse open, revealing beautiful D-cup breasts in a purple satin bra.

"Damn," he admired as he licked each mound, releasing her nipple and teasing it with his tongue. He was horny as fuck. He felt a fire in his loins like no other, and he mentally began to prepare himself for the sex to come. He had never seen Rodriguez with a man, or even heard her mention a boyfriend, so he knew her pussy was tight and ready. Sexing her would be a welcomed distraction. She made him feel wanted, and right now that was what Derek needed.

He stripped her, and she removed his clothes; then he picked up her petite frame and placed her directly on his dick, no rubber and no second thought.

She felt like heaven, and his dick filled her up nicely as she began to speak in Spanish while she bounced on his dick.

"Oh shit, Derek. Yes . . . fuck me! Fuck this pussy, *papi*!" she screamed.

His mojo was on point, until he began to think about what he was doing.

"Fuck me!" she moaned, but instead of hearing Rodriguez's voice, he heard his adoptive mother's, and just like all the times before, he nutted too quickly. Cumming after only five minutes of stroking, he pulled out of her and shot his fluid on her stomach.

Embarrassed, he stood quickly. “I’m sorry, Rodriguez.”

“Derek, it’s okay,” she said sincerely as she stood up and reached for him. She didn’t care that he had only lasted a short while. She didn’t know it was a recurring problem; she just thought that his nerves had taken over from the fact that he was fucking a long time friend.

“I’m sorry. I just need to get my head together,” he mumbled as he picked up his clothes and the envelope full of pictures, then rushed up the stairs to the bedroom Rodriguez had let him crash in.

Rodriguez ran her hands through her hair, unsure of what had just happened. She knew that she could not change it now, however, and hoped that she wouldn’t come to regret showing her true feelings.

Derek scattered the pictures out on the bed. He bit into his bottom lip until he drew blood. There were pictures of Derek hanging with Scar and his crew, and pictures of Derek leaving Scar’s club and house with duffel bags. There were also pictures of Derek with stacks of money in his hands as Scar handed them to him.

The most damaging picture was one Derek knew had known he would regret taking—him sitting behind Scar’s desk, surrounded by stacks of money and bricks of cocaine.

Scar had urged him to see how it felt to be a powerful drug kingpin for a minute. After a little coaxing and teasing from Scar, Derek reluctantly sat behind the desk. Scar’s crew was so hyped that there was a detective sitting behind the desk they all pulled out their cell phones and started taking pictures and video. Derek had barked at the little flunkies to stop snapping pictures with their cell phones, but obviously it had been too late. In return, Scar asked Derek for his badge so Scar could see how it felt to be a cop for a minute.

Again Derek was reluctant, but finally gave in. He let Scar take pictures with his gun and shield.

Now Derek could only blame himself for being so stupid and not trusting his instincts. He knew playing around with gangsters and taking pictures would come back to haunt him, but he didn't listen to his own conscience.

Derek grabbed up the pictures in a fury and began ripping them up. He took his gun out of his holster and put it in his mouth several times. He was seriously considering killing himself. There was no way he could risk the pictures coming out in the media. He would be fucked! Jail was not a place Derek was willing to go, especially over some shit like this.

Fuck that! Derek wasn't about to punk out and kill himself and let Scar win that easily. He had to make a move and make it fast. "Scar, you fucking piece of shit!" Derek growled.

As usual, Scar left out the back door of Derek and Tiphani's house. He had a smirk on his face, thinking about the serious pussy pounding he had just put on her ass. He also felt real good that she had done the deed of delivering a copy of his blackmail material to Derek. Scar knew Derek must've been shitting bricks after seeing those pictures. He figured his big brother should've known that he had video cameras everywhere that he could run back and make stills from.

Scar always had it in the back of his mind that shit would go sour with him and his brother one day. If truth be told, he had never really forgiven Derek or his mother for all of the torment he went through as a kid.

Scar walked through the neighbor's backyards and came around to the front of the house two doors down. He looked around and started up the street to his truck. He never parked right in front of Tiphani and Derek's house.

As he ambled forward thinking about his next move, he heard footsteps thundering in his direction.

"Scar Johnson, freeze! Police!" they screamed out.

"Not this bullshit again," he mumbled. Scar was suddenly surrounded by a swarm of police officers with guns drawn. He stopped dead in his tracks and raised his hands.

This was all too familiar, except this time it wasn't an acting job, nor did he know they were coming.

"Keep your hands up and turn around until I tell you to stop!" one of the cops screamed out.

Scar did as he was told. When he turned to face them— "Gun!" they screamed out.

Since Derek had busted up on them before, Scar never went over there without being strapped.

"Yo, be easy. I'm not gonna try nothing funny," Scar yelled out, knowing that if he didn't, those quick-to-shoot-ass cops would've filled his ass full of lead.

"Get on ya fuckin' knees and keep ya hands up!" an officer screamed out. Scar did as he was told. He could hear an officer approaching from the back. About sixteen others kept their guns trained on him, and he could see the glare from a red laser sight shining on his nose.

Scar suddenly felt a hand reach around the front of him and grab his gun out of his waistband.

"I got it," the officer yelled as he retreated away from Scar.

"Take him down," another one screamed. Suddenly Scar was pushed face down on the ground. Three or four officers dropped knees into his back and roughly grabbed his arms and pulled them around his back.

"Stephon 'Scar' Johnson, you are under arrest, and here is the arrest warrant!" an officer said, placing the paper up to Scar's face as they pulled him up off the ground. "You have the right to remain silent, anything—"

"Yeah, yeah, mu'fucka, I've heard it all before," Scar grumbled. Once again he was forced into a police car. This time Scar had no idea what probable cause they had to be locking him up. The only thing he could think of was that one of those weak-ass corner boys on his payroll must've been down at the station house singing like a fucking bird about Scar and his operation.

Scar flexed his jaw just thinking about it. Every time he felt he had gotten an upper hand on his brother, Derek came back with something else to bring him back to reality.

This was a real war, and although he knew he would have to temporarily get someone to fight for him, Scar was willing to do anything now. Derek had to be stopped.

"Make sure I get a phone call to my fucking lawyer," Scar spat as the door to the police car slammed shut.

Chapter 8

Man Down

Derek smiled when he heard that they had picked up Scar on the arrest warrant; however, he wasn't too happy to know that Scar was picked up on the block where he used to live with his wife. The officers that had been following Scar to prepare for the arrest were all buzzing about Scar being on Derek's street. They had been unable to see exactly which house Scar had gone into, though, since they had stayed a few car lengths away. Scar had parked down the street and walked through a bunch of backyards and disappeared.

Derek knew immediately that Scar had been in his home fucking his wife again, and the idea of it incensed him. His imagination started to run wild. He was picturing Scar fucking Tiphani; then he could see Scar cooking breakfast in his kitchen and picking up his little girl or playing video games with his son.

Derek slammed his fist on his desk, garnering a few strange looks from other officers and staff members around him. Derek wanted to clear his mind. He had been plagued with crazy thoughts and ideations. Once, he had even seen himself strangling Tiphani until the life went out of her eyes.

Shaking his head and trying not to stress, Derek stood up to go outside for a bit of fresh air. When he turned around to leave his desk, he bumped head first into Chief Hill. *Fuck!* Derek screamed in his head.

"Excuse me," Derek said, startled.

"Were you responsible for the arrest of Scar Johnson today?" the chief asked dryly, hardly fazed by Derek's nervous body language.

"Nah, um . . . I mean, he was picked up based on probable cause based on information from a confidential informant that we developed after the raids," Derek stammered.

He didn't fucking know why this chief unnerved him so badly, but it made him angry.

Derek didn't like the look the chief was giving him. Fuck it, he could admit it; he didn't like the chief at all.

The chief looked him up and down with a scowl on his face. "Do you mean reasonable suspicion, Officer Fuller?" Chief Hill said.

"Detective Fuller," Derek corrected him.

The chief ignored the correction. "I want to see the probable cause affidavit. I want to know everything about the informant too. I will not be embarrassed in a court of law. I'm hearing rumors already that the judges are agreeing that they will set bail for Johnson if he comes before them.

"This shit is starting to look like a fucking witch hunt now, Officer Fuller. You should've waited until you had concrete evidence of a crime. If Johnson walks again, shit might change for you. Like I said . . . Officer Fuller," Chief Hill said with finality. He turned his back and walked away before Derek could say anything in his own defense.

Suddenly the chief doubled back. "I hope all of this 'out for blood' shit you got going on with Johnson doesn't have anything to do with a certain affair and divorce," the chief commented.

Derek almost choked on his own saliva. "What?" Derek said in a low whisper, squinting his eyes with contempt.

"I'm just letting you know once again that there will be no bullshit on my watch," Chief Hill reminded Derek, leaving him standing there dumfounded.

Archie left the station house in a rush. It had been a long couple of weeks. Detective Fuller had been pushing them extremely hard to go after Scar Johnson, and then the deaths of Bolden and Cassell. Shit had been weighing hard on Archie's mind, even causing him nightmares. He wanted to get home—no, he needed to get home. Even the modified duty status didn't make shit better.

Finally making it outside, Archie revved up his motorcycle and used his foot to release the kickstand. He refused to drive his vehicle after the car bombings, and he checked and doubled checked his bike each time he was ready to ride it. Archie was super paranoid at home, too, and forbid his wife from driving any of their vehicles either.

With his mind heavy, Archie sped out of the station house parking lot and turned onto the street, heading for home. He made a left, and so did the car that was following him. Archie made a right; the car turned right as well. Archie was oblivious to the fact that he was being followed.

He never usually followed the rules of the road, and often cut in and out of traffic to bypass cars when he rode his motorcycle. After the deaths of his coworkers, he had an overwhelming fear of dying, so he began to follow the rules of the road.

Archie stopped at a red light and placed his feet on the ground to steady his bike. He flexed his back and wrists, which tended to get a little stiff when he rode for long distances. Staring straight ahead, he never saw the black van pull behind him and the bodies dressed in all black approaching him from either side. A lady blew her horn, trying to warn him, but a gun was put in her face.

The light turned green, and just as Archie lifted his feet back onto the bike's gear pedals, he felt something slam into the side of his head. He was hit with such force that he and his bike toppled over.

Archie opened his mouth, but no sound came out. He didn't even have time to fight or go for his weapon. A black bag was placed over his head, and he was dragged from under his bike, which had fallen on his legs.

Finally realizing he was in danger, he began to thrash and fight. Archie fought for air as his captors held him in a severely tight headlock.

"Mmmm," Archie groaned, his air supply being cut off. Swinging his arms and legs wildly, he tried to fight for his life. He was thrown into the back of a van, while his bike was left revving on the street.

Scar was laughing as the judge set his bail at ten thousand dollars. He thought he had to be the luckiest fuck in Baltimore. Either that or his payoffs were paying off. Ten grand was candy money to him.

Scar had his lieutenant pick him up and post the bail. On the ride from the jail, he was filled in on the latest war move. Scar was happy to hear about the capture of Archie. He knew this would be a low blow to Derek and the Maryland State Police. Another one of their men missing would definitely start ringing some alarms and bringing heat on Derek's dirty ass.

They drove to a secret spot near the beach in Baltimore that hardly anyone knew about, even members of Scar's own crew. Scar rushed inside to ensure he wasn't spotted.

"Where is he?" Scar asked.

Scar was led down into an old industrial wine cellar, and there he was. "Well, well, well. Looks like your boss let you down," Scar said, looking at Archie's battered and bruised naked body tied to a chair. "So, I heard you won't tell my little friends here who the informant was that snitched on me after the raids," Scar said, lifting Archie's downturned head so he could look into his battered eyes.

Archie's eyes were almost swollen shut. They were riddled with blue, red, and purple bruises, and blood was crusted all over his face.

"F . . . fuck you," Archie groaned out, barely able to get the words out. Archie knew he was going to die anyway, so he wasn't going to go out like a bitch and tell Scar what he wanted to hear. Once Scar's little henchmen had taken the bag off of Archie's head and showed their faces, Archie knew he would never leave there alive.

"Fuck me? Aw, that's just too bad. You and your little crew have been trying to fuck me for years, but guess what? Your precious leader, Detective Fuller, is really Derek Johnson—my fuckin' brother—and he has been on my payroll for years. So, all of your hard work would've never paid off anyway. He fucked you!" Scar said, lifting his gorilla fist and punching Archie across the face for emphasis.

Archie didn't even scream. He was so numb from the pain.

"Take care of him," Scar instructed, leaving Archie to the wolves. One of Scar's henchmen walked over, placed the jumper cables on Archie's two big toes, and sent enough of an electric surge through his body to restart a car battery.

Archie screamed so hard and so loud that the back of his throat began to bleed. He knew he was better off dead.

Derek was sitting in Rodriguez's home, drowning his sorrows in a bottle of Hennessy when he heard commotion downstairs. Startled, he stood up on wobbly legs and pulled out his weapon to investigate.

Creeping into the hallway, gripping his gun tightly, Derek slurred, "Who the fuck is it?" He lifted his gun up haphazardly. "Rodriguez? You better say something before you get a few in your ass," Derek continued, his words choppy.

Stumbling on the stairs, Derek finally made it downstairs without falling on his face. Looking around, he started flicking on lights. "Who the fuck is in here?" he belted out, but he didn't see anyone in the house. He stumbled into the kitchen—nothing. It was the same result in the living room. "Better had gotten the fuck outta here," he mumbled, walking over to the big bay window in the living room.

Derek pulled back the curtains on the window to continue his investigation, but he didn't see anyone on the porch either. Derek squinted and ducked his head to get a better view outside. He looked out into the street. He knew it wasn't raining, but he could see something dripping from the sky onto his car. It was like it was raining in one spot—on his car.

Out of the corner of his eye he saw movement. Maybe someone running away from the house? He couldn't tell; he was having trouble focusing. "What the fuck is that?" he spoke to himself, squinting harder. Finally, he unlatched the front door and stumbled down the front steps to the curb where his car was parked.

Gun in hand, Derek stood in the street in front of the hood of his car. Then he felt drops on his head too. Derek touched the liquid substance that was dripping on his car and then on his head. He looked at his hand and saw that it was covered in blood. "What the fu—" Derek slowly raised his head and looked up. He screamed, dropping his weapon and stumbling over the curb.

"Arrggghhh!" he screamed again as he looked up at the eviscerated remains of his unit member Archie. The sight of the blood and hanging intestines and guts caused Derek to pass out.

Scar's mystery stalker had been following him for weeks now, and this was the most gruesome thing the stalker had witnessed. The stalker had watched as Scar's henchmen took a beaten and bloodied body and strung it up outside of Detective Rodriguez's house. After the henchmen left, the stalker waited a few minutes before going to examine the body. The men had placed something in the pants pocket of the body and taken something out and thrown it onto the lawn. The stalker needed to find out what it was and who the body was. The war between Detective Fuller and Scar was in full swing, and there wasn't much for the stalker to do except make sure it went on long enough for both men to be destroyed.

As the stalker slowly snuck up on the crime scene, it became obvious that it was even more gruesome than it appeared from a distance. The body was strung up, gutted, and draining blood like a pig in a slaughter house. It was enough to send shivers down anyone's spine. Sure, the stalker had witnessed deaths and beatings before, but never anything so vicious. There was a split second where the stalker just wanted to turn around, leave, and forget about the mission. Hopefully Detective Fuller and Scar would just destroy themselves. But the stalker's obsession with payback and vengeance quickly put those thoughts to rest.

The first thing that was noticed were two big knots of bills, one in each front pocket of the body. The stalker took one, but it felt kind of damp, so the stalker thought better of taking the second one. It was left in Archie's pocket.

Next up was to investigate what was thrown on the lawn. It wasn't easy to see in the dark, so it took a while to find what had been thrown. Just as the stalker was about to stop looking and leave, the object was spotted. It was a cell phone. The stalker knew this could be beneficial to the one-sided war being waged against Scar and Detective Fuller.

Immediately, the phone was opened up and the contents were searched. There wasn't much on the phone that would help. Dejected, the stalker was about to put the phone away, but then a plan materialized.

It happened when searching through the contact list on the

phone. Detective Fuller's name and number were on the list. The stalker first dialed Scar's number and hung up immediately, then repeated the action, but with Detective Fuller's number.

Just as the calls were finished, the curtains in the bay window were pushed open, startling the stalker. Immediately, the stalker wiped the phone of fingerprints and ran. During the retreat, the phone was thrown under Detective Fuller's car so it would be easier for the cops to find.

About five minutes later, the police received an anonymous tip about a dead body hanging from a utility pole.

The lights and sirens flashed around Derek as he lay knocked out. When Derek came back into consciousness, he was on a stretcher surrounded by EMTs and a swarm of police. Derek recognized more than one of the crime scene investigators.

"Derek? What the fuck happened here?" Rodriguez asked when she noticed Derek had opened his eyes. Rodriguez had had enough. She wanted an explanation, and was starting to grow very suspicious about the deaths of her fellow unit members and Derek's strange behavior. It seemed to Rodriguez that each time shit went down, Derek was nearby, or had just been in contact with the officer before he was killed. Both she and Fuller had been involved in some shady shit before, but never would she have thought about killing one of her unit members. To her, that was the grimiest and most low-down things anyone could do. She didn't want to believe that Fuller could do something like that, but everything was pointing that way.

She also had reason to believe that Derek had motive for killing Cassell. The day that woman dropped off the envelope for Derek at her doorstep, there was also a note left for her. It simply stated Detective Fuller had a reason to kill Cassell. Check the warrant. At the time, she ignored it, thinking it was just his wife trying to stir some shit. Now she wasn't so sure.

"I don't know. I heard a noise . . . I think I came down . . . I don't remember," Derek said groggily. He was dazed and confused. The mixture of Hennessy and the hit he took on the head when he fell wasn't helping.

"What the fuck you mean, you don't know? Archie is fuckin' gutted open like a pig, hanging from a utility pole in front of my house! Blood is all over your fucking car and your hands! What the fuck is going on?" Rodriguez screamed, demanding an answer from Derek.

"Whoa, whoa. Take it easy," an EMT said, stepping between Derek and Rodriguez. Derek just stared ahead. He was numb and in shock. He didn't have the answers that she was looking for—or at least he wasn't going to tell her. He was not the man she thought him to be.

"If you don't start giving me some answers and start trusting me, I want you to get your shit out of my fuckin' house! Obviously you're bad luck, Derek. Either that or you're a murderer, since the bodies keep piling up around you," Rodriguez said to Derek, then turned and stormed away with tears clouding her eyes.

Chief Hill approached Derek just as Rodriguez breezed by him. "Fuller, we need a statement from you, since you were on the scene when the body was discovered," Chief Hill said.

"I already said I can't fuckin' remember what happened! I had a few drinks, and I must've heard something. I don't know why I came outside, and I don't know what happened after I was out here, okay! I know Archie is fuckin' dead, but I don't know what the fuck happened!" Derek yelled, the vein in his head visible at his temple.

He was tired of everyone being up in his face, blaming him for shit. Maybe he had made the mistake of getting into some shit with his brother, but he definitely didn't have his own men killed.

"I don't know what type of shit you're into, Fuller, but you better get your shit together. I will not have another fuckin' casualty or a fuckin' war that you started over a bitch. And I better not find out you're a dirty fuckin' cop," Chief Hill said, pointing an accusatory finger in Derek's face.

His words hit Derek like a sledgehammer. *What does this mu'fucka know?* Derek asked himself. It seemed like the chief knew a lot.

"Hey, Chief! You need to see this," one of the forensic crime scene investigators called out to Chief Hill.

"Remember what the fuck I said, Fuller. Your chances have run the fuck out," Chief Hill said in a harsh whisper and disappeared.

Derek closed his eyes and lay back down on the gurney. He

was wishing he was any one of his dead coworkers.

"Chief, look at this," the crime scene investigator said, showing the chief a rubber-banded stack of money sticking out of Archie's pants pocket. The money was covered in blood, so it made it almost impossible to see the denomination of the bills. The investigators took several pictures before removing the wad of money to place in the evidence collection bags.

"How much is it?" the chief asked as he watched. The investigator flipped through the bills quickly, careful not to contaminate the blood and DNA evidence. "Looks like it's about ten thousand or more," the investigator said.

"Why would an officer who is not even at top pay be carrying around that type of fucking money?" the chief asked quizzically. "Shit just doesn't make sense. Why hang the body here?" he murmured to himself.

"We got his cell phone!" another investigator called out as they scoured the street in front of the house. Chief Hill rushed over to where she had found the phone lying wedged into the sewer grate under Derek's car.

"Did it get wet?" the chief asked.

"Aside from a little bit of blood, I think we still got a good working phone," the investigator said.

"Turn it on," the chief demanded.

"Chief, I don't know if you want to disturb the evidence. It may cause us to lose something," she explained.

"No! Turn it on!" Chief Hill screamed.

She did as she was told. The chief snatched the phone from her hand and pressed the dial button to redial the last number called. The chief held the phone with a plastic glove over his hand and listened. It was ringing. Chief Hill was hoping that someone answered.

Just as he said that, Derek came limping over. "Hey, Grady, what ya got?" Derek asked the investigator that had found the money.

"Somebody worked him over really good before they gutted him like a Christmas pig," the investigator explained.

Derek shook his head in remorse. His phone began ringing. Derek fumbled with his pocket to get his phone out. He looked down at the screen. archie, it read. Derek crinkled his face and looked around.

He locked eyes with Chief Hill, who was walking in his direction, holding Archie's phone. Derek had a look of sheer terror on his face.

"Fuller, don't fucking move!" Chief Hill screamed as he handed Archie's phone back to the investigator.

Derek was dumbfounded. He had not remembered receiving any calls from Archie last night. Why would Archie be calling him?

"Can you fucking explain to me why Officer Archie had ten thousand dollars of what appeared to be drug money in his fucking pocket, called you last, and ended up dead, strung up to a pole in front of the house you reside in?" Chief Hill asked accusingly.

"Wait one fucking minute. I don't know what you are insinuating, but you better back the fuck up. I've taken a lot of shit off of you in the past couple of weeks, but accusing me of having something to do with the death of one of my men is the last straw!" Derek barked.

"We'll see about that. As soon as the lab comes back with something, I will be seeing you. Until then, stay the fuck out of my way!" Chief Hill spat, leaving Derek with something to think about.

Chapter 9

Payback is a Big Bitch

Tiphani had been a nervous wreck with everything that was going on between her and Derek and Scar. She often felt torn between what was right, saving her marriage, and her love of Scar's dick. Now things were falling apart for Derek and definitely out of her control.

She had agreed to help Scar take her husband down because she was selfishly thinking about her career and how it would look if she lost custody of her children. Tiphani was at a real crossroads. She had just as much to lose as Derek. Taking her husband down might save her career and let her keep her kids, or it might cause him to open up a can of worms that would make her lose everything, including her freedom.

Right now she was having a hard time seeing a way out of this mess. She had backed herself into a corner, and the only thing she could do now was to put all her trust in Scar and hope he knew what he was doing. Losing her kids, her career, and her freedom were definitely not an option.

With her mind heavy, Tiphani stepped onto the elevator inside the state courthouse building, where she worked in the district attorney's office. Being an assistant district attorney had been one of her life's dreams. As a child, she wanted to become a prosecutor so she could rid the world of all of the men who committed domestic violence and sexual molestation of children—men like her father.

Tiphani had grown up in a home filled with violence and pain. Her father was a serious alcoholic who often beat her mother, sometimes so severely she would be unable to walk or to see out of her eyes. Tiphani would watch helplessly, making promises to herself that the next time he did it, she would kill him and save her mother. Each time the beatings happened, however, Tiphani became paralyzed with fear, unable to do anything except run and hide to stay out of the path of her raging father.

When she would try to talk to her mother about it, her mother would make excuses for her husband and tell Tiphani that it was done because he loved her so much. Tiphani would say she wanted to kill him, and her mother would slap her for saying it and tell her to go to her room.

When Tiphani was fourteen, her father's abuse had finally taken its toll on her mother, and she suffered a brain aneurism and died instantly. Tiphani remembered thinking that although she would miss her mother, she was relieved that the poor woman would never experience pain at the hands of her demonic father again.

After her mother's death, Tiphani became like her father's wife instead of his daughter. She had to cook, clean, and basically take care of him like a woman would. Tiphani suffered in silence, constantly dreaming of the day she would leave home. The thoughts of killing her father were always there, but had been pushed to the back of her mind.

Instead, Tiphani replaced those thoughts of murder with thoughts of revenge through her own success. She was determined to become a prosecutor and find a way to put her father behind bars legally. It was going to be her father behind bars for abuse, and not Tiphani behind bars for murder.

She struggled to stay on top of everything through high school and college, fighting to stay awake during class because she was so tired from all of the work she had to do at home. Due to the lack of love and affection at home, Tiphani was constantly seeking love from men. She would do almost anything to get the love she wasn't receiving at home.

Over time, she came to equate sex with love. So, in order to fill that void in her heart, she would sleep with any man that showed interest in her. Tiphani couldn't stop searching for that love, and sex was her addiction. If a man made her cum, she thought he loved her. Sex made her feel wanted and needed.

After Tiphani graduated from law school, her father died from cirrhosis of the liver, and, of course, left her nothing but his debt. Unable to keep the promise to herself to see her father behind bars, Tiphani found herself struggling to make ends meet with her entry law clerk salary. It could have crushed most women, but Tiphani was not going to let her father win, especially not from beyond the grave.

Determined to move up, make something of herself, and leave her abusive past behind, Tiphani became the most driven budding attorney in Baltimore County. She would work extra hard, even when some of the white attorneys got over on her and took credit for her work. But Tiphani believed that cream always rose to the top, and that the people in charge would know and see that she was the one doing the best work.

Soon, the bosses did notice, and she began to make a name for herself and was asked to join the ranks of the district attorney's office.

When Tiphani met Derek, they had a lot in common. He was working hard to get to the top within the Maryland State Police, and he understood her need to overcome her past. Tiphani fell in love with Derek's charm. She thought he would make a great provider and family man.

The first time they had sex, she chalked up his misgivings to nerves, but she learned quickly that he couldn't meet her needs. Tiphani came up with a plan for herself. If Derek couldn't meet her needs, she would just make sure her needs were being met without Derek knowing. She was going to get some on the side. *Fuck it*, she thought. *Men do this shit all the time. Why can't I?*

There were some nights while they were dating when, after having their two-minute sex, Tiphani would put on her clothes, tell Derek she was going home, and go directly to a bar and pick up the biggest, sexiest guy there and fuck him in the parking lot.

After briefly dating, Derek proposed to Tiphani. She knew his sex was mediocre at best, but decided that she could try to look past it in order to have a good, trustworthy man who would take care of her. She would settle down and start a family and be a one-man woman.

Not even a year into their marriage, she was frustrated with their sex life and started to search for more dick to satisfy her needs. Tiphani did try to distract herself from her cravings for dick. She immersed herself into her work and continued her rise to the top of the ranks amongst her fellow prosecutors.

Her hard work caught the eye of the district attorney, and she began to get all of the high profile cases, even the ones her husband had worked. That was how much her bosses trusted her and her abilities.

As much as Tiphani needed sex, she never brought that part of her life into the workplace. That part of her life was for outside the office on her own time, without the prying eyes of her coworkers.

Snapping out of her reverie, Tiphani rushed out of the elevator, down the long corridor to her office. She could swear people were whispering and mumbling as she passed them, but she thought she was being paranoid. Finally reaching her office, she fished around in her pocketbook for her keys. She had her head down, and suddenly, the door swung open.

"Come on in, Mrs. Fuller," a man's voice boomed. Tiphani was startled. She slowly walked into her office, and her jaw almost dropped to the floor.

"Good morning. You don't look so happy to see me," he said with a sinister grin on his face.

Caught off guard, Tiphani swallowed hard, trying to find her words. The fucking mayor of the city was in her office, waiting for her to come in. What part of the game was that?

Why the fuck is he in my office? What does he know? These were the first things that came to Tiphani's mind. She shuddered, a chill running down her spine.

"Ahem." She cleared her throat, trying to compose herself. "It is . . . I mean . . . it is not every day the average Joe like me walks into her office and finds the mayor of Baltimore sitting behind her desk," Tiphani stammered, her words feeling like marbles stuck in her throat. A hot feeling rose from her chest, up her neck, and flashed on her face.

She looked around, unable to move or speak. Tiphani was very familiar with the mayor, but having him right there, right now, was not what she was expecting.

Tiphani was surrounded. Mayor Mathias Steele, a slick-talking Southerner who would probably throw his mother from a train to keep his job, was in her office, along with her boss, District Attorney Anthony Gill, another self-serving character driven by a name and the possibility of fame.

Tiphani felt like she'd walked into a bear trap, or like she was being ambushed by AK-47s and all she had was a butter knife to defend herself. Her body broke out in a cold sweat, with fine beads lining up at her hairline, threatening to take a dip down her face at any minute.

What the fuck do they want? How much do they know? The questions kept running through her muddled mind.

"Sit down, Mrs. Fuller. We need to speak with you about a serious matter that cannot wait," Mayor Steele said, leaning forward and folding his hands together on Tiphani's desk like it belonged to him.

Stay calm, stay calm, Tiphani kept telling herself. *They can't tie you to any of this shit storm.*

Tiphani looked at the mayor and immediately pictured him naked, and it wasn't because she was trying to calm herself down. She quickly closed her eyes to get the image to go away. When she opened them back up, Anthony Gill shot her an evil look. Tiphani knew he was probably really shitting bricks inside. Her boss hated to think he or any of his staff were in trouble or had brought negative attention to his office; but a personal visit from the mayor was a sure way to know that somebody's ass was in hot water.

Tiphani sat on the small black leather couch situated directly across from her desk. It was the same couch she usually had victims sit on to give her their story; or sometimes, defense attorneys sat there to convince her to plead their clients' cases out.

When she sat down, the leather on the couch made a noise, causing an ominous feeling to overwhelm her. Tiphani looked over the mayor's head at the wall where a large framed picture of her, Derek, and the kids hung. She swallowed the golf ball-sized lump in her throat and tried to be cool.

"Mrs. Fuller, I'm here because, as you may already know, your husband and his cohorts at the State Police Division One are being investigated. It has come to my attention that it seems Mr. Fuller is the ringleader of a group of dirty cops. We are finding out that he is into some high profile criminal activity. I'm not talking stealing evidence money from drug dealers or planting evidence, either. This is serious shit, Mrs. Fuller . . . serious, serious shit," Mayor Steele said, looking at her to gauge her reaction.

Tiphani stayed calm, although her heart thundered against her chest bone almost painfully. It was pounding so hard, Tiphani was surprised that no one in the room could hear it. Mayor Steele looked at her seriously. He wasn't there to undress her with his eyes like he usually did. Thoughts of the sexual trysts they used to have when she was trying to vie for her position didn't even come into his mind. He was there strictly for business.

"Tiphani, I understand that you may have some information to help the state's case against your husband. Is that true?" Mayor Steele asked, throwing one of those fishing questions at Tiphani to see if she'd bite.

She knew this game all too well, and was not about to take the bait. She looked into his hazy gray eyes and at his newly receding hairline. Biting down into her jaw, Tiphani prepared herself for the performance she was about to give.

"I have no idea what you're speaking about. As far as I was concerned, up until just a day or so ago when I heard about Officer Archie's death and that Derek may somehow be involved, I thought of my husband as a fine, upstanding citizen and a damned good police officer," Tiphani said, folding her arms across her chest. She knew she had to play the role of surprised or offended, because she was not about to tell the mayor and the fucking district attorney that she knew her husband was a dirty-ass cop and that the biggest drug kingpin in Baltimore County was his brother.

"Mrs. Fuller, I'm here to let you know that if you had even an inkling of what your husband was into, you'd better start talking and cooperating here and now. It won't benefit you one bit if we find out on our own," Mayor Steele emphasized, clicking his teeth. It was a habit he had that Tiphani now remembered she hated when they used to fuck.

"With all due respect, Mayor, you know me and you know my work in the past. I am a law abiding citizen, and I took an oath to uphold the law when I became a prosecutor. I did not know anything about Derek's dealings. In fact, I'm just as surprised by your presence here as you are by my obliviousness to his activities," she said coldly. Tiphani had put her game face on, and when she did that, she could be just as shrewd as any high-level government official.

Anthony Gill cleared his throat. "Tiphani, just so you are aware, the mayor and I have discussed this issue ad nauseum, and we have decided that we are going to bring any and all charges against your husband that will stick in a court of law. He will be prosecuted to the full extent of the law. We are not showing him any mercy. What he did was despicable. Like you and me, he also took an oath to up-hold the law, and because of his selfish and disgusting ways, three police officers and a fucking police chief are dead!" Anthony boomed, his voice picking up bass as he spoke.

Tiphani did not flinch. She kept a stony poker face and tried to stand her ground. All kinds of feelings were ripping through her. Tiphani was confused, torn between the reality of her failing marriage, which was her fault, and a potentially deadly deal she had entered into with Scar Johnson—and now this potential maelstrom was brewing.

The room seemed to be spinning around her. Tiphani felt hot, and her stomach muscles began to clench. *Do I lie and risk them finding out? Or do I tell the truth and have them lock me the fuck up right here and now?* She opted to stand behind her lie that she knew nothing about Derek's dealings with Scar.

Tiphani thought about Derek and about some of the underhanded things he had done in the name of loving and protecting his brother. She thought of how hard Derek had worked to make their marriage a success, and she immediately felt a pang of guilt. But there was no turning back now. She knew that the shit Scar had planted around to make Derek look guilty was surely going to put Derek behind bars for life. It was time for her to look out for number one. She couldn't afford to feel sorry for the man who was trying to take her kids and her life away from her. "Mrs.

Fuller, this case is as high profile as it gets here. The exposure of a ring of dirty cops in bed with a drug kingpin suspected of killing cops and government officials is a dead winner for this office, and under my watch, it will assure me a win in the upcoming elections. It is what everyone needs around here to recover from the failed attempt at bringing Scar Johnson down. Now we have someone to blame for that cluster fuck," Mayor Steele spoke, his pale white face filling with blood as he got excited about the coverage a case like this would garner for him.

Tiphani didn't understand why they were telling her their plans for destroying her husband. She just listened intently, waiting for them to drop the bomb on her.

"Tiphani, we know you are senior assistant district attorney here, but you will not be on this case," the mayor announced, dropping what felt, to Tiphani, like an atomic bomb on her.

Tiphani felt like he had slapped her across the face with an open hand. Her cheeks flamed over and her head began to throb at the base of her neck. Before she could speak, he continued.

"It's a conflict of interest, for one, and I just don't think you'll be able to separate your feelings enough. Although I think you are the most talented body Anthony has in this office, I'm taking you off of this, and as a matter of fact, I don't even want you to attend your husband's trial," Mayor Steele continued.

He might as well have fired her, as far as she was concerned. With everything that this case entailed, Tiphani knew it was going to be a high profile case, which meant she wanted to be on it. She wanted name recognition, just like the rest of them. It also didn't hurt that if she stayed close to this case, she could make sure that no one would find out about her connection to Scar.

"Ashley Simms is going to prosecute this case. She is the only other halfway capable assistant district attorney Anthony has in this office," the mayor announced.

Tiphani almost fell on the floor with shock. She was livid. Anthony knew goddamn well that Tiphani and Ashley hated each other. They had been each others' fiercest competitors in the office. She felt betrayed by Anthony Gill and the mayor.

"Derek being my husband didn't matter when I was working cases with him and making this office shine like the brightest star in the state, did it? What changed now? Do you really think I'm that emotional that I won't be able to separate my feelings? I'm disappointed that you and Anthony view me as that weak," Tiphani replied, shaking her head and halfway pouting. She was floored.

Not that bitch Ashley. She will definitely think she won my top spot in the office now. That bitch can't hold a match to me, Tiphani was thinking as she tried to put a hold on her feelings in front of these two white boys.

"Look, we can't afford one mistake on this case. We damn sure can't afford Derek's defense attorney standing up in court, pointing out the obvious conflict of interest and the fact that you may have some culpability in his crimes. No way!" Mayor Steele told her. He was seriously not budging on the issue.

Tired and feeling browbeaten, Tiphani just acquiesced.

She nodded her head in understanding and just remained quiet. Anthony Gill hadn't even tried to advocate for her, and Tiphani felt he knew exactly what the hell he was doing when he assigned the case to Ashley. Tiphani always felt Anthony might've been fucking Ashley anyway.

Weak-ass punk mu'fucka! Tiphani screamed in her head, shooting daggers at Anthony with her eyes.

"Mrs. Fuller," Mayor Steele began, standing up from Tiphani's desk and starting to make his way to the door, "I hope you understand what we are doing here and why. I just want to remind you that if I so much as get a sniff, one iota, so much as a fucking tick's dick worth of a hint that you had full knowledge, or even partial knowledge of your husband's dealings with Scar Johnson and the Dirty Money Crew, I will have your ass on a roasting stick in the same court of law you prosecute criminals like your husband in every day." He smiled at her evilly.

Tiphani felt like hawking up the biggest wad of spit she could muster and spewing it in his face, but she remained cool, knowing that shit could be worse. They could know about her and Scar, which would fuck her out of the game.

"Do what you have to, Mayor, but I'm a woman of dignity and my word. You of all people should know that," she said sarcastically, giving the mayor something to think about.

His face turned bright pink and he adjusted his tie. He broke eye contact with her, clearly uncomfortable. Without another word, Mayor Steele sped from her office, with little flunky-ass Anthony Gill on his heels.

"Punk-ass bastard," Tiphani mumbled. She rushed around her office collecting files and certain things that she needed. Tiphani had planned to take some time off anyway. Between the family court proceedings and Derek's constant attacks, she was overwhelmed.

Tiphani picked up all of the files that she needed, checked her voice mail, and decided she would just leave the office. As she prepared to lock up, her cell phone rang. It was Scar. She picked up immediately.

"Yo, I need to see you now," Scar huffed into the phone.

"I can't right now. The fucking mayor just left my office," she whispered, looking around suspiciously to make sure no one was passing by and could overhear her.

"Get at me as soon as you leave there," Scar demanded, disconnecting the line. Tiphani pulled the phone down from her ear and looked at it in shock. He had hung up on her, and he didn't sound too happy.

Not more fucking drama from him now, she said to herself.

Feeling the weight of the world on her shoulder, Tiphani carried her stuff and loaded into the elevator, where some of her fellow prosecutors were already standing. Tiphani was sure they'd heard about what was going on with her, and that her arch nemesis was getting to move into her senior spot. She rolled her eyes, not wanting to deal with another fucking piece of drama right now. She gave them her back and didn't even acknowledge them.

Tiphani could feel them staring at her, and hear them trying to whisper about her. When the elevator reached the lobby Tiphani turned on them. "You know, if you put as much energy into trying to be half the prosecutor I am as you do into being in my fucking business, you might reach my level one day," she spat, turning and storming out of the elevator.

With everything that was on her mind, all she wanted to do was get into her car and go the fuck home. She didn't want to see or hear from Scar. She didn't want to see or hear from Derek. Alone time is what Tiphani longed for; time to process the day's and week's events and figure out what her next move would be.

Walking toward her car, Tiphani noticed a tow truck parked behind her. "Now I'm gonna get blocked in. What the fuck else could go wrong?" Tiphani mumbled to herself. Then as she got closer, she noticed that her damn car was rigged to the back of the tow truck.

"Hey! Hey!" she screamed out, dropping all of her files and running toward her car. The tow truck driver looked at her strangely. To him she looked like another crazed lady running at him. In his line of business, he had seen this same situation play out a million times.

"What the fuck are you doing?" Tiphani huffed out, finally getting to where her car was being hoisted onto its two front tires.

"What does it look like, lady? I'm repossessing this car, duh," the driver said sarcastically.

Tiphani looked at his little acne-ridden teenage face and had to restrain herself from slapping the shit out of him.

"Repossessing it? There must be some fucking mistake. I'm a fucking lawyer. You think I can't afford my goddamn car note?" she shot back, the heat of embarrassment settling on her face.

"That's what they all say, lady. Blah, blah, blah, I'm sure you can afford your car, but right here on this order I have, it says this car . . . Mercedes-Benz E550 that belongs to one Derek Fuller is to be repossessed today at the request of the owner, who has refused further payments to your lien holder. Repossession is to take place today, Miss. Not tomorrow, not next week—today. And that's what I'm fixing to do," the smartmouth boy said.

"Let me see that shit!" she screamed, snatching the orders from his bony fingers. Sure enough, that bastard husband of hers had launched another missile at her. He had taken back the car he'd given her as a gift. That bastard was really trying to destroy her piece by piece—a low, painful take down.

Tiphani was seething inside. Her heart was about to explode, and tears burned at the backs of her eyes. Tiphani whirled around, feeling like all eyes were on her. She could see people stopping to look. Then she felt like dying when she spotted Ashley Simms and a bunch of the same coworkers she'd just told off looking and pointing. They were getting a kick out of her misery.

"Listen. Whatever the fees are, or whatever is owed, I will pay it. I have a bank account full of money. Trust me," Tiphani stammered, fumbling with her purse to get her checkbook.

"Miss, I can't even take your money if I wanted to. This car is not in your name, and I don't take bribes," the boy informed her.

"I can pay you more than that piece of shit job of yours could ever pay! Listen, you little shit, I need to get home. Now, if you don't take my fucking car off that rig, I will beat your ass right here and now," Tiphani barked. She had lost all sense of composure. It was not like her to come apart this way, but the ground was falling out from under her at this very minute. She was losing control of her life.

"Lady, if you want to go to jail, you can try that, but with all of these government folks watching, I don't think you will really do anything. Besides, you need to take this all up with this man, Derek Fuller, who I am assuming is your lover, boyfriend, or husband. Or you can simply call the car company and curse them out. But me, I'm just doing my regular nine to five job. Now, if you would move from in front of my truck, I would appreciate it." The boy climbed into the tow truck, leaving Tiphani standing there, looking like an ass.

She hung her head and tried to think of what her next move would be. All sorts of ideas were cramming into her brain at once; then something hit her like a bolt of lightning. There was only one way to solve this shit with Derek once and for fucking all.

Like a woman possessed, Tiphani stormed back toward the building.

"Show's over, bitches!" she screamed toward the growing crowd of coworkers that had been reveling in her undoing. Some of them laughed, some felt sorry for her, but Tiphani knew what all of them were thinking: How does a woman who was once at the top of her game, with everything you could dream of, suddenly lose it to the point of being looked at like one of the criminals she used to prosecute?

Inside the building, Tiphani pressed the elevator buttons with urgency. She planned to go back upstairs and give Anthony Gill a piece of her mind. Yes, she had stayed passive in their meeting with Mayor Steele, but she wasn't going to take this shit lying down. Derek was going to regret the day he was fucking born, much less the day his whack-dick ass crossed paths with her.

Tiphani paced the floor, thinking and waiting for the elevator. She rehearsed in her mind what she had to say to Anthony, and the fucking mayor, for that matter. The elevator doors opened with a dinging sound, and Tiphani went to rush inside. She bumped head first into Mayor Steele and his protective detail. Tiphani's chest was heaving and her hair was like a crazy bird's nest.

"Mayor, I need to speak with you," Tiphani said with urgency lacing her words.

"Mrs. Fuller, I think we've already discussed everything there is to discuss," the mayor said dismissively.

"I don't think so, Mathias," Tiphani said in a harsh whisper.

The mayor's eyes went squinty, resembling slits. He flexed his jaw and grabbed her arm, pulling her out of earshot of the officers in his detail.

"What the fuck are you doing?" he asked.

Tiphani had hit a nerve. She had always remained tight-lipped about their affair and all of the underhanded shit he did to become mayor. She had given him her word that if she was appointed as an assistant district attorney, she would never breathe a word of the things he was into or their little thing. Word getting out would make him seem like a philandering adulterer, and that would tarnish his chances of becoming governor.

"I am here to tell you that the fucking dirty cop case against my husband is the only chance I have left to try to put my fucking career back together and to be able to lift my head up with some dignity in this fucking town. I have worked extra fucking hard getting conviction after conviction to make you and Anthony look good! I have surpassed everyone is this godforsaken place, and the thanks I get is being pulled off the case of the century! I need this like I need food right now!" Tiphani said, her eyes low with contempt and her voice serious as cancer.

"You will have Anthony put me on the fucking case right away, or else, so help me God, I will tell it all. I will release the pictures and the video," she gritted out in a harsh whisper.

Mayor Steele felt like he would faint. His head was swimming. The day they videotaped themselves fucking, the mayor knew he would come to regret it. He wished he had a gun. He would shoot this bitch right in her smart-ass mouth.

"You know that it will look bad if you prosecute the case, Tiphani. Why are you doing this?" he asked her, also whispering and looking around to make sure no one could hear them.

"I am doing what I have to do, Mathias. You and all of the fucking men in this county are trying to destroy me, when all I've ever done was work hard. Now I'm willing to work extra hard on this case, husband or not, but I am out to save myself. If Derek did something wrong and needs to be prosecuted, right now I'm the only bitch that can make it happen.

"You and I both fucking know Anthony is fucking Ashley, and that is the only reason why he assigned this to her incompetent ass," Tiphani said with passion in her words. She was up in the mayor's face, showing him that she wasn't about to back the fuck down. This was her last chance, and she needed this to work. She had to get on this case, and she would do anything to make it happen.

"But you think threatening me will work in your favor?" Mayor Steele said, trying to act like he would let her reveal their lewd love affair.

"Oh, Mr. Mayor, all you would have to do is try me. Either you have Anthony call me no later than nine o'clock tonight and tell me that by some miraculous act of God I am now assigned to the case, or I will be all over the media tomorrow morning, and your chances at being governor and mayor, for that matter, will be over," Tiphani said. She turned and began walking away. It was her way of letting the mayor know exactly who the fuck he was dealing with when it came to her. The same way they had trained her to be a shrewd, relentless bitch in the courtroom was the same way she'd turn on them and use it against them. Tiphani was a woman possessed, and she was hell bent on revenge right about now.

"Tiphani, wait!" Mayor Steele called at her back.

She stopped in her tracks, but did not immediately turn around. She waited a few seconds and then heard his foot-steps approaching her. Tiphani turned around slowly, her face like a stone statue, hiding the real pain she was in.

"What is it, Mr. Mayor? How is it that I can help you?" she asked sarcastically, her voice cracking slightly.

Mayor Steele swallowed hard. He thought about all the times Tiphani had fucked him with a strap-on dildo and had him live out his fantasy of dressing like a woman during sex. He thought about how it would look in the papers, and what his little stuffy-ass wife would think. The images swarmed in his mind like a mini tornado, whipping his ass into submission.

"Tiphani, don't do this. You and I both know that a judge would never allow you to go on trial against the man you are currently in the process of divorcing. I know you are the best attorney we have, but keeping you off the case gives us our best chance at a conviction," Mayor Steele said in his smoothest, softest voice. The only thing he needed to do was get on his knees and it would have been outright begging.

"Yes, you're right, I am the best attorney you have, and no judge would allow me on a case with such a conflict of interest. But your best chance of a conviction is with me on the case. I can guarantee that. So, if you don't want the press to run front page stories about how the mayor loves women's clothes and strap-ons, you will find a judge and convince him that there is no conflict of interest and my divorce will not be admissible during trial." Tiphani knew she had the mayor in the palm of her hand, and she wasn't about to back down. Her life depended on it.

With his final attempt at changing Tiphani's mind failing tremendously, the mayor was backed into a corner: Risk bad press from losing a case, or risk even worse press for being outed as a sexual pervert. He chose the lesser of two evils in his mind.

"You are on the case. Get your shit together and bring your A game. I don't want to hear any excuses," he said with a worried look on his face. "Oh yeah, and get those divorce papers filed immediately," he continued, turning and rushing out of the building so fast that Tiphani couldn't even respond.

Chapter 10

Business Meeting

The Italian restaurant in Bowie, Maryland was Scar's favorite meeting spot. It was far enough away from the prying eyes of Baltimore to make it easy for Scar to conduct business undetected, but close enough that it didn't take up his entire day getting there. The layout was perfect for Scar to be able to see everyone coming and going, and at the same time give him the privacy that he needed.

As he sat with his eyes on the door and his back to the wall, he thought back to the first meeting he had there. Scar had come with his brother after Derek got his promotion to head the Narcotics Unit. From that point on, whenever they needed to exchange information and just catch up, this was the place they met. For obvious reasons, they had to be as low profile as possible. Being seen together would have been bad for business.

Thinking back, Scar couldn't believe all the ups and downs of his relationship with his brother. As he reminisced about the chain of events of their lives, Scar started to tear up a little. They had such a strong bond. They were a team, and nothing could keep them apart, not even the sheisty workers at the orphanage; but now they were so far apart nothing was going to bring them back together.

All because of some bitch, Scar thought to himself. With that thought, Scar immediately started obsessing over Tiphani. Yeah, he loved to fuck her and she would freak him whenever and wherever he wanted, but there were plenty of fish in the sea. Pussy was easy to come by, but having the brotherly bond that Scar and Derek had was sacred. Maybe if he took care of Tiphani, he could get his relationship with his brother back.

That's it. It's time to put this bitch to sleep, Scar thought as he started to hatch a plan to take out Tiphani. It would be perfect. Tiphani would be out of the way, Derek would get his kids back, and he and Scar could become the biggest players in all of Baltimore. He would also start planning a way to get Derek to become the next Chief of Police.

Just as Scar was daydreaming about his future with his brother, the current police chief walked through the front door of the restaurant. Scar watched as Chief Hill stood and scanned the dining room, looking for the person he was there to meet. Instead of sitting at a table, the chief went to the bathroom.

What is this mu'fucka doing? Did he see me? Scar thought as he watched the chief enter the bathroom.

Thirty seconds later, Chief Hill exited the bathroom and sat down in the same booth as Scar.

"What the fuck are you doing?" Scar asked Chief Hill.

"Making sure we aren't being watched, and taking a leak," Chief Hill calmly said as he looked at the menu.

Derek wasn't the only one Scar would meet at the restaurant. Chief Hill was also one of Scar's insiders on the police force, and a frequent guest at the restaurant. They first started doing business together when Scar was just a young buck coming up in the game. Their careers had been linked and on the rise ever since. At first Scar just paid him to stay out of jail, but as his street cred and power grew, the amount of his payouts also grew, and he started asking for favors from the officer.

"What's so important that you needed to see me?" Scar started in immediately.

"Relax. Let me order first," Chief Hill said as he turned to get the waitress's attention.

"I ain't got time for bullshit. I got a business to run. The fuck is it you want?" Scar asked, his impatience obviously increasing.

Chief Hill just ignored Scar's last comment and called the waitress over. When she arrived, he ordered his meal and tried his best to chat her up. The poor girl just wanted to take his order and leave, but seeing as Scar always tipped her so well, she had to stay and endure Chief Hill's weak-ass game.

"Would you stop embarrassing yaself? Yo game is weak," Scar said to Chief Hill as he turned to the waitress.

"Thank you, Lita. Just get my corny-ass friend his meal." With that, Scar handed Lita a twenty for her patience with Chief Hill and she walked away.

"Why do you always have to try and one up me? I was just having some fun. Is it so bad that I find the waitress attractive?" The chief defended himself.

"If you want pussy, go to a strip club. Shit, I own a few. Just let me know and I'll hook you up. Right now is not the time, though. There is some business that needs to be attended to," Scar said as he tried to move past the chit chat and get down to why he was there.

Chief Hill had reached out to Scar the day after Officer Archie was found strung up in front of Rodriguez's house.

Scar knew that Derek was staying there, and he wanted to send a message to his brother. He also wanted the news to get wind of Archie being a dirty cop, so he planted twenty thousand dollars in Archie's pockets.

Scar was well aware of the power of the press, and knew how to manipulate them to his advantage. He was the master at anonymous phone calls to the newspapers, or making sure that TV news crews happened to be in the right place at the right time. He believed the saying that even bad press is good press. It was one thing he learned from studying the Mafia boss John Gotti.

Scar was feeling good that his message was being heard after his disposal of Officer Archie. The papers and TV all covered the story, with little hints about Archie possibly being a dirty cop. Derek's name was dragged into the story as well; although, with his newfound plan of reconciliation, Scar was kind of regretting that aspect of the story. So, when Scar received the urgent message from Chief Hill to meet him at the usual spot, he was not happy. His plan was to kill Archie, set him up, and then lay low for a while. Meeting the Chief of Police for an urgent meeting was not laying low.

"Shit don't seem too urgent the way you actin' right now. If you here to shake me down for some cash, you're sadly mistaken, nigga." When Scar called Chief Hill "nigga," you know his anger was about to redline.

"Okay, okay. Let's start over. It is urgent, and we need to discuss the matter of Officer Archie."

"I heard about that. I had nothing to do with that unfortunate event," Scar said with a knowing grin spreading across his face.

"I'm not here to ask if you had anything to do with it. I'm here to discuss the calls made by Officer Archie to you and Detective Fuller," Chief Hill clarified, knowing full well that Scar had everything to do with Archie's murder.

Scar's grin disappeared. He wasn't expecting to hear that. He had no idea what the chief was talking about. "Fuck you mean?" Scar asked.

Chief Hill now knew he had Scar's full attention. It was time to get down to a serious discussion and figure out how much he could trust Scar—if at all.

"I mean that there was a cell phone found at the crime scene. You know, the crime scene you had nothing to do with," he said sarcastically. "Well, on that cell phone there were two calls placed earlier in the evening. The first was to you; the last was to Detective Fuller. Do you know anything about that?"

The chief looked directly at Scar to see if he could read any of his body language. Scar stayed calm, but you could see in his eyes that his mind was working to sort out the information just given to him.

"So you say. How do I know you ain't lying?" Scar's first instinct was not to trust anyone. He figured this must be some sort of scam to get him to pay up.

"Why would I lie about this? The detectives on the case already know the last call was to Detective Fuller because when I recalled the number, the idiot was standing right there and answered his phone. They are having a harder time tracking your number, but it is only a matter of time before they figure it out."

"How the fuck he get my number?" Scar said out loud, more to himself than to the chief. "If this is true, so what? It ain't no thang. You just make sure they don't find out it's my number, and we all good," Scar said, trying to act nonchalant and put a positive spin on a fucked up situation. At the same time, he was basically telling Chief Hill to fix the mess.

"It isn't that simple. There is about to be a huge investigation into Detective Fuller, his unit, and the whole department. The bad press from this has gotten the mayor determined to put someone behind bars. There's an election coming up, and the mayor wants heads to roll. He is not about to lose because he looks soft on crime and his police force is completely corrupt," Chief Hill said, trying to explain the seriousness of the situation to Scar.

"A'ight, give me some time to figure some shit out. In the meantime, you keep an eye on the detectives and make sure they don't find out it's my number."

"You don't understand. We don't have time. The investigation is going full steam ahead. Once the mayor heard about the phone call to Detective Fuller and the ten thousand dollars in officer Archie's pocket, he is determined to close this case in a hurry," the chief stressed, reiterating the dire situation they were about to find themselves in.

"Hold up, hold up. Did you say ten thousand dollars?" Scar asked.

"Yes. Ten thousand dollars in his front pocket. The news is going to go crazy once they find out that a cop was walking around with that amount of cash."

"There was twenty thousand when we left. You tryin' to tell me that ten thousand just happen to went missing?" Scar said. This time it was his turn to stare and try to figure out body language. He was certain that Chief Hill was not telling the truth and probably stole the money himself.

"It doesn't matter. Ten, twenty, thirty . . . it's all the same. It was a lot of money for a cop to be holding. The main thing is I'm not about to let any of this somehow be directed back to me, so I need to know why Archie called you, and what kind of business you had with him." Now Chief Hill was getting visibly agitated.

Their actions were starting to attract a bit of attention, not what either of them wanted or needed. Most people just ignored them, not wanting to get involved in other people's business, but there was one person there who was very interested in what was going on. Scar's shadow was back, and paying full attention to the pair and their reactions. Although not close enough to hear, the Shadow was still able to tell by the men's body language that the conversation was not an easy one.

After following Scar to the restaurant, the Shadow was surprised, pleased, and intrigued by the fact that Chief Hill was there to meet with Scar. If only there was a way to be able to hear what they were saying. The Shadow contemplated trying to get closer, but thought it best to stay away and not risk being spotted.

"We had no business. The only time I spoke to that nigga was when I was telling him to say his prayers before he was about to meet his maker. You best not be trying to pin anything on me. We're in this together," Scar said, letting Chief Hill know that if he went down, they both did.

"I know that we are in this together. I'm just saying don't try and fuck with me. We need to stick together. The investigation is moving forward, and Detective Fuller is about to go down. I just need to know what kind of business dealings you had with Officer Archie. I don't want any surprises coming at me during this investigation. The more I know, the easier it will be for me to steer the investigation."

"Away from you. You didn't finish the last sentence. Steer the investigation away from you. That's what you meant to say. You need to make sure you aren't involved. I hear what you're saying. You came here to warn me. Well, let me tell you something. However I go, you go. Got it?" Scar warned.

"That's not what I meant. I came here to make sure we are on the same page. I am going to personally get involved with this case, and I need to know everything you know," Chief Hill said, trying to defuse the escalating argument.

"I've told you everything I know, which is nothing. Somehow you stole ten grand from me, and that pig Archie somehow had my number in his phone. That about sums it up. Let's agree to stay away from each other for a while." With that, Scar stood, preparing to leave.

"Agreed. One last bit of information: I wouldn't trust that bitch D.A. you been fuckin'. Word is the mayor had a little sit down with her, and now she is on the warpath to clear her name. Watch your back," Chief Hill warned as he turned to the food that was just arriving at the table. "Won't you stay and eat with me?" he asked Scar sarcastically.

Scar was furious. Not only did he now have the chief to worry about, but he needed to keep his eye on Tiphani. To make matters even worse, his brother's head was now on the chopping block, and he didn't know if he could trust his own henchmen. If the chief was telling the truth, Scar didn't know who he could trust. He was becoming a solitary man, alone on an island, with no one to trust. Scar now knew that he needed to look out for himself and that his fantasy of reconciling with his brother was already not going to happen. The way it was starting to look to Scar, he was going to have to start playing everyone to make sure that he came out on top.

"Seems you already do most things solo. Eating alone won't hurt you," Scar said and walked straight out of the restaurant.

The Shadow was dying to know what was said between the two men, but could only guess. Maybe with a little more time and trailing Scar, the answer would reveal itself. But for now, the Shadow would just have to sit back and stay out of sight, orchestrating the downfall of Scar Johnson and Detective Fuller.

Chapter 11

Coming to a Head

Derek had stayed holed up in a hotel for two days, drinking himself into oblivion. On the third day, he finally decided to go to the station house to collect some of his things and let them know he would be taking some leave time without pay to get his mind right.

Derek pulled into the station house parking lot and noticed that the sign on his reserved spot had been removed and replaced. "Rodriguez? Hah! Ain't that a bitch? A niggah is gone for two days and the bitch he thought was his friend jumps into his grave," Derek said out loud. He knew that Rodriguez was hurt because he had never even mentioned their sexual encounter after it happened, but there was nothing to say. Derek had too much on his plate to stop and deal with a woman's problem.

He parked in a regular spot and went into the station house. All eyes were immediately on him when he walked in. "Hello to all of you mu'fuckas too," Derek said sarcastically, heading for his desk. Before he could even sit down for a second, Chief Hill was already standing over him.

"Fuller, I need to see you in my office, now," the chief said.

"Damn. Can I gather some of my shit first?" Derek asked, thrown off guard.

"No. You need to follow me now," the chief said with three uniformed officers flanking him, just in case Derek decided to act up.

Derek slammed the chair back into the wall as he stood up. He followed the chief to his office.

"Close the door," the chief instructed. Derek closed the door. His chest was heaving in and out. "Sit down," Chief Hill said.

"I'm 'aight. I'll stand," Derek said.

"Fuller, you are being placed on an indefinite leave until further notice. I'm sorry to tell you that you are under investigation for the murders of Archie, Bolden, Cassell, and Chief Scott," the chief said.

His words rang in Derek's ears like a fire alarm. Derek was too shocked to speak. After all he had done for the department, good and bad, he would never have had his men killed.

"You need to give me your gun and badge immediately and vacate the premises until further notice. You no longer have any police authority until, if, and when such time as you are sworn back in. Do you understand?" Chief Hill said.

Derek fought back tears. "I'm being framed. Can't you see that?" Derek croaked out. The chief just smirked.

Derek didn't know who to trust. Even his chief could have been on the take. He pulled his gun from his holster and placed it on the desk. He thought about blowing his own head off right there in the chief's office, but knew he didn't have the heart to kill himself. He also put his belt, badge, and credentials on the desk. Derek had been defined by his career for so many years that he already felt naked without his gun and shield.

"You and the entire Baltimore area will regret this. Scar Johnson will reign terror on you and the entire city, and I won't be here to stop him," Derek said, turning and storming out.

He stomped down the stairs and straight out of the station house. His mind was whizzing, and now that he didn't have so much to lose, he had a few people to pay a visit.

Derek went to his car, but was stopped before he could get in. "Excuse me, D," he heard a voice say. Derek spun around and looked at the person strangely. "I don't know if you remember me. I used to work for Scar," the boy said. His face looked kind of familiar, but Derek couldn't be sure.

"I'm Flip," he said.

"What the fuck you doing here, and what do you want?" Derek asked, angry at the intrusion.

"I want to help you set Scar up—not to go to jail, because he always beats the rap. I want him dead just as much as you do," Flip said, speaking like a little mechanical robot.

"Why should I help you?" Derek asked suspiciously.

"Because you and me are the only ones in this city that Scar don't got on his payroll now. You see that fucking chief you got up in there? Oh yeah, he has partied with Scar many nights. One time, you and him had just missed each other coming in and out to get y'all payoff money. Believe me, you need somebody who knows all of his moves inside and out, from what he eats for breakfast to what time that niggah goes to bed. That somebody is me," Flip explained.

Derek looked him up and down. The boy looked injured and hungry. Derek didn't have shit to lose by just listening to this young boy's plan. "Get in," Derek said.

Rodriguez was overjoyed with her temporary promotion. She pulled into her driveway, smiling from ear to ear. When she got out, she noticed Tiphani standing at her door.

"Hey. Derek isn't here," Rodriguez told her shortly.

"I'm not here to see him. I'm here to see you," Tiphani said, motioning to someone in a car. Scar stepped out of his Escalade with its darkly tinted windows.

"Look, I don't know what the fuck is going on," Rodriguez started, putting her hand on her gun.

"It's not like that. We just want to talk to you," Tiphani assured. All she could think about was her looming family court date. She would be ready for her husband this time.

"Can we go inside?" Tiphani asked.

"No, I don't think that's a good idea," Rodriguez said nervously. She realized she was the only one left from the original Narcotics Unit that had taken Scar down.

"Will this give you some assurance?" Tiphani said, opening a bag filled with money. Lying on top was a picture of Derek and Scar, smiling, side by side with their arms around each other.

Rodriguez couldn't believe her eyes. She knew Derek was under investigation, but she didn't really want to believe it.

When she saw the picture, she felt she had no choice but to listen. She hurriedly opened her front door and allowed Tiphani and Scar into her home.

Rodriguez moved away from them, never turning her back, and kept her hand on her gun. She was still not ready to fully trust Scar Johnson, Baltimore's most dangerous criminal.

"Listen, ma. If I wanted you dead, I wouldn't have any small talk. I would have blown your head off ten minutes ago," Scar said.

"What do you want from me?" Rodriguez asked with her hand still on her gun, unable to keep her eyes off the money bag.

"I guess you've figured out that your boss wasn't so clean. Well, we need to bring him down, all the way down for good, and we need your help," Scar explained.

"Shit, you got pictures of him with you. That's enough," Rodriguez said, growing angry. She felt she should've known Derek was dirty when that search warrant shit went down. She also felt like a fool because Derek hadn't trusted her with his secrets. They had both taken money from drug dealers in the past, but it never got to the point where any of the members of the unit were in danger of being killed—especially being killed by their own leader.

"No, it's not enough. You see, if Scar shows those pictures, Derek will just refute them. He will say Scar had them digitally made. He will say Scar is a liar. With Scar's reputation, whose credibility do you think will stand up in court?" Tiphani interjected, giving Rodriguez the lawyer-and-trial perspective on things.

"We need you to help us bring this dirty fuck down. Do it for your fallen friends. Do it for the good of the department," Scar said, trying to play on Rodriguez's morals. After waiting for her to respond and getting nothing, Scar then continued his mind games. "Better yet, do it for this," he said, dropping the bag of money at Rodriguez's feet.

"That's a half a million dollars in that bag. Nobody has to know if you just do what we need you to do. It's an easy decision. Your former unit members obviously didn't make the right decision."

Rodriguez looked like she was conflicted. That was money she could use, but that would make her no better than Detective Fuller. Rodriguez also knew that even though Scar was offering her this money for his help, he was basically telling her to get on board or she'd end up like Archie, Cassell, and Bolden.

Rodriguez's legs gave up on her, and she sat down on her couch as her thoughts went through her head a mile a minute.

Tiphani held her breath. She was counting on this last ditch attempt to amass something concrete on Derek. She needed this to work so she could distance herself so far away from Scar that no matter what Derek said, she would be safe.

"Why are you here? You working for Scar too? Why are you out to bring your own husband down?" Rodriguez asked Tiphani, suddenly realizing it didn't make sense for both of them to be there together.

Tiphani's lawyerly instincts took over, and she quickly responded to Rodriguez. "No, I am not working for Mr. Johnson. He is actually cooperating with the D.A.'s office to help bring in a crooked cop. As far as that crooked cop being my husband, it seems that I didn't know him as well as I thought. Because of my oath to uphold the law, I will prosecute anyone who breaks the law, even if it is my husband, and especially if that crooked cop has killed his own men." Tiphani threw in the last part to try to play on Rodriguez's loyalty to her fallen comrades.

"What do you need me to do?" Rodriguez asked. She felt like she didn't really have a choice but to get on board with Scar basically threatening her, and Tiphani making her realize that Derek probably killed his own unit because he was so entrenched in his own shit.

Tiphani smiled.

"You ain't gonna regret this shit. I can guarantee it. If shit works out, you can make enough money to retire from that fucked up place for life," Scar told her as he extended his hand for a shake.

Flip and Derek sat in Derek's hotel room, plotting. Flip drew a map of all of Scar's spots that Derek didn't know about. Flip told Derek the details of six murders Scar had ordered. He told Derek about stash spots where Scar hid money. He also provided Derek a long list of names of cops, lawyers, and government officials on Scar's payroll—one of which held a key position in the Baltimore mayor's office.

Derek shook his head. He would have had no wins against Scar no matter what he did, even if he was above board with his police work. Flip was all Derek had at this point, so he leaned in and hung on the boy's every word.

"Scar got this bitch name Julissa that does his hits for him. She is one bad bitch—beautiful, and she poses as a call girl, and then wham! She takes niggahs out," Flip explained. "I heard she gets rid of the bodies by pouring battery acid on the shits until they disintegrate," he continued.

"I guess all this shit you telling me leaves us no choice but to kill the nigga," Derek said, looking off into the distance like he was spaced out. "Which means I'm gonna have to kill my wife, too, or else that bitch will be a prime witness," Derek said seriously. He couldn't believe that things had spiraled so far out of control. The two people that he had loved most in the world, he now hated.

"Hey, Travis," Rodriguez said, flashing her credentials to the little old cop who guarded their evidence cage. The man was one of those cops that just refused to retire, so they assigned his half-blind ass to guard the cage so he could sleep on the job if he wanted to.

"Hello, pretty lady. How have you been doing?" the old man asked. He was old as shit, but wasn't too old to pay attention when a beautiful woman was in his presence.

Rodriguez laughed to herself. She knew the old man said that to all of the female officers because he didn't remember anybody and simply wanted to be nice.

"I'm good, old man. I need to pull some evidence for one of my cases," Rodriguez lied.

"Sure. Anything for you," Travis said, buzzing the gate open for Rodriguez to enter.

Rodriguez rushed through and went into the cage where all of the crime scene evidence was housed. She looked up and down the rows, making sure no other cops or detectives were in there. When she was sure she was alone, she walked down the aisle looking for the letters.

"Right here, baby," she whispered. She yanked a large box off the shelf and pulled off the top. Inside, she stared at plastic and paper bags that were numbered and labeled. She sifted through them until she found what she was looking for. She picked up the piece of evidence and replaced it with a piece that had Derek's blood on it. Then she exchanged another piece of evidence with something that she had gotten from his house with Derek's DNA on it. Next, it was Derek's fingerprints that she placed into the evidence. "Done," she whispered, rushing to put shit back the way it was supposed to be.

Rodriguez walked back to the gate and noticed Travis was fast asleep. She buzzed herself out and never woke the old man.

Chief Hill watched the closed circuit security screen in his office. He let a small smile spread across his face.

"Dumb little bitch. Did you really think this shit would be that easy?" Chief Hill whispered, rubbing his hands together.

Flip had given Derek a lot of information and a lot to think about. Derek was going to take this information and call some of his fed friends. The feds were notorious for putting hits out on dudes that they knew would keep beating the system. Derek had seen it over the years: from the Black Panther dudes to famous rappers, the feds would take a niggah out and make it look like black on black crime in a minute.

"A'ight, man. I will be in touch," Derek said to Flip, giving him five.

"Let me know what else I can do. I'm around. I wanna see that mu'fucka suffer for what he did to me," Flip said, holding up his hand and showing Derek his two missing fingers to make his point clear.

"I'll be in touch," Derek said. He closed the door behind Flip and pulled out his computer. It was time to make shit happen.

Flip stepped onto the elevator down to the lobby of the hotel. He felt good about what he had done. He got out of the elevator and walked through the lobby. As he stepped out of the hotel doors, he heard someone yell, "Yo, snitch!" Before he could run . . . Bang! Bang! Two shots to the dome splattered his brains all over the sidewalk. The doorman ran into the hotel, screaming for help.

Tiphani called up the Baltimore Sun and anonymously reported where they could pick up a package regarding a big breaking news story. Then she called the detective assigned to the murder cases of Archie, Bolden, Cassell, and Chief Scott, and told him the same thing. The package was on its way, and what was inside would turn the city of Baltimore upside down.

Tiphani looked over the pictures again and reviewed the gun ballistics report that Rodriguez had given her. Tiphani couldn't help but smile when she read that bullets from Derek's personal weapon, which he had forgotten in their home safe, were found in the bodies of all the dead officers.

Tiphani called Scar. "It's done, baby. I made all of the calls. We will live happily ever after." She smiled as she spoke into the receiver. "I love you too," she said, closing her eyes.

Hanging up the telephone, she shrugged into her coat on her way to mail her packages. She grabbed her keys and stepped out her door. When she stepped down her first step, she was hit from the side. She wasn't able to scream before she was dragged away.

To be continued . . .

Baltimore Chronicles

Volume 2

Treasure Hernandez

Prologue

Tiphani called Scar. "It's done, baby," she said. "I made all of the calls. We will live happily ever after." She smiled as she spoke into the receiver. "I love you too," she added, closing her eyes.

After hanging up the telephone, she shrugged into her coat on her way to mail her packages. She grabbed her keys and stepped out her door. As she took her first step, she was hit from the side. She didn't even have time to scream before she was dragged away.

"In breaking news, police report that Assistant District Attorney Tiphani Fuller has been reported missing. Police fear Mrs. Fuller may be in grave danger because of her husband's alleged criminal associations. ADA Fuller is the estranged wife of embattled Maryland State Trooper, narcotics detective Derek Fuller. Fuller, the former leader of the State Troopers' Drug Enforcement Section, was indicted by a grand jury last week on charges of conspiracy and first-degree murder. He is a suspect in the brutal murder of a DES officer. The officer's mutilated body was found outside of the home Fuller shared with a fellow officer. Detective Fuller, who is currently being held without bond, is also suspected of cutting deals with the Dirty Money Crew, a notorious drug syndicate headed up by the infamous Stephon "Scar" Johnson. Police would not confirm whether they believe ADA Fuller's disappearance is directly related to her husband's alleged crimes, but said they are putting out all of their manpower and resources to find her. The FBI is also involved. ADA Fuller was last seen dropping her children off to school two weeks ago. The children's where-abouts are not being disclosed, for their safety. We will continue to follow the story as it develops," the reporter said, staring into the camera.

Derek sat on one of the small, hard, plastic chairs in the dayroom of the protective segregation unit inside the Baltimore County Jail.

The room was pin-drop quiet. Everyone was interested in the infamous narco that sat right in the same jail with them; inmates and COs alike were glued to the television. In protective segregation Derek was surrounded by other corrupt cops under arrest, and other inmates who needed special protection. The warden knew there was no way Derek would survive in general population with people he had put behind bars.

Derek felt the heat of eyes on him, but at that point, he didn't care who was around him in the hellhole of a jail. The air around him was thick and threatened to suffocate him, even after he had finally exhaled. He was watching the television so intently, he didn't even realize he was involuntarily holding his breath.

He flexed his jaw at the news of Tiphani's disappearance and at the sight of his old home on the news, outside which every broadcast news station in Baltimore, Maryland was posted.

Derek was immediately drawn back to a time when his life was almost perfect. The two of them had everything, and within a second, boom! Their lives had exploded into chaos. Now, here he sat in jail for crimes he didn't commit. His wife was missing, feared dead, and their kids would surely end up in foster care.

He shook his head. What had he done to himself? To them? Just seeing his former home on the screen made his stomach muscles clench. What would happen to his kids? Where could Tiphani have gone? "She wouldn't just leave the kids like that," he mumbled under his breath. "Something had to happen to her." All of a sudden, a rush of anxiety filled his gut, and he raced for his open cell so he could throw up.

Derek had a fucked up feeling about this whole disappearance, and about everything in general that had happened thus far. He felt betrayed in more ways than one. He couldn't believe that his administrative leave had so quickly turned into an all-out witch-hunt against him, and now he sat rotting in a fucking jail cell with a bunch of trumped-up evidence compiled against him. The crimes he was accused of were unheard of, but Derek had been pegged as the scapegoat for the department for some reason.

Derek finished emptying his guts into the toilet and swiped the back of his hand over his lips, his mind crowded with thoughts of Tiphani. The news story had clearly shaken him. He had hoped that Tiphani would've come home by now. Every day that passed made it worse for her and damn sure made it bad for him. He had already been questioned about Tiphani's disappearance and didn't like the underlying innuendo in the voice of the detective who had interviewed him. It was like they were trying to blame him for her disappearance too. He had become so frustrated at the detective asking him the same question seventy-five different ways, he jumped into the detective's face, but the cocky detective still didn't back down.

"Mr. Fuller, we understand that you and your wife were going through a bitter and nasty divorce and custody battle," the detective had said, a sly smirk on his wrinkled, olive-colored face.

"Yeah. And what of it?" Derek squinted his eyes. "Well, sometimes when things like that are going on, one spouse, you know, may . . ." The detective's voice trailed off like he wanted Derek to fill in the blank with some crazy shit.

Even though Derek knew all of the interrogation tricks, he couldn't keep his cool. Blood immediately rushed to his head. "I didn't have anything to do with my wife's disappearance!" he screamed, his face turning almost burgundy as his heart hammered against his chest bone. He was used to being on the other side of the table, doing the interrogating, and discovered he didn't like being interrogated himself.

"Mr. Fuller, we are just trying to run down any leads that may help us find your wife," the detective said, his paper-thin lips moving in slow motion.

Every word seemed like flashbulbs of light to Derek, with nonstop images of Tiphani and Scar fucking exploding in front of him.

"I'm stuck in this fucking hellhole because somebody wanted me out of their way. My wife needs to be found now! My kids are all alone," Derek croaked out, the tears burning his eyes, and a sharp pain gripping him around the throat.

He couldn't erase the images of Scar ramming his wife in and out. Tiphani's face contorted with pleasure, pleasure that Derek was never able to give her. Derek's heart was breaking all over again. This was all too fucking much to handle.

"We are trying to find her, but I will tell you now. If she has in fact been kidnapped, and ends up dead, it only makes you look worse," the detective had said, as he rose to leave.

Derek shook the memories of that interrogation from his mind. That was almost two weeks ago, and still Tiphani had not been found. He'd heard on one of the many news stories that Tiphani's cell phone was found on the side of I-95. Not a good sign.

The night he was visited by the detective, just like today, he hadn't slept for even one hour. He hadn't been able to concentrate since. *If Tiphani turns up dead, I can forget my freedom. They will believe it was me, no matter what I do or say,* Derek thought as he paced up and down the pod. Although Tiphani had cheated on him, basically the catalyst for his downward spiral, he still worried about her whereabouts. He had a recurring thought since he'd learned about her disappearance—Scar could be the only person responsible for her kidnapping. He is the only muthafucka that would dare.

And just like everything else that had gone wrong in Derek's life as of late, Scar was behind it. Derek couldn't believe he was being labeled a cop killer for Archie's murder. Now Tiphani was gone, and he appeared to be the only one with an ax to grind, the divorce and custody battle making him the prime suspect, since no one knew about her affair with Scar.

Derek put his head in his hands and rocked back and forth. "God, if You exist, please let her be alive," he whispered.

Rodriguez let a smile spread across her petite face. *This must be it. It's really about to happen for me,* she thought to herself as she walked with a pep of arrogance in her step. She felt overly confident as she followed Chief Hill down to his office. Rodriguez was sure the private meeting requested by the chief would be the first step to promoting her to DES lead detective permanently, to officially taking over Derek's role.

The two walked in silence, both deep in thought. Once they arrived in the chief's office, the chief walked over to his desk and sat down. Rodriguez noticed that the chief's face was emotionless. To say that he had a poker face would be an understatement.

Suddenly, shit didn't seem like Rodriguez had thought. Watching the chief take his seat, a feeling of dread washed over her. Maybe she was wrong about the purpose of this meeting. The chief looked like he was about to bite her head off. Rodriguez couldn't figure it out, so she waited for the ball to drop.

"Nice artwork," she said, gesturing toward the chief's collection of black art paintings. She was trying to lighten the mood in the room.

The chief nodded, but inside he was laughing. *This bitch really thinks I'm stupid.* "Look, I didn't call you here for a social love call or no shit like that," Chief Hill said. "Have a seat. You'll need it."

Rodriguez sat down across from the chief. She placed her hands under her thighs to keep them from trembling. She knew now that she was definitely wrong about the purpose of this meeting.

"Look, I don't know what you got going on, or what you had against Derek Fuller, but I know what you did," Chief Hill said, staring Rodriguez down. He stared at Rodriguez so hard, his dark-brown, almost black eyes dug imaginary holes into Rodriguez's face.

Rodriguez started to say, "I don't know what—"

The chief put his hand up and cut her off mid-sentence. "You don't know what I'm talking about? Is that what you were going to say? That's the best you could do? The best lie you can come up with? C'mon, my six-year-old can do better than that!" Chief Hill spat, growing angry, feeling like Rodriguez thought he was stupid. More than anything, the chief hated to feel like somebody was trying to insult his intelligence.

"You fuckin' changed evidence in Fuller's case! Not only did you change it, you stole mitigating evidence that might help get him off! You also planted some shit," the chief said, letting Rodriguez know that she wasn't fooling him.

Rodriguez's face turned pale. It was like all of her color leaked from her face and pooled on the floor, buckets of sweat now dripping from her head. Rodriguez was frantic inside. She couldn't go out like this. *I'm taking shit to the grave,* she thought. She got defensive, the only way she figured she'd get around these accusations.

"You're fucking crazy!" she screamed, jumping up from the chair. "I would never do that shit! Fuller was my friend!"

"Sit the fuck down!" Chief Hill barked, the vein near his temple pulsing like crazy. "I'm not asking you if you did it. I know you did it!" He leaned back in his oversized leather chair and turned his computer monitor around so that the screen was facing Rodriguez.

Rodriguez swallowed hard, trying in vain to get rid of the huge lump that sat at the back of her throat. Finally able to breathe, she stood and stared at the monitor. She watched the computerized, grainy surveillance image of herself as she moved around the evidence cage. Her legs buckled, almost sending her five-foot seven-inch frame crashing to the floor.

"You look like you've seen a ghost. Sit down before you faint." The chief smirked. He had Rodriguez right where he wanted her—scared and willing to play the game.

Rodriguez flopped back down in the chair, exasperated and scared to death of what was about to come her way. "Chief, I swear . . ." Rodriguez started, her hands shaking so badly, she wanted to cut them off. Cold sweat now drenched her entire body, not just her head. Her bowels felt like they would release right there in her pants. This was the end of her career for sure, or so she thought.

"What made you do it? I mean, I thought Fuller was your friend . . . your supervisor and team member. I thought the DES was like a brotherhood? Didn't all you bastards go around professing this brotherhood shit?" Chief Hill shook his head left to right in a fake display of disgust.

Rodriguez hung her head at first. Then something hit her like a thunderbolt. "I—I was so mad about Archie's death. I mean, he didn't have to do him like that. His family couldn't even have an open casket. Then I started feeling like that mu'fucka Fuller had something to do with Bolden and Cassell's murders too. It was all too much to think about!!" Sweat dripped down her face, and she felt hot all over her body. She clenched her fists. At that moment, she wanted to see Derek in front of her. "I just wanted revenge. I didn't do it for any other reason, just revenge. I wanted him to suffer," Rodriguez fabricated on the spot.

"Bullshit! Nice acting job, Rodriguez." The chief smirked. "Scar Johnson is paying you too, ain't he?" Chief Hill stood up and leaned on his desk, toward Rodriguez. At that point, he was letting her know the gloves were off.

Rodriguez almost choked on her own tongue. *It's impossible for the chief to have figured that out,* she thought to herself. Rodriguez had only had one meeting with Scar, the initial meeting, and had always dealt with one of Scar's little workers when it came time to collect her money. There was no way Chief Hill would even associate her with Scar, unless he was on the fucking take himself.

"No. I don't know what you're talking about," Rodriguez lied, sticking to her take-it-to-the-grave philosophy.

"Don't bullshit me. I know all about it. See, I'm like God. Omniscient. I know everything that goes on in Baltimore," Chief Hill said, smiling evilly.

There was no need for her to continue fighting and denying her association. Her shoulders slumped, and she mentally gave up. It was time to level. "Please, Chief. This job is all I got. It's what I worked hard for all my life. I can't lose it. I can't afford to end up like Derek. I made a mistake . . . you gotta understand," Rodriguez pleaded, almost in tears.

"I hate to see a beautiful woman cry. Pull your skirt down and just fucking listen to what I have to say."

Rodriguez hung her head and listened. At this point, she didn't have a choice.

"I want twenty percent of whatever Scar is paying you, whenever he pays you. I want to know every time Scar contacts you. I will make sure my eyes and ears remain closed to what you're doing, but I expect my money. Don't ever think I can't find out how much you got, so make sure I get my twenty percent and you don't try to short me. We can all work together to bring Fuller down," Chief Hill said, leaning back in the chair in relax mode. "I never liked his ass anyway."

"Y-y-yes, sir, I can do that," Rodriguez stammered. She stood up and extended her hand toward the chief for a shake. "I can keep you posted, and the money is no problem. I can help you if you help me."

The chief accepted her hand, and they exchanged a brisk handshake, sealing their deal to help Scar put Derek away for life.

Chapter 1

The Best Laid Plans

Tiphani sat across from Scar and picked up her martini glass again. She was finally feeling a buzz. She still couldn't believe she was on a yacht, sailing off the coast of Florida toward the Caribbean. Scar sat across from her on a long black leather bench that was built into the yacht's upper deck wall. Tiphani stared at him with hazy eyes. She thought Scar looked hella sexy, rocking his Hermes boat shoes, a wife-beater that hugged his muscular chest, and a Gucci fedora sitting on top of his big head. She had conditioned herself to look past his ugly-ass scarred grill; his swagger was enough for her. It was more than her husband ever had.

Tiphani looked down at the feast set out in front of them. The table was full of all kinds of food prepared by Scar's own personal chef. There were lobster tails, huge freshly steamed shrimp surrounded by cocktail sauce, rich, leafy salads, tropical fruits, and the most expensive Beluga caviar money could buy. Despite all of it, Tiphani hadn't touched a bite.

"Why you not eating?" Scar asked her, picking up one of the huge prawns, ready to throw it back.

"I'm not really that hungry," Tiphani said in a low tone, swirling her liquor around in her glass. She wasn't interested in the food, Scar, or anything on the yacht at this point. She was missing her kids and having second thoughts.

"Shit speak for yourself." Scar wasted no time digging into the food he'd paid a grip to have his chef cook up.

Tiphani took another sip of her drink. She ran her fingers through her long, jet-black hair, like she usually did when deep in thought. The sun was beginning to set, and her mood was continuing to go down right along with it. The sea breeze kissed her beautiful face and whipped around her perfect, shapely legs. Between the dreamy scene—the sunset, the ocean, the ritzy yacht—and the buzz she was feeling, Tiphani was mesmerized. Flashes of her kids' faces played in her mind. She couldn't help but wonder if she'd done the right thing by letting Scar stage her kidnapping.

When Scar's little henchmen had snatched her from in front of her home, they had blindfolded her and put her in a van. Tiphani, not knowing it was a set-up, had fought ferociously, clawing hunks of skin from one of their faces, kicking and biting wildly. Scar had instructed them not to hurt a hair on her head, but she didn't make it easy, cursing, spitting, and bucking like a wild animal.

After she had finally worn herself out and sat still for five minutes, Scar's men tried to explain to her what was going on, but she wouldn't hear anything from them. In her mind she had been thrust into a fight to save her own life. Only after they'd told her what Scar had instructed them to say did she listen. She was informed that Scar had ordered the fake kidnapping, just in case neighbors or any other witnesses had been watching, and that there was a reason for everything. They also told her that Scar just really wanted her to meet with him and lay low for a while.

With all of the commotion, Tiphani was trying to make sense of it all. To her it seemed to be a bit much. She thought he could've just told her to come and disappear with him without all of the theatrics, but she figured Scar knew what he was doing. They explained that Scar knew when she didn't show up for her kids, her disappearance would be reported, and everyone would think she was missing. Scar had staged the kidnapping because he wanted it to seem like she was snatched, that it had something to do with her husband's dirty dealings.

After getting wind of the meeting between his brother Derek and his old crew member Flip, it wasn't lost on Scar that Flip had probably revealed a bunch of shit that could send Scar to prison for a long time. Which was why he had to shut Flip up permanently. He'd ordered the hit to take place publicly, to send a message to anyone else who had an idea to "flip" on Scar and the

Dirty Money Crew. The execution outside of the hotel definitely got everyone's attention. Word spread instantly about the fate of Flip, the snitch. Scar also knew that his brother Derek would be looking for a way to defend himself against all the charges thrown his way, which meant Derek would also be gunning for him. He knew it wouldn't be that long before the beast amassed enough evidence to finally make the charges stick.

Tiphani had protested Scar's staged kidnapping for the first couple of days, pouting and begging to go home to her kids. She was having trouble understanding the reasoning and desperately missed her kids. Knowing Scar was dangerous, she didn't push the issue as much as she wanted to. So, even though her kidnapping was supposed to be fake, she really did feel like she'd been kidnapped and was being held against her will.

Legally, she didn't think her disappearance would bring any value to the case against Derek, and she knew her kids were at risk of being forced into the foster care system in her absence. She'd even thought about Derek winning their custody battle, if he ever beat his case.

But Tiphani's protests and pleas fell on deaf ears. Scar used his charm and his dick to convince her that this staged kidnapping was the only way to put another brick in the wall against Derek. Ultimately, the dick had finally made Tiphani give in to Scar's plan. When his goons delivered Tiphani to Scar, he grabbed her and hugged her tightly. He was still playing the role of concerned lover, even though he just wanted to keep her close and keep an eye on her.

Staging the kidnap worked to Scar's advantage in two ways. One, he could make it look like Derek had something to do with it, and two, he could control Tiphani, while getting some of that tasty pussy.

After his welcoming hug, he led her down the pier, toward a line of huge yachts. Tiphani was confused, looking around in disbelief. She kept walking with Scar until he stopped in front of one of the massive boats. She read the hand-painted sign on the back of the yacht. It read "DIRTY MONEY." She looked up at Scar with furrowed eyebrows.

"I ain't gonna fake kidnap you and keep you in my basement, baby," Scar had said, smiling. He led her up the dock ramp into the boat.

Tiphani remembered her heart skipping a beat. She had quickly forgotten about her reservations about staging her own kidnapping. Scar welcomed her onto the regal boat. Inside Tiphani looked around in awe. It looked like a house. He led her into the fully furnished suite, which made her gasp. All of the furniture was pure white, and it immediately made Tiphani think about the way she envisioned heaven. There was a California king-sized bed, leather couches, plasma TVs, expensive throw rugs, mirrored walls and ceilings, and a Jacuzzi.

Tiphani was overwhelmed by the yacht. The luxuriousness made it feel like all of her worries had dissipated right then and there. She couldn't contain herself and had to let Scar fuck her right there on the spot.

After two days on the yacht, Scar thought it was time to put Tiphani onto his full plan and get her to buy in. When he told her they'd be gone for six months or longer, she cried, thinking about her kids.

Scar's plan was for her to go back to Baltimore, act as if she had been kidnapped because of Derek, and fake like she had fought to make a daring escape. Scar told her she could sell her story to every news program—*20/20; Dateline; Anderson Cooper*. Shit, even *Oprah*. They would all be fighting to cover the highly publicized reunion with her kids.

Knowing the law, Tiphani didn't think getting her kids back would be that easy. She figured there would be suspicion that she'd abandoned them and made up her story, which worried her immensely. She didn't think the whole thing was a good idea.

Scar reassured her he would pay whoever he had to pay to have her kids returned to her. He also told her she should always say that her captors kept mentioning her husband, and money he owed them. If she stuck to the story, it would make it seem as if Derek was the cause of her disappearance because he had been robbing drug dealers and selling drugs too.

The best part of the plan was, while she rode the wave of fame and notoriety, she would jump out of the box and announce her bid to run for circuit court judge. Scar told her that he had it all mapped out, and she would definitely win. In his grand scheme, Tiphani would be the one that would save him from all of the charges pending against him once and for all. A lot of pockets would be laced so that she would be appointed as the judge on his case when he finally turned himself in.

Being the driven, power-hungry career woman she was, at first Tiphani thought the plan was brilliant. She could sacrifice a few months without her kids for a greater career move. In her mind, becoming a judge would be great for all of them. But she didn't know Scar would never really be loyal to anyone, not even her.

Today, sitting on a yacht with a dangerous drug dealer, Tiphani was having second thoughts. The what-ifs had set in on her, and she sat, preoccupied with thoughts of all of the things that could go wrong—one of which was, she could be thrown in jail for fabricating a story so elaborate and would lose her children forever if anyone ever found out the truth.

"Damn! You been daydreaming for a minute," Scar said, breaking up her thoughts.

Tiphani let a weak smile spread across her face. Scar could see the second thoughts and doubt in her eyes. "I hope you dreaming about me and this pussy-pounding I'm about to put on you." He grabbed his dick through his pants.

Tiphani smiled just thinking about that good-ass dick.

When Scar saw her smile, he knew he had her again. He didn't care if he had to fuck her every minute of every day to keep her on course with his plan. He was going to do whatever it took to keep this bitch in line. Scar thought of Tiphani as the "queen of sorts." He saw her as one of the most powerful pieces in his game of chess against Derek and the Maryland State Troopers that had tried to destroy everything he had worked to build.

Before she knew it, Scar had swooped down on her like an eagle snatching up a little mouse as prey. The next thing she knew, Scar was carrying her like a little rag doll down the yacht steps to the lower deck. Once there, he reached under her dress and ripped her thong off with one forceful motion.

Tiphani began breathing hard, and a hot feeling came over her. She loved Scar's spontaneity. Nothing was all planned and boring, like with Derek. She giggled, the liquor tingling her senses. Scar forced his tongue into her mouth, she accepted, and they kissed wildly. Tiphani's cheeks were on fire. The heat their bodies generated was enough to cook something.

Scar pulled off his Ralph Lauren purple label shorts, freeing his beautiful, thick dick. Then he ripped his wife-beater over his head, exposing his chest, adorned by a diamond-encrusted Jesus piece. The platinum up against his ebony skin was sexy as hell. Tiphani licked her lips as he climbed on top of her. She buried her face in his neck and inhaled his scent. It was intoxicating. She felt like she was really falling in love with him.

Scar hoisted her sundress up and buried his face in her sopping wet pussy. He blew his hot breath on her clitoris and devoured her pussy until she was dizzy. Then he moved up, took a mouthful of her firm breasts into his mouth, and slammed his dick up in her like a bulldozer. Over and over again, Scar pounded into her flesh. Tiphani dug her nails into his back as he continued his mission. He rammed her with all his might and fucked her back into submission.

Tiphani accepted each of his thrusts for as long as she could. "Oh God!" she screamed, and then she came all over his dick.

Then Scar followed her, letting his juices saturate her neatly shaved triangle. Panting and out of breath, they collapsed in a tangled heap of flesh.

Just then Scar's cell phone rang. "Damn!" he panted. It was back to business just that fast. Although his ass was on a vacation of sorts, shit in the harsh streets of Baltimore was business as usual.

Scar still had a strong hold on the streets through his Dirty Money Crew, which was thriving and growing in numbers. He had groomed his little niggas well, and they were running shit back home, keeping his pockets laced. Niggas was hungry on the streets, and he was the only nigga offering to feed them, so they all remained loyal to him. Even in his absence, his presence was still felt.

"Speak," he wolfed into his cell phone. He listened for a minute. Then he sat up and pushed Tiphani away, turning his back toward her. Scar flexed his jaw as he listened intently. He balled up his fist on his free hand and squeezed it so hard, his knuckles looked like they'd bust through his skin. He pursed his lips and spoke. "Well, then kill the nigga. What you even second-guessing it for?" Disconnecting the line, he tossed his cell phone across the room, sending it crashing into the wall.

Tiphani jumped at the sound. "What's the matter, baby?" she asked, sitting up startled.

Scar ignored her question. He rushed out of the room to get his anger under control. He didn't want to unleash on Tiphani and risk having her fall out of line.

Tiphani lay back down, still hoping this plan was going to work in their favor.

Chapter 2

Business as Usual

"Yo, he said to kill this nigga," Trail said, no emotion behind his words as he hung up the phone.

"No. Please, Trail, help me, man. Sticks, please," the boy pleaded as he sat on a small chair in the middle of the floor, surrounded by members of the Dirty Money Crew.

The boy's begging and pleading for mercy amused the crew, who were laughing and making light of his impending doom, but he saw it as a last-ditch effort to save himself. Only fifteen, he felt he was too young to die. The day he took Scar's offer to join the crew, he'd made the worst mistake of his life, and he knew it now more than ever.

"Nigga, your trap was short seven fuckin' times in a row. Then you show up in the hood with a fuckin' brand-new-ass Escalade, paid out in cash! You can't afford that shit, nigga. You ain't move up in this game yet. Ain't nobody gonna surpass Scar's status. When you stole from that nigga and tried to floss like you was larger than him, you sealed your fate. You thought a nigga like Scar was gone, vamoose, and that you was gonna get away with having larceny in yo' heart. Well, nigga, I just got word from the king of these streets. The order has been given—you're a dead man." Sticks' face curled into a hard scowl, stiff and emotionless like stone.

"Yo, I can pay it back. It wasn't that much, I swear. I just been saving for a minute," the boy begged, shaking his legs back and forth.

All of the Dirty Money Crew members began laughing uproariously. They thought this little begging-ass boy was amusing, and they were particularly anxious to see him get his punishment, even if it meant murder. In Scar's absence the crew all looked to

Sticks for their orders, and he knew he definitely had something to prove.

"Yo, now a nigga wanna cop a plea," Timber said. He was one of the new members of the crew. "Let me kill him, slow and painful like. I will cut off his eyelids so the nigga can't blink. I will remove that nigga's fingernails and toenails one by one while he watch." Timber got menacingly close to the boy's face.

Timber was a wild boy, and he was helping the Dirty Money Crew wreak havoc on the streets of Baltimore. He had relocated from Alabama to Baltimore with his mother, and it wasn't long before he got knee-deep into the streets. He had told Sticks and Trail that he got his nickname Timber because one night when he was eleven, he went out into his backyard, sawed off a tree branch and beat his stepfather to death with it for hitting on his mother. When the word spread about him to all the gangs in Alabama, they started calling him Little Timber after that, and the name stuck. (Tim-ber!" was what the tree cutters in Alabama called out when they cut trees down.) After Timber felt the power surge from his first murder, it became nothing for him. He was ruthless and was into torture. In fact, he craved the sensational rush he got from committing heinous acts.

"Nah, I'ma do this shit Scar-style—short and sweet, no need for a bunch of blood and guts and shit," Sticks said. He really just wanted to assert his power and show off his bravado in front of the younger dudes in the crew. Murder and mayhem was what he wanted on his tombstone.

"Yo, Scar always gives a nigga his chance to have last rites. So what is it gonna be?" Sticks said to the boy. "You got a choice, nigga—call a bitch, call your moms, or you wanna chance to pray to God? Don't think too long, nigga. I ain't got all day."

Staring death in the eyes, the boy thought to himself, *This can't be real.* Crying like a baby and trembling like a leaf, he agreed to a call to his mother to say good-bye. He figured at least she would know he was thinking of her before he died. He couldn't imagine how she would react if he had gone missing for weeks, or when the police finally came to the door to tell her they had found his body. He wanted to tell her good-bye himself. In his mind, he was saying, Fuck God, because if there was a God, He would save him right now.

"I'ma call my moms," the boy whined through the tsunami of tears that covered his face.

Sticks kept his gun trained on the boy. "Tell this nigga the number to dial," he instructed the boy. The boy did as he was told, and Trail punched the numbers in on one of their many disposable track phones they used to communicate about their business and to speak to Scar, to avoid being traced.

Trail put the phone on speaker, and after three rings, the boy heard his mother's melodic voice filter through the speaker.

"Hello?" she answered.

"Ma! Ma!" the boy cried out.

"Anthony? What's the matter? Where are you?" his mother said, concern streaming through her words.

"Say bye, nigga," Sticks whispered, placing the cold steel up against the boy's temple.

"Bye, ma! I love you forever!!" the boy screamed.

"Anthony!" his mother screamed.

Trail disconnected the line.

Bang! One shot to the temple, and the boy's body slumped from the chair and hit the floor with an ominous thud.

"One down, two more Frank Lucas snitch-ass niggas to go," Sticks said. Temporarily put in charge by Scar, Sticks had vowed that the streets would be sorry for the day he was born. He remembered all the ill-treatment he'd suffered at Scar's hands in the training phase of his comeup. Now he was prepared to take it out on anybody who got in his way, even members of the crew.

Sticks, Trail, Timber, and four new young members of the Dirty Money Crew loaded into two black Suburbans. Sticks drove slowly through the streets of Baltimore, blasting Drake and Lil Wayne. The bass and the lyrics had them all hyped. All except Sticks, who was silent and intently focused on his mission, while the other members were laughing and cracking jokes on each other.

"Yo! Y'all gotta shut the fuck up!" Sticks screamed. "We about to go handle some serious business. If Scar was here, y'all niggas would be like church mice up in this bitch, scared to fuckin' make a peep!"

An immediate hush fell over the vehicle.

"Now, we gonna ride out slow and easy. This nigga Bam think shit is one hun'ed. I wanna scope out his spots first." Sticks spoke calmly, as if he didn't just scream on them. He was a perfectionist when it came to a mission. For him, failure wasn't an option.

Sticks was a hungry dude from day one; he'd never had shit given to him. When Scar had met him, he could tell the boy would do almost anything to put food in his starving stomach. Which was why Scar had chosen him. Scar had groomed him much like a trainer would groom a prize fighter. So when Sticks collected his first couple of stacks, his loyalty to Scar was sealed. Scar figured he was the perfect one to run shit, allowing him to lay low.

They drove down a block and were careful to stay two or three buildings away from their destination.

"Look, there go that nigga right there," Trail said in a low tone, pointing out a hustler named Bam that had been on the crew's radar for some prime real estate he owned in the Baltimore drug trade.

Before anybody else could do or say anything, Sticks accelerated and rolled up on the rival dealer without warning. The truck tires screeched against the street, startling everyone on the block.

Before anyone could react, Sticks threw the truck in park and was out in a millisecond. He ran up to Bam, his gun drawn. "Yo, I thought I told you we staging a takeover of this set!" Sticks screamed as he rushed towards Bam.

Bam threw his hands up in surrender.

It was too late. He had been caught slippin' and clearly not prepared for the huge .45-caliber gun sitting in his face. "Your choice was to get down or lay down, like that dude Beanie Sigel said. You chose to lay down, muthafucka," Sticks growled.

Boom!

One shot to the dome, and Bam's body crumpled to the ground, leaving the other members of Scar's crew in shock. Screams erupted everywhere.

"Go in the mu'fucka and clean it out. Drugs and money!" Sticks barked, whirling around with his gun, swinging to ward off everybody.

The rest of the crew members raced into Bam's trap house and looted as fast as they could.

Sticks had always instructed them that they had eight minutes from beginning to end to do a "jux." He had timed the nine-one-one response, the time it took the police to get up and out on a call.

He looked at his watch. They were almost on schedule but not quite. He could hear the distant wail of sirens. "Let's go!" he ordered. "We ain't got no witnesses." He called out to the crowd of onlookers and to Bam's little crew. "I saw all y'all faces—Anybody snitch, I will be back!"

Sticks and the rest of the Dirty Money Crew loaded back into their vehicles and rolled out.

Trail was fuming mad. He didn't understand why Sticks didn't give him any forewarning that he was going to murder Bam. He huffed, "Nigga, how you just gonna jump the fuck out and not say shit? No heads-up or nothing?"

"Hesitation leads to reservations. One ounce of doubt and you a fuckin' dead man on these streets," Sticks said calmly. He didn't give a fuck about anyone's feelings. This game and all its little quirks was all about a paper chase and power for him.

"You could've still said something," Trail told him. "Let a nigga know what you was about to do and shit."

"Damn, mu'fucka! Pull your skirt down. I can't take no bitchy whining and complaining shit. If we gonna be on this new shit, taking down all the other niggas in Baltimore, we don't have time to run our mouths like bitches. Now drop the fuckin' subject and follow my lead, nigga. I mean, you either get down or lay down!"

Trail did as he was told and shut his mouth, but he didn't like it. He twisted his lips to the side and bopped his head to the music in an effort to keep himself quiet. Shit was definitely different than when Scar was home. Trail noticed that since Scar had left, Sticks was more ruthless than ever. He was letting the young'uns run wild in the streets of Baltimore, killing any person—man, woman, or child—that got in their way. They were collecting money almost every hour. All of the street contracts and territorial agreements Scar had made with rival hustlers was out the window once he left. Sticks had single-handedly dismantled a commission of hustlers that Scar had put together years ago to divide up the drug territories and put an end to a war that was going on at the time. Although Scar had assigned himself the most lucrative spots and the biggest piece of the pie, the other hustlers got down with the commission because they were afraid of the consequences if they refused. Shit on the streets was all good after that. There were a little jealous spats here and there, but whenever niggas heard Scar wasn't happy, those little sidebar fights quickly turned into truces.

Now, Trail was worried that Sticks, if he wasn't careful, could start one of the biggest drug wars in Baltimore's history, even bigger than the one Scar put an end to where seventy street dudes had been killed in a five-month span.

Finally, Sticks pulled the vehicle up on the other side of town. Trail bit down into his jaw. He knew that this entire south side belonged to Tango, another big hustler in Baltimore. Tango and Scar had finally settled their beef over streets years ago with the formulation of the commission, drawing imaginary lines in the Baltimore streets.

"Yo, Timber, you ready to earn your wings, nigga?" Sticks asked.

"I was born ready. Where they at?" Timber said with his thick country accent.

"That's their main hub right there. I heard they collect like six hundred thousand stacks every eight hours. We about to take their day's work." Sticks laughed like he was a damn maniac.

"A'ight, let's get it," Timber said, pulling on the truck's door handle with one hand, while he gripped a stolen AK-47 in the other.

Danielle rolled her eyes as her mother rambled on with another lecture. She was thinking, her mother just didn't get it. The more Dana told her to stay away from boys, sex, and drugs, the more Danielle was drawn to them. Today though, it was a different lecture. Her mother was trying to convince her to go and spend more time with her older sister. Ever since she had turned sixteen, Danielle had begun to smell herself, thinking she was grown.

"Why should I go spend the weekends at her house, Ma? She's a cop, and I hate the police! " Danielle said. "Plus, she's boring. Ain't nobody trying to sit up in her face all day talking about nothing at all." She folded her arms across her ample breasts and shifted her weight from one foot to another.

Dana was determined to get her to focus on something other than the streets and she wasn't trying to hear it. "First of all, your sister has a very good job. She helps pay most of the bills in here and keeps you in all of that expensive stuff you like to wear. You can show her you appreciate her. She loves you, and besides, you used to like to spend time with her."

Danielle rolled her eyes as she applied a full face of makeup. At sixteen, she resembled a grown-ass woman. Thirty-six D cup breasts, a small waist, plump round hips, and an ass you could set a glass on made her a hot commodity in the hood. She got a million attempts at getting with her a day, and knew just how to play the game. Danielle wasn't interested in traditional school. She was from the "use-what-you-got-to-get-what-you-want" school, having learned from the best—her mother. And she damn sure didn't have time to spend with her lame-ass sister.

"Look, you're becoming too spoiled, Dani. One day your sister is going to cut you off, and then what you gon' do? Huh?" Her mother took a long drag off her cigarette.

Danielle sucked her teeth. She always felt unloved because she never knew her father. And ever since she could remember, Maria had been like a second parent.

"Fine. I'll go with her for the weekend, if you let me go to a party with Veronica and my friends first."

"She will be here on Saturday morning to get you, so have your ass back up in here. You act like spending time with her is going to kill you. You should try to appease her, as much as she does for us. When she cuts us off, your lips gonna be poked out. If that happens, your hot ass ain't gonna get those little stripper-ass outfits you like to wear." Dana blew a ring of smoke toward her daughter.

"Whatever. I'll be here. Yeah, sure," Danielle said, grabbing her purse and heading out the door.

Danielle rushed up the street, switching her hips as hard as she could. She smirked to herself at all of the catcalls she received from the little hoodrat dudes in her neighborhood.

"Yo, Dani, I will fuck those poom-poom shorts right off that fat ass," a little corner boy called out.

"Nigga, pa-lease! I fucks with real hustlers. Hand-to-hand is played out!" Danielle screamed, craning her neck in true ghetto-girl fashion.

She finally made it to the end of the block, where she spotted the person she was expecting to meet. Her heart jumped in her chest. He was so damn sexy. Danielle let a smile spread across her face at the sight of the gleaming silver Benz S550 he sat in. She rushed over to the passenger side and slid in.

"Damn, baby girl! You got my shit on wood with them li'l shorts," Sticks said, licking his lips. *I have something for this little hottie,* he thought to himself.

"Two weeks and you can't handle seeing me in shorts?" She leaned over to kiss her new man.

Everybody in Baltimore knew Sticks was down with the Dirty Money Crew, including Danielle and her little friends. But she was so excited when Sticks had stopped her in a party. In fact, she felt extra special that he had chosen her out of all the girls in the club that night. Sticks had told her she reminded him of Lauren London, a comment she got all the time, but coming from him, it made her blush.

That night Danielle gave Sticks her number. Her best friend Veronica had stayed up with her all night waiting for him to call, but he never did. Three days had passed, and Danielle had gotten a little depressed. Then, when she least expected it, Sticks showed up at her high school. It just so happened, that day she'd decided to attend classes. She'd rolled her eyes at him and told him off.

Sticks laughed at her and told her he liked the way she looked when she was mad. He grabbed her hand and led her to his car. He started calling her every day since.

"Where you wanna go, *mami*? The world is yours," Sticks said, tossing a money stack into her lap.

Danielle's eyes lit up. She didn't want to seem too thirsty by picking up the stack and counting it, but she wanted to so badly.

"I wanna be wherever you are. We could sit in this car all night and I'd be happy," she replied.

That's exactly what Sticks wanted to hear. He liked the little pretty girl, but he also had bigger plans for her. Before he put her to work, he wanted to run up in that fat ass. He took her to get something to eat at Ruth's Chris, one of his favorites.

Danielle had never been to a real restaurant like that. The closest she'd come was when her sister had taken them out to eat at the local Olive Garden.

"Thank you for dinner, baby. I really appreciate everything you do for me." Danielle smiled, causing her deep dimples to show.

"Yo, ma, you know I keep it one hun'ed, right?" Sticks asked, his tone serious.

"Yes. Why? What's the matter?"

"I want you, ma. I know I said I wanted to wait until you was seventeen and shit, but I think a nigga fallin' for you."

"Ohhh, Sticks, I already fell for you," Danielle said, leaning over into the driver's seat so she could kiss him.

"Come home with me."

"Okay. Anything for you." Danielle had never felt the warm feeling she was feeling inside right now. *It must be love,* she thought.

Sticks knew as soon as he gave Danielle a taste of the dick, her young mind would be his to mold.

He and Danielle entered the doors to his luxury condo wrapped together. They were in a tangle of arms and legs, kissing and licking each other hot and heavy.

Danielle straddled Sticks around the waist, and he held onto her plump ass. As Sticks carried her up the stairs toward the bedroom in a rush, they thrust their tongues down each other's throats. Her breathing was labored, her heart hammering against her chest bone, and her ears were ringing, she was so excited. See, Danielle had only had sex with two other guys, and they were young boys, so she was scared to death.

Sticks lay her on the bed and started kissing her bare butter-colored thighs. Her shorts were hitched up so far into her crotch, she had a serious camel toe. The sight turned Sticks on immensely.

Danielle's thighs trembled. No matter how hard she tried to control her nerves, she couldn't. Sticks licked down her thighs to her calves. Then he lifted one of her legs and licked behind her knee, sending needle pricks all over her body.

"Mmmm," she moaned.

Like an expert, Sticks stealthily removed her shorts before she even knew what had happened. He stared down at her young, fresh, pink, unblemished flesh. "That's a pretty pussy," he grunted as he slid his hands up her shirt and pulled it over her head. He unsnapped her bra with one hand as he kissed her deep.

Danielle felt so hot, she thought she would explode. She didn't know what to expect, but she knew she wanted it badly. She just wanted Sticks to keep touching her and taking her.

When Danielle was fully naked, Sticks got off the bed and stood up to look at her. He stared at her like she was a fine meal that he was about to devour.

Danielle had her eyes closed. When she didn't feel him anymore, she opened them. "What's the matter?" she asked, closing her legs.

"Nothing, ma. I just wanted to admire your beauty. You are really gorgeous." Sticks didn't tell many chicks they were gorgeous, but Danielle really was. Her skin was smooth and seemingly untouched. He thought she looked so pure, unlike some of the scarred-up, sagging-tit chicks he fucked with normally.

Sticks removed his clothes and climbed back onto the bed. He placed his mouth over hers, and they kissed again. This time it wasn't wild and lustful, but slow and steady. It made Danielle feel loved.

While he kissed her, Sticks used his knee to part her trembling legs. He grabbed his rock-hard dick and guided it to her flesh, making Danielle jump.

"I'm not gonna hurt you," he said. Then he gently entered her.

"Aghhh!" she gasped. A sharp pain shot through her pelvis.

Sticks moved in and out of her slowly at first. His eyes popped open from the feeling he got from her body. He was shocked. He didn't expect her pussy to be so tight. She really felt like a virgin. Sticks was even more enamored with her now.

"Aghhh, aghhh!" Danielle grunted, biting down into her lip.

The sounds of her moans, and the suction Sticks felt from her tight walls made his head spin. He pulled out of her to keep himself from busting a nut. "C'mere," he whispered. After pulling Danielle up off the bed, he lay down and guided her on top of him.

She straddled him and sat down on his dick. "Aghhh!" she screamed out from the pain. Paralyzed with pain, she wasn't ready to take all of his thick, long tool.

Sticks grabbed onto her hips and guided her up and down on him, until she started feeling more pleasure than pain. "That's it, ma. Slow and steady. You like this dick, or you love it?"

"I love it!!" Danielle screamed. "I love you!!"

Sticks didn't return the four-letter word, but he was damn sure glad she had said it. He could feel the nut welling up inside of him. He began pumping his hips, causing Danielle to bounce up and down. Her titties bouncing in his face was turning him on even more. He lifted his head slightly and took a mouthful of one of her nipples.

"Oh, yes!" she screamed.

Sticks sucked hard and fucked her even harder. He felt it welling up. He moved faster. Faster.

"Aghhhh! I feel something!" Danielle hollered. She had never had an orgasm. The feeling busting through her loins made her pump on the dick even harder and faster. She didn't feel pain anymore, just pure, hot, wet pleasure.

"Uggghhh!" Sticks growled, his body stiffening and jerking as he released his hot load.

Danielle felt his liquid dripping back out of her. She was too hot and too in love to think about any consequences. "Oh my God," Danielle cried, and she lay on top of Sticks' perfect chest.

Sticks was silent, his usual manner when thinking hard. He couldn't believe this little, inexperienced girl wound up giving him the best sex he'd ever had.

Chapter 3

Sealed Fate

Derek felt like he had eaten a jar of paste. His mouth was dry, and his throat ached. He swallowed hard, trying to fight his nerves as the court officers led him into the courtroom. He had almost shit on himself when his lawyer came to the court cells earlier that day to tell him that the jury had reached a verdict in his trial. Derek knew a fast verdict like that could go either way, for conviction or acquittal. He could only pray that the jury was made up of reasonable citizens who would take into account his service to the community and city of Baltimore.

As he was led in, Derek saw Archie's whole family seated in the front of the courtroom. His wife, kids, and parents were all there waiting to see justice being served. Derek's heart jerked in his chest. He still couldn't believe everyone would actually think he had something to do with Archie's murder. Derek was an usher in Archie's wedding; he'd brought the entire DES hand-rolled cigars when Archie had his first baby. He thought it was just crazy that none of those facts was allowed to be brought out during the trial. Instead, the prosecutor's office had made Derek out to be a demon who killed to cover up his mis-deeds, painting him as a lowlife that worked for the very criminals he was supposed to be putting away.

Although Derek had gotten into some dirty shit with Scar, he would never kill one of his own men. No one knew the reason he worked with Scar. Scar was his baby brother. Derek normally hated drug dealers and what they stood for, but he'd made a promise to his mother to always take care of Scar. He had taken that promise to heart, and now it had landed him in hell.

Embarrassed, nervous, and angry, Derek averted eye contact with any of the other Maryland State Troopers in the courtroom, including Chief Hill and Rodriguez. The walk to his seat felt like an eternity. He took his spot behind the defense table and sat down. The lights in the courtroom felt super bright, as if a huge stage spotlight was shining right on him. The air in the courtroom seemed so thick and stale, Derek felt like he'd suffocate. To get some relief, he adjusted his tie to get some air.

Derek couldn't help but think the worst. He was going to jail for life. He said a silent prayer. He could feel sweat sliding down his forehead, dampening the underarms of his shirt. As the news cameras rolled, he swore he could feel the heat of the entire world's eyes on him through the camera lenses. He was usually cool under pressure, but at this moment he thought he was about to lose it completely. The tension was too much. He wasn't sure he would be able to handle life in prison, especially for something he wasn't guilty of. His fate was in the hands of the jury now.

"All rise. The Honorable Judge Irvin Klein presiding," the court officer called out.

The sound of wood creaking and bodies shifting seemed unnervingly loud to Derek as everyone in the courtroom stood up. Once the judge was behind the bench, everyone took their seats again.

"Remain standing, Mr. Fuller," Judge Klein instructed. "We might as well get this over with as quickly as possible."

Derek felt his legs weaken then buckle. He took a deep breath to try and calm his nerves, which didn't work.

"Jury, have you reached a verdict in the matter of the State of Maryland versus Mr. Derek Fuller?" the judge asked.

A sickening hush fell over the room, and Derek's stomach let out a loud growl. He had nervous bowel syndrome. He hunched over slightly, which was all he could do to keep himself from throwing up or shitting on himself.

"We have, Your Honor." The jury foreman, a rail-thin white man who'd been a military police officer, stood up slowly.

Derek's defense attorney had tried to dismiss the man during voir dire, arguing that he would be prejudiced and overly sensitive to a police murder, but the prosecutor had fought to keep him and won.

"Jury, what say you?" Judge Klein asked, looking over the edge of his wire-rimmed glasses at Derek.

"As to count one of the indictment, murder in the first degree, we the jury find the defendant guilty," the foreman read.

Derek's legs buckled, and he fell back into the hard-wood chair.

The courtroom erupted in pandemonium. Cameras zoomed into Derek's face as he sat there in shock. His worst nightmare had come true. Archie's wife cried out in part joy and part agony, while other officers in the room began cheering and jeering.

The court officers rushed over to Derek and grabbed him up out of the chair. At first he put up no fight, but then, suddenly, flashes of anger sparked through him. He knew he didn't stand a chance at sentencing.

"I gave my life for this fucking city! I am a cop and this is how you mu'fuckas repay me? I was the one who gave the DA details about Scar Johnson! I'm innocent, you bastards! Can't you see this is a setup? I didn't kill Archie! I didn't kill anyone!!" Derek screamed as the court officers manhandled him, thrashing against their grasp violently. He wasn't going down without a fight. "You all will regret this shit! I'm fucking innocent!"

The court officers finally got him into a tight arm bar and forcefully removed him from the courtroom, but Derek continued his rant, which fell on deaf ears. The entire city of Baltimore had pegged him as a cop killer.

Chief Hill smiled and gave Rodriguez a pat on her back. "I guess you did it," he said, chuckling a little.

A pang of guilt flitted through Rodriguez's stomach. She knew, without the evidence she had planted, Derek's attorney would have been able to establish reasonable doubt in the case. She hung her head in shame. Here it is, one of her fellow officers was just falsely convicted of killing one of his peers, and their fucking chief was celebrating. The department was being racked with corruption and disloyalty, and she didn't know who to trust anymore. She really believed some criminals were more loyal than some cops.

When Chief Hill had threatened to blackmail her, Rodriguez got a harsh reality check that every cop had a price, that in Baltimore, dirty justice was up for sale to the highest bidder.

Thinking about the money, Rodriguez looked down at her Bulova watch. She had to meet up with one of Scar's workers for her final payment. Part of her agreement with Scar was, if Derek was convicted, she would get an extra fifty thousand dollars. Yes, she felt bad about Derek getting convicted, but she still felt like she needed to look out for number one. She damn sure wasn't about to turn down an extra fifty grand because Derek pissed off the wrong people. Rodriguez just figured she played the game better than he did, and she wasn't about to try and change a system that had been in place for years before she came around and would still be in place after she left. But after this she was done. The guilt she felt wasn't worth the money. She had enough and was ready to get out of the corruption game. She told herself that after she collected the money she would not play on Scar's team anymore. She had other plans for her life, including trying to be a good daughter and big sister. She was the leader of her family.

Rodriguez rushed out of the courthouse. She wanted to pick up her loot and then go pick up Danielle. *Maybe I'll take her shopping to celebrate,* she thought.

Rodriguez definitely knew a little something about the hard-knock life. When their mother had escaped their abusive father and ran to Maryland from New York, all she had was her children and the clothes on her back. Being Puerto Rican down in the South wasn't easy. Her mother did odd jobs cleaning people's houses and waiting tables part time, to take care of her children the best she could. The entire family was teased and ridiculed for being Hispanic, including Rodriguez, who worked little odd jobs as a kid and through high school to help her mother out. When she decided to join the police force, it was as if she had struck gold. They were used to living pisspoor, so having a stable income, no matter how modest, was better than living paycheck to paycheck from dead end jobs.

Just thinking about the turn her life was taking made Rodriguez angry with herself. She swore that this was going to be the last crooked thing she did.

Her mind heavy, Rodriguez drove up to the new warehouse where Scar's new crew of young gunners had set up shop. She felt more comfortable coming to the deserted warehouse because it was on the outskirts of the city, and since it was a new spot for the crew, the police didn't know about it yet. So she didn't have to worry about anyone associating her with drug dealers.

She picked up her cell and sent a cryptic text to the phone number Sticks had provided her. It was a code to let Sticks know she was outside to collect her money. While waiting, she heard, Bang! Bang!

Rodriguez almost jumped out of her skin. Someone had banged on her car window. Inhaling deep and exhaling slow, she tried to calm the thundering in her chest. She was finally able to control her trembling hand long enough to press the window button. "Why the hell are you sneaking up on me like that?"

She touched her gun for assurance.

"I just like fucking with you, that's why," Sticks said, cracking up like he was watching the funniest comedy show. "Ay, yo!" He called out a little code he and the crew used, and suddenly the iron gate to the warehouse slowly began rising.

Rodriguez put her car in park and stepped out. As she got closer, she heard rap music blaring and could smell the weed smoke coming from inside the warehouse. There had to be about twenty guys in the warehouse. Some were at a table counting money, some were bagging drugs, while some were in different stages of sexual acts with girls. But most of them were standing guard with huge assault weapons in hand.

Rodriguez thought it was a shame the way Scar was leading the youth of Baltimore astray. Almost none of the Dirty Money Crew members were older than seventeen, because Scar knew that meant they would be charged as minors for most of the crimes they'd commit. Rodriguez felt like shit inside for being a part of the city's destruction.

"Yo, Trail, get this bitch her pay," Sticks ordered. Trail gritted his teeth. He fucking hated that Sticks tried so hard to act like Scar, ordering him around like they hadn't started out together on the same level. Sticks was taking this standing role as leader to the head, and Trail was growing more and more fed up by the day. Trail walked slowly to retrieve the money.

Rodriguez looked around. She thought back to a time when she was running up in a spot like this, taking everybody to jail. She scanned the room in disbelief, and then she spotted someone, which almost made her faint. She squinted and blinked her eyes, thinking that they were deceiving her. *That can't be her,* she thought to herself.

Just then Danielle rose up from the chair and turned around. "Baby, I'm done with this stack," she yelled to Sticks. She locked eyes with Rodriguez, and she stopped breathing for a minute. Then she started coughing.

Rodriguez let an evil look take over her face as she stared at her, and Danielle quickly turned around and walked in the opposite direction of where her sister stood. She was shocked to see Rodriguez there. Rodriguez was equally shocked, but she knew she would risk putting Danielle in grave danger if she grabbed her up like she wanted to. That would give the impression that Danielle was affiliated with law enforcement and put her in harm's way. Rodriguez was fuming inside, and she couldn't stop staring at her little sister.

"See something you like over there? I didn't know you liked to lick pussy. Yeah, you look like one of them dike bitches," Sticks said.

Rodriguez snapped out of her trance. "No, I'm just admiring how you are keeping stuff together while Scar is away," Rodriguez fabricated on the spot.

Just as she said that, Trail returned with a small knapsack and threw it at her feet. "Fifty, like Scar told you," Trail said dryly, quickly turning his back and walking away.

Danielle sat down on one of the couches and looked her sister up and down. She put her head to the side and twisted her lips. *I can't believe her ass is a dirty cop. Oh, I'ma have a field day with her paper now. She gonna pay me. I betcha Mama don't know about this,* she thought to herself.

Danielle knew she could never let Sticks find out she was so closely related to Rodriguez. Being down with a cop—something she would never reveal to the crew—was a sure way to get herself killed. Especially with the big day they'd all been planning for coming up. It was going to be Danielle's chance to finally establish herself and get out from under her sister's controlling ass. After their upcoming lick, Danielle figured she would get enough money that she wouldn't have to spend time with her lame-ass sister. She would be able to support herself and buy herself all the fly shit she wanted.

Rodriguez took one last look at Danielle before she turned to leave. Danielle saw her looking, so she got up, walked over to Sticks, and began tonguing him down. She wanted her sister to know she was grown, that she was establishing her own independence.

Back in her car, Rodriguez slammed her hands on the steering wheel. She was livid. How could Danielle be so stupid, getting involved with a crew of criminals? She was even more mad at herself. She had sold her soul to the devil, and now the role model she tried to portray to her impressionable sister was shattered.

"She can't be involved with Scar's crew," Rodriguez mumbled to herself. "I will put a stop to this shit."

It took her a while to pull out. She kept contemplating getting out of her car, storming back into the warehouse, and snatching Danielle out of there by her hair. She could picture herself shaking her until her damn brain stem came loose. She was just that angry.

Finally, Rodriguez rationalized that it would be way too dangerous for them both, because the Dirty Money Crew weren't afraid to kill a cop. Feeling totally helpless, she pulled out and drove off. Her new mission was to save her sister before it was too late.

Watching from across the street, the person trailing Sticks witnessed the whole scenario that just played out. When Scar was in town running the Dirty Money Crew, he had a shadow trailing him and plotting to take him down. Now that he was missing in action, the Shadow was now following Sticks, the apparent heir to Scar's empire. It was surprising to see Rodriguez at the warehouse. The Shadow figured she would have been at the courthouse watching to see the outcome of the case against Detective Fuller.

As Rodriguez drove off, the Shadow thought, *Apparently no one has any loyalty in B-more. Is anybody on the straight and narrow in this city?* Making a mental note to find out what shit was in the warehouse. The main focus right now was to take down the Dirty Money Crew.

Tiphani lowered her head as she heard the news reporter's words.

"Today, former Maryland State Trooper DES Detective Derek Fuller was found guilty of first-degree murder of DES officer Christian Archie. Fuller's sentencing will be held next month. The prosecutor's office is seeking the death penalty in the case."

Tiphani, torn between a whirlwind of emotions, had a frail smile on her face. She thought about her life with Derek and how hard he'd tried to please her. She felt slightly guilty and responsible for his entire downfall. Then she thought about her kids. How would she explain all of this to them? Tiphani felt horrible that they would grow up without Derek, that their only memories would be of the media reports that their father was a crooked cop and a murderer.

Tiphani closed her eyes and tried to make herself feel better. It was hard. She tried to think of negative things about Derek. Then she remembered that he'd tried to take her children from her. That was enough for the moment. She clung to that one thought because it helped ease her guilt.

She thought about the way she was going to look in her judge's robe when she returned to Baltimore. That alone made her feel much, much better. She was finally smiling. Then she let out a small laugh. "He just got what was coming to him," she whispered. "That's all."

Tiphani looked over at Scar's sleeping form, watching him as he took each breath. She felt all dreamy inside. She sometimes couldn't believe that she was really in love with Scar. The time on the boat had proved him to be more attentive and charming than she thought he could be.

While with her, he had put aside the tough-guy exterior that he displayed on the street, doing little things for her, like rubbing her feet, or making her little animals out of paper to cheer her up when she was missing her kids. He would hold her when she cried, stroking her hair gently, and kissing the top of her head to comfort her. Tiphani felt that Scar was more than just some street thug that killed people. He was the man she was in love with. She often thought about what it would be like if she could have an open relationship with him, or if they could get married. Tiphani wanted to be with Scar all of the time for the rest of her life and could only hope he felt the same way.

Tiphani reached over and turned the TV off. She slid into the bed and eased her body behind Scar's. Then she threw her arm around him and hugged him. This was where she wanted to be forever.

Chapter 4

The Return

Six Months Later

Tiphani stumbled into the emergency room at Baltimore General Hospital. "Help! Help me!" she screamed, her eyes wide and dazed, blood dripping down her face. "Please help me!" she squealed again.

Everyone inside the bustling county hospital ER turned and stared at her. One lady put her hands over her mouth in shock.

The triage nurse jumped up and rushed toward Tiphani. "Get a team!" she yelled into a small handheld radio device.

Tiphani screamed again, "They are gonna kill me!" and then she collapsed to the floor.

A team of doctors and nurses rushed to her side. They worked together and hoisted her up off the floor onto a gurney. "She's got a large laceration on the head," the lead surgeon said to the team. "Appears to have bruising everywhere. Looks like somebody worked her over pretty good."

"Help me!" Tiphani screamed, seeming to come back alive. Clothed in only a dirty, ripped white tee-shirt, she started thrashing her bare legs wildly. Her hair was matted, her entire body bruised, and the soles of her feet were filthy like she'd walked a thousand miles barefoot to get there.

"Strap her down!" the doctor demanded as Tiphani bucked and thrashed wildly. "She appears to be going into shock!" The team rushed to strap her to the temporary bed.

Once inside the examination room, Tiphani began screaming again, this time, just a high-pitched shriek.

"We need to sedate her in order to treat her," one of the nurses said.

After a nod from the doctor, the nurse skittered away to retrieve a syringe filled with a mild sedative. She plunged it into one of Tiphani's thighs, and Tiphani's body quickly went slack. She was knocked out.

For the next hour, the nurses and doctors examined her limp body, her face riddled with bruises. Since she had no identification, the hospital staff treating her had planned to take fingerprints while she was knocked out so they could try to identify her.

Before they could get a technician to take the prints, one of the nurses looked at Tiphani closely. She crinkled her eyebrows and mumbled to herself, "This lady looks very familiar. I know I've seen her somewhere before."

She rushed out of the room and went into the ER's lobby. She ran over to the bulletin board that displayed all of Baltimore's WANTED and MISSING posters. The nurse looked up and down at each row of pictures. "I knew it!" she screamed, snatching Tiphani's picture off the board. She ran back to Tiphani's room like she was on fire. "Doctor! Doctor!" she called out, waving the MISSING poster in front of her. "Somebody needs to call the police!"

Tiphani's eyes fluttered as she came into consciousness. She could hear voices around her. "Help," she rasped out.

Somebody moved toward her quickly. "Mrs. Fuller?" a man said. "I am Detective Hanson."

"Mmm, save me," Tiphani croaked.

"No one can hurt you now, Ms. Fuller. We will protect you," the detective said, standing at the side of Tiphani's hospital bed.

After a minute of staring at her, the detective got right to the point. "Ms. Fuller, do you know what happened to you? Who hurt you like this?"

"They hurt me. They said they would kill me. They said it was because of him," she said through tears.

"Who? Ms. Fuller, tell us who," Detective Hanson replied, his eyes sympathetic.

Detective Hanson was drawn in, and Tiphani knew it. She could tell by the concern written on his face that her Oscar-worthy performance had worked like a charm. She had everyone at the hospital fooled. Once again, Scar had steered her in the right direction. Tiphani had endured the most painful part of her role—the self-inflicted injuries—just so the entire plan would come together realistically.

Derek almost choked on his own spit when the breaking news report streamed across the TV screen and interrupted his daily dose of *The Maury Show*. The breaking news was that Tiphani had made a daring escape from her captors after six months and ran for her life right into the Baltimore County Hospital room. It was also being reported that the police were questioning Tiphani, and so far they believe her kidnapping is directly related to her husband's crimes.

Derek couldn't take anymore. He rushed into his cell, his mind racing once again. Although he was pissed off that he was being blamed once again for something he didn't do, a feeling of relief settled over him. At least his kids would not be in the system and they'd have their mother, he reasoned. Derek thought the entire kidnapping had Scar written all over it. He could only wonder if his wife would stoop so low as to be a part of it as well.

Tiphani's recovery went quickly but not quickly enough for her, as some of the scars from the injuries she and Scar inflicted on her body were still slightly visible. The day Tiphani left the hospital, she was swarmed by reporters from all over. Even the BBC wanted a piece of her. A hailstorm of questions were thrown at her as soon as she stepped through the hospital's revolving doors.

Secretly, Tiphani was loving every minute of the attention. She was one hundred percent sure the District Attorney Anthony Gill and Mayor Mathias Steele had been watching the reports on her.

She stood at the podium and fielded question after question.

"I am just happy to be alive. I was held for months with little to no food. I was beaten and verbally abused," Tiphani said, her voice cracking as she acted like she was choking back tears. The crowd that had gathered was hanging on her every word.

"Although I cannot identify my abductors because they kept themselves hidden behind masks, I am sure that the police will find them and justice will be served. I have no further comments." Tiphani waited to be escorted into the black Lincoln Town Car that was waiting for her.

Tiphani's popularity soared. She was booked on every news and talk show. When *Oprah's* show producers called her, she'd jumped up and down when she hung up the phone. Her reunion with her kids was highly publicized as well, one reporter even commenting that the entire thing seemed "staged."

Tiphani was dubbed a heroic survivor. On every show she appeared on, she made sure to act as if she was very saddened by Derek's conviction. But she always made it a point to say that his actions had put her and her children in harm's way and that she was filing for divorce. Tiphani touted herself as an upstanding citizen on the right side of justice. She would quote the law and ensure that she appeared not only as a strong and brave victim, but also a sharp, well-versed attorney ready to take her career to the next level. She was establishing a solid platform to announce her political plans.

Tiphani appeared on *Oprah* dressed in a red two-piece skirt suit, red being the power color for female candidates running for public office. Tiphani sat up straight, folded her hands in her lap, and made sure she gave the proper amount of eye contact. She answered Oprah's questions without a hitch. She also shed a lot of fake tears when she had to speak about Derek and her so-called ordeal at the hands of people he was mixed up with. Then, without warning, she announced her plans to run for Baltimore County circuit court judge right there before millions of viewers. Even Oprah was caught a bit off guard by Tiphani's abrupt announcement. She told Oprah and the entire world that she was committed to public safety and justice, which was her reason for running for one of the circuit court judgeships. Tiphani smiled brightly when she received a standing ovation from the crowd.

She could only hope Scar was watching their plan in action.

After almost two weeks of having no contact with Scar, Tiphani was going through withdrawal. She hadn't seen him since he had dropped her off a few miles from the hospital the day she'd reappeared. The night after the taping of her appearance on Oprah, Scar contacted her and told her that he would return to Baltimore as soon as she won her seat.

"I miss you so much," she cried into the phone. Scar just listened with no response. All he had on his mind was helping her win so that he could finally beat these cases against him and live the rest of his life in peace.

Chapter 5

Setting It Off

Danielle sat with her arms folded, her head cocked to the side as she looked across the table at her big sister Maria in disgust. The scowl on her face spoke volumes. Her older sister had been calling her and showing up at her house almost every day since she had seen her inside of the Dirty Money Crew's warehouse. Finally Danielle had agreed to meet with her because she couldn't take the pressure from their mother, and she damn sure couldn't stand her pig-ass sister blowing up her cell phone while she was with Sticks.

Danielle had decided she was there today to tell her sister that she wanted her to get the hell out of her business. She didn't need her sister sniffing around and blowing up her spot. She was loyal to Sticks, and Maria could kick rocks if she didn't understand that. At sixteen, she decided that she'd rather ride or die with Sticks, who she had fallen deeply in love with, than listen to her overbearing and overprotective sister. *This bitch thinks she's somebody's mama,* Danielle thought.

"Are you going to eat?" Maria asked softly. She could read Danielle's body language very well. It didn't take a rocket scientist to figure out that the teenage girl didn't want to be there.

"Yup. When I leave here I will eat. My man will buy me food. I don't want anything from you, including the food that you buy."

Trying to remain calm, Maria lowered her eyes and shoveled a forkful of pasta into her mouth. What she really wanted to do was reach across the table and slap the taste from her little sister's mouth.

"Why would you get involved with a crew like that? Do you really know who they are? They murder people, Danielle. Do you even know who Scar Johnson is? What he is capable of? Not only is it dangerous to be associated with people like that, it's stupid," Maria whispered harshly, letting her feelings drip through every word.

"You don't know nothing about me or them. You think you wrote the book because you're a fuckin' crooked-ass cop that takes bribes and shit!" Danielle screamed out, garnering looks from other patrons inside the restaurant. Danielle thought her sister was a big hypocrite. She was already regretting that she let her mother strong-arm her into meeting with her, knowing their mother always took her big sister's side.

"Don't worry about what I do. Do as I say, not as I do. I am a grown-ass woman. I can handle myself. This street shit is not a game to be played by little girls." Maria gritted her teeth, squinting her eyes into slits. She figured if she was hard with her little sister, it would show her concern.

Rodriguez was truly troubled by her sister's new affiliations. They had come as a surprise. She obviously didn't know Danielle as well as she'd thought. Both sisters were stubborn as mules, so Maria knew telling Danielle what to do wouldn't work, but still she tried.

"What? Don't' tell me what to do. I'm never going to do as you say! Who the fuck are you? Don't try to play the big-sister role. This game is also not for crooked-ass cops. You don't fit in anywhere. I have one mother," Danielle barked, rolling her eyes. "I don't need you on my back."

"Danielle! I forbid you from seeing Sticks, and you also need to stay out of their warehouse. Don't you know if the police run up in there and find all of those drugs and guns, you're going to jail for a long, long time. I won't be able to help you," Rodriguez spat, feeling like it was her duty to school Danielle.

Danielle began laughing. "Look, stupid, how many ways I gotta say it? Sticks is my man. Read my lips– I . . . love . . . him. You can't stop that. Now after sixteen years you think you can tell me what to do and who to see? Well, you can't!" Danielle screamed. "Why don't you just fuck off and leave me alone!" She pushed her chair back so hard, it hit the floor.

Everyone in the restaurant was watching and whispering about them now. Rodriguez tried to smile weakly to get the attention off of them, but it was too late. She and the onlookers watched as Danielle stormed out of the restaurant.

Danielle walked a few yards and suddenly felt physically sick. Her sister had aggravated her so much, her stomach started cramping. She felt a flash of heat come over her entire body then an overwhelming wave of nausea hit her like a Mack truck. She hunched over and threw up. She was hurling her brains out. When the entire contents of her stomach was out on the ground, she stood upright and tried to be strong on her weak legs, wiping her mouth and inhaling in an effort to get herself together.

Just then her phone began vibrating. She snatched it out of her bag; she wasn't in the mood for her sister or her mother. She looked at the screen and saw that it was Sticks calling. "Fuck!" she cursed under her breath. Her heart almost skipped a beat with fear. She knew if she answered it, he would ask where she was, and he'd probably say he was coming to get her.

Danielle started thinking quick about what she would say. Not wanting to be associated with Rodriguez at all, there was no way she could tell Sticks she was at a restaurant with her sister. She also couldn't risk lying to Sticks and saying she was in school because she never knew when he would show up. Unable to think of a lie quick enough, she decided to ignore Sticks' call. She figured she would get her head together and then call him back when she was calm and had thought out her lie.

Immediately Danielle dialed Veronica's number, the only other person Sticks found acceptable for her to hang out with. Sticks had forced her to cut off ties with all her other friends, both male and female. She nervously shifted her weight from one foot to the other as she waited for Veronica to pick up her phone. If Sticks was looking for her and couldn't find her, it wouldn't be long before he started scouring the streets.

After what seemed like an eternity, her friend answered, and a feeling of relief washed over her.

"Veronica, I need you to come get me. I'm downtown, and Sticks is already looking for me. I was with my lame-ass sister, and now I won't be able to explain to him where I was at. Get your ass here as soon as possible," Danielle said nervously. She was so focused on her phone call, she didn't notice she was being watched.

After paying the bill, Rodriguez came outside. She was surprised to see her sister still standing out there. Trying to seize the opportunity, she rushed over to Danielle and tried again in vain to speak with her.

Not wanting anything else to do with her sister, Danielle began to walk away. Getting the hint, Rodriguez extended an envelope to her, which stopped Danielle in her tracks. Danielle knew it was the money for her mother. The money was the whole purpose of her meeting with her sister. Danielle may have been pissed off at her sister, but she wasn't about to mess with her mother's money. Reluctantly she snatched the envelope and threw it into her pocketbook.

Neither sister spoke. Danielle had more pressing issues to take care of, namely, how she was going to lie to Sticks.

Maria was too stubborn and knew she was wasting her breath, so she walked away feeling dejected.

"What the fuck is this bitch doing meeting with a fucking cop? Ain't this about a bitch? She is probably a fucking snitch! That's why that mu'fucka was staring at her the other day," Sticks mumbled to himself.

Sticks had seen enough. He gripped the steering wheel of his car, willing himself not to get out and just shoot Danielle in the head right then and there. He had watched her go into the restaurant, with Rodriguez following right behind. At first, he figured it must've been a crazy coincidence, but then he remembered the way Rodriguez was staring at Danielle at the warehouse like she knew her. When Danielle came out alone, Sticks figured they'd planned it that way, just in case anyone was watching. But seeing her take the envelope from the cop was all he needed to draw a conclusion. *That was how snitches rolled.* He was really convinced she was a snitch when he saw her throwing up. She sick because she is nervous as hell. *I got something for that bitch. Can't believe I fell in love with this traitor-ass bitch,* he thought to himself as he watched the first girl he'd ever loved betray him.

Sticks wasn't the only one doing surveillance at the restaurant. The Shadow, like always, was there following Sticks. Since Scar's disappearance, the Shadow had been constantly trailing Sticks. In his inexperience, Sticks didn't even for a second think about anyone following him. He was starting to feel invincible in his new role as unofficial leader of the Dirty Money Crew.

All the same, this current situation was confusing to the Shadow. Why did the cop from the warehouse hand an envelope to Sticks' woman? What was the connection? It was getting hard for him to figure out all the different players and side deals going on in the Dirty Money Crew. He started thinking there was only so much information he could gather from the outside, that it might be time to infiltrate the crew, start taking them down from the inside. *It's time to join the Dirty Money Crew,* the Shadow thought. *But how?*

Not knowing how to handle the situation, Rodriguez sat inside her car for a little while. Her conscience was eating at her as she thought about losing Danielle to the streets. She blamed herself. *Maybe if I was a better sister she wouldn't need to be in the streets. Maybe I should've never gotten down with Scar's crew and betrayed Derek.* All of these thoughts ran through her mind one after the other, like an electronic billboard sign.

Rodriguez closed her eyes to try and stop the images from scrolling. She had to admit that she knew all along that Scar and the Dirty Money Crew were a huge problem for the city of Baltimore, but she still fell victim to the allure of easy money. When she'd started taking his money, she didn't like Scar but could justify his actions and the reason to take the money, but now that he and his crew were influencing her family, she was growing to hate him and everything he stood for. She was ashamed that she'd never thought to do anything about the Dirty Money Crew, until they hit too close to home.

As she prepared to finally pull out of the restaurant's parking lot, she started thinking of ways to get Danielle away from the Dirty Money Crew's tight grip. As if a light bulb went off in her head, she thought of it. The perfect plan. She peeled out and began driving like a woman possessed.

***

Danielle had made it all the way home before calling Sticks. She and Veronica went over their lie a thousand times with a fine-tooth comb. They tried to think of every possible thing Sticks could ask. Danielle knew Sticks was just bold enough to call Veronica and interrogate her as well.

She dialed Sticks' number and nervously waited for him to pick up.

"Hey, baby," she said sweetly, desperately trying to hide her nerves. She lied and told him she was in the mall with Veronica when he had called her, that her phone didn't have a signal. From what Danielle could tell, it seemed as if Sticks had bought the story. He didn't ask as many questions as he normally did, which set her at ease. Sticks told her to be ready in two hours because he was coming to get her.

Danielle hung up from Sticks and rushed into her bathroom. She looked around to make sure her mother was busy counting the money from Maria. When she was sure her mother was good and distracted, she closed the door, ripped her pants down, and took a piss in a cup. Before she could even think about getting dressed to see Sticks, she had to have a question answered. She needed to be one hundred percent sure.

The last few days had been hard on Danielle. She was throwing up the second she woke up, a sure sign of pregnancy. She tried to ignore it, but the feeling didn't seem to be going away. Danielle nervously stared down at the little white dipstick and waited, her heart beating like horse hoofs at the Kentucky Derby.

When the two lines showed up so quickly, she thought she was reading it wrong. She retrieved the box out of the garbage and read the back for the twentieth time. "Two pink lines mean pregnant," she said out loud. She grabbed the hair at both sides of her head and shook her head from side to side in disbelief. She and Sticks had been having unprotected sex, but he'd made her feel so damn good, she never worried about the consequences.

What the hell am I going to do now? she thought. Danielle put her back up against the bathroom door; slid down to the floor, and cried her eyes out. There was no way a baby would fit into her life right now. Besides, she didn't know what Sticks would think or say.

For the next two hours Danielle was walking around like a zombie, and before she knew it, Sticks was blowing up her phone again. She pulled herself together and went outside to meet him. Her mother's warnings as she left the house fell on deaf ears. Danielle was too distracted to even hear her. Her legs felt like they were made of melted butter as she walked to Sticks' car. She wasn't dressed like her usual sexy self, and by the look on his face, Sticks took immediate notice. She tried to smile to hide the fact that something was wrong, but her smile still appeared forced and fake.

"Hey, baby. I missed you," she sang as she slid into the passenger seat of the car.

Sticks was unmoved and unnervingly short with her. Danielle took notice too. Her mind started going crazy with wild thoughts. *Maybe he knows I'm pregnant,* she thought as butterflies danced in her stomach. She willed herself to stay calm.

"Yo, where you been?" Sticks asked out of the blue. He wanted to test her, to see if she would tell him a lie to his face. Loyalty was everything to him. He kept trying to give Danielle the benefit of the doubt. He really did love her, but being a snitch was unacceptable in his book, no matter who the person was. Even if it was his mama.

"I-I told you. I was at the mall with Veronica. You know how those fuckin' dead zones are up in that raggedy-ass mall. No signal." Danielle, unable to look Sticks in the eyes for fear she would burst out crying because of her secret, lowered her head and eyes. She knew it was his baby, but she was afraid he wouldn't take the news so well. She was scared he would accuse her of trying to trap him, and then he would leave her, or worse, beat her down like he had done twice before.

This bitch can't even look me in my eye. She is lying to my fuckin' face. I should murk her ass right here, Sticks thought to himself as he flexed his jaw. He hated when people lied to him, but what made this worse was, he truly loved this girl. He was seriously considering marrying her. Now he had no choice but to put an end to their relationship, and her life. Their relationship was now business, and no one fucked with his business. He had to think of something real good to take care of her ass.

"Yo, we moved the operation up to the day after tomorrow. You gonna be the front person," Sticks informed her.

"Me? I can't—I—I mean, I wouldn't be any good at that."

Danielle had only agreed to be a lookout or a driver for their upcoming operation. She had helped with the planning and logistics but wasn't ready to go to the front line. In fact, Sticks had told her she would be behind the scenes—a driver or a lookout—that she wouldn't ever have to get her hands dirty because he wouldn't want to put her in harm's way. But now he was changing up the game plan. Something didn't feel right to her. *Maybe it's just the pregnancy,* she thought.

Danielle's immediate hesitation and ultimate refusal was enough for Sticks. He was sure she was a snitch now. She'd always been down for whatever, since he had started fucking with her. That's why he loved her so much. Aside from the tight wetness she was walking around with between her legs. Sticks thought she was the most beautiful ride-or-die chick in all of Baltimore.

Sticks had watched her rob grown-ass hustlers in broad daylight. He had witnessed her beat down two female crackheads that owed him money, and he saw her exert authority over some of the real young crew members, keeping them in line like a mother hen. *Why the sudden change of heart?* he wondered. He quickly concluded that it was because she was working with either the feds or the local police and couldn't get her hands dirty.

Sticks had plans for Danielle. Knowing she was snitching had hurt him deep down inside. He didn't take lightly to anyone hurting his feelings, especially somebody he trusted so deeply. Good pussy or not, love or no love, in his eyes, Danielle was just like any other snitch and she would be handled as such.

They were both silent as Sticks drove toward the warehouse, each of them wondering what the other was thinking.

Danielle's hands were sweaty. She contemplated just telling him about the baby right then and there, but when she noticed his mood, she decided against it. She knew firsthand how violent Sticks could get when upset, so she opted to remain silent. *Maybe he will marry me and we can be a family,* she thought to herself.

Danielle promised herself to tell Sticks about their baby when he was in a better mood. Right now she would just try and ride out his mood.

Sticks looked over at the side of Danielle's beautiful face. A fucking waste of beauty. Too bad. *Shake it off, nigga,* he thought to himself. *She is a snitch.*

The nervous energy inside the Dirty Money Crew's warehouse was crazy. Some of them paced the floor, others drank liquor or lit up blunts, trying to calm their nerves.

"Yo, I'm ready to make this paper, dog," Timber said, rubbing gun oil on the outside of his favorite gun, the AK-47 Sticks had given him.

"Calm down, nigga. We need to have this shit well thought out. I didn't think we were even fuckin' finished planning anyway." Trail didn't understand why Sticks was breaking out the gate with this shit when they were still in the planning phase.

Sticks, on edge for the past two days, barked, "Yo, you a bitch-ass nigga, and I'm sick of your fuckin' whining and complaining! Shut the fuck up and stop actin' like a straight bitch! The shit is as planned out as it's gonna get!"

"Fuck you, nigga! I'm tired of you tryin'a punk me in front of the young'uns," Trail shot back. It was like he had drunk a glass of liquid courage. He knew how crazy Sticks could get, but he was really fed up. For months he had watched as Sticks and the new members of the crew terrorized the city, bringing heat on all of them.

"What? What you say, nigga? I will body you right here and right now, word to everything. You punk bitch, you lucky Scar likes you," Sticks said, pointing his gun at Trail's head.

"Fuck this shit! Do this shit without me. We ain't ready yet." Trail stormed out of the warehouse. He had finally hit his breaking point. There was no way he was going to be a part of something as big as this without a well thought out plan of action.

"Go then, you scared-ass pussy!"

Sticks started having a bad gut feeling about going through with their plans too, but he couldn't let the young'uns see him sweat or think he was scared.

Deep down he knew Trail was right. There needed to be more planning, but with the thought of a snitch in his crew, and his hunger for power, he couldn't call it off. He mentally shook off his doubts and made his weapons ready for war.

"Fuck anybody who ain't down!" Sticks growled as he looked around into the faces of the young crew of gunners. All too afraid to reject his ideas, none of them dared to speak or express even a little bit of doubt. "A'ight then. Let's roll out," he yelled.

Danielle's heels clicked against the shiny marble floor of the bank. Dark shades covered her eyes as she stood behind a small counter and acted as if she was filling out a deposit or withdrawal slip. She carefully transcribed the note Sticks had provided to her word for word onto the bank's withdrawal slip. She looked around, trying not to show her nerves. She had a precise time to act. If she made one false move, everyone would be thrown off their role. She was the point person and everything going as planned depended on her.

She swallowed hard as Timber walked in, then Sticks, then two more of the crew. They fanned out and got into their rehearsed positions. Now all four corners of the bank were covered and being watched.

Danielle looked at her watch and exhaled. Ten seconds left. Slide the paper under the glass. Tell the teller, "No funny business," and show her the gun. Slide the paper under the glass. Tell the teller, "No funny . . ." She rehearsed her role over and over again in her head. She also thought about the alternate plan, just in case.

Danielle had been charged with shooting the little old security guard that stood by the customer service tables running his mouth, if something jumped off and he tried to break bad. Timber and the others would then take the counters and snatch as much money as they could get.

Sticks was there just to ensure everything went according to the time frame. He usually had these things mapped out. Eight minutes was all they had from the time they walked in until the time they reached their getaway car.

Danielle swallowed hard. She felt sweat dripping down the sides of her face as her stomach did somersaults. The time had finally arrived. She walked slowly to the middle teller, as she was instructed. See, Sticks had found out from an insider at the bank that the middle teller didn't have the panic button in front of her station. She would either have to lean left or right, which would tell them if she was trying to push it.

"Good morning, ma'am. How can I help you today?" the teller asked, not really paying too much attention to the customer standing in front of her.

Danielle silently pushed the slip of paper under the small opening in the glass. The teller's eyes popped open and she looked around nervously as soon as she read the words. Now she was paying attention to the customer standing in front of her.

The teller immediately looked left and locked eyes with Timber, who smiled at her and patted his waistband to let her know not to try anything funny. Then the teller started to notice the other members of the crew sprinkled around, sticking out like sore thumbs amongst the regular bank customers.

"Ma'am, how would you like your bills counted out?" she asked, trying to remain calm.

"I don't have a preference," Danielle coolly replied. "I have to get some more tens," the teller said. "I will be right back."

Danielle figured the teller was probably getting a bag to put the stacks of money in because she had been warned in the note about panic buttons, dye packs, and calling the cops.

Sticks watched the teller from a distance. He noticed her give the teller to her right a little side glance. Then the other teller looked down and reached for something. Sticks tapped his foot impatiently. He figured whatever the middle teller had said to Danielle was a code for the other teller to push her panic button.

That was enough for Sticks. He walked over to Danielle, who looked up at him as if to say, What the fuck are you doing? Are you crazy?

"Honey, we gotta go. We can stop at another bank on the way out of town," he said, grabbing onto Danielle's arm.

"On the way out of town" was the signal to abort the robbery. Danielle quickly followed Sticks' lead and split.

When Timber noticed them rushing to try to get out of the bank, he lost it. "What the fuck is you doin', nigga?! I ain't leavin' outta here without some paper!" he screamed loudly, pulling his gun from his pants.

Screams erupted all over the bank. People began running for the doors, and some got down on the floor.

Meanwhile, the little old security guard tried to draw his weapon, but before he could even hoist it up, one of the younger crew members shot him dead. Bang! Bang! Bang! "Yo! Let's go, nigga!!" Sticks screamed to Timber.

Danielle began running for the door, but the other security guard tried to grab her. Timber lit him up with his semi-automatic, and the guard's blood sprayed on her face and clothes, making her sick and weak. The adrenaline pumping through her body and the baby in her belly was a bad combination. Danielle felt like she would faint at any minute.

Timber continued to spray at random. The inside of the bank was pure pandemonium now, with bodies dropping from his reckless bullets. He jumped up on the counter, but the bulletproof glass was too high for him to climb over it. When the tellers had all fled to the bank's emergency robbery shelter, Timber got so angry, he started shooting more of the bank's patrons at random.

Sticks heard the distant wail of sirens. He was finally out the door. Whoever wasn't with him would just be left behind.

Danielle was right behind him but starting to fall farther behind. Trying to keep up with him, she kicked off her heels and tried running barefoot, but she was too weak to pick up speed.

Sticks knew they had a car waiting for them one block up, but they hadn't given the driver the signal to come get them from the front of the bank. He took off down the street, but the block was beginning to fill up with cops.

Timber was now hot on Sticks' heels, but Danielle had fallen farther back, her chest burning with each step.

"Police! Drop your weapons!" a cop screamed at them.

Timber turned and opened fire, hitting the officer right in the head.

"Get the fuck in, nigga!" Sticks screamed to Timber as he and Timber got to the getaway car.

Danielle was still coming toward them, trying hard to make it. Winded, she continued struggling, running for her life. She heard loud pops as the cops opened fire on them, and bullets whizzed by her head.

Sticks jumped into the truck, and so did Timber. "Wait!" Danielle screamed, tears and makeup streaking her face. It looked like they were leaving her. "Put it in reverse! Reverse out the block!" Sticks screamed.

The driver did as he was told.

Danielle was almost there, but then they started moving away from her. "What are y'all doin'?" she screamed. "Sticks!" The faster she ran, the farther away the getaway truck went.

"Do it now, nigga!" Sticks yelled.

Timber extended his arm out of the window and opened fire on Danielle. The police were also shooting at her.

Danielle felt hot metal searing through her skin.

Her eyes bulged in shock and pain. She was in disbelief that her own crew had set her up. As her legs stopped moving, she thought about the baby she was carrying and the great betrayal she had just suffered. Then she gave up. Her bullet-ridden body lurched forward and hit the ground with a splat. She felt the life leaving her. "Why, Sticks, why?" She gurgled as blood spilled from her mouth.

Within no time her limp, lifeless body was surrounded by the police.

Sticks, Timber, and the driver jumped out of the truck they were in and changed to a smaller car they had stashed a few miles away, just in case something like this had jumped off. Sticks knew at least three members of their crew were dead and the rest of the young'uns were going to be hemmed up by the cops. He couldn't look back now. He knew he wouldn't have trouble recruiting replacements into the Dirty Money Crew. But the thought of replacing Danielle gave him instant heartburn.

"Damn, man, I thought Dani was your main bitch," the driver said.

"That bitch was a snitch," Timber replied before Sticks could say anything. "We was gonna kill her ass after this anyway. We just wanted her to help us get this last big lick before we murked her informant ass."

Sticks didn't really have the heart to stand in front of her and just kill her, so he had instructed Timber to make sure her death looked like it was a result of the bank robbery. He still had too much love for her. In his own world, thinking about Danielle, Sticks remained silent as they rode in the opposite direction of the racing police cars. He was hurting inside.

"Who the fuck is banging on my door this time of night?" Dana grumbled as she rushed to her front door. "Better not be this Danielle talking about she forgot her damn keys. Who is it?" Dana called out.

"Baltimore County Police!" a booming baritone on the other side of the door replied.

Dana screwed up her face and yanked the door open. She thought maybe Danielle had been picked up for something.

"Ms. Rodriguez?" the officer asked.

"No. My last name is Thomas. My daughter's last name is Rodriguez," Dana said nervously. A sick feeling washed over her.

"Can we come in, ma'am?" one of the officers asked. Dana moved aside, and the officers stepped into her home.

"Ma'am, we are sorry to tell you that your daughter Danielle Rodriguez has been killed."

Dana's ears started ringing, and she couldn't move. A scream was welling up inside of her, ready to erupt. She opened her mouth, and the sound that escaped was almost like that of a pig at slaughter. She fell to her knees and screamed, "Nooooo!" at the top of her lungs.

The officers tried to help her up, but Dana would not move from that spot. She was wracked with sobs, and her body trembled.

After a few minutes on her knees wailing uncontrollably, she allowed the officers to help her up. "What happened?" she yelled. "Why my child?"

"Ma'am, your daughter was killed fleeing the scene of a bank robbery. She was with a group of men that tried to rob the bank," one of the officers informed Dana.

"You must be mistaken! My daughter wouldn't do something like that! She is a good girl! Danielle knows better! I don't believe you!" Dana belted out, flailing her arms at the officers.

"Ms. Thomas, I'm afraid it was your daughter." The officer shoved a picture of Danielle's bloodied body toward Dana.

Dana placed her hand over her mouth. It was Danielle in the picture. "Would you please call her sister? She is a cop too," she managed to say.

The officers looked shocked, like they thought she was lying.

"Her card . . . it's on the counter. Please call. I can't . . . I just can't," she said, breaking down with tears all over again.

Maria Rodriguez was in her bed when her cell phone began vibrating. She looked at the screen and saw a strange phone number. "Hello?" she answered cautiously.

"Yes, this is Officer Rodriguez," she replied to the strange caller. Rodriguez sat up in the bed. "About my sister? What about her? Has something happened?" she asked, a pang of nervousness punching through her gut.

After the caller instructed her to come down to the hospital, she jumped out of the bed and began throwing on any piece of clothing she could find. She instinctively grabbed her gun and badge and busted out the front door. She raced her car through the streets of Baltimore, running all red lights on the way as her heart beat out of her chest. *Please let this girl be okay,* she thought.

When she arrived at the county hospital, she flew down the hallways, almost knocking people down several times. She finally noticed a gathering of cops and rushed over to where they stood.

"Hi, I'm Officer Rodriguez. Someone called me about my sister?" she said, trying to catch her breath.

Rodriguez didn't recognize any of the Baltimore County officers there. As a state trooper, she sometimes worked with the local county cops, but not often enough to know them on a first-name basis or by sight.

"Officer Rodriguez, I am Lieutenant Brady, Baltimore County." A tall, white-haired man extended his hand for a shake.

"What is going on with my Danielle?" Rodriguez asked, ignoring the lieutenant's hand. She was feeling worse about this whole scene by the second.

"I'm sorry, Officer Rodriguez," the lieutenant said in a low tone, trying to soften the blow. "Your sister is gone."

Rodriguez thought she hadn't heard correctly, so she asked the lieutenant to repeat himself. When he did, she hollered, "No!"

Rodriguez began banging the wall next to her so hard, her hand felt as if it would break. Even with the pain, she couldn't stop punching. She wanted to rip somebody's head off. She had warned Danielle, had told her about that crew. She had promised herself since she was a child that she wouldn't shed tears. This was different, uncontrollable. She couldn't keep them from falling.

"How did this happen?" she croaked out, tears burning at the back of her eyes.

"Our initial reports say she was shot by her own people while they ran from the scene of an attempted bank robbery," the lieutenant explained.

Rodriguez immediately knew who was responsible. She could only wonder if they'd found out Danielle was her sister and took it out on her.

"I want the autopsy, toxicology, and DNA reports back as soon as possible," Rodriguez told the lieutenant. "I want to be involved and informed about all the developments in this case. I am her sister."

The lieutenant didn't argue.

Rodriguez knew right away who she would make pay for Danielle's death. The Dirty Money Crew had taken away her only sibling. She stormed out of the building. She needed time to think and regroup.

Once outside, she immediately began plotting the downfall of the entire Dirty Money Crew, including Scar Johnson.

***

Rodriguez and Dana sat in the front row together at the funeral, hand in hand, hoping they could make it through such a tragic day. As Rodriguez stared at Danielle's stiff corpse, she found new fervor to take Scar down.

Rodriguez hadn't slept in a week since finding out about Danielle's death. Wracked with guilt, she could hardly stand to look at herself in a mirror. She had always thought of herself as a standup cop, but now she doubted herself as a cop, a sister, a daughter, and as a person in general. She realized she hadn't been strong enough to stand up to Scar and say no when he'd approached her the first time. Blinded by the money, and fearing for her own safety, she took part in Scar's web of murder, lies, and deceit. Well, things had changed. She wasn't afraid anymore. She was pissed, and didn't care if Scar exposed her and the deal they had cut. She didn't care if she lost her job. She just wanted to avenge her dear sister's death by getting Scar and his little murderous crew off the streets.

What devastated her most was when the medical examiner told her that Danielle was pregnant. Not only did Rodriguez lose her sister, but she also lost her chance to be an auntie. She didn't even bother to tell their mother about that because her mother wanted to be a grandmother more than anything and wouldn't have been able to handle it.

Rodriguez needed some sort of redemption. Suddenly, it was now her mission in life to help get young kids off the streets and to show that life under Scar's direction wasn't the American dream but really a nightmare.

Chapter 6

Closure

Derek stared at Tiphani in shock and awe. He was so surprised she had come to visit him, he could hardly keep his mouth closed. She looked extra beautiful to him now. Derek missed seeing her beautiful face with its exotic features. He still thought she was the most beautiful woman in the world. Her perfume filled his nostrils and made his dick hard.

Derek sat frozen, holding out hope that his wife had come to tell him she wanted him back. He didn't even care whether or not she ever apologized; he just wanted his life back. And he knew Tiphani was talented enough a lawyer to help him get out of jail.

"Well, I know this is awkward," Tiphani started. She could barely hold eye contact with Derek, who looked horrible in the orange prison jumpsuit. His skin was ashy and drawn up, and he looked like he had lost fifty pounds. His full beard swallowed up his face, and she could see the signs of stress in his red, hopeless eyes. She did notice that his eyes lit up when he saw her, which didn't flatter her at all, but made her feel sorry for him for a brief moment.

"Thanks for coming to see me. I don't get many visitors, unless my attorney decides to come," Derek said, half-jokingly, trying to lighten the tension between them.

There was an awkward silence. The air in the room felt much the same way the courtroom did the day Derek was convicted, thick and almost suffocating.

"How are my little ones? Are you all right? Do you know who did the kidnapping? Did they hurt you at all?" Derek rattled off, trying to fill the awkward silence.

Tiphani ignored every one of his questions. "I came for a specific reason. This," she said, sliding a set of newly drawn up divorce papers across the table toward him. She didn't have time for small talk, nor did she want to have any with her soon-to-be ex-husband. She wanted to get to the point and get out.

Derek was in shock when he looked down at the papers. Seeing them took his breath away and he stopped breathing for what felt like a few minutes. They'd had their fair share of ups and downs and even an ugly, drawn out custody battle when he was a free man. But somewhere in the back of his mind, he'd always thought they might work things out.

He lifted his shackled hands and picked up the papers to examine them more closely. DIVORCE DECREE, it read. Derek felt like his heart split in two. If being in prison hadn't broken him, this did.

"Tiphani, I'm sorry. I don't know what else to say. I still love you. I need you. You and the kids are all I've got. Can we please work things out?" Derek gripped the papers in his hand so tightly, he was inadvertently crumpling them.

"Look, let's just get this all over with," Tiphani replied, a smirk on her face. The more Derek begged, the weaker he looked to her, which turned her off all over again. Tiphani wasn't stupid. She knew her husband's manipulative ways well. She knew he just wanted somebody to stick by him and help him try to appeal his conviction.

Tiphani was still bitter. She couldn't forget the way Derek had treated her after the incident with Scar, calling her all types of whores in front of her colleagues in family court. She wasn't going to forgive him. They were done.

"Tiphani, why don't you think this over and reconsider? Think about the kids." Derek felt tears welling up, but he refused to let her see him cry. He felt like he had been stripped of his dignity in enough ways already.

"Look, Derek, what don't you understand? We are done. Over. I don't want you anymore. I have moved on, so you should do the same. I am over you and all of this. I am just here to make it official and legal. Now sign the papers and do us both a favor."

Derek hung his head in defeat. He could tell by her callous attitude that his wife had been corrupted by his brother. He knew it was a strong possibility that she and Scar were still together, maybe living like one big happy family with his kids, now that she was home safe. The thought of Tiphani and Scar together made Derek's insides boil. He still found it hard to believe that the woman that once loved him so much could now hate him so deeply.

Biting down into his jaw, he picked up the pen and began signing the divorce papers. As he wrote his name on the line, he thought more and more about his brother's betrayal. About Tiphani's betrayal too.

"This is what you and Scar had planned all along, isn't it? To destroy me over lust? Is dick that important to you? You know good and damn well where Scar is. You probably faked the whole fuckin' kidnapping too, you cold-hearted bitch!"

Derek's sadness had now turned to unbridled anger that he needed to let loose. If he wasn't shackled, he felt like he probably would've punched Tiphani until her face caved in. Because of the commotion he was causing, the COs began moving toward the table as his voice rose higher and higher.

"I hate you, bitch!" he screamed. "You know what goes around comes around! You and Scar will get yours! You think he is gonna love you like I did? He won't! You hear me? He won't! He is using you just like he used me! I'm his flesh and blood, and he betrayed me, so imagine you! You're just a piece of pussy to him! You are replaceable in Scar's world! You better think about what you're doing! Don't be stupid!"

The COs grabbed his arms and began dragging him out of the room.

Tiphani remained composed. She heard what Derek was saying but gave it no thought or credence. Scar loved her, and she knew it. Derek was just jealous.

She gathered up the signed divorce papers and watched as her husband made a total ass of himself. She felt relieved when she looked down at his signature. Cutting off all ties with him was what she needed to succeed.

Tiphani felt good inside. She finally had closure.

Chapter 7

Out of the Shadows

The Shadow was lying in bed thinking about the news that the Dirty Money Crew had lost a few bodies in a botched bank heist. Now was the perfect time to get on the inside. They were short of men and were going to need to fill the ranks. But how was the question. You couldn't exactly just walk up to the front door and say, "I want to join."

Many different scenarios were playing out in the Shadow's mind, but none seemed right. The Shadow had done such a good job of keeping a safe distance from Scar and his crew that there was no contact with any of them.

Taking down Scar's crew was an obsession that was turning maniacal. It was all the Shadow thought about, and now the time had come to take it to the next level and destroy Scar and the Dirty Money Crew. There was no more surveillance to be done, no more information to be gathered. Everything that could be known from the outside was known. Now, the information obtained had to be put to use on the inside.

Throughout his surveillance, the Shadow kept following Scar and his crew to a specific check cashing place. He thought the Dirty Money Crew was looking to take the place down. Some of the younger bucks tried forcing their way in through the front door but were quickly met with some retaliatory force and had to run because the cops had been called. After that incident, the Crew backed off the place, which seemed to be the Fort Knox of check cashing places. No one was going to get in. The Shadow figured robbing this place would be the way into the Dirty Money Crew.

It had been three weeks of watching this place all day, every day, from the front of the store to the back. They ran a tight ship, and robbing it seemed damn near impossible. The more the Shadow watched, the tighter the security seemed to appear. In fact, the Shadow saw no weakness. Almost all hope was lost, and the Shadow had decided he was just going to try and blast through the front door.

But then the Shadow observed something. While staking out the back alley, he saw the woman who worked at the check cashing walk out the back door of the nail salon two stores down. It had never occurred to him, but the workers at the check cashing place never left the building all day. There was no back door, and none of them ever left through the front, not even to get lunch.

When he saw the worker leave through the back door of the nail salon, it finally made sense. Somehow the nail salon and the check cashing place were connected. That's how they were getting in and out during the day. He just had to figure out how they were connected. That was the way in to the check cashing and the Dirty Money Crew. The Shadow was hyped and couldn't wait to take this place down.

Immediately the Shadow thought it was a good day to get a manicure. His nails were looking a little raggedy. After bullshitting with the ladies at the nail salon and gaining their trust, he went to the bathroom, which was conveniently located in the back of the salon. There wasn't much time to snoop around. A person could be in the bathroom for only so long before people started checking on them.

The Shadow started opening every door that was visible. Nothing but supply closets and tanning booths. He stood in front of the back door and tried to figure out how the two stores were connected. That's when the Shadow saw it. It wasn't easy to spot, but there was a door that looked exactly like the wall. No doorknob, just a little hole so a person could grab it and slide it. It was a pocket door that slid sideways into the wall.

Sensing he didn't have much time, the Shadow quickly opened it. He saw a downward set of stairs. He ran down the stairs and saw that they led to a long tunnel that ran underneath the store next to the salon. *I bet this leads right to the check cashing place,* he thought. Back up the stairs and into the bathroom he went.

Almost instantly one of the salon workers came knocking on the bathroom door to make sure everything was okay.

"Just have an upset stomach," he said. "I'm finishing up in here." The Shadow came out of the bathroom, said good-bye, and walked out of the salon. He was now one step closer to taking down the Dirty Money Crew.

Dressed in all black with a wool knit face mask, the Shadow easily broke into the salon in the middle of the night and was now hiding in the tunnel, where he was going to wait until morning. The plan was to ambush the first person to come through the tunnel. Since it would be first thing in the morning, whoever came through the tunnel was definitely going to be surprised. Another advantage to doing the stickup first thing was, there wouldn't be as many people working, or waiting to cash checks. The Shadow was hoping to get in and out.

After waiting several hours, the Shadow couldn't stay awake. The long hours of following Scar, Sticks, and anyone involved with Dirty Money Crew nonstop were taking a toll. It was a much-needed rest.

Deep in sleep and dreaming of the good life, the Shadow was startled awake by the sliding open of the door to the tunnel. Immediately the hand went to the gun. He was ready to pounce.

Crouching down in the darkest part of the tunnel, he waited as the unsuspecting victim walked right into the trap. When they were in range, the Shadow jumped up and pointed the gun in the face of the middle-aged woman who worked at the check cashing place, catching her completely off guard.

"Hands up, bitch!" the Shadow growled. "You wit' anyone?"

The woman lost control of her bowels and shit herself right there on the spot. Speechless, she just stood there with her hands up, eyes bulging, staring at him.

"Speak!" he demanded.

"I—I—I'm alone," she stuttered. "I come early to open up from the inside. Please don't hurt me," she said through heaving sobs. "Please."

"Do what I tell you, and no one will get hurt. Start walking."

They made their way through the tunnel and up into the back room of the check cashing place, the woman crying and pleading for her life the whole time. The smell of shit was getting awful. Once inside, the Shadow directed the woman to open the safe.

"I can't. I only know the combination to the mini safe."

"Who can open the main safe?"

"Big Mike. But he won't be in for at least thirty minutes."

The Shadow had a decision to make. Wait for Big Mike, or just take what was available right now and hope it was enough to impress Sticks. "What's in the mini safe?"

"Not much. Just the cash we use for the drawer."

"Open it!" The Shadow stuck the gun in her face for maximum effect.

The woman was so nervous, her hands were trembling, and she kept messing up the combination.

"Hurry the fuck up!" The Shadow hit the woman upside her head with the butt end of the gun, opening a gash in her head.

Blood soaking her hair and pouring down her neck, the woman yelped like a dog and started back to the lock. This time she was able to open the safe.

As soon as it was open, the Shadow reached in and took the contents out. There was three thousand dollars in cash and about forty thousand dollars in calling cards, which made the Shadow more than happy. He placed the calling cards and cash in a duffel bag. Then before leaving, he hogtied the woman with electrical tape.

Being careful to avoid being seen by anyone coming into the nail salon, the Shadow snuck out the back door and walked to the waiting getaway car a block away.

Word about the robbery spread through the streets like wild fire. The Dirty Money Crew was trying desperately to find out who did it, but no one knew.

Sticks was starting to become paranoid. He thought one of his guys did it and wasn't telling him. If word got out that one of his guys was doing something behind his back, it would signal to the streets that he didn't have control, and the streets would lose respect for him, meaning, he would now have a bull's-eye on his back. He felt like his very life depended on finding out who robbed the check cashing place.

Timber was standing guard outside of the warehouse, passing the time by working on his rhymes. He had dreams of becoming a rapper and thought he could someday use his connections in the crime world to get him a record deal. He figured, a lot of other rappers had started out slingin' rocks and then went on to stardom, so why couldn't he do it?

As he spat his lyrics, a figure walked up to the gate of the warehouse. Timber stopped rapping. "Got a problem, mu'fucka?" He stared directly into the person's eyes, letting them know he wasn't afraid.

"I wanna come in."

"Who the fuck is you?" Timber put his hand on the pistol in his waistband.

"I robbed the check cashing spot."

Timber wasn't expecting to hear that. "Who says?" Staying calm, the Shadow opened up the duffel bag and showed Timber the calling cards. "I want to fence these."

Seeing the calling cards made Timber a believer. Not taking his eyes off the Shadow, he yelled out, "Ay, yo," which was the code for the other workers to open the gate to the warehouse.

The warehouse, as usual, had about twenty guys in it, all smoking blunts. Some were counting money, others were bagging dope.

This was the first time the Shadow had ever been inside. He was taking mental notes, just in case this was the last time as well.

"Yo!" Timber barked at the top of his lungs, "this the nigga that took down the check cashing spot."

Everyone in the warehouse instantly stopped what they were doing and turned to look at the person who did what none of them was able to do. All talking and movement stopped. The warehouse got so quiet, it was as if no one was even breathing.

Timber and the Shadow stood in the middle of the warehouse in full view of everyone, like animals in a zoo. The Shadow was just taking it all in, the exits, how many dudes were there, how many guns, everything. If this was gonna be his only time in the warehouse, he wanted to be sure to remember every last detail.

The silence was broken by footsteps at the back of the warehouse. It was Sticks coming from the back office. He slowly walked across the warehouse. The tension in the warehouse was thick. All of the crew just watched and waited to see what he would do.

Sticks knew that everyone was watching him, which made him walk slower. He was trying to show this new jack who was boss, that he didn't have to hurry for no one. "This nigga here?" Sticks said, a condescending smirk on his face.

The tension in the air dissipated as everyone in the warehouse laughed. With that one little remark, Sticks let everyone know that he wasn't afraid of this new jack, that he had the situation under control. All of the young bucks in the crew were reassured that they had put their trust in the right man, that no one would be gunning for Sticks anytime soon.

"So you the man that took down the check cash spot?" Sticks eyed the Shadow with caution.

"That's right, and I want to fence these calling cards." The Shadow came back cool as ice. "You interested?"

"Come back to the office where we can discuss business in private," Sticks countered.

The two men were playing a game with each other, both striving to gain the upper hand, neither man wanting to show weakness. They made their way through the warehouse and into the office, where Sticks sat at his desk and directed the new jack to sit across from him.

"First off, who the fuck are you? I ain't never seen you before."

"Day. My name is Day."

"Day. A'ight. Where you from, Day?" Sticks wasn't ready to trust this dude yet. He was thinking, *Some guy just shows up out of the blue, robs a spot, and no one knows who he is. That's not exactly someone you just welcome with open arms.*

"I'm from Pittsburgh. Hill District. Was born here, so I decided to come back. Needed a change of scenery. You know how it is, kind of wore out my welcome. Five-O may be on the lookout for me up there."

"I hear you. You know, we been wantin' to take that spot for a minute," Sticks said, starting to feel more at ease with this dude.

"No, I didn't know. Great minds think alike," Day joked.

Sticks smiled then got serious. "How you do something alone that my whole crew couldn't do together?"

"Careful planning and execution." Day didn't want to give up too much information. He figured, the less he had to say, the better.

"Why that spot? And why come to us?" Sticks was being very cautious with Day. He was intrigued by this guy but still on guard.

"The spot was random. Everyone knows you the only game in town. You want to do business or not? I'm not a cop, so there's no need for all these questions. If you don't want these calling cards, someone else will. I just came to you because you the most professional niggas in B-more. I figured it'd be easier dealing with you than some of these wild-ass niggas out there." Day opened his bag to show Sticks the calling cards and move the proceedings along. He didn't like all the questions and was hoping that his bluff about taking business elsewhere would work.

But Sticks liked getting his ego stroked. Being told he was the only game in town and the most professional made him feel like a king and took him off his guard a bit. When Day opened his bag, Sticks saw the calling cards and did some quick math in his head. The cards could easily be sold on the streets for a nice little profit.

Sticks, thinking about what to do, sat back and stared at Day. He knew he was going to take the cards, but was he going to actually buy them or take them by force? On the one hand, no one knew this dude, so no one would miss him, but on the other hand, Sticks kind of liked this cat. He was obviously smart, and he definitely had some balls, robbing a spot that none of his crew could. And Sticks admired that.

"A'ight, I'll take the cards—"

"For how much?" Day said, cutting Sticks off before he could finish his sentence.

"Whoa! Hold on, young buck. Relax. I'll take the cards, but let's talk real business first." Sticks leaned forward in his chair. "You need to join the Dirty Money Crew."

Day sat there in shock, but stayed stone-faced throughout. This was exactly what he wanted and was much easier than he thought it would be. In fact, he couldn't believe it was actually happening. *I need to play this right,* he thought. "I don't know. I'm kind of a lone wolf. I do my best work alone," he said, trying not to sound too eager.

"Word. I hear that, but why be a lone wolf, when you could have the protection of the whole pack?"

Day nodded his head like he was really giving it some thought.

"Look at it this way. You could have the whole pack with you or against you. Do you want to be the hunter or the hunted?"

Just what Day wanted to hear, a threat from Sticks. He already knew he was going to hook up with the crew, but he needed Sticks to feel superior and in charge. He wanted Sticks to feel as comfortable as possible around him, and thought one way was to let him feel smarter and tougher.

"You make a persuasive argument. I'm no match against you and your men. Seems to me the only smart decision here is to say yes."

Sticks smiled. He wanted to keep this dude close. He envisioned big things for the two of them together. Every boss needed a right-hand man, and Sticks thought he might have just found his. "I like your thinking. Now, let's smoke a blunt to celebrate," he said, pulling out a bag of weed and dropping it on the desk.

Day smiled at Sticks. "I think that's a good idea." As Day sat there calmly watching Sticks roll a blunt, all he could think was, *This is the beginning of the end for you, you dumb mu'fucka!*

Chapter 8

Politics as Usual

Mayor Mathias Steele stood at the podium, signaling the beginning of the press conference. It was time to announce the Baltimore County judgeships. He was confident in the appointments that had been made. The media had cameras started rolling, and he was ready to proceed. "It is my honor to present the newly appointed justice of the Baltimore County circuit court, Ms. Tiphani Fuller." The mayor flashed his winning smile.

Flashbulbs sparkled in the crowd as Tiphani took her place next to the mayor on the stage. Dressed conservatively in a navy blue Anne Klein suit, she already resembled a government official. Smiling from ear to ear, she put her hand up and waved to the crowd. She was amazed at how smoothly things had been going for her.

"First, I'd like to thank God and my children for giving me the will to live and to fight through my ordeal. Fighting my captors off wasn't easy, just as I know helping the city of Baltimore fight crime will not be easy either. I am honored to be appointed as your circuit court judge. I plan to serve you with integrity and dignity. Surviving a violent kidnapping has made me a stronger person. I promise you, I will enlist justice to a system that has been broken and marred with corruption. I just thank you again for trusting me," she said, smiling and waving again like a newly crowned beauty pageant contestant.

More bulbs flashed as Tiphani and Mayor Steele posed for the perfect photo op. He pulled Tiphani close to him, a fake smile plastered on his face. Tiphani and Mayor Steele had history, and in order to keep what they shared in the past, he'd agreed to grant her whatever she needed.

Mayor Steele was expected to win the state senate seat, but he knew one wrong move or one bit of dirty information being leaked could cost him. He was just hoping that his support for Tiphani didn't backfire on him.

Tiphani was also in full support of Mayor Steele's bid for the senate seat. She knew that if he won she would definitely be able to help Scar become the biggest, most connected player in the game.

Tiphani had four gowns laid out on her bed for her victory celebration. She planned to be the center of attention at the party being held in her honor. Sometimes she still couldn't believe how her life was going. It seemed that everything just fell into place for her, and she was the first to admit, she deserved every bit of what she got. She picked up a lavender-colored Badgley Mischka from the bed and held it up to herself. She twirled around in the mirror like a little girl who had just gotten a new dress for Easter. She would be stunning, and she knew it.

Tiphani's personal hair stylist put her jet-black hair up into a neat bun, and her makeup artist gave her a very natural look, which accentuated her high cheekbones. The pair of professionals had made Tiphani look and feel like a million bucks.

After her assistants were done making her up, she slid into her dress and examined herself carefully. She hadn't felt this good about herself in a long time. Staring at herself in the mirror, she thought she looked gorgeous. She kissed her kids good night and headed out to the party.

When Tiphani arrived at the city's largest catering hall, she made a grand entrance. There were hundreds of people in attendance—politicians; high-profile attorneys; several of her former colleagues from the DA's office, and a small group of police officers and state troopers. Everyone was there to support her, but more importantly to make sure they got face time with her. The private attorneys and prosecutors wanted to make sure she liked them, so things would go their way in the courtroom; the cops wanted to make face with her, so she'd always sign their search warrants, even in the middle of the night; and the politicians needed to keep Tiphani as an ace in their pockets, not knowing when their dirty dealings would be exposed.

Tiphani smiled and waved and made her way through the crowd. She felt better than she had on her own wedding day. As she worked the crowd, saying hello and accepting congratulations, she noticed Rodriguez, who was standing alone watching her. *What the fuck is she doing here?* she thought to herself, but she kept her plastic smile plastered on her face as she dodged bodies, making her way across the room.

Tiphani always had the feeling that Rodriguez never really cared for her. At first she thought it was because of Rodriguez's loyalty to Derek, but when Rodriguez had gotten down with her and Scar to set Derek up, she knew that wasn't the case. She just couldn't figure out what it was about Rodriguez that gave her the creeps.

One thing was for sure. Tiphani wasn't worried about Rodriguez revealing anything about her and Scar right now. She and Rodriguez both had secrets about each other that could easily destroy one another. The difference now was that Tiphani was not aware that since Danielle's death, Rodriguez was at the point that she did not care if her corrupt behavior was made public. Rodriguez was ready to face the consequence of her actions. She just wasn't ready to tell on herself.

Tiphani was smiling and speaking to some of the other judges when she noticed Rodriguez making her way toward her. She kept the fake smile plastered to her face. "Excuse me," she said to the group of people she had been speaking to, her face becoming serious. "Tiphani, how are you? Congratulations. You look great," Rodriguez said, grabbing her into a rough, awkward hug.

"Rodriguez, I'm surprised to see you here." Tiphani giggled.

Rodriguez let her out of the hug and looked into her face. Her expression was serious. She moved her face closer to Tiphani's. "I hope you're finished with your little affair with Scar Johnson, now that you are a big-time circuit court judge," she whispered, leaning into Tiphani's ear.

Tiphani's body stiffened, and she pursed her lips. The air swirling around them was thick with tension. "I am glad to see you, Rodriguez. Thank you for coming out to support me. Please don't hesitate to let me know if you ever need anything," she said, straightening out her gown. She started to turn around as several more of her supporters approached her.

"Funny you should ask. I will be contacting you real soon about a person we both have in common," Rodriguez called out loudly, garnering stares from others in the crowd. "Do I need to make an appointment, Judge Fuller?"

"Just get in touch with my clerk," Tiphani replied, rushing away.

Tiphani spent the rest of the night showing good face with her supporters. She even danced a few times.

Although Tiphani seemed fine, Rodriguez' visit and words were gnawing at the back of her mind. She left the hall and climbed into a waiting black Lincoln Town Car. She eased into the backseat, pulled off her shoes, and leaned her head back. The driver already knew where to take her.

I could get used to this, she thought to herself. *I just wish Scar was here to celebrate our work.* Her cell phone began buzzing inside her clutch. She hadn't looked at her phone all night long. She lifted her head off the backseat and retrieved her phone from the slim bag.

"Hello," she answered in a sultry voice, a mixture of happiness and exhaustion. "Hello?"

Still there was no answer on the other end. She looked at the screen, and the call disconnected.

She placed the phone up against her chest and smiled. She knew immediately it was Scar calling to let her know that phase two of the plan was about to go into effect. Scar was about to reappear, and before she knew it, he would be sitting in front of her in her new courtroom.

Tiphani felt like she owed Scar everything. Not only did she feel a great sense of loyalty to him, she loved him. She vowed to do everything in her new judicial power to help Scar clear himself of the charges against him.

Scar hung up his cell phone and turned his attention back to the beautiful woman lying in his bed. He walked over and gave her a deep kiss. She returned his kiss and opened her legs to allow him into her. Scar thought about Tiphani briefly. He knew he didn't love her or want to be with her, but he was hoping that she believed that he did.

As Scar moved his dick in and out of his newest beauty, he only hoped that he had Tiphani wrapped around his finger as much as he thought he did.

Chapter 9

I'm Back

Sticks and Trail embraced Scar with a hug, pat, and pound. "Damn, nigga! You look relaxed," Sticks commented, giving Scar the once over. Trail was smiling at Scar just for good measure, but he was seriously biting his tongue. He was waiting to get Scar alone, to fill him in on his boy Sticks' power trip.

"Lots of good sun, good food, and good pussy will do that to a nigga," Scar said, laughing at his own joke.

"I'm glad you back, my dude. Shit has been different without you," Trail said, casting sidelong glances in Sticks' direction.

Scar climbed into his Escalade and allowed Sticks to drive. As they rode down the highway, Sticks blabbed on and on about how the Dirty Money Crew was on the serious comeup under his direction, painting a picture of himself like he was the hardest gangster since Pablo Escobar. Trail just listened and laughed to himself, feeling like Sticks would eventually get his.

Scar, listening to Sticks' grand stories, suddenly spotted a trooper's car hiding in the bushes. He quickly reached over and grabbed the steering wheel, causing Sticks to swerve.

"Oh, shit! Nigga, what you doin'?" Sticks screamed out.

Scar knew exactly what he was doing.

The next thing they knew, blue and white lights were flashing behind them, just as Scar expected. He was extra calm and collected, mentally prepared for what was next. He had purposely not alerted his little henchmen to his plans, thinking they would try and stop him, and he didn't feel like dealing with their bullshit.

"Awww, fuck! What's up with this shit, Scar?" Sticks asked, his entire body shaking.

Trail was calm. He knew Scar must've known what he was doing.

"Give me y'all burners. Hurry the fuck up!" Scar instructed.

Sticks and Trail quickly took their guns and handed them to Scar, who put one gun in his waistband and one in the back of his pants.

The state trooper finally approached the car and knocked on the window. Sticks slowly rolled the window down. Before the trooper could ask for the registration, he noticed Scar in the passenger seat and fled back to his patrol car, where he went over the radio and called for backup. He didn't even have to say why he needed backup once he said he had Scar Johnson pulled over. Scar was back!

In less than five minutes his truck was surrounded by state troopers with their guns drawn and ready. Scar was called out of the car with at least fifteen guns trained on him. Before his feet could fully touch the ground, he was wrestled to the ground and searched.

"Gun!! Gun!!" one trooper screamed out.

All of the other troopers got on high alert. Soon helicopters hovered overhead and the cast iron SWAT truck could be heard in the distance. They were not playing this time. Scar was going back to jail.

Sticks and Trail were detained and released. The cops didn't really have anything on them, and besides, the one they really wanted was Scar, who gave his boys orders to continue running the business until his permanent return, of which he was very confident, this time cleared of all charges against him.

Derek got word of Scar's return and arrest. Watching the media coverage had made his day, giving him a pep in his step. He went back to his cell and retrieved a very important phone number. Then he used his daily phone call to call his new ally.

"Hi, may I speak with Mayor Steele please?" he whispered into the phone, leery of his surroundings. He didn't know who to trust up in the jail and he wasn't taking any chances. He was placed on hold.

When the mayor picked up the line, Derek's heart jerked in his chest with excitement. "Scar Johnson is back," he said. "I want you to watch it all unfold. When you're ready, I will give you the location of my safety deposit box key with the tape," he whispered. "But first I need your assurance that you will make me a free man once I hand over the evidence you need to bring her to her knees."

"Yes, you have my word. If you have what you say you have, I'm going to need it if I am to take her out once and for all. I love it when a plan comes together. Especially when somebody thinks you're the one in the dark and in fact they are the ones walking blind," Mayor Steele commented.

Derek could feel the mayor's huge smile through the phone. "So we got a deal then?" he asked, himself smiling.

"Yes, we have a deal," Mayor Steele said before disconnecting the call.

"See who gets the last laugh now, you bitch!" Derek mumbled as he walked back to his cell. "I'm back!"

When Rodriguez saw the news report on Scar's return to Baltimore, she was beside herself with anger. She had almost wrecked her car speeding down the streets and highways to the station house like a maniac. When she arrived, she haphazardly parked her car and stormed into the stationhouse. Panting and out of breath, she busted into the cell area and began searching up and down the rows of cells. She didn't see Scar anywhere, which angered her even more.

"Where is Scar Johnson?" Rodriguez huffed, speaking to the little skinny rookie trooper who sat guard at the cells.

"He already went to see the judge for a bail hearing," the little trooper answered.

"A fuckin' bail hearing? There is no way he should get bail! He is a fuckin' flight risk. For God sakes, he just came back into town after being on the run!" she screamed.

As she turned to head down to the courthouse to catch Scar's hearing, she ran headfirst into Chief Hill. The chief had overheard her rant and knew exactly where she was going.

"Rodriguez, I'm warning you. You need to mind your fuckin' business on this one," Chief Hill gritted.

"This is my fuckin' business. My fuckin' sister is dead because of this bastard. You wanna expose me, go right ahead, but believe me, I will not be going down by myself, if you know what the fuck I mean," Rodriguez growled in the chief's face. She pushed past the chief and stormed out of the station house. She wanted to see the whites of Scar Johnson's eyes. Rodriguez arrived at the courthouse and found out that Scar Johnson's bail had been denied. She sighed. *Maybe Tiphani is done with Scar and she is going to be on the up and up with this case against him,* she thought to herself.

District Attorney Anthony Gill had a permanent hard-on since he'd gotten word of Scar's arrest. Anthony saw this as a golden opportunity to finally bring Scar Johnson to justice for years and years of crime. Anthony had already made it up in his mind that he was not assigning the case to any of the assistant district attorneys that worked for him; instead, he planned on prosecuting the case himself, which was almost unheard of. Anthony knew he'd take some flack from the media, and that his assistant DAs would be mad with him, but he didn't care. His appointment as DA was on the line, and he couldn't risk another foul up with Scar's prosecution.

Anthony sat at his desk studying every single detail and piece of physical and documentary evidence in Scar's case. He wanted every stone turned before he got into court again. His goal was to have so many charges stick that Scar would be in prison for life.

"Mr. Gill, we have just received word from the court on which judge you're going to have for the case against Stephon "Scar" Johnson," his paralegal said in a light voice. She saw Anthony's face and suddenly became nervous.

"Who is it?" Anthony asked, almost holding his breath. He was so nervous, he almost started hyperventilating.

"I'm afraid the judge is going to be Judge Tiphani Fuller," the paralegal said, looking at Anthony.

"Fuck! This shit is ridiculous! Either this bastard Johnson has nine lives, or he is paying out a lot of fucking money to stay on the streets!" Anthony slammed his hands on the desk, knocking over the case file and all the stacks of papers in front of him. Tiphani hated him and had only tolerated his presence at her party because of the mayor.

Anthony's stomach began hurting. This was the worst possible news he could have heard. He was sure Tiphani would let all of the calls in the courtroom go for the defense just to spite him. But one thing was for sure. Anthony would not waste anymore time. He instructed his paralegal to call the courthouse and put in for an immediate start to the trial. He planned on giving new meaning to "the right to a speedy trial."

Scar slipped into his suit jacket. The jury selection for his trial had taken almost two weeks. He had heard through his attorney that Tiphani was being extremely tough on the prosecutor during the jury selection process. He just had to smile to himself after hearing this.

Today Scar was being transported to court to face the revenge-hungry district attorney and, most likely, more than half the residents of Baltimore, who all hated him with a passion. He had gotten word that Tiphani was a little pissed at him for getting himself arrested as soon as he returned, instead of coming to see her first. She had wanted him to sneak around and hit her off with some dick before he made his presence back on the streets known. But Scar had other plans. Frankly, he'd grown tired of fucking Tiphani to get what he wanted. Scar was a man who couldn't be held down, and he could tell that Tiphani wanted more out of their "thing" than he did. She had even mentioned marriage one time when they had just finished getting busy. Scar thought she was straight crazy for even considering that shit.

Scar wanted to start distancing himself from her, but he couldn't cut her completely off and out of his life until he was a free man.

"Let's go, Johnson," a CO called out.

Scar got his game face on, shrugged his shoulders to shake off his little bit of nerves, and headed out of the cell, confident things would go his way.

***

Tiphani sat in her chambers preparing to see Scar for the first time since they'd separated from the yacht. She examined herself in the mirror for what must have been the fiftieth time. Kind of nervous about seeing her man after so long, she kept checking her makeup and hair closely to make sure not one hair was out of place. She put on her black judge's robe and struck several different poses. She smiled, made serious faces, then practiced banging her gavel. Tiphani chuckled at herself, behaving like a high school teenager about to go on her first date with a boy she'd had a crush on for years. Finally satisfied that she looked great, Tiphani took one last look in the mirror and winked. She thought she looked very good as a judge. She just hoped that Scar thought she looked as sexy as she thought she did. "Showtime," she whispered to herself.

Rodriguez mixed in with the crowd and settled in on a bench at the back of the courtroom. Her plan was to be present at the trial every single day until she saw Scar get what he deserved. When Sticks and Day walked through the courtroom doors with a few other members of the Dirty Money Crew, she had to count to twenty to keep herself from jumping over the aisle and beating Sticks until he was unconscious. She knew he was the mastermind of the bank heist that got Danielle killed and she had something for him, but first she needed to see Scar get his.

Sticks noticed Rodriguez. He looked over at the crooked cop and smirked. He hated Rodriguez for turning Danielle into a snitch. He just didn't know that Rodriguez hated him just as much. It was definitely a volatile situation in the courtroom that could explode at any minute.

"All rise. The Honorable Judge Tiphani Fuller presiding," the court officer called out.

"Let the games begin," Rodriguez whispered, eyeing Sticks.

Tiphani slid onto her chair. She swallowed hard and tried to calm down. As hard as she tried, she couldn't keep from looking over at a very calm and relaxed Scar, who looked sharp in a charcoal Brooks Brothers suit.

Tiphani had long since stopped seeing Scar's ugly scars. In fact, in her eyes he was gorgeous. Just looking at him and thinking about his dick was turning her on right there in the packed courtroom. She then looked over at her former boss, District Attorney Anthony Gill, who looked frazzled, like he hadn't slept in days. She smirked to herself. She could definitely tell that he was nervous. All the same, she planned on making his life a living hell in her courtroom.

"Shall we begin? Mr. Gill, you have the floor."

Tiphani looked over at Scar and spoke to him with her eyes. The message was, You don't have anything to worry about.

Scar confidently folded his hands on the table in front of him like he was about to watch a dramatic play or some sort of sideshow attraction. The back and forth between the prosecution and the defense was amusing, to say the least. Even more amusing was the way Tiphani practically abused Anthony on every objection he made, and kept him from asking the state witnesses a lot of pointed questions. Even the reporters in the courtroom had to moan at her overruling of some of Anthony's objections. Tiphani was having a field day.

At the end of the day's proceedings Tiphani raced back to her chambers and locked the door. She ripped off her robe and began touching her clitoris. Her pussy was drenched. She slid her fingers into her own wetness and pleasured herself while she envisioned Scar's muscular body and his thick dick. Tiphani masturbated off the images in her head until she came.

"Oh God. I don't know how I'm going to stand seeing him every day like this. I need him," she mumbled to herself. "I have to make fast work of this trial shit. I need this to be over, so I can get my gotdamn fix," she grumbled under her breath.

Rodriguez had left the courtroom that day sure that she had fulfilled her suspicions about Tiphani's and Scar's relationship. She was very alert to the little glances and smirks Tiphani floated Scar's way.

Rodriguez also noticed that Scar and his attorney were unbelievably calm, even though he was facing enough charges to send him to prison for life. Rodriguez, hell-bent on destroying Scar, was going to continue her hunt to get to the bottom of things, and if Tiphani got in the way, she'd just be a casualty of war.

Chapter 10

Trial and Error

"Your Honor, can we approach the bench?" Anthony Gill was coming apart. His shirt was wrinkled, he looked like he hadn't shaved or cut his hair in weeks, and he had bags under his eyes, hinting he hadn't slept a single hour in the three weeks since the trial had begun.

"Approach," Tiphani said dryly. She couldn't wait to shoot him down on whatever he was going to ask. It had become a daily occurrence in the courtroom to the point where the spectators in the gallery began to look forward to what kind of spectacle she would make out of him every day.

"Your Honor, the State planned on introducing two evidence exhibits today, and, and, well, um—"

"Get to the point, Mr. Gill." Tiphani already knew what he was trying to say, but she had to play dumb. "Our evidence has gone missing, Your Honor," Anthony blurted out. He looked like he was about to cry.

"Mr. Gill, is this some sort of sick joke?"

"We registered the evidence exhibits with the court as State exhibit 1 and 1a. I'm sure of it; my paralegal has the stamped receipt. But, but . . ."

Anthony was really not doing well. His eyes wide and pleading, he looked as if he would just faint right then and there.

"Mr. Gill, you have made so many errors during this trial, I am very tempted to call a mistrial. Either you get it together, or I'm going to end this circus right here and right now." Tiphani loved the attention of being on center stage and was putting on a show for the courtroom.

In response to Tiphani's berating, Anthony could hardly muster a rebuttal. He just slumped his shoulders in defeat.

Scar's defense attorney pounced on the opportunity to further embarrass Anthony. "Your Honor, with all due respect, we need to continue the trial with or without the State's so-called evidence. It's just too bad the bungling fools at the DA's office can't keep up with their own exhibits."

"I agree. The trial must go on. Mr. Gill, I guess that evidence just won't be admitted. Either find something else, or pick up where you left off." Tiphani had to try very hard to keep a smile from spreading across her face. She felt more powerful than God when she sat up on that bench. Being able to manipulate lives made her pussy wet, and she squirmed in her seat, opening and closing her thighs to create friction around her clit.

Tiphani knew exactly what had happened to the State's exhibits. She had facilitated the disappearance of two weapons that Scar had allegedly used, one in an assault so severe, a store owner almost died, and the other, he had used to kill a police officer. She wasn't about to let those come into her courtroom.

Anthony Gill rushed back over to his table. His list of witnesses was dwindling. All of the witnesses who were supposed to testify against Scar began backing out when they heard Scar was actually back in town. Anthony was scrambling to keep the case against Scar together and wasn't doing a very good job of it.

Tiphani looked over at Scar and gave him the same little eye signal. Just as she took her eyes off Scar, she spotted Rodriguez staring right into her face. She cleared her throat and held her gaze for a few seconds. Rodriguez's presence at the trial every single day made Tiphani uneasy. She couldn't figure out why she was so interested in Scar's trial. Especially since she had taken dirty money from him.

Tiphani rolled her eyes at Rodriguez and turned her attention back to the trial. She secretly hoped that Rodriguez hadn't noticed her little signals to Scar, but Rodriguez wasn't the only one who noticed.

Day, who was also at the trial most days with Sticks, showing support for Scar, saw the same thing. He and Scar hadn't officially met yet, but they had a history that went way back. As Day sat in the courtroom for another trial against Scar, he couldn't help but get a feeling of déjà vu. The feeling that Scar was going to inevitably get off permeated both trials. He just sat in the trial and thought to himself, *These government mu'fuckas always fuck these trials up. If you want something done right, do it yourself. I'll have to take Scar down myself.*

Rodriguez was convinced there was something going on between Tiphani and Scar. She watched the little exchanges between them and watched Tiphani use the same number of eye blinks each day, the same cough, and a little fingertap to signal things to Scar. She couldn't prove it yet, but she knew for damn sure that something fishy was going on between Scar and Tiphani, and she planned to continue attending the trial until she got something concrete. She had to be careful before going public with her suspicions, knowing firsthand how far-reaching Scar's power was. She didn't want to end up like the rest of the DES unit—either dead or in jail.

"I am asking that you convict Stephon Johnson on all charges. He is a menace to society. Mr. Johnson has ruined the lives of hundreds of young kids. He has been responsible for ninety percent of the drug distribution on the streets of Baltimore, and he has engaged in bribery, racketeering, and murder. He needs to be off the streets immediately. Only you can do that. The State rests its case," Anthony said to the men and women of the jury in his closing argument. Anthony just wanted the entire debacle to be over. He had failed the city of Baltimore. He was suffering from severe insomnia and had gone home at least four nights, put a .22-caliber in his mouth, and contemplated pulling the trigger. He knew his career wouldn't survive if Scar was acquitted, and he'd been made a fool of enough already.

As Anthony made his way back to the prosecutor's table, he looked over at Scar and shook his head. Without words he acknowledged that Scar was more powerful than himself. He had basically thrown in the towel.

Scar looked over at the jury and saw two members yawn while Anthony was speaking. He chuckled to himself. He felt like the king of Baltimore. Scar was so sure he would get an acquittal, he was unfazed by the proceedings. He even slept with ease in the jail at night because he knew it wouldn't be for long.

Scar's defense attorney barely had to say anything during his closing remarks. He basically harped on the fact that Anthony had bungled the State's case against Scar. It looked like it was working. The jury was attentive, and a few members had even shaken their heads in agreement with the defense. The court proceedings were adjourned while the jury deliberated.

Tiphani raced back to her chambers after she sent the jury out. She paced up and down the floor of her grand office space silently praying that the jury would come back with a quick acquittal. She couldn't wait much longer to have Scar touch her body. As a judge, she couldn't interfere with the jury, but she really wanted to send them a note saying, "Hurry the fuck up."

She jumped when her desk phone rang. "Hello," she answered, anticipation evident in her voice. The jury had reached a verdict. "Okay, I'll be right out," she said. She rushed into her robe so fast, she tripped over it and almost busted her ass. "Calm down, Tiphani, calm down," she said to herself.

Tiphani was back on the bench within minutes of the call. "Jury, have you reached a verdict in the case of the State of Maryland versus Stephon 'Scar' Johnson?" She felt all tingly inside when she said his name.

"Yes, we have." The foreman handed the judge the verdict in a sealed envelope.

Tiphani ripped it open, her hands shaking with anticipation. As she read the words, a hot flash of relief came over her. She handed the paper back to the foreman and immediately gave Scar an eye signal.

"Mr. Johnson, would you and your attorney please rise for the reading of the verdict?" Tiphani stared right into Scar's eyes. She knew right then and there she was definitely in love with him. If she had any doubts before, they had all been erased now.

Scar stood up and adjusted his suit jacket. He looked over at the jury and awaited his fate. Scar's attorney didn't break a sweat. He already knew what it was going to be.

"We the jury find the defendant, Stephon Johnson, not guilty on all charges," the foreman read. "Noooo!" a woman screamed from the back of the courtroom. It was Flip's mother. "He murdered my son! He stole my baby from me." The woman continued to scream, and some of her other family members had to pull her up off the floor.

Rodriguez jumped up and almost impulsively ran up to the front and started beating Scar in his head. Meanwhile, Chief Hill had a huge smile on his face.

Sticks, Trail, and all of the members of their crew who showed up were cheering and exchanging pounds, thinking about the big-ass party that was sure to take place after the trial. Day celebrated with them, but he was thinking of the next step in his mission.

The courtroom was a riotous mess. News reporters raced down the aisles to get the first pictures of Scar. Some snapped quick shots of the defeated and beaten down district attorney. The trial had turned the city of Baltimore on its ass.

"Order! Order!" Tiphani called out. She wanted to officially dismiss Scar, to be the one to tell him he was a free man. The noise in the courtroom quieted to a slight hush as she continued to bang her gavel.

When order was restored, Tiphani said, "Mr. Johnson, the jury has found you not guilty on all charges as listed in the indictment. These charges are dismissed by this court. Mr. Johnson, you are a free man," Tiphani said with another telling bang of her gavel. Scar turned toward the crowd of haters and supporters. He flashed a bright smile, adjusted his suit, and started walking out of the courtroom.

When Scar passed Anthony Gill, he leaned over to him. "Damn, man. Maybe you'll be able to get me in your next life." He let out a loud laugh.

Anthony stared at Scar with a deep hatred. Scar felt untouchable just knowing that his rights under the Constitution against double jeopardy protected him from being prosecuted for the same charges again. He felt like he was as smart as Albert Einstein for the way he had planned and executed his entire acquittal, outsmarting all of these government officials who had big-time degrees from Harvard and Princeton, including Tiphani. He had cleaned up his mess and vowed he'd be more than extra careful from that day forward, which included cutting ties with all of the people around him that he considered deadweight. Like Tiphani.

Tiphani rushed into her chambers, grabbed up her cell phone, and began dialing Scar's phone number. She couldn't even wait until he left the building before trying to contact him. She got the computerized voice mail on Scar's phone. She disconnected the call and redialed again. Again, Tiphani didn't get an answer. She called again and again.

"Okay, Scar, I know you're celebrating, so I will wait for a little while," Tiphani mumbled out loud, tossing her cell phone onto her desk when she really wanted to scream.

"I fuckin' knew it! I knew this bitch was dirty!" Derek screeched as he got news of Scar's acquittal. When he had learned that Tiphani had been appointed circuit court judge and then was miraculously assigned to Scar's case, he became very suspicious of all of the past occurrences. He had sat in his cell for an entire week and written out all of the events involving Scar and Tiphani. Since Derek had nothing but time on his hands, he was able to examine the events one by one, and eventually, like a puzzle, it all came together for him.

Derek placed his last call to Mayor Steele, who did as Derek instructed. The mayor was kind of skeptical when he retrieved the DVD from the safety deposit box, but when he put the DVD into the player, he was pleasantly surprised to see Scar fucking Tiphani's brains out.

"Aghhh! I got you now, you bitch! You just thought you could threaten me. Now let's see who has the upper fucking hand," Mayor Steele spoke out loud to the TV screen as he admired

Tiphani's firm titties and round ass. He shuddered, just thinking about how good her pussy felt to him when they'd had their affair. "If your husband only knew what I used to do to you," he whispered, talking to Tiphani's sexy image on the screen. "Well, now he and I are going to destroy you."

Chapter 11

Fatal Attraction

It had been five days since the trial had ended, and Tiphani still couldn't reach Scar. She was having difficulty concentrating on the case before her. In fact, after Scar's acquittal, she wasn't even interested in being a judge anymore, adjourning her cases and giving short breaks so she could go into chambers and call Scar over and over again.

But Scar wasn't accepting her calls. Either that, or he'd gotten a new phone number. She looked at the call history on her phone. All of her outgoing calls were filled with Scar's number. Not even a call to her babysitter or any of her friends was listed.

Tiphani was becoming undone. She wore her hair pulled back into a dirty, ratty bun, and she barely wore makeup these days. She was beginning to feel like Scar was purposely avoiding her, which made her feel like she was going to slip into a deep depression any day now.

She decided she wasn't going out like that. She wanted and needed Scar, and that's what she was going to get. Tiphani went back into the courtroom and adjourned all of her cases being presented for the rest of the week. She had places to go and someone to see, and she wasn't going to stop until she did.

Scar looked down at his buzzing phone for the one hundredth time that morning. "This bitch just won't give up," he mumbled as he rolled over and moved the arm of the beautiful young girl sleeping next to him so he could stand up. He was thinking about changing his cell phone number but had more urgent things to take care of, like running his empire. Scar was sick and tired of

Tiphani blowing up his phone like a mad woman. She had left him at least twenty desperate messages begging him to call her back, and not once did she get a return call. Scar didn't feel one ounce of remorse for not calling her, or not wanting to have contact with her.

Scar mumbled to himself, shaking his head in disgust. "Did this bitch really think I would wife her after she cheated on my brother with me? She suppose to be so fuckin' smart, but she couldn't figure out I was using that dumb ass." As he thought more and more about it, he had to smile. He didn't realize his dick could be that powerful. "Maybe I should sell my shit." He chuckled to himself.

Scar was done with Tiphani. Now that she had served her purpose, he didn't need her any longer. Scar was hoping she would've gotten the drift by now, but since she was still calling, he knew she was still on it like that. "Don't tell me I'ma need a fuckin' exterminator for this pest." Scar sighed, looking down at yet another call.

Tiphani sat in her chambers after her day in court. She could barely keep her eyes open. She had been spending her nights sitting outside of some of Scar's old spots and still had not spotted him. It seemed to her like he had changed up all of his regular hangouts and drug houses. It was getting to be too much for her to handle.

The thought of Scar avoiding her was driving her insane. It got to the point that she had been crying so much, her eyes were swollen. Then she lied to her court clerk, saying, she was having an allergic reaction to something.

Again, she called Scar. This time she was crying so hard, her face was a mess of makeup and tears, and she could hardly see the number pad on her phone. "Scar, why won't you call me back? I need to see you right away. Please, please!" she whined into the phone, leaving yet another message on his voice mail.

Tiphani was beginning to feel like a fool. She had given up her entire family, sent her husband to jail for crimes he did not commit, and changed her entire career, all for the attention of her own brother-in-law. She was starting to realize that her priorities had been all fucked up. Now Scar was acting as if he didn't even know her.

She pulled her hair and bit her lip until she drew blood. "If he thinks he is rid of me that easily, he is fucking wrong. He has not seen the last of Tiphani Fuller," she spoke out loud to herself. Tiphani just had to come up with a plan to get Scar to see her again, and she knew exactly what drove his every thought too. Money.

Rodriguez sat outside the courthouse in an unmarked police car. She watched as Tiphani left the building and got into her car. Rodriguez waited for her to pull out and was on her ass, following her to several different houses and clubs in the seediest parts of town. Finally, Tiphani jumped on the highway. She was heading toward one of the richer parts of Baltimore. Rodriguez was confused, until she saw Tiphani pull up to the gates of a huge mansion.

Rodriguez followed and parked her car down the street. She was going to sit there and wait to see if Tiphani came out with her man. This was her only mission in life, and she had nothing but time. She pulled out her camera and began snapping pictures of Tiphani as she got out of her car and walked up to Scar's door.

When Scar pulled back the door, Rodriguez was able to zoom in and get a great shot of Tiphani throwing her arms around Scar's neck and kissing him deeply.

"That's the money shot, bitch!" Rodriguez said to herself. Within no time she definitely had what she'd come there for.

"Oh my God!" Tiphani screamed. "I thought I would never see you again, baby. Why haven't you been answering my calls?" She held onto Scar like she never wanted to let him go, her heart thumping wildly with excitement. If she got caught at Scar's mansion, it would mean the end of her career, and probably her freedom, but Tiphani didn't care. She felt she had been forced by Scar to take this chance. If he had just answered her calls, she wouldn't have gambled like this. Seeing and touching Scar, Tiphani felt like she'd cream in her pants right there on the spot.

"I needed some time to myself. I mean, damn, I just came off trial. Plus, I figured you would be more worried about your kids and spending time with them, since you were away from them for so long."

The only reason Scar had agreed to see Tiphani was because she had left him a message telling him she knew a foolproof plan to make a large sum of money at one time. She had said it would be enough money that Scar could retire from the street life. When Scar heard that, he didn't call her back. Instead, he made Sticks call her and tell her to meet him at the mansion. Scar was about to sell the mansion anyway, so after he used her once again, he would be gone without a trace or a forwarding address.

"I need you. I need you to touch me, baby. It's been so long, and we've been through so much. I did all of this for you. Please . . . Scar, I need you," Tiphani pleaded, rubbing on his dick through his pants.

Scar hated bitches that whined and begged. She was like a desperate drug fiend. He grabbed her wrists roughly and removed her hands from his body. "You came here to talk about business right now, so let's talk about that." He released his grip on her and shoved her away.

Tiphani crinkled her forehead. She couldn't understand his rejection. She figured the faster she gave him the information she had, the faster he would give her what she wanted. "I had this case come across my desk," she began.

Scar was listening attentively.

"There are several armored trucks coming into the capital building at night, every night. These trucks are filled with all of the government money from each little city in Maryland. I'm talking millions of dollars. The trucks all come together. It's about six of them. I've been told that each truck holds at least ten million dollars. They make deposits into the state's treasury vault. Two of the trucks make deposits to the state's gold repository, so the trucks with a certain insignia also have gold bars inside. The market for gold is unbelievable right now."

"But what makes you think they don't have the entire fucking army coming with those trucks?"

"Because the case involved one of the guards, and he gave up all the details. He said there were only a few guys guarding the trucks. He was suing the government because he got hurt on the job and was saying the government put him in harm's way." Tiphani was desperate to get Scar back in her life.

"How am I going to be able to plan this out? I mean, we need times, dates, amounts, types of guns, all that shit," Scar said, already calculating the money.

"I'm going to help you, baby. I'm going to help us," Tiphani said softly.

"I missed you, girl," Scar lied, grabbing her and pulling her into his chest. He knew just what to say and do to wrap Tiphani around his finger.

A feeling of relief came over Tiphani's entire body. She hugged Scar tightly and began to cry. "Please don't leave me like that again," she cried into his chest. "I love you so much, Scar Johnson."

Scar stroked her hair, but behind her back, he rolled his eyes. He really couldn't stand her weak, silly ass. Sometimes he still couldn't believe he would probably never speak to his brother again all because of this trifling bitch.

Tiphani moved out of Scar's embrace and dropped to her knees in front of him. "Please, let me taste you. I've missed you so much," she whispered. Then she took his thick black manhood into her warm mouth.

Scar inhaled deeply. Her head game was on point. He let Tiphani suck his dick until he came all over her face. Just another way to degrade her, and she was all for it. He looked down at her as she rubbed his cum all over her lips and tongue.

"You want some of this dick up in you now?" Scar huffed.

Tiphani shook her head and rushed to take off her clothes. Scar grabbed her, manhandling her, threw her onto his desk, and rammed his dick into her so hard, she almost choked on her own saliva.

"Agghh!" she screamed out in ecstasy. That was just what she wanted. She was hoping he would reward her sexually, once she gave him the information.

Tiphani was elated to be back in Scar's good graces and never wanted to be without him or his dick ever again. But for Scar, no matter how good she made him feel sexually, he still had it in his mind that he would get the armored truck information from her, and that would be it. Besides, although it was all a part of his plan, now that she was a judge, she was too much of a liability to have around.

Tiphani had barely left Scar's mansion and he was already back to business.

"Yo, Sticks," he called out.

Hearing Scar call his name, Sticks immediately jumped and ran into Scar's office.

"What's that dude's name you grooming?" Scar asked as Sticks entered the room.

"You mean Day?"

"Yeah, that nigga. Tell him I want him to follow Justice Fuller and report back to me with what he sees."

Sticks looked confused. "Who's Justice? I don't think I know that nigga."

"You stupid mu'fucka—Tiphani. Justice Fuller is Tiphani. She a judge, so you call her justice. Niggas these days are stupid."

"Oh, word," Sticks replied, embarrassed. "A'ight. I'll holla at him."

"Now get out my face!"

Sticks just turned around and walked out. He thought it best just to shut up and do what he was told before he made himself look like more of a fool.

Scar, intrigued by Tiphani's information, had Day follow her to make sure nothing would get in the way of his chance to live the rest of his life on some tropical island.

Chapter 12

Watch Your Back

Day walked up behind Tiphani in the parking lot of her local supermarket. He had been following her like Scar wanted, but it was also to his benefit as well. Here he could get on Scar's good side and at the same time gather information to destroy him.

"Justice Fuller," Day called out.

Tiphani turned around to see who was calling her. She loved it when people recognized her on the street, and especially when they referred to her as Justice. It actually kind of turned her on. "Yes?" she replied to the stranger.

Day said quietly, "Justice Fuller, I am an associate of Scar Johnson."

Tiphani got nervous. She looked around to make sure no one had heard what was just said.

Day added, "He informed me that you will be gathering information regarding some armored vehicles."

"Who did you say you were?" she asked, not wanting to give any information to a stranger.

"I work for Scar. He and Sticks are grooming me. Scar told me what you are doing, and I want to do it for you."

"Oh, you want to take my glory and get in good with your boss. Well, I promised my man I would deliver, and I will."

"No, I don't want to take credit for it. I just want to make sure you are out of harm's way. See, Scar told me he was concerned for you. He is afraid you will get caught. I just want to ensure that you don't. Yes, I want to keep Scar happy, not by giving him the information, but by keeping you safe. You see he loves you." Day was playing on Tiphani's emotions, knowing how much she loved Scar.

Tiphani was beside herself. There was nothing in the world she wanted to hear more than that. "Did he say that—he loves me?"

"Yes, he did," Day said, laying it on thick now. "That's why I propose that I gather the information, but you can relay it to him. That way Scar stays happy because you are safe."

Tiphani thought it over in her head for a few seconds. She could keep Scar happy by being safe and also giving him information that would make him tons of money. Then he would keep fucking her like she wanted. But what she thought of most was that Scar said he loved her.

"Okay. If it will keep Scar happy, let's do it. I don't want my love to be too worried about me. But I will lock your ass up if you try and take credit."

"I won't, I promise. I'm just trying to make my cash, and it's easier to do that when the boss is happy."

After exchanging a few more details, they agreed on a meeting place and time when Day could gather all of the information from Tiphani. Day walked away happy that he now had more control of his position in the crew, and Tiphani walked away thinking about how in love she and Scar were with each other. In Tiphani's mind they were going to be the ultimate power couple.

Scar was banging into Tiphani's ass from the back. This time she had on her judge's robe. The black material hung around her hips while he moved in and out of her rapidly.

"Who fucks you the best, Your Honor?" Scar said. Tiphani couldn't even answer him, she felt so good. Scar felt the nut building up, so he quickly pulled his dick out and squirted his load all over her robe. "Now, that's that reverse Bill Clinton shit! Fuck justice!" Scar said, laughing as Tiphani collapsed on the bed.

Tiphani and Scar had been meeting up in some of the seediest parts of town to ensure that none of her professional colleagues saw them together. It had been a week since he'd accepted her back, and she had been getting fucked lovely every day since. Scar had even fucked her one time in his truck in a dark-ass alley in the hood. Tiphani could care less, as long as she was getting the dick.

"So what's up with that info?" Scar knew her mind would still be cloudy from the good sex, so she would tell him everything he needed to know.

"I drew you a little diagram," she said, laying on Scar's chest now. "It has the times, which guard has what weapon, their whole routine."

"That's wassup. I knew it was a reason I always thought you was the shit." Scar really did think she was smart, but he didn't respect her one bit.

"So when is it going down?" she asked, leaning up on her elbow and looking into his face.

"We doin' the shit tomorrow night, if everything is gravy. I'm sending my crew out there to scope shit out tonight. As soon as I get the word from them, we will set shit into motion."

"Oh, so you don't trust me and my information?" Tiphani pouted, a little offended.

"C'mon, baby girl. You know me better than that. I'm a thorough nigga. It's business, not personal."

"All I want is ten percent of whatever the take is." Tiphani had kind of thrown Scar off. He wasn't really expecting to give her shit, but her demand made him have slightly more respect for her.

"A'ight, ma. We can do that. You better get a foreign bank account. Shit, ten percent of millions is gonna be hard as fuck to hide. You damn sure can't stuff those kinda stacks under your bed."

Tiphani hadn't thought that far ahead, but Scar was right. She needed to open her foreign bank accounts immediately. She didn't plan on staying in town after the heist anyway. Her heart was set on disappearing with Scar and her kids to start a new life somewhere with beautiful beaches and constant sun.

Rodriguez took more pictures of Tiphani coming out of the seedy short-stay motel. "Damn, Tiphani, you have reached a new low over dick. You and your little boyfriend will be very sorry," she said aloud, as if Tiphani could hear her.

Rodriguez put her camera down and picked up the stack of pictures she had just printed out at Wal-Mart. She shifted through all of the pictures of Tiphani and Scar together. She even had pictures of her naked in the back of Scar's truck.

Hell-bent on revenge for her sister's death, Rodriguez knew what she had was so strong, Tiphani would probably do anything to keep her from releasing the pictures to the media.

She flexed her jaw when she spotted Scar leaving shortly after Tiphani. "Fuckin' coward!" She gritted. She still couldn't believe she'd helped them to bring Derek down, something she considered one of the worst mistakes of her life, but since she was the last DES member standing, she had personally taken on the responsibility of getting revenge on Scar, whatever the cost—be it prison or death.

Anthony Gill put the barrel of his .22-caliber pistol in his mouth and pulled the trigger. Part of his brain busted out of the back of his skull, and his body dropped to the floor like a metal anvil. After being publicly humiliated, Anthony saw his life as being over anyway. Already removed as DA, he knew it was just a matter of time before he was fired all together.

Anthony had sent a note to the mayor explaining that Tiphani and Scar Johnson had made a fool of him, that he didn't want to live any longer. He also sent some of Tiphani's old case files, the ones where she had made side deals.

When Mayor Steele received the letter from Anthony a cold chill had shot down his spine. He read it over and over again. Tiphani was ruining lives one by one, and he wanted her out of the way once and for all.

Mayor Steele, in a close race for the senate seat, with the polls showing him behind by only a few points, needed something to bolster him into the limelight, so he would still have a chance to pull into the lead. With dirt like that on the new circuit court judge, he could portray himself as being tough on government corruption, which would give him a fighting chance at winning the senate seat. But since he was the one who'd appointed her, the situation was a delicate one.

The mayor had been trying to wait before revealing Tiphani's secret, keeping it as a trump card. He really didn't want the evidence to leak out. As he had always done, he wanted to make a behind-doors deal to get her out of the way for good. But as the race went on, he needed a smoking gun, and it looked like Tiphani was holding it.

I'm not waiting anymore, he thought. *Fuck this bitch. Now my friend Anthony is dead because of this bitch. Her husband is in jail. This bitch is like a black widow spider, and I'm about to cut off all eight of her fucking legs.*

"Marsha! Marsha!" the mayor called out.

The young intern rushed into his office. "Yes, sir," she huffed.

"I need you to send out all of these packages with a return receipt. Do not open them and do not fuck this up!"

"I won't, sir. Yes, sir." Marsha took the stack of oversized manila envelopes from the mayor and rushed out of his office. Once she was on the elevator she read the addressee information on each envelope: NBC; ABC; CNN; FOX. She could only wonder what was inside those envelopes.

Mayor Steele needed to get Tiphani's phone number. After being appointed to the judgeship, she had changed her cell number. He wanted to let her know which day to watch the news, so when the world saw her bare naked ass, she would too.

When the CO came to the cell to tell Derek he had a visitor he was shocked. He knew damn sure Tiphani wouldn't be coming to visit him again, and he didn't have anyone else. All his friends were either dead or had turned on him.

Derek's mind raced as he followed quietly behind the CO. When he finally walked into the visiting area, his jaw almost hit the floor.

"Let me just start by saying I am so sorry," Rodriguez said in a low, remorse-filled voice.

Derek sat across the table from his visitor, at a loss for words. If there weren't so many COs around, he might've jumped across the table and tried to strangle Rodriguez to death for turning her back on him.

"It's all a part of the game, I guess," he replied.

"I'm here about Tiphani. She is into some heavy shit—"

"I already know all I need to know about that conniving bitch. It was all of you that didn't believe me when I said I was being set up."

"I need your help. I need to know what makes her tick. I need to know everything about her. She was the judge on Johnson's case, and all along she was fucking him."

"That's old news. She was fucking him, and I busted them. That's what started this whole fuckin' war to begin with. Unfortunately, me, Cassell, Archie, and Bolden ended up being casualties. You were our only hope, but you let them convince you to turn on the DES," Derek growled. The more he thought about it, the angrier he got.

"I swear, I didn't know. I didn't know who to trust. I am sorry. I had to take care of my sister," Rodriguez said, her eyes welling with tears.

"What does she have to do with this?" Derek asked softly.

"She has everything to do with it. My mother couldn't afford to take care of her, to keep a roof over their head, none of that. They needed me. She was sixteen, and they killed her, Derek!" Rodriguez whispered, hot tears in her eyes.

"Who killed her? Scar?"

"Scar's little crew. I think he ordered the hit. They may have found out she was my sister. I swear I will not rest until that mu'fucka Scar is dead or in jail for the rest of his black-ass life. And, Tiphani, she is going down with him. She made it easy for him—all over some dick," Rodriguez said through clenched teeth.

"I can tell you everything you want to know about her, but you gotta promise to help me win my appeal."

Rodriguez extended her hand for a shake. "Deal." They had struck a deal, but they didn't realize that, in the Baltimore County Jail, the walls had ears.

Derek was feeling good on his way back to the tier after his meeting with Rodriguez. He had his fellow officer on his side and the mayor. He was sure he would make it out of jail before he could be sent to the state penitentiary.

As he walked along with a smile, he noticed that the CO took a different turn than their usual path to the protective segregation unit. The CO was new, one he hadn't seen in the jail before. "Yo, ain't you goin' the wrong way?" he asked.

The CO didn't answer.

They turned another corner, and suddenly—blackness. Derek tried to scream, but he had a pillow case put over his head.

"They told you to watch your back, nigga!" his attacker mumbled.

The next thing he felt was cold metal piercing the skin of his back, arms, legs, and neck. Derek had been stabbed with a shank over forty times and was bleeding all over his body.

When the deed was done, the fake CO shed his stolen uniform and rushed through the hallways to the escape route his inside contact had given him. He was outside in no time.

He picked up his cell phone and called a very important person. "Yeah, it's done," he said. "Where do I go for my paper?" Satisfied with the answer, he hung up.

Chapter 13

All Good Things Come to an End

Sticks and Trail lay side by side in the bushes on the side of the state capitol building in their assigned positions. Scar had given all of the crew members detailed assignments.

Trail's heart began hammering in his chest when, like clockwork, he saw two armored trucks pull up to the building. And just like Tiphani had said, the armed guards were all laughing and playing around as they unloaded the bags of money. Sticks got up on his knees for a better view.

"Get down, nigga," Trail whispered.

Sticks, anxious to play cowboys and Indians with the guards, ignored him. He was an attention-seeker for real, and he loved a good shootout, but that wasn't part of the plan.

Trail was pissed. He added this incident to a laundry list of shit he wanted to tell Scar about Sticks.

Sticks and Trail watched as two of the armed guards disappeared into the building, while the others hung around talking shit outside.

Trail saw the two black Suburbans approaching in the distance and took that as his signal. Staying low, he quietly ran across the grass and grabbed the guard with the shotgun around the neck, from the back. The guard didn't have time to react, his air supply completely choked off by Trail's tight grip rendering him completely powerless.

Sticks did the same with the other guard, who held a long gun. Except, Sticks used a safari knife to cut his throat.

That wasn't part of the plan either. Trail almost threw up from all of the blood.

Just like a well run assembly line, their plan fell into place perfectly. As soon as Sticks and Trail had the two biggest threats down, Scar jumped out of one of the Suburbans and shot the other two guards with his Glock, muffled by his homemade silencer.

Then the little young'uns jumped into the back of the armored trucks and began grabbing bags and bags of loot.

After about five minutes, the other two guards were seen talking as they came back out of the building. They immediately noticed that something was wrong. In unison, they both went to draw their weapons, but it was too late. They were ambushed on either side by Timber and another little young boy.

It all happened so fast. All of the guards were dead, and the area looked like a horror film massacre scene, with blood everywhere. Scar had made sure Day got rid of the building's outside surveillance camera prior to the setup.

Everyone piled into the Suburbans, and they raced away from the scene, the SUVs filled with cash.

"Yo, I thought that bitch said it would be six trucks?" Sticks was still on a high from the murder he had committed. But he didn't think they had enough money from just the two trucks. A bunch of people had to get a cut, and he knew Scar would be taking the lion's share.

"Six trucks or two trucks, we got paid, nigga, so stop complaining," Timber said.

Some of the other little crew members started laughing. Nobody was showing Sticks the same respect since Scar's return.

"Who the fuck you talkin' to?" Sticks growled, feeling the heat of embarrassment rising in his chest.

"I'm talkin' to you, bitch-ass nigga!" Timber barked.

Sick and tired of Sticks' shit, some of the others instigated the situation, chanting, "Ohh!"

Timber went on talking to another crew member about the money.

Suddenly, Bang! Bang! Two shots rang out inside the truck. Timber's body slumped down in the backseat. Everybody in the truck knew he was dead.

Day almost swerved off the road. "Yo! What the fuck, nigga?" he screamed, his ears ringing.

"You asking questions, or you driving? You can be added to the list of niggas that got caught by the Grim Reaper, if you want to," Sticks said calmly.

When the crew arrived back at the warehouse, Scar got out of the other Suburban. No one dared to say anything to him.

"Where is everybody?" Scar asked when he didn't see Timber.

There was silence.

Finally, Sticks stepped up. "I had to murk that nigga, boss. He was talkin' about all the shit he was gonna do with his paper and I saw him as more of a liability than an asset. A nigga that run his mouth like that ain't worthy."

The other little young'uns looked around at each other in amazement, but they were too scared to tell Scar the real story.

"My nigga. Always lookin' out," Scar said, giving Sticks a pound. "Now let's count up this paper."

They unloaded the bags and poured out the money on the floor of the warehouse.

"Daaammn!" Scar exclaimed, looking at all of the money stacks. They had to have at least two million dollars in stacks of big bills there. The money had come from so many places and was unmarked.

Tiphani had come through for real. Scar was smiling from ear to ear. He was so happy, he even contemplated keeping her around a little while longer. He picked up his phone and called her.

Tiphani put a hundred-dollar bill between her ass cheeks and told Scar to take it out with his mouth. She giggled like a high school girl when he followed her instructions.

"I always wanted to be able to have enough money to wipe my ass with it," she said, laughing even harder.

Scar climbed up behind her and swiped his dick up and down her ass crack.

"I'd much rather wipe my ass with that though," she purred.

Scar parted her ass cheeks and wet her asshole with his spit. As Tiphani arched her back and lifted her body to accept him, he slowly eased his dick into her anal opening.

Tiphani bit down into the pillow, and tears leaked from the sides of her eyes. The pain shooting through her ass was almost unbearable.

But the more of his manhood he put in, the better it felt to her. Soon, she was matching Scar pump for pump, and he was moving in and out of her asshole with ease, like it was her pussy.

Tiphani reached under her stomach and put her fingers into her vaginal opening. Having both holes filled made her go wild. She bucked and slammed into Scar even harder now, sending the money that surrounded them on the bed flying all over the place. "Agghhhhh!" she screamed. Her body shuddered and she fell onto the bed. She'd just had the best orgasm of her life.

Scar was next. "Arrgghh!!" he growled, shooting his load into her tight asshole.

Tiphani lay almost paralyzed on the bed, and Scar fell to the side next to her. She smiled to herself, feeling like her life couldn't be more perfect. She had already made her deposit into her overseas account in the Cayman Islands and was enjoying the fruits of her labor.

Sticks waited outside of Trail's baby mother's house. He watched as Trail kissed his little girl and his baby mother at the door. He felt a pang of jealousy. He didn't have any family, and he couldn't hold down a relationship after what happened with Danielle.

Sticks had been watching Trail ever since Scar had told him that Trail was complaining about him behind his back. The crew had another job planned for that night, and Sticks just didn't trust him.

Trail skipped down the front steps of his house, feeling good. He had money stashed now, to take care of his two favorite girls. Trail had come a long way in the game, but after the heist tonight, he planned on getting out and moving far away from Sticks, Scar, and the entire Dirty Money Crew. Preoccupied with his thoughts, he wasn't looking at his surroundings. He went to open his car door.

Sticks stepped from behind it. "What up?" he said, appearing out of nowhere.

Trail jumped so hard, he dropped his keys. "Nigga, what the fuck is you doin' sneaking up on a nigga like that?" Trail could feel his heart beating in his throat. He didn't trust Sticks either.

"What? You ain't happy to see me?" Sticks asked with an evil smile. "Let's take a ride. Scar wants us to do a job," he lied.

"He didn't hit me and tell me shit about a job. What kind of job?" Trail could barely get his nerves under control.

"Just c'mon, nigga. Get in the car. Follow my lead."

Sticks moved his shirt slightly to show Trail his gun, and Trail reluctantly got into his car with Sticks.

Sticks gave Trail directions, a left here, two rights there, and finally they ended up riding down a desolate one-lane road in the country part of Baltimore.

"What the fuck is this, nigga? What could Scar possibly have out here?" Trail asked, looking around.

"We suppose to do a pickup. Scar didn't wanna risk shit getting out in the city," Sticks lied again. "See that car up there? That's them niggas we suppose to meet up with. Pull right behind that car."

Trail felt slightly better. At first, he thought Sticks was doing some snake shit, but when he saw a car parked ahead of them, a feeling of relief washed over him, and he thought maybe Sticks was telling the truth.

Trail stopped his car behind the parked vehicle. "Yo, it don't look like nobody in that shit." He squinted to get a better look.

The next thing Trail felt was cold steel up against his temple. He jumped, and his first instinct was to reach for his own burner.

"Don't even try it, mu'fucka! Get the fuck out the car!"

"Yo, nigga, you on some real bullshit," Trail said, raising his hands.

Sticks kept the gun on Trail, reaching around and taking Trail's gun from his waist. "Now get the fuck out the car!" he barked again.

"Just tell me what the fuck you want, and let's get this shit over with, nigga."

"You a bitch-ass nigga. I heard you was running your trap about me. You think I'm a power-hungry mu'fucka, huh? Well, you know what . . . you're right." Sticks slammed his gun into Trail's head.

"Agghhh!" Trail screamed out as blood spurted from his head. He fell to the ground, holding his head.

Sticks stood over him. "Stand up and face me like a man."

"Yo, nigga, I don't want no beef with you, man. You can have whatever you want. You want my share of the loot, so be it." Trail wiped blood out of his eyes.

"Nah, nigga, I don't need your money. Although after I fuck your bitch and kiss your baby girl, I might just take that shit." Sticks laughed like a maniac.

Trail tried to drag himself up off the ground to attack Sticks. He couldn't bear to think about Sticks going to his home and putting a hand on his wifey and baby. "You bitch-ass nigga!" he screamed.

Bang! Bang! Bang! Bang!

Trail's efforts to attack Sticks were short-lived. His eyes popped open wider and wider with each shot that pierced his body. He placed his hands over his chest, and his body involuntarily jerked as the life went out of him.

"Who shot ya? Separate the weak from the obsolete!" Sticks sang the Biggie verse as he looked down at Trail's dead body. He spat on his crew member and got into the getaway car he had stashed there.

Sticks drove back into the city to get ready for their job. He had no remorse, and he was ready to murk any other nigga that tried to get in his way. Including Scar.

Tiphani rushed out of her car to get to court. She had a few hearings scheduled that she wanted to get over with. Tonight was her and Scar's biggest heist. She couldn't stop thinking about how much money she would get from this job. In fact, she was hoping it was enough to set her up for life.

Just as Tiphani approached the judge's entrance at the back of the courthouse, she was confronted.

"Good morning, Your Honor," Rodriguez said, stepping in her path.

"Rodriguez, what, what are you doing back here? The police entrance is at the front."

"I'm not here on police business. I'm here on judge business." Rodriguez grabbed her by the arm and pulled her out of the view of the court officers standing guard at the back door.

"Get your hands off of me! What is the meaning of this shit?" Tiphani yelled.

"I know all about you and Scar Johnson," Rodriguez began.

Tiphani opened her mouth to speak, but Rodriguez cut her off.

"Don't try to deny it. I'm not asking you, I'm telling you," she said. She pulled a manila envelope from her jacket. "You might want to take a look at these before you say a word." She handed Tiphani the envelope.

Hands shaking, Tiphani slowly opened the envelope. She became hot all over her body at the sight of the pictures inside. "Where did you get these?" she gasped, barely able to speak.

"Don't worry about that. Just know there are more where that came from. Now, can we talk business?"

"What do you want? If it's money, how much? Just tell me," Tiphani whispered. She was drenched in sweat.

"I want you to set Scar up and help me bring him down once and for all. He killed my sister, he is killing kids on these streets, and he set Derek up."

"How?" Tiphani croaked out, tears streaming down her face. She was caught up. She had no choice but to comply with Rodriguez to save her own ass.

"I want you to tell me where the next heist is going down, so we can have teams waiting. Scar will not make it out alive this time."

"W—w—what about me and my children?" Tiphani whined, a mess of tears, sweat, and nerves. "We won't be safe if I give you the information."

"Scar won't know it was you that snitched. I'm not that coldhearted that I'd tell him it was you. But once I help you get away from him, you have to help me free Derek of all the charges against him. Tiphani, you and I both know he is innocent."

Tiphani hung her head. Her so-called good life and fantasy love life was falling apart right before her eyes. With pictures like that, she would be thrown in jail for helping Scar get off on his trial. Not to mention, her face would be plastered all over the media as a crooked judge who slept with defendants. Tiphani had to save herself and think about her children. "Okay. I will help you bring Scar down," she said, barely able to get the words out.

"Good. Let's talk about a plan. This has to happen sooner rather than later. I will not wait another minute to bring him down to his fucking knees."

All of Mayor Steele's packages must have arrived at the television networks at the same time. The telephone lines in his office were ringing off the hook. Marsha, his intern, could barely answer one before the other starting buzzing. The mayor had instructed her to take every single call and confirm that the DVD contained in the package was in fact authentic.

Mayor Steele sat in his office smiling. He had cleared his calendar so that he would be able to watch when all the news programs started airing Tiphani's dirty laundry. It wouldn't be long before she was exposed. He had purchased a brand-new suit for the press conference that was sure to follow Tiphani's little unveiling.

The mayor would have to speak out against Tiphani and her crimes. This scandal would put him in the media's eye, and he would get the pre-election boost he needed. Shit was going according to plan. He had already paid somebody in the jail to get rid of Derek.

It was bad enough that the woman he had appointed to circuit court judge was corrupt. There was no way he could risk Derek revealing that he, the mayor of the city, had struck a deal with a convicted dirty cop, who was a cop killer himself. In Mayor Steele's assessment, Derek should be dead, or at least, that is what he had paid for.

***

"Yo, man, I saw her talking to a cop, my nigga. I'm telling you, Scar, it was her," Day said.

"Nigga, you better have yo' fuckin' facts straight," Scar barked as he paced the floor.

"I'm tellin' you, boss. I followed her just like you told me to. She went to that court building, but at the back door. I got out the car and watched her talk to that Puerto Rican bitch that was coming here before. She was crying and shit, and then after a minute, she shook hands with her."

Scar punched a hole in the wall. He was angry at himself for letting Tiphani back near him. "I should have trusted my first instinct after the trial and deaded that bitch! I had a brand-new start, and I let this dick-hungry bitch weasel her way back in. She is as good as dead."

"Yo, nigga, let me take care of that bitch," Sticks ranted. "I can't tell you how much I wanna murk that bitch. She been a casualty in my book."

"Nah, I got something else in mind for her," Scar growled. "I want everybody to gear up. Tonight is gon' be bigger than I expected."

As Scar continued stalking up and down the warehouse, all of his little workers were silent. No one dared to even make eye contact with him. They knew he was highly unpredictable when angry, and no one wanted to be the one he took his anger out on.

Scar made his way back to his office and sat at his desk, his blood boiling that, against his better judgment, he let Tiphani back into his life. He hated being lied to. He demanded loyalty, and if he wasn't getting it, then that person deserved to die.

"Boss, can I say something else?" Day stood in the doorway to Scar's office.

"Nigga, what? I ain't in the mood, nigga."

"A'ight, when you ready," Day said in his most soothing voice. Scar was volatile, and Day needed him to listen. "I've got a plan to set Tiphani up and pull off the heist at the same time."

"Nigga, I'm always ready. Speak."

Day proposed, "I was thinking I could find Tiphani and tell her the plans of our next heist then make sure she tells that Puerto Rican bitch and flip the script on them bitches."

Scar sat and listened intently, going over the pros and cons of the plan in his head. He liked the idea. He liked it a lot. He gets revenge, and he gets his money. “I like that shit,” he said, a sinister grin on his face. “Get Sticks and go find that bitch.”

“I think I should do it alone,” Day said. “Not sure Sticks is the man for this job.”

The grin disappeared from Scar’s face. “What you sayin’, nigga?”

“I just think Sticks should stay away from this one,” Day said, leading Scar on.

It was a fine line between snitching and just giving information. If Scar thought Day was snitching, then Day’s whole plan would be shot, and he would be in danger of being shot.

“Why, nigga? Stop being so cryptic. Just tell me. This ain’t no twenty questions.” Scar was falling right in line with what Day needed.

“I ain’t no snitch, but Sticks has been buggin’ lately. Timber wasn’t talking about how he would spend his money. He clowned Sticks, and Sticks murked him for no reason. And I don’t know for sure, but I think he murked Trail. He’s been dropping a few hints around the warehouse.”

“I hear you. I’ve had my eye on that nigga. I have my suspicions about him murdering Trail.” With his suspicions about Sticks being confirmed, Scar’s body was tensing up.

Sensing he had Scar on his side, Day pushed his luck and went for the one thing Scar would definitely react to.

“But the thing that got me wanting to stay away from him is, I think he’s got his eye on your throne, boss. I know you ain’t gonna let that happen, and I don’t want to get caught in no crossfire when you gotta take that nigga down. He’s a loose cannon, boss, and I don’t want no part of his craziness.”

Scar’s heart was about to pound out of his chest, he was so furious. Another person in his life was now betraying him. His brother was the one person he could trust, and he fucked that up by fucking his wife and getting him thrown in jail.

“Fuck that nigga!” Scar growled. “You stay away from him. Do your shit with Tiphani alone. What was said in here stays in here. If I hear that you said even one word of what was said in here to anyone, you as good as dead, nigga. Got that?”

"You can trust me, boss," Day said, trying to appease Scar. "This shit stays in this room."

"Get the fuck out my face!"

Not wanting to push his luck any more, Day got the fuck out of the office as fast as possible. He left the warehouse without speaking to any of the other soldiers and made his way to Tiphani and their meeting spot.

Chapter 14

What Goes Around Comes Around

Tiphani and Rodriguez sat across from each other in a hotel room talking about their plan. Tiphani explained all of the nuances to Scar's methods. She drew a small map and told Rodriguez where each of Scar's henchmen would be posted. She laid it all out, with ease.

Rodriguez grew more and more excited by the minute. It would just be a few short hours and she would have Scar Johnson by the balls once and for all.

"You said Scar killed your sister. I didn't know you had a sister," Tiphani said, changing the subject.

"Yeah, a baby sister. Her name was Danielle. She was a good girl, until she got caught up with that boy. He's a part of Scar's crew. No matter how hard I tried to get her out of it, she didn't listen. When I found out she was running with Scar's crew, doing jobs right along with them, I tried to demand that she stop. That backfired and drove her even further in. They set her up to get killed, probably because they found out I was her sister. I don't have anything left to live for if I don't bring Scar down. It was all my fault. All of this was my fucking fault." Rodriguez ended her rant by slamming her fists on the table. She didn't want Tiphani to see the tears welling up in her eyes.

Tiphani was speechless. She had always pictured Rodriguez as a hard ass, but this emotional side was refreshing. She was more encouraged to help Rodriguez now, understanding her sudden quest for revenge. Besides, she had her money tucked away, and there would be other men to fulfill her every need, so she figured it better to save her own ass and help Rodriguez. *Maybe getting rid of Scar is what I need to get over my shortcomings and my sex addiction,* she thought, feeling better about helping take Scar down already.

"Call him. I want to make sure he is still planning to do the job tonight before I send out all of our resources," Rodriguez told her.

Tiphani knew for sure that the heist was still going down, Day having told her all of the details. Nonetheless, she picked up her cell phone and dialed Scar's number.

"Hi, baby," she sang into the receiver. "I'm at the courthouse getting some last-minute work done," she lied. "Is everything still on for tonight?"

"Yeah, everything's on," Scar replied.

"Ohhh! That's so good. I'm so excited. Can't wait to get more of that cold cash in my hands. Maybe after this we can retire to Mexico or even Africa."

Tiphani was laying it on thick with Scar. A little too thick for Rodriguez's liking. Rodriguez used hand signals and motioned to her to hang up the phone. Taking her cue from Rodriguez, Tiphani cut her call short.

"He said everything will go as planned."

"Oh, yeah? And what did he say about your share of the money?"

"He said it would be waiting for me," Tiphani replied, lowering her eyes.

Tiphani didn't care that Rodriguez and the state troopers planned on busting up Scar's heist. She had enough money from the first two heists to be comfortable if she had to go on the run with her kids. Tiphani had already moved her money and closed her foreign accounts to make sure that her money was safe and that she could not be implicated in any of the crimes if Scar decided to try to take her down with him. She planned to outsmart all of them, including Rodriguez.

What Tiphani didn't know was that Derek had provided Rodriguez with her social security number and all of her computer passwords. Rodriguez knew where she had wired all of her money, knew every transaction she made with a credit card, and even what types of snacks she bought for her children. Rodriguez didn't fully trust her either, so she was always one step ahead.

Bringing Scar down was only part of the plan. Tiphani wouldn't get away completely free. She would also have to pay. Literally.

"Where the fuck is Trail?" Scar asked Sticks.

Sticks was caught off guard. He had always had slight suspicions that Scar had a soft spot for Trail, but he could never really confirm it or figure out why. "That little nigga ain't show up today. I haven't seen or heard from him," Sticks lied.

"Call the nigga. He needs to be here. I'm not trying to do no major shit without one of my majors, you feel me?" Scar gave Sticks the once over.

Scar wasn't stupid either. He knew Sticks was kind of jealous of Trail, so he'd purposely told Sticks about Trail's complaints to see what Sticks would do. He wanted to test him, see if he was a capable and trustworthy number two. The bitch-ass thing for Sticks to do would be to try to show Trail some malice, but the man-up type of thing to do would be to have a man-to-man sit-down with Trail. That Trail was missing, Scar felt like Sticks had taken the bitch-ass way out.

When Scar was just seventeen he had fallen in love for the first and only time with a woman named Rita. Rita just couldn't be kept. She was a wild child and loved to party and get high. Rita got caught up but not before giving birth to a son—Scar's son.

"I called that nigga, and he ain't answering," Sticks said.

"It's just not like that nigga not to show up for something as important as this. I better not find out that nigga dipped on us with that fuckin' money." Scar gritted, playing it off.

"He probably did. I told you already, when you was gone, this nigga was tryin'a take over the game like a one man show. He even went down on the south side and muddied the waters with those cats, Tango and them. I'm telling you, Scar, you thought that dude Trail was quiet. He was a fuckin' quiet menace and a liability." Sticks wanted so badly for Scar to feel for him like he felt for Trail.

"It's all good. The show must go on," Scar said in a low whisper.

Scar needed Sticks for what he had planned for tonight, but there was no fucking way he would let Sticks slide. As soon as he found out what was up with Trail, he planned to get at Sticks in a deadly way. *This nigga better hope not a hair was harmed on my boy's head, or he is a fuckin' dead man,* Scar thought to himself as he eyed Sticks.

Tiphani sat in front of the police van with Rodriguez. She was shaking like a leaf.

"Why are you so nervous? Didn't you do this same shit to help Scar out?" Rodriguez asked her.

"What same shit?"

Tiphani felt her heart sink into her stomach. With all of the precautions she had taken to help Scar, she'd never thought about the human factor—that somebody could be following her and making note of all of her actions.

"Whatever," Tiphani whispered, looking straight ahead out of the window. She watched as all of the unmarked police cars got into position. She noticed the undercover cops strategically placed near the buildings. Tiphani thought about Scar. She was sorry she had to do this to him. She was truly in love with him, but she was more in love with herself.

"What time do you have?" Rodriguez asked her. "Ten minutes past ten," Tiphani answered.

It would only be a few more hours before that entire street would look like a scene out of a movie. Tiphani's stomach began to cramp. Then her cell phone rang. It was Scar.

"Hello?" she answered, trying hard to keep her voice from quivering.

"What's up, baby girl?" Scar asked, knowing exactly where she was at.

"I'm just here with the kids about to go to sleep and wait for you to come through," she lied. She closed her eyes as she felt her heart breaking.

"That's good. Tonight is gonna be perfect, so have your bags packed and ready to go. I'm bringing you a couple of million tonight. Fuck being a hundred thousandaire. You gonna be a millionaire," Scar said.

"Good! I can't wait," Tiphani replied. They hung up the phone.

"Boy, he must really be in love with you, or is it the other way around?" Rodriguez said.

Tiphani, frustrated and nervous, ignored her comment. "I just want this to be over with. I don't even know why you need me here. I'm a damn judge!"

"I need you here as collateral. I couldn't trust you to be somewhere that you could let Scar know what's going on. I've seen your sex sessions with him up close and personal. You are in love with his dick, and up until now, dick has made you do some crazy things—Judge." Rodriguez didn't have an ounce of respect for Tiphani's ass and wasn't pulling any punches.

"By the way, did you start thinking about how we're going to get Derek out of jail? I know you must have some strings you can pull down at city hall."

"I will sort things out when this is all over. But let's get one fuckin' thing clear. After I meet all of your demands, I don't want to see your fuckin' face ever again!" Tiphani was tired of Rodriguez putting all of this pressure on her. All she wanted was to meet her demands so she would turn over that pack of pictures.

Tiphani had fallen asleep in the van when she heard Rodriguez's watch alarm going off. She jumped up and wiped sleep out of her eyes.

"It's time," Rodriguez told her. Awake and wired, there was no way she could even think about sleeping on a night where she was so close to bringing Scar Johnson down.

"You better say a prayer. I know Scar very well, and he is not coming without some heavy artillery," Tiphani told her.

Rodriguez instructed Tiphani to climb into the back of the van, not wanting to risk anyone seeing her face through the windshield. She also instructed her to climb into the back and use a long scope to watch for Scar's arrival. Rodriguez had her men in place, and everyone knew the precise time shit was going to jump off.

Tiphani had warned Rodriguez that Scar was very prompt and thorough when it came to these jobs, the main reason he was so successful at it.

The time had finally arrived. Rodriguez watched through a scope as the armored trucks arrived. Her heart thumped wildly as she watched the drivers and guards unload the bags of money. "Scar and his little band of misfits should be rolling in another minute or so," she whispered.

According to the way Tiphani had explained it, Scar and his little men would hit, once two of the guards had gone in to do the drops. Rodriguez held her breath for a minute in anticipation of Scar's arrival. But nothing happened. She looked down at her watch. It had been almost five minutes since the guards disappeared into the building, and there was still no sign of Scar.

"Where the fuck is he?" Rodriguez asked, growing antsy.

Another two minutes passed, and still no Scar Johnson.

"Officer Rodriguez, where the fuck is your band of thieves?" one of the SWAT guys asked through on the radio. They had been in position for so long, they were tired of waiting.

"He was supposed to be here already," she responded.

More time passed and still no Scar. Now the guards that had gone into the building returned, and all of the guards began preparing to roll out.

"What the fuck did you do?" Rodriguez screamed. "You fucking told him, didn't you? You slimy bitch!" She dropped her scope and grabbed Tiphani around her throat.

"No! I didn't. I—I d—did not," Tiphani croaked out. Rodriguez continued squeezing her neck. She had lost all control. The opportunity to bring Scar down was slipping away, and she thought Tiphani was responsible once again.

"I will kill you," Rodriguez growled, spit dripping out of her mouth. She looked like she was possessed by a demon. She continued to squeeze until she noticed Tiphani's eyes rolling up in her head. Tiphani made gurgling noises like she was about to die. Rodriguez snapped out of it and let her go.

"Ahem! Ahem! Ahem!" Tiphani was coughing like crazy, trying to catch her breath, tears streaming down her face. She instinctively sucked in gulps of oxygen as she held her throat. Everything had gone wrong, but she hadn't tipped Scar off. She was worried that Scar not showing up might mean he was on to her. If that was the case, she knew she'd be marked for death.

Once the armored trucks pulled out, Rodriguez, feeling defeated, slumped down in the back of the van.

"Officer Rodriguez, was this some fuckin' kind of joke?" one of the undercover officers blared through the radio.

Rodriguez ignored the questions that came through the radio one after the other. She felt like a total fool and a failure. Again. She looked out of the van's windshield and noticed that all of the state troopers she had enlisted for the bust began coming out of their hiding spots. Rodriguez guessed it was to discuss what had gone so damn wrong. She knew she had to eventually get out and try to calm them all down, but she was so damn embarrassed, she hesitated.

"You fucked up, Tiphani," Rodriguez said in a harsh whisper. "You are going to be ruined."

"I swear I didn't tell him anything. I wouldn't be sitting her like a sitting duck if I had tipped him off. You have to believe me. I held up my end of the bargain, but something must've happened to keep him from coming here."

"No! Something doesn't just happen! Somehow he must've fuckin' found out!" Rodriguez screamed. "My first guess is, you fuckin' told him, so he would fuck your brains out. My second guess is, you're so stupid, you didn't notice that he fuckin' had a tail on you the whole time."

Just then there was a knock on the van door. They both jumped.

"Officer Rodriguez, it's me!" the SWAT team leader screamed.

Rodriguez pulled back the door and climbed out of the van. Tiphani sat inside listening to their conversation. Rodriguez was pleading for forgiveness, telling the other enraged troopers, she had everything planned out to the minute and didn't know what happened.

One of the SWAT members stepped in front of his boss to give Rodriguez a piece of his mind. Suddenly, the SWAT team leader dropped to the ground, a perfect hole in the center of his forehead.

"Oh, shit!" Rodriguez screamed.

Next, the other SWAT team member fell to the ground. Same thing, a perfect hole. Then two more officers were down.

Rodriguez looked around on the roofs of the surrounding buildings, but she didn't see anyone. Then she noticed a red dot on her arm. She raced to get back into the van. She knew then that there was a sniper firing from somewhere. "Everybody get the fuck back to their cars now!" she screamed into her radio, and all of the officers began scattering.

Scar was once again one step ahead of them.

A bullet whistled through the air and hit the side of the van as Rodriguez was about to climb into the front to drive away. She dropped down on top of Tiphani, who was crying hysterically, to shield her. Then more bullets hit the van, one shattering the passenger side window this time.

"Oh, God! He is going to kill us! What about my kids?" Tiphani screamed, covering her ears.

Rodriguez knew she had to take a chance to get out of there. She jumped into the driver's seat and started the van. Just as she went to pull out, Bang! A bullet pierced the windshield, and Rodriguez's body slumped over, blood leaking from her head.

"Agghhhh!" Tiphani screeched. If she didn't act fast, she would never make it out of there alive. From the back of the van, she struggled to pull Rodriguez's limp body from the seat. By now she could hear more police coming onto the scene and more bullets flying. She struggled with the dead weight until Rodriquez's body finally fell far enough over that she herself could climb into the driver's seat.

Tiphani struggled behind the wheel and hurriedly threw the van into drive. With her hands shaking fiercely, she pulled out like a mad woman. Just as she made it out of the spot, another bullet hit the side of the van. They had missed her again. She sped down the street and away from the scene, crying and shaking so hard, she could barely maintain control of the car.

"Oh, God! What have I done? What have I done? Somebody help me!" she squealed. She didn't know where she was going or how she would ever get her kids so she could disappear.

Tiphani kept driving and driving. When she thought she was far enough away from the scene, she picked up her cell phone. That's when she noticed a flashing text message—You just fucked up. Make sure your will is up-to-date, bitch.

Tiphani threw her phone down. She knew exactly who the text was from. Scar was out for revenge, not just any kind of revenge. He would have a high bounty on her head. She couldn't stay in Baltimore. She just had to figure out a way to get out before Scar and his little crew members found her.

Tiphani thought she knew somebody who could help her. She picked her phone back up and dialed the mayor's phone number. The mayor had told her to meet him at the courthouse, that he would gladly help her.

Tiphani watched as the sun came up on another day. She knew it would be her last day in Baltimore, Maryland.

Derek clung to life in the jail's infirmary. The nurse came in and shifted him in the bed, so he wouldn't get bed sores. He'd heard the doctors say he had barely made it.

The small television that hung over his bed had the news on. Derek stretched his eyes when he heard a reporter say that there was breaking news regarding Judge Tiphani Fuller. He knew right then that Tiphani's indiscretions with Scar would be aired that day beginning on the six o'clock news.

Wincing in pain, he fought against the drowsy effects of the painkiller to watch the news. He planned to be glued to the television for every single news broadcast. Derek hadn't figured out who'd tried to kill him yet, but he also planned to await Rodriguez's return with the information needed to help him get free. If Rodriguez didn't come through, he knew he still had the mayor's loyalty for helping him. Derek was happy to still be alive and took comfort in the fact that all of Tiphani's lies would finally be brought to light. In his assessment, he would be a free man in no time, and the first place he would go is to see his brother, eye to eye, man to man.

Tiphani had managed to sneak into a drug store and purchase a Halloween costume wig, some oversized shades, and a new shirt. She couldn't go to the courthouse in a shirt with Rodriguez's blood splattered all over the front of it. She took a cab to the court building, and as she exited, she looked around. Tiphani noticed all of the cameras and the podium set up at the front entrance.

"This is all I need today," Tiphani mumbled to herself. "A fucking high-profile case in front of the court. I need to get inside to meet with the mayor. Just gotta make it inside." Tiphani didn't notice that she was once again being watched like a hawk.

When she got to the back entrance, the guards didn't recognize her. One court officer told her, "Ma'am, this entrance is for judges only."

"I am Judge Tiphani Fuller," she said nervously, pulling the sunglasses down slightly to reveal her face a little more.

The guard's eyes grew wide, and he swallowed hard. He looked like he'd just seen a walking dead person.

"Stay right here, Judge Fuller, um, one minute." The guard ran behind the desk and picked up the telephone. He mumbled something into the receiver as he eyed Tiphani, who rolled her eyes at him, tapping her foot impatiently. Tiphani was fuming. She didn't have time for this shit today. It was all too risky standing there. The longer she waited, the less time she had to make it out of Baltimore alive.

"Judge Fuller, they have instructed me to escort you to the front entrance of the building," the court officer told her.

"What? What the fuck is going on?" Tiphani screamed as four other court officers emerged and put hands on her. She began fighting them, bucking and thrashing. "I'm the fuckin' circuit court judge! What the fuck is the meaning of this?" By now her wig had come off, making her identity readily apparent. "You are making a mistake!"

When the guards emerged through the front doors with Tiphani, she was met by a crowd of media and Baltimore citizens. Mayor Steele was standing behind a media podium, all dressed up and looking debonair.

The crowd began jeering and booing Tiphani. "Murderer!" a lady screamed out.

"Dirty judge!" screamed another.

Tiphani felt her stomach muscles clench. There was basically a mob of people after her. "Mathias, what is going on here?" she shrieked.

"Here she is, ladies and gentlemen. The crooked judge who sleeps around with defendants and gets paid to hand down acquittals," Mayor Steele announced in a serious tone.

"Mathias, I can ruin you!" she screamed.

It was too late. She listened to a loudspeaker blaring her voice. "Aghhh, Scar, fuck me! You fuck me so much better than Derek."

Tiphani's bladder released right there on the spot. The entire world knew she had fucked Scar Johnson and that she had been on the take the entire time.

"Just like I promised, I will be tough on government corruption. There will be no dirty cops or judges when I'm elected to the state senate next week," Mayor Steele boomed into the loud speakers. "Take her to jail where she belongs!" Mayor Steele shouted. With that command, the court officers roughly carted Tiphani to the cells inside the courthouse.

Tiphani was screaming, but no one could hear her over the loud jeers of the crowd, which was now turning into a mob.

Scar watched from a distance. He was pissed. Now he would have to use other connections to get to Tiphani. One thing was for sure, he wouldn't let her get away with setting him up. He had two of her most precious commodities to hold over her head.

"Uncle Stephon, when will we meet up with Mommy?" Tiphani's son asked.

Scar looked at Tiphani's daughter, who was sleeping in the backseat of his truck, Sticks sitting next to her, his gun on the ready. "Soon, baby boy, very soon." He picked up his cell phone to call in a favor.

Chief Hill raced out of the stationhouse. He had received a call that spurred him into action. He arrived at the courthouse in record time, flashed his identification, and rushed to the cell area where Tiphani was being held. "I'm here to pick up our prisoner," he announced. "Judge Fuller."

The captain of the court officers asked, “Who said she is the state’s prisoner?”

“I fuckin’ said it, and the mayor fuckin’ said it. You want to question us? Or maybe Judge Fuller is fuckin’ you and payin’ you too,” Chief Hill gritted through clenched teeth.

The decorated court officer backed right down.

Tiphani was sitting in the corner of the cell when they came in and told her she would be going with the chief. She remembered Chief Hill’s face from somewhere, and it wasn’t in court. She slowly walked out of the cell and out of the courthouse with Chief Hill, who led her to an unmarked car.

Tiphani thought that was very strange. “If I’m so bad, why don’t you have a squad car? And since when does a chief come out to pick up prisoners?”

Chief Hill was silent. He held onto Tiphani’s arm tightly as he led her into the back of the car. Once she was seated inside and he was in the driver’s seat, he turned on his car radio.

“Uncle Stephon, when are we going to see Mommy?”

Tiphani heard her son’s voice coming through the speakers. “Noooo! Help me!” She began to scream and buck in the backseat. She tried banging her head on the windows to get the attention of anyone on the outside, but it was of no use. She continued to scream. “Please! Not my children, pa-leeeessee!”

“No need to cry now, Judge. You brought this all on yourself,” Chief Hill said calmly.

Just then it came to Tiphani remembered where she knew the chief from. She had seen him meet with Scar several times to pick up payments. She had also remembered seeing him in the courtroom when Derek was convicted. All along she’d thought of him just as the chief of Division 1, but as it turned out, he was another of Scar’s paid aces.

Tiphani knew her life was over. She figured she would never make it to any prison. The chief was surely going to be driving her straight into Scar’s hands.

Her throat sore from screaming, Tiphani finally gave up on her cries for help, and began concentrating on trying to ease her hands out of the handcuffs. She kept struggling. She felt like her wrists were bleeding already, which was exactly what she wanted—something wet and moist to help her squeeze her small, bony wrists out of the cuffs. She kept on maneuvering as the chief continued driving.

All Tiphani could think about was her children, who were old enough to identify Scar, so she knew he would kill them too. Tiphani felt a flash of anger in her chest, as her motherly instincts suddenly started taking over, her need to save her children becoming overpowering.

Tiphani had always thought of herself as a shrewd career woman with the skills to keep rising to the top. But now, riding in the back of a cop car with a crooked-ass police chief on her way to meet death face to face, it looked like the "Maryland blues" was bringing her right back down. But Tiphani had other plans. If she was going to die, she would die trying to free her kids first.

As she looked at the back of Chief Hill's head, Tiphani felt like it was now or never. She pulled the handle on the door, and it flew open.

"Oh, shit!"

Chief Hill screeched as he swerved the car, causing him to slow down a bit, all part of Tiphani's plan.

Tiphani jumped out, and her body hit the road like a sack of potatoes and rolled. She could feel her skin ripping open with "road rash," as the wind was knocked out of her. After a few seconds of excruciating pain, she got her bearings enough to run down the highway screaming for help.

Chief Hill pulled over on the shoulder of the highway and got out of his car. He kicked the tires. "Fuck!" he screamed. He scrambled to his car and picked up his police radio. "Chief Hill, Division 1, on the air!" he screamed.

"Go, Chief," the operator answered immediately.

"I have an escaped prisoner on I-95. Female, black—aww, fuck it! It's Judge Tiphani Fuller, and she is to be considered armed and extremely dangerous. I want her taken down by any means necessary! I repeat, she is to be taken down!" Chief Hill barked. If Tiphani got away, Scar would simply kill him, chief of police or not.

Tiphani ran down the highway like a mad woman. Her legs and chest burned as she ran as fast as her legs would take her. "Help me!!" she screeched.

Finally, a longhaul truck driver stopped. He thought maybe the crazy woman was running from a john that was trying to beat her up or kill her. He reached over and pushed open his passenger side door.

Tiphani climbed up into the cab of the eighteen-wheeler. "Please, help me!" she huffed. "I'm a judge. The police are trying to kill me!" she gasped.

The truck driver was stunned, not understanding what he got himself into. Then he noticed all of the police cars whizzing down the highway. "Oh shit! You need to hide up in the back of the cab," the truck driver said with a thick country accent. "I got some blankets back there you can cover up with."

Tiphani did as he said.

"I'm gonna keep on driving the hell outta Maryland, but I know they gonna eventually block off this here road."

"Just keep driving, please. My life is on the line," she cried, burying herself in the back of his cab.

Day was getting nervous. He had been waiting at the meeting spot for half an hour, and still there was no sign of his girl, which wasn't like her. She was always right on time. The war on Scar Johnson was getting heavy, and Day was afraid that his girl had been found out. He vowed to look out for her and keep her safe, and if she wasn't, his guilt might push him over the edge.

Then, out of the shadows she crept. She was being very careful not to be spotted by anyone, and to make sure it was Day in the car.

Day pushed the button to roll the automatic window down. "Get in quick, Halleigh."

Halleigh ran to the passenger side door and got in the car. "Dayvid, I'm sorry I'm late."

Dayvid and Halleigh had met when Halleigh moved to Baltimore from Flint, Michigan. Dayvid was being groomed by Halleigh's man, Malek, to take over his drug business, and the three formed an immediate bond. When Malek had asked Dayvid to take care of Halleigh when he was gone, he didn't need to ask twice. Dayvid would do anything for Malek.

Malek was killed in front of his house with Halleigh watching as Detective Derek Fuller shot him. From that moment Halleigh had vowed revenge on Detective Fuller. After she started following him, she realized Detective Fuller was an associate of Scar Johnson. That's when Dayvid realized that Scar probably had Detective Fuller kill Malek because he was moving in on Scar's territory.

Ever since then, Halleigh and Dayvid had been shadowing Detective Fuller, Scar, and anyone associated with the Dirty Money Crew. They fancied themselves a cross between Bonnie and Clyde, and Robin Hood. They had made a pact and were determined to destroy the persons responsible for the death of Malek, the one person they both loved.

"I followed Tiphani to the courthouse, and shit was a circus over there," Halleigh told Dayvid. "There were camera crews and reporters everywhere. They grabbed her up and propped her up in front of everyone as the mayor made a speech about cleaning up corrupt police and judges."

"What? Slow down. What happened?"

"They played the tape we made of Tiphani and Scar fucking, right there in front of the whole city on a big screen so everyone could see. Detective Fuller must have leaked the tape we sent him. Holy shit! I can't believe this, Day. Our plan is working!" Halleigh was about to jump through the roof, she was so excited.

She reached over, grabbed Day, and kissed him passionately. Then they both separated and just stared at each other for a second, both stunned by the sudden passion. Before, it had just been more of a business relationship. Although Day definitely had a thing for her, he would never disrespect Malek like that. Not knowing how to handle the situation, he just moved on like it was nothing.

"We need to keep on track. I told you this would work. I have to get back to Scar. You go home, and we will meet up later to figure out our next move. Stay hidden in the shadows. Don't let no one see you."

"Okay." Halleigh got out of the car and ran into the shadows.

Dayvid sat there and watched her disappear. He whispered, "I love you. Be safe."

***

Derek was elated when he'd heard of Tiphani's arrest at the courthouse. He was just waiting for the day the COs walked into the infirmary to tell him he was a free man. Today, when the COs knocked on the little metal hospital bed to tell him he had a visitor, he just knew it was someone sent by the mayor's office to let him know he would be free in no time.

When the visitor stepped into the room, Derek's heart started racing. It was Sticks who was ambling toward his bed. Derek almost shit his pants. He shot Sticks an evil look. He wasn't fully recovered from the stabbing, so he knew he had no chance of winning a fight with Sticks.

"What the fuck are you doing here?" Derek growled in a low voice, so the guards wouldn't overhear his conversation.

"Scar sent me, nigga. You know the drill. He wanted to me to send you a message. The same strings you pulled to ruin your ex-wife and bargain for your freedom is the same ones you need to pull to help him get out of Baltimore unscathed," Sticks whispered harshly.

"Tell Scar I said fuck him!" Derek spat. He winced. Raising his voice caused him pain.

"I don't think you will have the same attitude once you see this." Sticks dropped some pictures onto Derek's chest.

Derek reached out with his one free hand and picked the pictures up. They were face down. He examined them, almost choking on his own spit as he stared down at pictures of his kids sitting on Scar's lap. He crumpled the pictures as he balled up his fist. "What the fuck does he want?" Derek gritted, his body throbbing with pain.

"He wants your ex-wife dead. He also wants it to be arranged that he gets out of Baltimore without the beast breathing down on him. Scar knows about your little agreement with the mayor, soon-to-be senator, so he figures you can throw some words his way. It's either that, or receive your kids' body parts one by one as a care package here at the jail," Sticks said with finality. He didn't even give Derek a chance to answer. He just stood up and walked toward the door, and the CO standing guard let him out.

"CO! CO!" Derek called out frantically. The CO rushed to his bedside.

"I need a phone," Derek said, struggling with his words. "I have an emergency at home."

Tiphani and the truck driver made it through the police road block without a hitch. A few state troopers had climbed up into the truck's front cab to take a look, but they hadn't seen anything. Besides, the smell of the truck driver's cigars and his musty underarms had driven them right back out.

She came out of hiding when the truck driver announced they had made it all the way down to Fort Lauderdale, Florida. She climbed into the passenger seat of the truck and stared out at the water. She began to cry. The reality of her situation had started setting in. She would be spending the rest of her life on the run. Not only was Scar Johnson looking for her with plans to kill her, but every single police entity in the state of Maryland had a bounty on her head as well. As she said a silent prayer for her children, she realized the truck driver had been speaking to her.

"So what you gonna do from here?" he said. "I'm headed back home to Texas to my family."

"I don't know. But if you leave me your name and some contact information, I will make sure you are compensated for all of your help."

"That won't be necessary. Let's just say a guardian angel sent me to save you from the boys in blue," the man said.

Tiphani let a weak smile spread across her face. Then she opened the truck door and climbed out onto the street. She looked around at her new surroundings. She smelled the salt air, looked at the palm trees, and said to herself, "I will have the last laugh, you mu'fuckas," as she walked to the beach to begin plotting her comeback.

Baltimore Chronicles

Volume 3

Treasure Hernandez

Acknowledgments

It has been a crazy ride so far. I never thought I would write books, and there are so many people to thank for making it happen.

Momma and Daddy, without you I would be nothing. Thank you for always being there.

My homegirl Marpha, you a trip, girl! You gave me the courage to write, and now look what you've done! LOL.

To my biggest fan, Sue: You give me some of the most amazing inspiration at some of my darkest hours. Ain't no one like you and never will be, girl. You gotta teach me them karate kicks you're famous for.

Katie, you're the best cellie I could ask for. Who knew a white girl could be so down? LOL.

Dan Broccoli, you my boo.

Cushing Hill Gang forever! Still suckin', Hue Grizz! Urban Books, thanks for believing.

All my girls in lockup, keep ya heads up. They can only keep you down if you let 'em.

To all the corny-ass COs: I'm gettin' paid, suckas.

To my business associates up in Boston: Keep sweepin' it under the rug.

To each and every one of my fans: Thanks for reading and enjoying my stories. I won't stop 'til you had enough. I got nothin' but time.

And last but not least, to God Almighty: Thank you for putting the power of imagination in my head and making it come out through my fingertips.

Chapter 1

Manhunt

"Have you seen this shit?" Mayor Steele showed Dexter Coram, his chief of staff, the headline of the newspaper he was gripping. He was pacing backstage, waiting to go in front of the press and give them an update on the progress of the manhunt for Scar Johnson and Tiphani Fuller—which to this point was nothing.

"Yes, I have, sir." Dexter referred to the headline, which read City Now Needs Mayor to Disappear. The article described the disappearance of Tiphani Fuller, a corrupt circuit court judge who had escaped from police custody. As the headline screamed, the newspaper was calling for the resignation of the mayor over this fiasco.

"My opponent is going to jump all over this. These sons of bitches are blaming me for this corrupt bitch." The mayor threw the newspaper on the floor. He was in a tight battle for state senator, and his opponent was gaining ground quickly. This type of damaging headline could be the nail in the coffin for his hopes of election.

"God, I wish I never fucked her," the mayor muttered to himself. It was scaring the shit out of Mayor Steele that Tiphani could come forward at any time with information on their affair. It was the reason he had recommended her in the first place when the governor was looking for someone to promote to circuit judge. Mayor Steele needed to find her and make a deal with her, because if she wasn't willing to cooperate, then she would just have to be taken out permanently.

"We can spin this, sir," Dexter encouraged.

"How?"

"We bring focus back to Scar Johnson and his ambush of the SWAT team."

"Jesus, are you insane? The man is responsible for killing half the SWAT team. How is that better?"

"Well . . ." Dexter had nothing.

Scar Johnson was a notorious criminal in Baltimore. Along with his drug empire, he had been robbing armored cars—with the help of Tiphani Fuller, who just so happened to be sleeping with him—until she started working with the police and tried to set him up. Before they could arrest him, Scar got wind of her deceit and hatched a plan. He intended to kill Tiphani along with the SWAT team. Unfortunately for him, he was only able to take out half the SWAT team, and Tiphani escaped the ambush. Now both Scar and Tiphani were in hiding, and the mayor was left to answer to the public for this failure.

"Damn! Don't we have any new developments to tell these cocksuckers?" the mayor snapped at Dexter.

"No, sir, I'm afraid we don't." Dexter was used to the mayor's outbursts, especially these days.

"Well, fuck it. I'll just have to lead these leeches on and give 'em enough to think we're making progress." With that, the mayor stepped out from behind the stage to begin the press conference.

The energy in the room was palpable. This was the biggest news story to hit Baltimore in a long time. A circuit judge accused of sleeping with and aiding a known criminal to avoid prosecution, and a mayor losing control of his city; it had all the makings of a Hollywood thriller. The members of the press knew they would be getting a lot of mileage out of this story, and their excitement was obvious. As soon as the mayor entered, the cameras clicked all around, as rapid as gunfire, and reporters rushed to pull out their recording devices and notebooks.

"I know you all have a lot of questions, so let's just begin," the mayor announced.

The questions crashed down on him like a tidal wave. Every reporter spoke at once. From the other side of the door, it sounded like an angry mob about to riot. They all wanted their questions to be heard and answered. One female reporter stood up and yelled her question at the top of her lungs. To take some sort of control of the situation, the mayor pointed at her to signal that he would entertain her question first. Seeing this, the rest of the reporters quieted down and let the woman speak.

"Sir, are you any closer to finding Judge Fuller and Scar Johnson, and is there any evidence that they are hiding together?"

"We have many new leads that I am not at liberty to discuss right now."

The mayor was lying. In fact, there were no leads as to the whereabouts of Tiphani or Scar. It was as if they had both disappeared off the face of the earth.

Again the room erupted in questions. The mayor pointed to another reporter.

"Mr. Mayor, Scar Johnson has been terrorizing this city for too long. He killed half the SWAT team, was sexually involved with a circuit judge who presided over his case and set him free, and he is said to have members of the police force on his payroll. Why haven't you done anything about this?"

"I really do not like to dwell on the past," the mayor said weakly. "Let's move forward and focus on the present and why we are all here."

"There is a manhunt for two fugitives who disappeared—a murderous drug kingpin and a judge who escaped from police custody. This is why we are here. What are you doing to keep the citizens safe?" the reporter demanded.

"Again, I am not at liberty to discuss the specifics of our investigation." The mayor appeared calm to the reporters, but inside he wanted to kill every one of them. He had nothing to give them, yet they were just going to keep on pushing with their bullshit questions.

Another reporter yelled out, "Is there anything you can tell us about any new developments?"

"We are working around the clock to bring these two into custody."

"What exactly are you doing?" an obviously irritated reporter asked.

"I have answered that."

"Are you being paid off by Scar Johnson?" someone yelled out.

"Is it true that you had an affair with Judge Tiphani Fuller?"

The questions were coming rapid fire now. They weren't even waiting for him to respond. It was clear that all the reporters were starting to get annoyed with the mayor, who, they suspected, was avoiding questions and not answering truthfully.

"Now we're getting into gossip and slander territory." The mayor jumped in to slow down this line of questioning. The last thing he needed was for it to be printed in the paper that he was screwing Tiphani Fuller and was as corrupt as she was. "If you continue this line of questioning, I will be forced to end the press conference."

Scar was sitting on the couch watching the news coverage; his exposed torso still glistening with sweat from the marathon threesome he had just engaged in. He was sandwiched in between two women while the television played the latest on the manhunt for him and Tiphani. The rest of his crew was all hanging around in the other room, cutting and bagging coke. Even though there was a manhunt for Scar, it didn't mean business had to stop. Scar didn't become the most notorious gangster in Baltimore by slacking off and running scared.

During sex, Scar had been distracted, thinking about how the fuck he was going to get out of Baltimore. He was feeling the pressure of the manhunt and was watching the news every chance he got to keep up to date on what the police were doing. So far, no one in his crew or on the street had heard anything that would make them think that the police were close to Scar at all. Still, he wanted to play it safe and stay hidden until he knew for sure he was getting out undetected.

All of Scar's safe houses had been raided, so Scar picked a new safe house that would be the ultimate "fuck you" to the police force; he took over Detective Rodriguez's house. After killing her in the ambush, he thought it only fitting that he should hide out at her house.

Scar was also watching the news to see if there was any information about that bitch Tiphani. He was mad at himself for fucking her. He should have known that any woman who fucks her husband's brother is a snake. Scar loved fucking her, and it turned him on that he was fucking his brother Derek's wife, but the second Tiphani ratted him out to that crooked cop Rodriguez, she sealed her own fate. She was a dead woman in Scar's eyes, and when he finally caught up with that lying, scheming bitch, she would be joining the other lying, scheming bitch Rodriguez in hell.

He had ordered the Chief of Police to take her out while she was in police custody, but that bumbling fool fucked up everything and let her disappear without a trace. For all Scar knew she could be in Cuba right now, spending all of the money he had stolen from the armored cars and given to her—money that Scar considered his and now wanted back. He wanted to put an end to her trifling ass for good.

"Get out." Scar ordered the two women to leave as the mayor made his appearance on the TV. "I need to watch this alone."

Scar had been violent lately, and the women didn't want to be the ones to get a beating, so without saying a word, they put their clothes on and left the room, no questions asked. As long as Scar provided them with coke, some money, and good dick, they would do whatever he said. It also didn't hurt that they would be out of harm's way in the next room, where all the coke was.

The mayor started his press conference with a brief statement and then took some questions from the press. Scar sat motionless and listened intensely, hoping to read between the lines and figure out what moves the mayor's office was trying to make.

"Yo, Day!" Scar screamed into the next room. "Come here."

When Day entered, he saw Scar sitting back on the couch with one hand in his lap, the other arm draped over the back of the couch, and both eyes glued to the TV.

"What's up?" Day asked.

Without taking his eyes off of the television, Scar said, "Come here and listen to this crooked motherfucker. Tell me if I'm right and they don't have shit on me. It's like they a chicken with its head cut off, running around in circles with no rhyme, reason, or direction."

Day sat down in a leather recliner. The two of them sat there in silence, watching the mayor give non-answers to the press. He was bobbing and weaving from questions like Muhammad Ali would bob and weave from punches in his prime.

When the press conference ended and the mayor left the podium, Scar picked up the remote and turned off the television.

"What you think?" Scar asked.

"Seems like this nigga don't know shit. I don't think he answered one question. Sounded like if they asked him his name he wouldn't give them a straight answer," Day joked.

"For real, nigga. Don't joke. You think I'm right?"

"In all seriousness, yeah, I think you right. I think if they was close to us, we would know. I got every nigga out there keeping they ears open. We straight," Day said, trying to calm any doubt that might be creeping into Scar's head.

Day needed Scar calm. He needed him in Baltimore. Day wanted revenge on Scar in the worst way, and he didn't want the revenge to be Scar getting picked up by the police. He wanted street justice. He wanted to be the one to take Scar down, just like Scar had been trying to take down Day's mentor, Malek—before Detective Derek Fuller shot him in cold blood. Day was going to make sure they both paid for Malek's death.

Malek was more like an older brother to Day. He had taken Day under his wing and showed him the hustle. Malek was planning to set up shop, make his cash, and then get out. He'd promised to give his operation to Day for his own. Day was getting ready to become a big player in the game, but Scar and Derek put an end to that. Now Day wanted to return the favor.

If Scar got spooked and tried to run without thinking it through, there was a good chance he would get nabbed. The police were pissed and they were working around the clock to find Scar. He had shot and killed several of their own, and when you rattle the nest, the hornets start attacking.

"Stay here until we get the new safe house ready," Day continued. "In the meantime, you worry about the business and stayin' on top. I'll worry about keepin' you outta the eyes of the police."

"You right. They can't touch me! I'm Scar mutha-fuckin' Johnson! I'm the new Teflon Don. I got more than nine lives;

I got hundreds," Scar boasted as his face contorted into an evil grin, the scar on his cheek making him look even more sinister.

"What's the word with this bitch Tiphani? Don't seem like the police know anything. What do we know?" Scar asked.

"To be honest, I don't know, boss. Sticks was handling that for you. I didn't really get on top 'cause I was lettin' him do his thing. Seem like he ain't handlin' his business right." He wanted to make sure that Sticks got the blame for it. This was all playing into his plan to disrupt the organization from the inside.

"You need to start knowing, nigga. I need you on top of all of it." Scar was a little agitated with Day.

"Yo, Sticks!" Scar shouted into the other room before Day had a chance to respond and defend himself.

Immediately, Sticks popped into the room, almost as if he had been standing directly on the other side of the door, waiting like an eager puppy to be let into the house.

"What the fuck, nigga? I barely finished saying your name and you standing in front of me." Scar had a disgusted look on his face.

"I was just walking by the room when you called."

"Whatever. Don't be lying and tryin' to eavesdrop like some bitch. You find out where Tiphani is yet?" Normally Scar would have shot a nigga for acting like that, but right now he needed Sticks alive and on his side. Scar didn't like Sticks and thought he might be gunning for his throne, but he was a businessman and knew that Sticks was willing to do shit none of his other crew would. Sticks was wild and would murk a nigga in a second. So, Scar had to put up with him for now, but kept him at arm's length while keeping an eye on the shifty nigga.

"Nah. After she escaped from the back of the chief's car nobody has seen hide nor hair of that snake bitch. I mean, she still got to be in B-more. With all the roadblocks the cops set up, there ain't no way she got through. If she in B-more, I'll find her." Sticks added a little bravado at the end.

It seemed to Sticks like he constantly had to prove himself to Scar. Sticks had been loyal to Scar since he was a young buck, and he was feeling less than appreciated lately. Scar seemed to be hiding shit from him, and it was starting to really piss Sticks off.

It used to be Timber and Trail that were Scar's main dudes. Sticks was jealous of their position, so he did what he had to do and took those niggas out. After they disappeared, Sticks just played it up to Scar that they were disloyal to him. He thought that after he murked Timber and Trail he would be the main dude Scar turned to for advice, but that shit didn't happen. This punk bitch Day started hounding up on Scar.

Sticks was over this disrespect and was feeling like he could run the crew better himself. He needed to start getting support from some of the new young bucks in the crew and then maneuver his way to the top spot. If that meant deading some niggas along the way, so be it. If that meant going toe to toe with Scar, even better.

"Well then, do it. Find her. Do what you get paid for, nigga. Bring her to me," Scar snapped at Sticks.

"Don't worry. I'm gonna smoke that bitch out of hiding," Sticks replied, trying to keep Scar's confidence in him.

"It ain't gotta be that hard. We got the bitch's kids. When I was fuckin' her on my yacht, she kept talkin' the whole time 'bout how much she missed her kids. Well, I bet she really misses them now," Scar said with a smirk. "As a matter of fact, let's get them little rugrats in here."

He turned his head and yelled, "D.J., Talisa, get your little butts in here."

A few seconds later, the door opened and in came Scar's niece and nephew.

Addressing Scar by his birth name, his seven-year-old nephew said, "Yes, Uncle Stephon?"

"Get your butts over here and give your uncle a hug." Scar softened at the sight of the two young children.

The children ran over to their uncle and Scar scooped them up in his big arms. The kids had been with Scar since he took them the night he ambushed Tiphani, Rodriguez, and the SWAT team. It was easy for Scar to get the kids to come with him since he was their uncle. He just told them that their mommy was on vacation and he was going to take care of them for a while. They loved their uncle and thought he was fun, so they easily went along.

Scar's thinking that night was that he was going to kill Tiphani, take her kids, and then use them as leverage to control their father—who just happened to be Scar's brother. Well, Tiphani escaped death, but he still got her kids and could use them to force his brother Derek, who was a cop, to help him escape from Baltimore. One thing he didn't plan was that the kids would be so damn cute. They were the only people in Scar's life that he could genuinely trust. Their love for him was the only unconditional love Scar had felt ever since he was placed in foster care at the age of four. This clouded his judgment when it came to them. He wanted to use them and toss them like every other person in his life, but he wasn't sure if he would be able to do that to them. His emotions might get in the way.

Day and Sticks both stood there feeling a little uneasy. Neither one of them had ever seen any softness in Scar whatsoever, so standing there while he showed this softer side made them uncomfortable. They were actually afraid that if Scar realized he was being watched while letting his tough demeanor fade, he would lash out with double the usual venom and they would be the recipients. It was not something either one wanted to experience.

Despite their uneasiness, though, they both took note, thinking that they may be able to use this weakness against him later. Day not only wanted to destroy Scar physically, but also mentally, and this might be one way to make Scar feel the mental anguish that he felt when Malek was killed. Even though Sticks didn't care if the little shits lived or died, he wanted to take everything that Scar had, and seeing Scar's reaction toward the kids made Sticks want them.

"Y'all want some ice cream?" Scar asked his niece and nephew.

"Yeah!" They screamed in unison.

"Yo, Sticks, take these two out for some ice cream."

"You want me babysittin' now?" Sticks wrinkled his face in disgust.

"No. I want you to take them out for some ice cream," Scar said methodically as he mean-mugged Sticks. He didn't want to alert the kids to any problems since they were still wrapped up in Scar's muscular arms.

"Why can't Day do it? I got some shit I got to take care of," Sticks replied, sounding like a thirteen-year-old trying to get out of doing his chores.

Scar put the kids down and told them to go and get ready. After they left the room, he spun around and rushed Sticks.

"Muthafucka, don't you be cursing in front of them kids!" Scar got right up in Sticks' face. "When I tell you to do something, you do it. I don't give a fuck what you gotta do. Right now you taking them for some fuckin' ice cream. I oughta bust you in the jaw for that shit." Scar was heated and looked like he was about to go ballistic.

Day was standing there watching the drama escalate, and he jumped in to calm the situation. He wanted to make Sticks look like an ass as well.

"Yo, yo, yo! Chill. I'll take 'em. It ain't all that," he said, trying to get between the two. It was useless, since by this point they were nose to nose.

After a few seconds of silently staring at each other, Sticks gently backed away from Scar. "No, no. You right. My shit can wait. I'll take them little ones for ice cream. It's all good," he said, while in his head he was screaming, *Fuck you, nigga! I should murk your ass right here and now!*

"That's right. You will." Scar turned his back on Sticks and returned to the couch to watch the news coverage.

Sticks wanted so bad to pop Scar, but he knew he needed to make sure that some of the crew would have his back. If he were to kill Scar right now, most niggas in the crew would retaliate and dead his ass for doing so. He was going to have to play this smooth. It would take some time and planning, but Sticks was more determined now than ever before. This disrespect was the last straw. Making a nigga babysit was some disrespectful, punk-ass shit. Before he did something that wouldn't be in his best interest, Sticks thought it best if he got out of there.

"Ay yo, I'ma go." Sticks turned to leave.

"Me too, boss." Day said.

"Wait."

Both Day and Sticks stopped in their tracks. Sticks was thinking, *What the fuck this nigga want now?* Day was thinking, *Oh fuck. What?*

"Day, you stay with me," Scar said, still looking at the television.

This almost sent Sticks into a full-on rage. He was furious that Day was getting special treatment over him. He thought to himself, *I'ma do both these niggas!* He played it cool and stayed calm on the outside, while his insides were erupting like a volcano. Without saying another word, he left to get ice cream.

After Sticks left the room, Scar waited a minute or two and then had Day make sure he wasn't eavesdropping. Day opened the door and saw no signs of Sticks. He figured Sticks was furious but wouldn't be stupid enough to stay and listen. He was probably halfway to the ice cream parlor by now.

"No sign of him, boss," Day reported.

"Something ain't right with that nigga. He on edge. I want you to watch him. Ever since Trail been missing, I ain't trusted his ass," Scar calmly said, looking off into space like he was trying to figure it out in his own head as he was saying it.

"Whatever you want," Day agreed.

Chapter 2

Back from the Dead?

Immediately following the press conference, the mayor went to his office and gathered his staff for an emergency meeting. With his campaign for state senator in danger of spiraling out of control, and his struggle to keep order in the city, the mayor was in desperate need of some good news. He was hoping that one of his staff members would deliver it.

The mayor sat behind his large oak desk and watched as the members of his staff entered the spacious office. Everyone took their respective places, and the mayor leaned back in his leather chair and surveyed the room. They just sat there staring at the mayor, waiting for him to say something. The longer no one said anything, the more nervous the staff started to become. With the tension and confusion mounting, Dexter Coram finally broke the ice.

"Well, I think that went well," the ever positive chief of staff began.

Everyone in the room could feel the collective sigh of relief as the tension was finally released. Following Dexter's lead, the whole staff nodded their heads in agreement. They all wanted to stay positive and encourage the mayor. To put it plain and simple, their futures depended on the mayor's future. If the mayor lost his job, they would also be losing their jobs.

Truthfully, they knew that before the mayor would allow himself to go down, he would take any one of them down first. In order to save his own ass, he wouldn't hesitate to blame one of his staff for what was going on. Therefore, they all wanted to kiss his ass to avoid becoming the sacrificial lamb.

They had good reason to believe that the mayor would throw any one of them under the bus based on what they saw him doing to Tiphani Fuller. Back in the day, it seemed like Tiphani was always getting special treatment from the mayor, no matter how many times she fucked up a case, or how unprofessional she acted. None of the mayor's staff liked her because they felt that she was a detriment to their office, but the mayor would ignore their pleas to fire her. There were always rumors of an affair between Tiphani and the mayor, but when he went so far as to recommend her for a promotion to the circuit court, that pretty much confirmed it in everyone's eyes. They were sure that he was screwing her.

Now, all of a sudden, when his campaign for state senate was in trouble and he needed a boost in his public perception, Tiphani was being outed as a corrupt judge, and a statewide manhunt was on for her. When it was his career on the line, he had no problem airing her dirty laundry to the world. Obviously the only person the mayor cared about was himself. His actions left the staff feeling like it was every man for himself.

"Oh, you think it went very well, huh? I should fire your ass for saying that," the mayor responded to Dexter. "Does anyone have anything to say? Any information?" The mayor was losing his patience.

After a few more seconds of silence, Chief of Police Hill cleared his throat and finally spoke up. He had hoped to perhaps go unnoticed and get out of this meeting without having to say anything, but that wasn't about to happen. Everyone in the room was staring at him.

"Well, sir, as you know, this is our top priority. All other cases have been put on hold. Everyone on the police force is working overtime to find and capture the two suspects. We have called in every favor we have to every agency in the state to assist us in this manhunt—"

The mayor let out an exasperated sigh. "Yes, I know all of this. Most of this was done on my request. Tell me something I don't know, you imbecile!" His patience was gone.

Knowing the mayor was definitely not going to like what he was about to hear, the chief continued. "That's it, sir. Unfortunately, with all of the manpower and hours we are spending, we have nothing. No trace of either one of the suspects.

"One theory is that they escaped the country together. There were some rumors that Judge Fuller had an overseas bank account, but we can't find any evidence of that." Chief Hill stopped for a second to watch the mayor and gauge any reaction.

Hoping to put some sort of positive spin on it, he continued, "I'm working my men to death on this one. We haven't given up, and we are certain we will come up with something eventually."

This pissed the mayor off. Blood rose to his face and he turned bright red. Then, at the top of his lungs, he started screaming, "Eventually! When the fuck is that going to be? You stupid son of—"

"Mr. Mayor, you have a phone call," his secretary announced over the intercom, interrupting him before he could really lay into Chief Hill.

"Not now, Susan."

"But, sir, he won't stop calling. He says it's extremely urgent."

"I don't care! Take a message!" Mayor Steele screamed into the intercom.

"He told me to tell you it's Derek Fuller calling from prison."

The mayor's day had just gone from bad to worse. All the blood that had rushed to Mayor Steele's face disappeared instantly, and a look of shock swept over his face. He was not expecting to hear that name, especially since he had ordered Derek Fuller murdered and had gotten word that the job had been done. Did the guy he paid to kill Derek lie to him? How was this possible? Was this really Fuller, or someone pretending to be him? The mayor's mind was racing with hundreds of different scenarios.

"Everybody out," he commanded.

Happy to have an excuse to leave and end the mayor's tirade, the whole staff got up and out of the office without any hesitation. Being around the mayor right now was a nightmare, and every minute in his presence was just another chance to get screamed at and possibly fired.

As the staff rushed out of the room, the mayor added, "Chief Hill, you can stay in the waiting room. We're not done yet." The rest of the staff was relieved not to hear their names. They were safe from the mayor's wrath for now.

As the door shut after the last staff member exited, the mayor put his hand on the phone receiver, took a deep breath, and picked up the phone.

"Derek!" he said in his most jovial tone, trying to mask the shock he was actually feeling. "How are you? What can I do for you?"

He was cursing himself on the inside for not following up and checking with the prison to confirm that Derek was really dead. He had gotten the phone call saying the job was done, and normally he would have double checked it. With everything going on and being so distracted, he didn't have time and just took the information as fact.

"It's about time you fucking answered! I've been calling, and your bitch secretary wouldn't put me through. I need to get the fuck out of here right now! You promised me weeks ago to get me out. You know I was set up by Scar and I didn't kill Archie. Now, get me out of here!" Derek demanded.

Staying calm, the mayor answered Derek. "Well, I'm not sure how easy that's going to be. I don't know if you've seen the news, but right now I have my hands full with your ex-wife and her lover, Scar Johnson."

"I don't give a fuck!" Derek was starting to sound desperate. "You need to get my ass out of here now! Scar Johnson has threatened my family and tried to have me killed here in prison."

Hearing that put a smile on Mayor Steele's face. Derek thought that the attempt on his life was ordered by Scar, not the mayor. This was the best bit of information the mayor had received in a long time. Even though the attempt on Derek's life didn't work, at least the blame wasn't being put on the mayor. Just to make sure he was in the clear, he wanted to get Derek to clarify. He wanted to be certain there wasn't another attempt on Derek's life that Scar actually did order. So, he asked, "What do you mean, Scar tried to have you killed?"

"There was some fake-ass CO who set me up and stabbed me like forty times. I nearly died. I spent, like, thirty days in the fuckin' hospital ward in ICU before I finally woke up from a coma. When they found out I was still alive, he sent over one of his boys to threaten me. He told me that if I didn't cooperate and help Scar get out of Baltimore, they would mail my kids' body parts to me one by one."

This phone call kept getting better for the mayor. Not only was he not being blamed for Derek's attempted murder, he just found out that Scar Johnson was still in Baltimore and looking for a way out. At the rate it was going, the case would be solved and the mayor would be guaranteed his senate seat by the end of the call.

"Did they say anything about Tiphani's whereabouts?" the mayor eagerly asked.

"No. I don't care about that deceitful whore. I need to get out of here and rescue my kids!" The urgency in Derek's voice was evident.

"I don't know if that's possible. How will it look if I release the crooked cop husband of the crooked, whoring Justice Fuller? Don't forget, you are in jail for conspiracy and first degree murder. The citizens will have me hung in the town square." The mayor referenced an old custom from medieval times.

"I don't give a fuck! My kids are in danger! You need to find Scar, he needs my help. If I get out, he will find me. Get me out and I will find Scar Johnson. I can also guarantee that Tiphani will appear from the hole she's hiding in." The intensity and desperation from Derek were coming right through the phone.

The mayor remained silent and contemplated this last offer. He was weighing his options. Within this five minute phone call, an incarcerated Detective Fuller had given him more information about Scar than the entire Baltimore police force could. What more would he be able to find out if he was a free man?

As desperate as Derek was to find his kids, the mayor was just as desperate to capture Scar and Tiphani. He needed to take this chance. He would find a way of releasing Derek quietly. If he was lucky, the press would be so consumed with the manhunts that they wouldn't even realize that Derek had been released.

"Okay. Give me a day or two. I'll get you out," the mayor replied.

"Thank you. Thank you. We will get Scar. I promise." A relieved Derek ended the call.

The mayor hung up the phone and leaned back in his chair, thinking, *I hope I don't regret this.*

"Susan, send Chief Hill in here," the mayor said into the intercom.

A moment later, the door to the mayor's office opened and the chief walked in. He was expecting the mayor to pick up where he left off and start screaming at him again. So, to try to stop it before it started, he began to speak immediately.

"Sir, about before . . . we—"

"Sit down, Chief," the mayor interrupted. "I just had an interesting conversation. It seems that this son of a bitch Scar Johnson is still in Baltimore."

A surprised chief asked, "How do you know, sir?"

"Detective Derek Fuller told me. He knows more from prison than your whole police force. Doesn't say much for you or Baltimore's finest, does it?"

"With all due respect, sir, he's a crooked cop. How do you know he's telling the truth?"

"Because he is. You have fucked this whole investigation up. I don't see why I need you around if I can get the answers I need from prisoners. Do you want your job, Chief Hill?"

"Yes, sir, I do. Do you want me to interview Detective Fuller and see what he knows?" Chief Hill felt like he was fighting for his job at this point.

"No. Detective Fuller is going to be quietly released. When he gets out, I want you to know his every move, and after he leads us to Scar Johnson, I want you to kill both of them. Then I want you to find Judge Fuller and kill her too," Mayor Steele calmly ordered.

He wanted Derek dead to make sure he definitely stayed quiet. The mayor couldn't risk Derek revealing that he, the mayor of the city, had struck a deal with a convicted dirty cop who was a cop killer himself.

Chief Hill was stunned. He couldn't tell if the mayor was serious. In order to not get into any more trouble, he decided to stay silent.

"Do you understand? If this doesn't happen, I will personally make sure that you not only lose your job, but that you get publicly humiliated as well. I may even make it look like you were involved with Scar and Tiphani in some way. Hell, you shouldn't have a job right now after you fucked up and let judge Fuller escape," the mayor threatened as he coldly stared at the chief.

"Yes, sir, I understand. I can do that," Chief Hill reluctantly agreed. He was so nervous he didn't even realize that he had been gripping the arms of the chair so tight that he started to put marks in the leather. He was stuck. He had to say yes, and he had to come through. If the mayor went through with his threat, Chief Hill would never be able to get a job again, and even worse, would probably be thrown in jail for conspiracy. He knew that a Chief of Police in prison would not last very long. Every inmate in the joint would be gunning for his ass so they could make a name for themselves.

"Now, get out of here. I need to figure out how to get Detective Fuller out of jail without the press finding out."

"Yes, sir." Chief Hill was so anxious to leave he practically leapt from the chair. How did he end up in this situation? Another life fucked up by Scar Johnson.

As Chief Hill walked down the corridor of City Hall, he contemplated how he had gotten so involved with Scar. If he hadn't been so greedy and taken those payoffs, he would be fine. He was thinking he should have killed Scar when he had the chance. Well, now was his chance, and he wasn't going to fuck it up this time. Chief Hill was prepared to kill anyone he needed to in order to keep his position of power—starting with Derek, Scar, and Tiphani.

Chapter 3

Accidental Family

Halleigh walked out of the bedroom and down the hall toward the living room. She had been napping. Between taking care of her son, following members of Scar's crew, and worrying about Dayvid, she wasn't getting much sleep at night. So, any chance she got during the day to catch up on some rest, she did. All of it was wearing her down, but she was determined to follow through with her promise to exact revenge on Scar for the death of her husband, Malek.

After fleeing from Flint, Michigan to start a new life with Halleigh, Malek just wanted a small piece of the streets so he could support his family, but Scar wouldn't allow it. In Halleigh's eyes, Scar was greedy. He could easily have let Malek have his small share and still ruled Baltimore, but instead, Malek ended up dead. So, Halleigh was going to teach Scar a lesson. She was going to teach Scar that greed kills, motherfucker.

As she approached the living room, she heard sounds of cheering coming from not only the people in the room, but from the television as well. She stood in the entryway and leaned against the door frame with her arms crossed in front of her, smiling at what she saw. Sitting on the couch with their backs to her were Dayvid and her son, Malek Jr., watching the Ravens game. She stood there for a few minutes just taking it all in, and it made her happy. To see her baby boy mimicking Dayvid, cheering every time Dayvid did and having such a great time with a positive male role model was the best thing in the world.

Malek Jr. would get extra energy and happiness whenever Dayvid was around. For those few minutes, she forgot about everything else going on in her life and she began to daydream.

She started to picture that it was Malek and his son sitting there cheering on their favorite football team while she was in the kitchen cooking dinner for her family. When she snapped out of her daydream and realized Malek wasn't there, she got a little sad. She missed him, and hadn't realized just how much until then. She had been so focused on her revenge plot with Dayvid and taking care of little Malek that she hadn't allowed herself any time to think about the past. Now it all hit her like a ton of bricks.

She thought back to all the events in her life that had led her up to this point, from the moment she met Malek to losing contact with him to being forced into prostitution, and then finally reuniting with Malek. When they had a son and escaped from Flint, Halleigh thought her life was on track to be happily ever after—until Malek was gunned down in their front yard right in front of her. It was all too much for her to handle. If she allowed herself to think about it for too long, she would lose control, and she couldn't afford to do that. She had a beautiful baby boy that she was determined to raise right. She wasn't going to let him make the same mistakes she made in her life.

Malek Jr. was about the same age as Halleigh was when she lost her father. The one thing she wished growing up was to have a dad around the house. She always felt her life would have been so much better if a loving father had been in the picture. Her mom wouldn't have gotten hooked on crack, she wouldn't have had strange men coming in and out of the house all the time, and Halleigh wouldn't have gotten raped by a few of those strange men. She wished now that Malek Jr. could have a loving father in the house, but Scar Johnson and Detective Derek Fuller took that away from him.

"Mommy! They're winning!" Malek Jr. excitedly exclaimed when he saw Halleigh standing behind him.

"I see, baby," she said, breaking out of her own thoughts and putting a smile on her face for her boy.

"Watch. It fun." Malek Jr. scooted closer to Dayvid to make room for Halleigh on the couch.

"Yeah, it's fun. Come watch." Dayvid smiled.

"How about I make you some popcorn first?" Halleigh asked.

Malek Jr. and Dayvid turned to one another with wide eyes and smiles across their faces and gave each other a pound. "Yes!" they both said, not so much as an answer to the question, but as an agreement with each other at how awesome the idea was.

Halleigh chuckled at the sight of Dayvid's big fist and Malek Jr.'s tiny fist bumping into each other.

A few minutes later, Halleigh came back from the kitchen. "Popcorn's ready," she said as she entered the room and sat in the space that Malek Jr. had made for her on the couch.

The three of them sat there eating popcorn and watching football. It was an exciting game that kept them riveted to the action. Somewhere around the middle of the fourth quarter, Malek Jr. starting getting sleepy. He was fighting to stay awake and watch the end of the game. He snuggled his head into his mama's chest as he reached over and grabbed Dayvid's hand.

"I like this," he said as his eyelids became heavier with every passing second.

"You like the game, baby?" Halleigh asked her sleepy little boy.

"No," he replied.

Before Halleigh could even ask what he meant, little Malek was asleep. Halleigh looked down at her now sleeping boy and then over at Day, who was already looking at her. They stared at each other. Halleigh didn't understand what her baby boy was referring to. Then Dayvid said, "I like this too," and grinned.

Suddenly, Halleigh became a little nervous and looked down at her boy in order to break eye contact with Dayvid. His words helped her understand what her little boy meant. It wasn't the game he was referring to; it was the moment. Malek liked everything about that moment—watching football, eating popcorn, and sitting between a man and his mama. To his little mind, it felt like a family—the kind of family Halleigh had been daydreaming about no more than an hour ago.

"I'll take him to bed." Not knowing how to react and already feeling a bit uncomfortable, Halleigh started to gather Malek Jr. in her arms.

"Okay." Dayvid helped her with her son. "Good night, M.J." he said as he kissed the boy on his forehead.

He watched Halleigh carry the boy down the hall and into his bedroom. Even though she was carrying a child in her arms, Dayvid still couldn't help but check out Halleigh's bangin' body. Dayvid had always thought Halleigh was fine, but lately it seemed to him that he was maybe feeling a little more than just sexual attraction to her. He would never say anything to her about it, though. He wouldn't disrespect his deceased friend Malek like that. Besides, he saw how Halleigh just reacted when all he did was agree with her son and say how good it felt to be on that couch with them. She obviously wasn't feeling the same thing that he was.

"Well," Halleigh said as she sat back down on the couch after putting her son to bed. "That little man was out."

"Yeah, he sure was. That little dude is mad fun to watch the game with. He know nothing about what's happenin' on the screen, but he still be rootin'," Dayvid said with a smile on his face.

"Yeah, he's cute," she agreed, trying to decide if she should mention anything about the awkward moment that just happened between them or just leave it.

Dayvid sat there thinking the same thing, but decided he wasn't going to be the one to say anything about it. He just sat there waiting for Halleigh to break the silence. After a few seconds, Dayvid checked the time on his phone.

"I should go. Gotta see Scar and keep up this charade. Don't want him to stop trusting Day," he said, referring to the name that he used with Scar. "I think he's getting paranoid. Seems like he ain't trustin' no one right now. 'Cept me, of course." He finished with a mischievous grin across his face.

"Good. Fuck him." Halleigh pursed her lips. "We should just ice him now. Make it look like the cops did it."

"It ain't that easy. He never leaves his place. I can't make it look like the cops unless he go outside, and that shit ain't happenin'. He playin' it real safe right now."

"I don't know how much longer I can wait." Halleigh was getting impatient and wanted Scar dead now.

"It won't be long. We just have to hold out. He has me stayin' real close to him. It's just a matter of time."

Dayvid was trying to stall Halleigh and keep her satisfied as to the progress of their plan. As he became more involved in Scar's crew, he started thinking that he could take over, if not all of the business, at least a part of it. He saw that he could live a nice life with a piece of that action. He was afraid that Halleigh wouldn't go for that, so he kept that part of his plan to himself. Her only focus was to make Scar suffer while he died. She didn't care about his money or his empire. In fact, after they had destroyed Scar, she wanted nothing to do with the streets. Malek had left her with a nice chunk of change that she could live on.

"It better be soon," she warned.

"It will, I promise. I gotta go," he said as he put on his coat and rushed to the door, leaving Halleigh sitting on the couch.

Chapter 4

Planning my Comeback

The midday Florida sun was shining through the window. Tiphani lay on the bed naked, next to Cecil, with their legs intertwined. They had just finished another one of their marathon fuck sessions. Even with all of the stress in her life, Tiphani was still just as insatiable as ever. She couldn't get enough dick.

Cecil needed a breather. He had never met a woman so sex crazed that she wore him out. It was usually the other way around. He could go on all night, usually ending with the women begging him to stop because they couldn't handle it anymore. But not Tiphani. She was an animal; it was never enough for her. What he didn't know was that Tiphani had other motives. She knew that if she kept fucking Cecil this good, she could probably get him to do whatever she wanted.

Tiphani had ended up here in Florida after escaping from the back of Chief Hill's car in Baltimore. She had run down the road until an understanding truck driver picked her up. Without asking any questions, he let her hide in the back of his cab under some nasty old blankets.

When the driver had to stop at the roadblock leading out of Maryland, the cop who was to check the truck's interior stuck his head inside the window, took one sniff of the funky body odor emanating from the driver, and decided not to investigate any further. The officer was not about to subject his nose to the nastiest stench he had ever smelled for any longer than he had to. He let the driver pass through without searching the truck.

To Tiphani's surprise, the driver never once made a move on her or demanded sex in return for helping her. He was a happily married, churchgoing man, who loved his wife and never once thought of cheating on her. He just wanted to help those in need and never passed judgment on any human. He told Tiphani that he left the judgment up to God and the person's own conscience. He followed in Jesus' teachings and loved all men equally.

The driver transported Tiphani across several state lines, all the way to Fort Lauderdale, Florida. She felt like he was her guardian angel.

The first thing she did in Florida was to make contact with her offshore bank accounts. She needed money to set herself up with a place to stay. She was going to be dealing strictly in cash from here on out. The offshore bank was more than happy to wire her money. They took the information for the Western Union that Tiphani provided, and within minutes, she had several thousand dollars. Every few days, she would have them send more money, each time to a different location.

Having more than enough to live on, she started in on her plan to get back to Baltimore. She rented an apartment overlooking the water in Fort Lauderdale, bought a computer, and got to work. Every morning, she would catch up on the news coming out of Baltimore. It seemed to her that they were really fucking up and nowhere near finding her or Scar.

Her afternoons were spent searching the databases of all the prisons in the area, carefully researching certain prisoners who were about to be released. She had a plan, and she would need someone with some special skills. The easiest place she could think to find someone like that was in the prison system.

When she would find a prisoner who seemed like he might be a candidate, she would go to the prison to visit as a lawyer. She had some fake IDs and fake business cards made up, which made it easy for her to go in and out of the prisons. Tiphani would visit under the premise that she was a defense attorney looking to do pro bono work. She would say she thought that there might be grounds to sue the government on behalf of the prisoner, due to a technicality in their case. Little did the prisoners know that it was basically one big audition to see if they fit in with what Tiphani needed.

After a while, Tiphani was becoming frustrated. There had been several prisoners she made contact with, but none were good enough. One was just too damn stupid and would never be able to help her, one had clearly turned into a punk and was now some other inmate's bitch and was too worried about looking pretty, and one was so butt ugly that she couldn't stand to look at him for even a second. She was starting to think that she would have to move her search to another state.

This wasn't what she wanted to do. Moving around too much and crossing state lines would give more people an opportunity to recognize her. Finding another apartment to rent where the owner would be willing to accept cash with no questions might not be as easy. She was taking a huge risk already, and with her escape being national news, Tiphani knew visiting prisoners wouldn't be safe for much longer.

She decided she would give her search through the Florida prison system one last chance before coming up with a new plan—and she was happy she did.

Deciding to go back through prisons she'd already researched proved to be fruitful. She locked on to one prisoner in particular that looked on paper like the perfect candidate. He was a former Army sergeant who was in prison for aggravated assault and about to be released.

When Tiphani first laid eyes on Cecil, she got wet between her legs. He was six foot four of pure muscle, bald and full of confidence. His eyes were what really made him stand out. Not only were they the perfect almond shape, but they each had their own color. His left eye was light hazel, and his right eye was dark brown. Tiphani realized this must be why he had the nickname Two-tone.

He walked in the empty interview room and his energy immediately filled the space. The way the guards were reacting to him, he obviously commanded their respect. She knew right away that she had found her man.

He sat down across the metal table from her and looked directly into her eyes. She felt like he could see right through her into her soul. She shivered a bit, but immediately composed herself and went into lawyer mode. She shuffled a few papers around before she began. He stayed silent and just watched her with suspicion.

She folded her hands in front of her on the table and began. "So, you know why I am here?"

"I know why you say you're here."

"Good. So I don't need to go into specifics."

"I think you do." Cecil looked her right in her eyes as if he were daring her to convince him.

"Okay. I see you're a man who demands all the facts before making a decision." She then proceeded to tell the same bullshit story she told to every other prisoner she had interviewed.

Cecil continued staring at her as he remained silent. His apparent self-confidence was turning Tiphani on, but also throwing her off.

"Well, ah, I was a . . ." She reached down and fumbled with her briefcase that sat on the floor beside her chair and pulled out some folders. Cecil still said nothing.

Tiphani continued, "I was, ah, looking through some files of some old cases, and yours was of particular interest to me." She placed a file on the table in front of her.

"Why?" Cecil asked.

"Well, I am doing pro bono work."

"That doesn't answer my question. Why is my case interesting to you?"

"I believe very much in justice, and in your case, I think there has been great injustice. There seems to be some discrepancies in your case and in the evidence provided against you."

"Like what? Can I see my file you have in front of you?"

"Oh, this is confidential material, and I can't show you unless we actually start working together." She put the folder back in the briefcase. "There are many things that interested me about your case, but I don't want to get into specifics right here. You never know who could be listening." Tiphani whispered the last sentence and gave a flirtatious smile.

"We are in this room alone. No one is listening but me. Tell me about these discrepancies." Cecil still had not averted his eyes from Tiphani.

"Okay. I believe some of the evidence might have been tampered with. Some of the testimony given was perhaps false. There are other things, but now is not the time to go into all of that. I am here to speak with you about your side of the story. I want to take this case when you are released, which I believe is going to be soon. Am I right? I just want reassurance from you that you will be in it one hundred percent once we start going forward with the lawsuit. I can foresee a big payday for you. "

Her story was well rehearsed, and to someone not versed in the law and not paying close attention, it would sound legitimate. All of the other prisoners bought into it, but not Cecil. He was skeptical. Her story didn't sound right to him. It sounded too rehearsed and unnatural. This was perhaps because he had made her nervous and flustered and had thrown her off her game. The entire time she was giving her speech, she couldn't stop imagining riding his dick.

"So, what do you think?" she asked.

"Sounds like bullshit to me."

"I assure you it's not."

"Look, stop lying. Why are you really here? Did someone send you?"

Tiphani thought for a second. How else could she come at him? Let's try a different approach, she thought.

"What did you do in the Army?"

"Explosive Ordinance Disposal. E.O.D. specialist. Is that why you are here? I don't have time for this." He turned to call the guard.

Tiphani knew it was no use in trying to keep up the lie. He was too smart to fall for her story, and besides, he had her way off her game.

"Wait. I'll tell you why I'm really here." She paused, looked down to stall for time so she could think up something. Nothing was coming. He waited a few moments then turned again for the guard.

"I wanted to meet you," she blurted out.

"Why?"

"Honestly?I saw your picture and I thought you were fine. I was hoping that we might get together when you get released." It was the first thing that came to her head. Anyway, it was based in truth; it wasn't all a lie.

"You sayin' you want to fuck me when I get out?" Her knees got weak. She got hot all over, and she was speechless for a moment.

"Yes."

"Why should we wait 'til I get out?"

Tiphani said nothing. She wasn't sure what he was saying. She thought she knew, but she wasn't sure.

"Let's see how fine you think I am." He got up from his seat and walked over to the guard. They exchanged a few whispered words and then the guard stepped out of the room.

Cecil walked back over to Tiphani and stood next to her chair. She remained silent and turned her head toward him. He placed his hand on her chin and lifted her face so their eyes met.

"If you want to fuck, then let's fuck," he propositioned.

She slowly stood up from her chair like she was in a trance. When she stood fully erect, time briefly stood still; then they started kissing each other. Cecil didn't waste any time. He pulled Tiphani's skirt above her waist, ripped open her stockings, and yanked her panties off. With her pussy exposed, Cecil spun her around and powerfully bent her over the table. He pulled down his pants, unleashed his dick, and forcefully plunged into her.

She gasped at the abruptness of it, but took it all in. She loved it. She hadn't been fucked like this since she was with Scar.

"Fuck me hard."

He pounded into her with authority. He had complete control over her. She was pushing back, trying to get every last inch of him.

"Oh yeah, daddy. Spank me."

He obliged by smacking her ass several times, leaving hand prints. He spread her ass cheeks and continued his assault.

The harder the better was Tiphani's motto. She needed this.

Finally, Cecil pulled out of her with a groan and shot his cum all over her ass. She reached around and wiped it all up then licked it off her hand. She stayed bent over the table with her arms and legs spread out until he told her to get up.

"Is that what you wanted to do when I got out of here?"

"Mmmm. That was better than I could have dreamed."

"Give me your card. I'll holla at you when I'm sprung." She pulled her skirt down then took a business card from her briefcase.

"You can call me at this number. It's my private cell." She wrote her number on the back of her fake business card. He took it and walked to the door and had the guard let him out. She composed herself, gathered her things, and left shortly after.

Cecil "Two-tone" White was released a little over a week later. He called her the second he stepped foot outside of Everglades Correctional Institution. She picked him up drove him back to Fort Lauderdale, and they hadn't been away from each other yet.

Now, here they were, naked and in bed, the place they spent most of their time. When they were hungry, Tiphani would either order in or send Cecil out to get food. She didn't see the need to take the chance to go outside and be recognized. She was happy to stay inside, get fucked, and begin her psychological breakdown of Two-tone.

Tiphani figured it was time to put her plan in motion. She got up from the bed and stood in front of the window that looked out over the ocean. Standing there naked, with her arms crossed in front of her, she took in a deep breath and let out a heavy sigh.

Cecil rolled over when he heard the sigh. "What's wrong, baby?"

This is too easy, she thought. "Nothing."

"Something's on your mind. Tell me."

Like an Oscar-winning actress, she took a dramatic pause, kept staring out the window, and let a few tears fall from her eyes. "It's just . . ." Another pause. "I'm thinking of my children." Tiphani had yet to tell Cecil anything about her past. This was the first he was hearing anything about children.

"You have kids? Where are they?"

"They were taken from me."

Cecil propped himself up on his elbows. "By who? What do you mean?"

She turned to him with tears in her eyes. Her act was pulling him in. It was much easier than she had expected. *Maybe I should be an actress,* she thought then quickly got back on track. She was going in for the kill now. She was going to tug on his heartstrings.

"I have a confession to make. Promise you won't be mad."

"Of course not. Tell me." She had his full attention now.

"I have a past that I haven't told you about."

"We all do."

"Mine is complicated and twisted."

"Can't be any worse than mine. I'm a convict," he joked, trying to lighten her mood.

She smiled a bit to let him know she got his little joke.

"Well, first I want to tell you I'm down here hiding, and that I'm wanted by the law."

"So you're not a lawyer?"

"No, I am a lawyer. In fact, I'm a judge, but I was set up, and now they're looking for me. See, I was married to a man, Detective Derek Fuller—he's the man I had my children with. We had a fine marriage, except for one problem. He was awful in bed. I mean, he was the worst fuck ever. He was the ultimate minute man. Heck, I was lucky if he lasted a minute.

"Anyway, he has a brother, Scar Johnson, who is a major drug dealer in Baltimore. Those two don't get along. Well, they did get along, until Derek thought that Scar was fucking me."

Tiphani looked Cecil in the eyes to reinforce this next lie. "He wasn't." She paused to see if Cecil believed her. He seemed to, so she proceeded. "I thought he was just being a good brother-in-law and listening to my frustrations about my husband. Little did I know he was using me so I would help him in his trial and keep him out of prison. I was so gullible." She looked to Cecil with puppy-dog eyes to gain his sympathy.

"So, after Scar avoided jail, he turned on me. I think he and the mayor started working together to ruin my career and my life. Somehow, they made up a tape that sounded like Scar and I having sex and played it for the whole city of Baltimore to hear." She started crying.

"Wait, why would the mayor do anything like that? And why would he work with a drug dealer? For that matter, why would Scar turn on you? You're his brother's wife." Cecil became skeptical of this tale.

Tiphani sniffled and wiped her tears. She took a second to compose herself and think of how she could explain all of this and still look like she was just a victim.

"I walked in on the mayor fucking one of the district attorneys. He's been having an affair with her for years. He kept sending his chief of staff, Dexter, this squirrely creep with hairy ears, to threaten me and keep me quiet. He probably worked with Scar because I'd just set him free. They probably worked out some deal and made the tape so I would look like a corrupt judge. Scar wanted me out of the picture because he thought I turned on him."

Pretending that she was about to break down again, she took a deep breath like she was gathering her emotions and continued. *This was turning into a masterful acting job.* "He thought I was ratting him out for robbing armored cars, but I was just talking with my friend, who happened to be a detective. Next thing I know, he killed her then came after me, but I escaped—not only once, but twice.

"When I got arrested for corruption, the police chief came and said he was transferring me, but I knew better. He was going to kill me. I wriggled out of the handcuffs and jumped out of the back of his moving car and ran away. Some trucker picked me up and drove me here to Florida."

"What about your husband?" Cecil was trying to keep everything in this story straight. So far it seemed legit to him.

"He was threatening to kill me too. He ended up going to jail for murder. He killed the entire unit he was in charge of. I knew he wasn't the straightest cop out there, especially since he had a drug dealing brother, but I didn't think he would resort to murdering his friends. I'm such a fool." She broke down in tears and heaving sighs of woe. "My kids were kidnapped and now are God knows where. They had nothing to do with anything."

"These crooked mu'fuckas." Cecil slowly shook his head in disbelief. He was getting angry at the injustice he thought had been done to Tiphani.

Cecil hugged her with his massive arms. He tried to calm her down by stroking her hair and rubbing her back. She continued to sob. She wasn't about to stop this act now.

"I just want my children back and for them to be safe. I don't know what to do. I'm wanted, I have no friends left, and I'm not strong enough to fight them," she said through more tears and heaving sobs.

"You have me."

She looked up at him with those same puppy-dog eyes. "Really? My story doesn't scare you away?"

"Hell no."

She kissed him. "I'm afraid. I don't know how to go up against those men." Now she was playing to his manly ego.

He took it bait, line, and sinker. "I have a few ideas. I can help you, girl."

"You mean it? You'll help me?"

"I will do whatever it takes to get those kids back for you and to take revenge on all those mu'fuckas."

She hooked him. She couldn't believe how easy it actually was. She guessed it was true that men think with their dicks. To reward him for being so kind and gullible, Tiphani started kissing her way down his chest to his dick and gave him head.

Chapter 5

Man against Man

"Where the fuck you been?" Scar asked Day as he walked in the room.

"Watching the Ravens game." As always, Day had his alibi down pat.

"Why you ain't watch it here, nigga? I got the high-def flat screen." Scar gestured with pride to his sixty-inch television.

"I watched it at Friday's. You know I be tryin' to fuck the bartender there." Day continued his alibi.

"What's his name?" Sticks punked Day.

"What?"

"What the dude's name you tryin' to smash?" Sticks said with a smirk on his face.

Day instantly went after Sticks. "I'm gonna knock you the fuck out!" he barked as he charged toward Sticks. He wasn't going to let Sticks disrespect him like that. Day was going to make him shut his mouth with a hook to the jaw.

Before Sticks could do anything, Day was on him, but Sticks blocked the wild punch that Day threw. Sticks grabbed Day by the neck, and the struggle for control was on.

"Back the fuck up, punk!" Sticks screamed as he pushed Day backward. He pulled his gun from his waistband and pointed it at him.

"Fuck you! You the punk pulling your piece in a fist fight," Day shot back.

Bang! A gunshot went off inside the room. The argument immediately stopped and the room fell silent. Almost instantly, the door to the room was kicked in, and storming through the door came three of Scar's crew, with guns drawn, ready to blast.

"Drop yo mu'fuckin' gun, nigga!"

"Drop yo piece!"

"Drop that shit!"

They were all screaming and pointing their guns at Sticks when they saw him standing there with his gun drawn.

"Yo, chill, my li'l niggas. Chill! It's cool!" Scar yelled over all of their screams.

Everyone turned their attention to Scar and saw him standing there holding a gun at his side. He had fired his gun into the ceiling to put an end to the fight.

"Yo, Scar, we heard a gunshot." Flex, one of the newest members of the crew, said. He had gotten his name because he was so jacked it looked like he was always flexing his muscles.

"I was trying to keep these two fools from killing each other," he said, pointing with his gun in the direction of Day and Sticks. "It's all good. You on point coming in here like the mu'fuckin' cavalry, yo."

"We got yo' back. Whenever. Bet," Flex said as he gestured with his head for the other two to follow him out the door.

Scar turned to Day and Sticks. "Now, you two mu'fuckas stop acting like bitches. Put yo' gun away."

Sticks complied and put his gun back in his waistband. "I was just joking around. Who knew this nigga was so sensitive?" he said. "Unless the truth hurts." Even though he was joking, he knew it would piss Day off.

This last little remark pushed Day over the edge again. He had put up with Sticks' bullshit long enough. It was time this nigga got taught a lesson for real. He was going to break his jaw so he couldn't talk any more shit.

"Fuck you!" Day started toward Sticks again.

"Enough!" Scar wolfed out, which stopped Day in his tracks. "This shit is dead now! Now, sit the fuck down, both of you."

They both hesitated, and then obeyed like children who just got scolded.

Scar lectured the two. "I'm not gonna make you two hug it out or any corny shit like that. You both men, so handle it like men. We all want the same thing, mad paper, so let's make that shit. We don't need to be fightin' like bitches."

"Word," they both mumbled, but this was far from over. Neither Sticks nor Day were about to drop it. They both sat there, already plotting out ways to murk each other.

Scar stayed standing in front of the two. He stared at them with a look of disgust and confusion on his face. He couldn't understand why niggas were so stupid and childish sometimes.

"We have a new safe house yet? I'm sick of staying inside this place all the damn time. I might as well be in the joint."

"I got my man looking for a place in that nice part of northern Baltimore County. We be lookin' for, like, an estate. Mad land for you to walk around on. You won't have to leave yo' property," Day said. In reality, he was stalling. He hadn't been looking for a place at all. He thought it would be easier to keep an eye on Scar if he stayed in Baltimore.

"Nigga, you sound like a real estate agent. Just get it done." Scar was scowling.

"Yo, one problem, though." Sticks wanted to be involved as well.

"What?" Scar asked

"The cops still have mad roadblocks up. This city is on lock-down. It might be risky," Sticks warned.

"Fuck," Scar said under his breath as he began to slowly pace. He was trying to figure out a way to get out of Baltimore risk free. Sticks was right; it was risky without knowing exactly when and where they would be stopping cars. Though he didn't want to do it, he figured the best way would be to get Chief Hill on board. After the fiasco with Tiphani, Scar was reluctant to ask the chief to do anything else. He couldn't have fucked that up any worse. Scar had told the chief to take Tiphani out of the city, shoot her, and stash the body; but he somehow let her escape from the back of his car and disappear.

"Sticks, go talk to the fuckin' idiot chief and tell him he needs to help us." Scar was unsure if this was really the best idea, but felt he had no other choice.

"Word? I'll do it now." Sticks stood up. He was eager to get the hell out of that room. The whole time he was sitting there, all he wanted to do was bitch-slap Day and murk his ass. He was happy to go speak to the chief and show Scar he was capable of doing his business. Day seemed to be fucking up with the safe house, so it was a perfect time for Sticks to step up. He wanted to be close to Scar to learn everything he could about his empire. Then when he took Scar down, he could triple the operation.

"Not yet. I need to tell you what to say. Chill for a minute," Scar said.

"You want me to go with him? It would be more intimidating with the both of us," Day asked.

"Nah. You two need to be separate for right now. Sticks got this. You get that safe house in order," Scar said.

"A'ight. Whatever you say, boss." Day played the good soldier, but on the inside he was pissed. He wanted to go so he could get an angle on the chief for himself.

Scar just stood there staring at Day, waiting for him to get up and go. "What the fuck? Don't be sittin' there. I'm sick of being up in this bitch. These walls are pissin' me off. I mean now. Find me a new place."

"Oh yeah, right. I'll take a drive north and see what's happening." With that, Day got up and out the door.

After Day was gone, Scar turned to Sticks, who was sitting down rolling a blunt.

"Stop that for a second and listen to me," Scar ordered.

Sticks stopped rolling the blunt and leaned back on the couch. "What you need? What you want me to say to the chief?"

"I'll get to that. First thing, I want you to keep an eye on that nigga Day. Something don't feel right. I ain't never seen him with a bitch, and now he talkin' about fuckin' some bartender," Scar said as he twisted his lips.

"A'ight, I can do that. I feel you. Something off about that nigga. I can murk that nigga if you want. You know I ain't got a problem with that," Sticks said, hoping the answer would be yes. He was definitely sick of the attention Day was getting and was happy that Scar was questioning him. If Scar gave him the go ahead, Sticks thought it would make his life so much easier.

"Not yet. He still my nigga. I just need to know what's up," Scar said.

That was not the answer Sticks wanted to hear. Sticks knew what was up. Day was a kiss-ass who needed to be murked.

"Now, roll that blunt," Scar said as he sat on the couch. He was going to get these two to play against each other. In his mind, it was a masterful plan that would keep both of them in line and on his grind for a while. He would keep flipping the script on them. One day he would favor Sticks, then the next he would favor Day; make them each think he wasn't really feeling the other one. If they both thought they had a chance, then they would be trying to out do each other. When they would see the other getting more attention, they would then work harder and be more loyal soldiers. Scar thought of it as a type of psychological warfare.

Chapter 6

Follow the Money

Chief Hill sat in his car in the parking lot, replaying the events that happened earlier in the day. After Hill's morning meeting with the mayor, Sticks had approached the chief in front of City Hall. It was a risky move by Sticks. He knew every agency in Baltimore was searching for Scar, and since he was a known associate of Scar, they would probably be looking for him as well. He didn't give a fuck, though. Sticks wanted to send a message to the chief that he wasn't scared. He also wanted to make a point to Flex that he was a real nigga, not afraid of shit.

Flex and Sticks had been in a car outside of the massive marble building, waiting for the chief to appear. After about an hour, the chief finally came walking out of City Hall. Sticks stayed in the passenger's seat and watched Chief Hill descend the steps and head down the street toward his car.

Sticks came up behind him before he could open his car door.

"Ay yo," Sticks said, standing on the sidewalk. The car created a barrier between them. Chief Hill looked up and knew right away who the person standing on the opposite side of his car was, but acted as if he didn't. They had met plenty of times before, while Chief Hill was receiving bribe money from Scar.

"Can I help you?" he asked.

"We need to talk," Sticks replied.

Still acting confused, the chief furrowed his brow. "I'm sorry. I don't believe I know you."

"Stop fuckin' around, nigga. You know who I am and why I'm here." Sticks was putting an end to the chief's little charade. He wanted to get on with it and get out of there. Even if he wanted to act like he wasn't scared, Sticks knew that standing in front of City Hall wasn't the safest place for him to be at the moment.

The chief slowly looked around, trying not to draw attention to himself while he searched for anyone who might be watching them. The last thing he needed right now was to be caught speaking with a known associate of Scar Johnson. Satisfied that no one was watching them, he turned back to Sticks.

"Where is Scar?" he asked in a hushed tone.

"Don't worry about that. You and me is gonna talk. Let me in your car."

"No. Not here and not without Scar."

"Nigga, that ain't happenin'. We talkin', and if we don't, you gon' be sorry," Sticks warned.

The chief knew that Sticks' threat was credible. After years of working with Scar and taking his money, the chief saw firsthand what Scar was capable of doing. He also figured that if he played along, he could get to Scar and do as the mayor wanted—find him, kill him, and put an end to his stranglehold on the city.

"Meet me at midnight at the twenty-four-hour diner up on I-95," Chief Hill directed.

Sticks had met the chief at that diner plenty of times to give him his bribe money, so he knew exactly where he was talking about. It was far enough outside of the city that they wouldn't be recognized, and it was just dirty enough that no one really gave a fuck about anything. They could meet there, conduct their business, and not be bothered by anyone.

"A'ight. If you don't show, it's yo' head. Don't be tryin' to set me up, neither."

"Bring Scar." The chief gave an attempt to get Scar out of hiding.

Ignoring the chief's request, Sticks said, "Just be there at midnight." And with that, Sticks walked away, leaving the chief standing at his car.

Snapping out of his replay, Chief Hill looked at his watch. It was 11:55 p.m., five minutes until he was supposed to meet Sticks—and hopefully, Scar. He reached over, opened the glove compartment, and removed the Glock .45 GAP. He took the gun and tucked it in the waistband of his pants. He wasn't going to take any chances with this meeting. If Scar showed up, he might just try to shoot him on the spot.

Even if Scar didn't show up, he thought Sticks might try to set him up, which was why he got to the diner an hour early. He wanted to stake it out and make sure there was no one waiting to ambush him. With it being so close to the meeting time and none of Scar's crew seemingly anywhere in sight, he figured he wasn't about to be ambushed.

While he sat there waiting for the final five minutes to pass, he gave one last look around the parking lot. It seemed clear to him, so he got out of the car, walked across the parking lot and into the diner.

After their encounter with the chief, Sticks had Flex drop him off and then go immediately to the diner. Sticks wanted Flex to make sure the police didn't set up any sort of trap. Flex had picked up a nondescript Nissan Maxima at a chop shop and put out-of-state plates on it so it wouldn't stick out at the roadside diner. Flex had been in the parking lot ever since. He had been sitting in the backseat of the car all day.

He had watched Chief Hill drive and walk around the parking lot a few times and then sit in his car the rest of the time. When Chief Hill would get anywhere near his car, Flex hid under a blanket on the floor. The tinted windows made it difficult for the Chief to see inside, so he didn't inspect it as carefully as the other cars in the lot.

Watching from the back seat through the dark tint windows, it didn't seem to Flex that the chief was planning on any trap. If anything, it looked to Flex like the chief was searching for a trap that might be set for him. When the hour passed and the chief walked into the diner, Flex called Sticks on his throwaway cell phone.

"Yo, he's just goin' in now. Everything look good."

"Good lookin', my nigga. I'll be there in a minute. Just chill there, make sure nothin' goes down. I'm gonna reward you nice for your work," Sticks answered, feeling good. He had found the crew member he was going to groom and get on his side. Flex would be the first one Sticks would recruit when he started forming his own crew. Sticks' plan was to start giving Flex jobs like this one and pay him enough cash to keep him wanting more. That way Sticks could convince Flex that he could make more money with him and not Scar.

Sticks, who had been parked at a rest stop about a mile away, ended the call and made his way to the diner. A few minutes later, he pulled into the parking lot, parked his Escalade, and walked into the diner.

As he was entering the diner, Sticks saw the finest girl he'd seen in a while heading to the entrance as well. She had all the right curves in all the right places, and she wore clothes that accentuated them perfectly. Sticks couldn't take his eyes off her firm breasts and round, perfect ass.

She saw him looking and gave her ass an extra little bounce as she walked. Sticks sped up his walk so he could reach the door at the same time as she did. She reached for the door, but Sticks beat her to it.

"Let me get that for you, ma." He opened the door for her and seductively looked into her eyes.

She matched his gaze with an equally seductive look of her own. "What a gentleman."

"Anything for a fine young woman as yourself."

"Manners, charming, and sexy. I think I like you."

She winked at him and walked into the restaurant, making sure he had a nice view of what she knew he wanted—her ass.

"Yo, ma. Let me holla at you."

"You want my number?" She batted her eyelashes and played coy. She knew this game all too well.

"That ain't all I want." He rubbed his chin.

"Ooh, and a sense of humor. I definitely like you." She reached in her Gucci purse and pulled out a pen and paper.

Sticks looked around the restaurant and saw Chief Hill staring at him, so he cut their encounter short. He wanted to keep pushing up on this chick, because she seemed down to fuck. If he kept working on her, she'd be fucking him in the bathroom in no time. But he had business that couldn't wait.

"I'ma definitely holla at you real soon." Sticks took her number.

"I hope so." She grabbed his hand and looked in his eyes one last time.

Sticks got so turned on he practically busted a nut right there. He turned and headed straight for the back booth, where the chief was already waiting.

With no emotion showing on his face at all, Sticks sat down across from Chief Hill. He was trying to get his mind off that woman. He needed to focus on what he was there to do—but damn, she made him horny.

The two men sat there staring at each other. Neither one said a word, not wanting to be the first to speak. Each one was trying to intimidate the other. After about a minute, Chief Hill finally broke the silence.

"Well, I take it Scar won't be joining us."

"That's right," Sticks said, still without emotion on his face or in his voice.

"That's too bad," the chief responded.

Each man was being very careful not to give anything away in this little game of cat and mouse that they were playing with each other.

The chief continued, "You said you wanted to talk. So?"

"You wearing a wire?" Sticks asked. He wasn't about to say anything until he knew for sure.

"No. Are you?" the chief shot back without hesitation. "How I know you ain't lying?" Sticks was being very cautious.

"You could pat me down, but that isn't going to help. I could have planted mics in the diner. So, I guess you'll just have to trust me," the chief said with a smirk on his face.

"How about we each ask an incriminating question and we both answer truthfully," Sticks responded with his own smirk.

The chief chuckled. "Okay." He had a look of amusement on his face, but he was thinking he may have underestimated Sticks. Maybe Sticks was smarter than he was giving him credit for. He would have to proceed with caution.

"You first." The chief sat with his hands folded on top of the table.

Sticks started right away. "Were you going to kill Tiphani Fuller when she escaped from the back of your car?"

"Yes," the chief answered immediately. "Were you involved in the ambush of the SWAT team that resulted in the death of Detective Rodriguez?"

"Hell yes." Sticks' whole face lit up with a huge smile. The chief got pissed at how pleased Sticks was to answer that question. Now he just wanted to get this over with before he lost his cool.

"Satisfied? Can you finally tell me why we are here?" Chief Hill asked to move things along.

"Scar needs to know when and where the roadblocks are in Baltimore."

"I can't tell him that."

"He says he will make it worth your while."

"I can't do it," Chief Hill said, shaking his head. Sticks wasn't surprised by the chief's resistance. Scar had told him that Chief Hill would probably try to get more money out of the deal by saying no at first.

"He said he has paid you a lot of money over the years. For this information, he will triple what he normally pays you." Sticks said what Scar had coached him to say.

"So, Scar is still in Baltimore?"

"I didn't say that."

Sticks answered so quickly that the chief could safely assume that Scar was still in Baltimore. The chief sensed now was his opportunity to try to get Scar out of hiding.

"I need to speak with Scar in person if this is going to happen."

"You speakin' with me now. I got the cash in my trunk. Scar says, you do this, this is the last thing he'll ask you to do. You never have to work for him again."

This angered the chief, that Scar thought he could dictate when and how he could end their relationship. Chief Hill knew working for Scar was wrong, but he always felt that it was his choice, not Scar's.

"Well, you tell Scar, if he wants to get out of Baltimore, he needs to speak with me in person. He doesn't decide when I stop working for him; I do."

"He ain't gonna like hearing that. You should just take the cash, son. Simple and easy, then you out."

"If we don't meet, he can expect the roadblocks to be doubled and the manhunt to intensify even more." The chief was pissed.

"You makin' a mistake," Sticks said matter-of-factly. "I don't think so."

Chief Hill got up and walked out the door. He was hoping that his aggressive tactic was going to work. He thought about following Sticks, because he was almost certain Sticks would be going directly back to Scar, but when he got to his car, he looked back at the diner and saw Sticks watching him from the front door. He would just have to wait and see how Scar would react. Chief Hill started his car and drove away from the diner.

After the chief was out of sight, Sticks walked over to Flex, who was still sitting in the Nissan Maxima. As Sticks approached the car, Flex stepped out of the backseat to greet him.

"What's good?" Flex asked as they greeted each other with a pound.

"Walk with me," Sticks said as he started toward his Escalade. He didn't say anything to Flex as they walked.

After the chief took off, being the opportunist that he was, Sticks had hatched a plan. Now he was consumed with what he would tell Scar and how he could use all of what just happened to his advantage. He needed to come up with a story that would keep Scar off his back.

When he got to his Escalade, he pushed the button on the remote to open the trunk.

"You done good today," he said as he leaned into the trunk and opened the briefcase that was sitting there. This was the bribe money that was intended to go to Chief Hill.

"Oh shit! That's some serious paper." Flex had never seen so much cash.

Sticks took about a quarter of the money and handed it to Flex. "There's plenty more where this came from. You know Scar ain't never be givin' you loot like this. Remember who this come from. Someday you might have to declare who your loyalty lies with."

"Yo, good lookin', B! You ever need anything, I'm yo' man! I'm the loyalest nigga out there." Flex couldn't hide his excitement.

That's exactly what Sticks wanted to hear. The almighty dollar worked its magic on Flex. Sticks now had him where he wanted. A few more payouts like this and he would be following Sticks and not Scar.

"You earned it, nigga. Just don't be flauntin' this shit in front of the other young bucks. This is coming from my own stash, and I don't want every nigga tryin' to do me favors so they can get a piece of my cash. You feel me?" Sticks lied, trying to make sure that Scar would never find out that he took the money for himself.

Flex assured Sticks, "You ain't gotta worry. I don't want none of them tryin' to get their paws on my shit neither."

"I hear you. I'm out." Sticks laughed as he closed the briefcase and then the trunk.

Sticks needed to take the rest of the money and stash it before he went back to Scar. He also needed a little bit of time to get the story straight in his head. It had to sound legit when he told Scar that Chief Hill took the money.

"The fuck you mean, he stole the money?" Scar clenched his jaw.

"He up and took that shit. He told me he ain't helpin' us, then he stuck his mu'fuckin' pistol in my face." "Why the fuck you ain't fight him back?"

"I would have, but he took me by surprise. I turned my back for a second, and when I turned back around, he was pointing that shit in my face."

"Why you ain't hit the gun out his hand?"

"I couldn't. He was just outta my reach. I tried, but he just stepped back." Sticks demonstrated the movement.

"Nigga, you need to fight fire with fire. Pull yo' shit out and blast that fool." Scar was becoming so tense that his body was starting to ache.

"That's the fucked up thing. I wasn't strapped. I left my piece at my crib." Sticks couldn't tell if his lie was working.

"So, you just let this nigga walk with my cash?" Scar's breathing was starting to sound like a thoroughbred after the Kentucky Derby.

"Hell no! I chased after this mu'fucka. As soon as this nigga took off, I ran to my car and followed. We was speeding all over the road like *The Fast and the Furious* until he drove right into a roadblock. He sailed right through that shit, probably flashed his badge then laughed like a mu'fucka. I had to stop chasing him and go the back roads. You know they be lookin' for me too. I wouldn't be no good to you if I'm locked up. "

Scar went ballistic. The remote control flew across the room, slammed into the wall, and smashed into a million pieces. He shattered the glass coffee table by stomping on it, and he kicked in his beloved sixty-inch flat screen.

“I want this mu’fucka dead! He took my money. I’ma take his life!” Scar wolfed as his crew tried to avoid all the debris flying about the room. “Gimme yo’ gat. I’ma do this nigga myself!” Scar barked at one of his young crew members. “No one steals from Scar Johnson!”

The young crew member handed Scar his 9 mm. Scar was pacing back and forth, practically foaming at the mouth, he was so heated. He was like a caged, rabid pit bull.

In all of his years in the Dirty Money Crew, Sticks had rarely seen Scar this mad. None of the young crew members in the house had ever seen him like this. They had no idea what to do, except just stand there and hope they didn’t become a target of Scar’s wrath.

“Y’all get the fuck out!” Sticks ordered to the other crew members.

They didn’t waste any time scurrying out of the room. They looked like a bunch of cockroaches running back behind the walls when the lights get turned on. Sticks remained in the room, waiting for Scar to calm down a little. When it seemed as though Scar was ready to listen, Sticks began trying to talk some sense into him.

“Scar, we need to think about this,” Sticks said calmly. He didn’t want Scar having any contact with Chief Hill and finding out who really stole the money.

Hearing Sticks, Scar knew he was right. They did need to think about this. He needed to keep a low profile, and going after the chief of police would bring too much heat. His pacing started slowing down, but his mind was still moving a mile a minute, trying to figure out what they should do.

When Scar’s pacing stopped altogether, in a calmer, more rational tone, he spoke. “You right. This mu’fucka did the one thing he thought would piss me off so much that I would come after him. He knew I wouldn’t just come and talk to him face to face. I’m too smart for that. So, he stole my money to try and get me out. We lost him. He ain’t with us no more.”

"Exactly," Sticks reassured.

"He almost got me. Damn." Scar was sort of impressed that the chief was that smart. He was more impressed with himself that he figured it out and saw the chief's plan.

"What you want me to do?" Sticks asked.

"Nothin'. You good for now. Since we ain't got the chief, we gon' have to put the heat on my brother Derek now. A little birdie told me he gettin' out tomorrow." Scar was going to reinforce to Derek that he had his kids and it would be in his best interests to help him escape the city.

"I can do that."

"Nah. I want him to see some new faces. Show that nigga we an ever-expanding unit. I'ma get Day on that," Scar said. "Hand me yo' phone."

Sticks reluctantly did as he was asked. He couldn't understand why Scar wouldn't just let him handle everything. He was getting fed up and didn't know how much longer he could stand being disrespected by Scar.

Scar took the phone and dialed Day's number. "Yo. Where you at?" he asked when Day answered.

"I'm up north," Day lied. He was still in the city. "Get your ass down here."

"It's gonna take me a minute. Tryin' to work some shit up here." Day easily lied again.

"Fuck that! I'm tellin' you to get back here," Scar snapped.

"A'ight, I'm on my way. Be there in a few hours."

"Nah, you know what? Just go straight to County and pick up Derek Fuller. He gettin' sprung tomorrow."

"I'll be waiting for him."

"I'ma text you two pictures later—one of Derek, and one to show him. When you get it, call me so I can tell you what to say to this nigga," Scar instructed.

"Bet," Day said and ended the conversation.

Scar tossed the phone back to Sticks, sat on the couch, and started rolling a blunt. He was on edge and needed to chill out. With the manhunt for himself and Tiphani still going strong, he felt like Bin Laden hiding out in a cave in Pakistan. He needed to get the fuck out of that house and Baltimore soon or he was going to go crazy.

He took a hit from the blunt then said, "I'ma kill this mu'fuckin' Chief Hill," as smoke came pouring out of his mouth like smoke from a fog machine.

Chapter 7

The Kids Are All Right . . . For Now

Day sat outside of the Baltimore County Jail, looking up at the gray sky and thinking about Halleigh. He was really starting to feel her, and he couldn't stop thinking about her bangin' body. The more he pictured her firm breasts and perfectly round ass, the more he got turned on. It was starting to make him horny as shit. He wanted to bust a nut so bad, he actually thought for a second that he should take a chance of leaving the jail to go fuck one of the Dirty Money Crew's hoes real quick.

Get your head on, nigga. She's way off limits. You're here to do a job, he thought as he snapped out of his daydream.

To try to occupy his mind with thoughts other than Halleigh, Day reached over and turned the car radio to his favorite station, 92Q. He took out his cell phone and looked at the picture Scar had texted earlier of his niece and nephew sitting on his lap. It was like a family portrait where everyone has huge smiles on their faces—except for the fact that Scar was holding a gun and pointing it at the camera, and the kids had looks of terror on their faces. This didn't really help Day get his mind off of Halleigh. When he looked at Scar's nephew, it reminded him of Malek Jr., which, of course, made him think of Halleigh.

He was just about to drive away from the jail when he saw the gates start to open. Thinking it might be Derek, he waited. Sure enough, when the gates fully opened, Detective Derek Fuller came walking out. He walked to the edge of the curb, stopped, and looked around.

Derek stared as a black Cadillac Escalade slowly came toward him and stopped with the passenger side door directly in front of him. He couldn't see inside because of the tint on the windows, but he thought it might be someone the mayor had sent. Just before he reached for the door handle, the passenger's window slowly came down. When he saw the person sitting behind the wheel, he knew it wasn't someone from the mayor's office. Someone from the mayor's office would have been wearing a suit. This guy was wearing a purple-and-black leather Baltimore Ravens jacket with a white tank top underneath.

"Scar sent me. Get in." Day leaned on the passenger's seat so he could see out the window and into Derek's eyes.

"I can take the bus." Derek started walking away. Keeping pace, Day drove next to him so he could keep talking. "You're going to want to hear what I have to say."

"I doubt that."

"You want to see your kids?" Day showed Derek the picture of his kids with Scar.

This stopped Derek in his tracks and he leaned in the window. "You son of a bitch! Where are my kids? Where the fuck are my kids! They better not have one hair on their heads harmed or I will kill you!"

Day just sat there silently, watching Derek lose his mind. He let him keep screaming until he was finished, then calmly said with a slight smirk on his face, "Don't worry. Your kids are fine. Now, if you will get in and listen, you will be that much closer to seeing them again."

Derek was glaring at Day with hate in his eyes. If he had a gun, he would have shot him right there. Little did he know that Day wanted to shoot him just as much. Day would never forget that Derek was the one who shot and killed his mentor, Malek. If Day didn't need Derek's help, he would have shot him the second he saw him.

After a few seconds staring Day down, Derek got in the SUV and they drove away from the jail. Day hopped on I-83 and headed north.

"Where are we going?" Derek asked impatiently.

Day ignored him and just kept driving. He wanted to fuck with Derek and knew this would piss him off. Since he couldn't shoot him, he figured he could at least have some fun. Making Derek angry and uncomfortable was going to be entertaining for Day.

"I asked you a fucking question." Derek was losing his patience.

"You hungry? I know you ain't had any decent food in a while." Day was still fucking with Derek.

"Cut the bullshit! Where the fuck are we going?" Derek yelled. When it came to his kids, his fuse was very short.

"You better chill the fuck out, nigga. You in no position to be gettin' an attitude." Day said, reminding Derek who was in charge.

Derek got it. He wasn't about to jeopardize his kids. He remained silent. He couldn't believe that his brother was threatening the life of his kids. How had their relationship gotten so bad? He remembered back to how happy he was when he found his brother after being separated all those years. Their lives had gone in totally opposite directions after they left the foster home, but that didn't matter. When they reunited, their bond was just as tight as when they were kids—until Scar broke that bond by fucking Derek's wife. Now their brotherly bond was shattered beyond repair.

They drove a little farther without speaking and Day pulled into the Mondawmin Mall parking lot. Since it was a weekday afternoon, there weren't many cars in the lot. Day drove to a particularly deserted section and parked his SUV far away from any other vehicle. He sat there for about a full minute, not saying a word. This was killing Derek. He wanted to scream and punch this dude in his face, but if he did, it would jeopardize his children, and Derek was going to do everything in his power to make sure those two beautiful children remained safe. So, he sat there biting his tongue.

"Scar needs your help," Day began.

"When can I see my kids?"

"After you help Scar."

"I want to see my kids and I want to see Scar," Derek demanded.

Day ignored the request and continued with what Scar wanted him to say. He wasn't about to go into detail about why he couldn't see Scar or his kids.

"Scar needs you to get the mayor to pull some strings and get him out of Baltimore."

"I suppose he wants to escape with his whore Tiphani, too. Tell Scar I'm not doing shit until I see my kids and I meet with him," Derek said coldly.

"Tiphani's on her own. She disappeared into thin air. He wants that bitch dead," Day corrected Derek.

This surprised Derek. He thought for sure that they would be together considering the way Tiphani fell for Scar and how addicted she seemed to his dick. She was always clingy, and Derek knew that Tiphani needed that dick constantly. Unless, of course, this dude was lying. There was no way to tell for sure, so Derek figured he just needed to assume it was true.

"I can find her. I promise. Just let me have my kids back," Derek pleaded.

"If you do as Scar says, you'll have your kids."

"Fuck him," Derek said more to himself than to Day. Day didn't say anything. He waited for an answer from Derek. Derek was staring out the window, watching a mother and her two children walk across the empty parking lot and into the mall. His heart was aching for his children. He needed to figure out a way to get them back. He was between a rock and a hard place. "Just do it. Time's running out." Day took out his phone and showed Derek the picture one more time.

Derek started to tear up when he saw his kids. They were tears of sadness and anger. Seeing their faces made him sad, but seeing that Scar had guns around them infuriated him.

"You tell my brother Stephon that I will do what he wants. Then I'm coming for him and Tiphani, and I will kill them both." Derek was seething with anger.

He had no intention of really helping Scar. He only said it to protect his children. He figured if he could string Scar along, it would buy him some time to find out where he was hiding, and buy his kids more time to live. His children were the only thing in this life he cared for anymore. He was prepared to kill anyone who came in between him and his children, and he would start with Scar and that cheating, conniving bitch Tiphani.

Day handed Derek a throwaway cell phone. "Keep this on you. I'll call when we need to meet again. You better have made some moves when I come callin'."

Derek stepped out of the SUV determined to save his children and annihilate his brother. Stephon "Scar" Johnson was going to regret the day he betrayed his brother.

Chapter 8

A Picture is Worth a Thousand Words

The waiting room to Mayor Steele's office was silent except for the steady clicking of his secretary's keyboard. Susan was diligently typing up the mayor's next speech. Derek sat on a leather chair against the wall, watching her. Susan had stopped him from going directly into the office, telling Derek that the mayor was on a very important phone call. Derek had been waiting for fifteen minutes, and he was getting impatient. He just wanted to get this meeting over with so he could get on with saving his children.

"Hello, Susan. You are looking lovely as usual." The mayor's chief of staff, Dexter Coram, walked into the room.

"Hi, Dexter." Susan glanced up at Dexter and went right back to typing.

"When are you going to finally have dinner with me?" He was leaning over with his hands flat on the desk.

Without looking up from the computer screen, Susan answered, "Never."

Susan didn't understand why Dexter insisted on always asking her to dinner. It was obvious to her that Dexter was one of those down low brothers. He acted as if he liked women, but she had seen him flirt with guys enough times to know that behind closed doors, Dexter liked to get nasty with other dudes.

"One of these days you'll say yes." Dexter winked at her, but Susan ignored him.

"The mayor's busy," she told him. "You'll have to wait." Dexter shrugged. As he turned away from Susan's desk to go sit down, he noticed Derek sitting there.

"Is that who I think it is? Mmmm . . ." he whispered to Susan with his eyebrows raised.

Susan just rolled her eyes and kept typing. To her, Dexter was the epitome of sleaze.

Dexter kept staring at Derek as he went and stood directly in front of him with his hand reached out. "Hi. I'm Dexter Coram."

"Derek." He shook Dexter's hand.

"I like that name." Dexter was smiling and wouldn't let go of Derek's hand.

"Thanks." Derek ripped his hand from Dexter's.

"My friends call me Dee." Dexter stayed standing in front of Derek.

"Good for you." Derek looked to Susan.

Dexter went to sit in the leather chair directly across from Derek. He was looking at Derek like he was waiting for him to say something.

"Get it?" Dexter asked.

Derek really didn't feel like having a conversation with this freak, so he just kept staring at the wall and didn't respond.

"Dee Coram. It sounds like the word decorum." Dexter had a little grin on his face, getting a kick out of his own corny joke. It was a lie anyway; no one ever called him Dee.

There was still no response from Derek, who just wanted this guy to shut up.

"Yeah, I don't think it's that funny either," Dexter said, sounding disappointed.

Susan continued to type while listening to this sad attempt at flirting by Dexter. She was grossed out by the chief of staff, and when he did this kind of stuff, it made her dislike him even more. She had never been around someone so weasely, smarmy, and sleazy. Nothing would make her happier than to never have to speak to him or see him again.

After a few minutes of silence, Dexter couldn't help himself. He had to say something to Derek.

"You were in jail, right?" he asked, staring seductively at Derek.

Derek was losing his patience. He just wanted to be left alone until it was time to go in to see the mayor. Derek ignored the comment again, but the dude wouldn't stop.

"Must have been scary with all of those guys in there." Dexter paused for a response and again got nothing. "I can tell you worked out while you were locked up."

This shit was getting out of control, and Derek was at his breaking point. Dexter's compliment was an obvious lie. Derek had lost weight, and his body was nowhere near as ripped as it used to be. He spent most of his time in the infirmary trying to recover from his stab wounds.

"You have nice shoulder definition. I like it. How do you get that? I work out, but I can't get my shoulders as nice as yours. The ladies must love you." Dexter couldn't stop himself. "What do you think, Susan?"

Derek let out a small moan and shook his head in disgust. His face was starting to tighten up with anger. He looked over at Susan, who had a look of disgust on her face too.

When she made eye contact with Derek, she shrugged her shoulders as a sign of camaraderie. She could tell that Derek was just as irritated by Dexter as she was. She wanted to say something to Dexter, but he was her superior and she would risk being fired if she did. So, she said nothing, figuring that one day Dexter would get his.

When Derek wouldn't answer him, Dexter finally took the hint and stopped talking. That didn't stop him from staring, though. He was trying desperately to make eye contact with Derek. He was checking him out from head to toe. As he was sitting there, he discreetly reached into the inside pocket of his suit jacket and pulled out his BlackBerry. He surreptitiously started taking pictures of Derek's crotch while pretending to check emails.

Susan had seen Dexter do this before and realized right away what was happening. She started clearing her throat in order to get Derek's attention. He was too busy trying to ignore Dexter, so he wasn't picking up on her signals. Seeing he wasn't catching on, she continued a little louder. Derek still didn't look her way. She started coughing, and that finally caused Derek to look at her. With her eyes, she signaled toward Dexter, while making a motion with her hands like she was pushing the shutter button on a camera.

Dexter was so consumed with his picture taking that he had no clue of anything going on around him. He was in his own perverted world.

Derek didn't really understand what Susan was trying to say, but when he looked over at Dexter, he realized right away what this freak was doing. That was definitely the final straw. Derek leaped from his chair and lunged at Dexter.

"What the fuck you doing, nigga?"

Derek didn't want to cause any trouble in the mayor's office, so he'd tried ignoring Dexter, but a dude taking a picture of his dick was cause for a beat down. Derek tried grabbing the BlackBerry from Dexter, but he wouldn't give it up. He held on with all of his strength. He wasn't about to let Derek see what was on there. They struggled back and forth, each trying to gain control of the phone.

"Cut it out!" Dexter squealed like a girl. "Give me the phone, motherfucker!"

Finally, Derek let go of the phone with one hand, cocked it, and punched the shit out of Dexter's face. Dexter let out a high-pitched scream and let go of the phone. While he was hunched over trying to protect his face from any more of Derek's punches, Derek took the phone and hurled it against the wall as hard as he could. As the phone smashed against the wall and Derek turned to beat on Dexter, the mayor's office door swung open wildly.

"What's going on out here?" Mayor Steele yelled. Susan was a little disappointed to see the mayor come out of his office and interrupt the beating. She had been watching the whole episode with delight. Dexter was getting his comeuppance sooner than she expected, and she was hoping he was about to get more. When Derek punched Dexter, she thought, *Karma's a bitch, you sleazeball.*

"This freak is taking pictures of me on his cell phone."

"I am doing no such thing. This man attacked me for no reason."

"I should kick your ass for lying." Derek stepped toward Dexter with his fist cocked.

"Hey hey hey! Stop it! Both of you in my office, now!" the mayor bellowed.

"I'm not going in there with this fruitcake," Derek said.

"Ugh." Dexter rolled his eyes and pursed his lips. "Either he comes in here, or no one comes in here. Take it or leave it." The mayor turned and walked into his office.

Derek looked at Dexter, who was sitting there with a smug look on his face; then he looked at Susan, who had a sympathetic look on hers. He decided he should just get the meeting over with. *Fuck it,* he thought and walked into the mayor's office as Dexter followed.

Susan watched the door to the mayor's office close then went back to typing, this time with a little grin on her face.

The mayor stood behind his desk and watched the two men enter his office. He was not happy with either of them.

"Sit down, both of you." He waited for the two men to sit before he continued. "I don't know and I don't care what just happened out there, but you two are going to have to learn to work together."

"Why is he even in here?" Derek asked.

"After today, you and I will no longer have any contact. Dexter will be representing me. Anything you and I have to say to one another will go through Dexter," Mayor Steele said.

"How do I know I can trust this sneaky, down low creep?" Derek protested.

Dexter didn't say a word. During the exchange between the mayor and Derek, he had made his way to a mirror on the wall and was tending to the bruise forming on his face.

"Again, take it or leave it," Mayor Steele told Derek. Derek didn't like it, but he had no choice. He needed the mayor on his side and whatever help the mayor could give. His children were his only concern at this point. He would do anything to get them back. If it meant having to deal with a punk like Dexter, then so be it. He would do it.

"Fine."

"Good," Mayor Steele said.

"I look forward to our time together." Dexter cocked his head slightly and grinned as he looked at Derek's reflection in the mirror. Dexter could swear that he was watching the bruise swell up on the spot. He was concerned about how it was going to affect his looks. All he wanted to do was get some ice and try to stop the swelling.

It took everything in Derek's power to not stand up and kick that grin off of Dexter's face. Instead, he just clenched his jaw and said nothing.

The mayor chose to ignore the blatant taunt as well. He had seen Dexter do his thing before, but didn't feel like dealing with it. Even if he was a bit of a kiss-ass at times and sort of creepy, Dexter was loyal to the mayor, and right now, the mayor needed as many people on his side as possible.

"As we discussed, I got you out of prison, so now it's time for you to do me a favor." The mayor leaned back and folded his hands in front of his chest.

"How much does he know?" Derek said, referring to Dexter.

"Everything. Feel free to talk," the mayor said.

Derek was still skeptical of Dexter and didn't feel comfortable saying what he wanted to say. "Everything?" he asked.

"Ugh. Yes, I know everything. I'm the chief of staff. I know the deal you two have, so just say whatever it is you want to say." Dexter was still facing the mirror as he spoke. He would have turned around, but he wanted Derek to see his booty. He thought it was his best asset.

Derek was so frustrated by Dexter and his tone that he just blurted out what he had to say. "Fine. Before I can help you kill Tiphani, I need help killing Scar."

"Oh please. Just because he fucked your wife doesn't mean we should help you kill him," Dexter announced, still checking himself out in the mirror. He thought the bruise made him look tough. Maybe Derek would think it looked sexy and become attracted to him.

Derek was seriously on the verge of giving this freak a beat down that would put him in the intensive care unit. "Shut the fuck up. I'm in a meeting with the mayor. After today I will speak to you, but right now, you don't exist in my world." Derek faced the mayor. "Look, I can get Tiphani. I just need my kids to get her to show her face. Scar is holding my kids hostage, and he isn't going to give them up easy."

"Do you think Scar is still in Baltimore?" Mayor Steele was interested.

"I know he is. He sent one of his men to pick me up from jail. He thinks I'm going to help him get out of Baltimore. I told him I would speak to you about it. If he's watching me, he probably thinks that's why I'm here."

"What does he want me to do?" the mayor asked. "He wants to know about the roadblocks."

"Dexter, double the roadblocks in the city," the mayor directed.

"Yes, sir." Dexter was still surveying his face in the mirror, though his mood was improving. He wore makeup at home all the time, but had been too afraid to wear it to work. Now he could use the bruises as an excuse to wear makeup in the office for a week or two.

"So, what can we do? We have no idea where he is. We've been looking for this son of a bitch everywhere," the mayor continued.

"I'll find him, and when I do, I'll take him out. I just need access to the police department files and a few men to help." Derek waited for an answer.

The mayor wasn't going to give an answer right away. Derek's offer sounded good, but he wanted to think it over. He spun around in his chair and looked out the window onto the streets of Baltimore. The people had no trust in him and no respect for his police force. He was losing his city, and he blamed it all on Scar Johnson. He needed to do something to take back control of the city.

"Okay. I'll have Chief Hill get in contact with you. He can help you with whatever you need." Mayor Steele stood up.

"Thank you." Derek stood up as well and shook the mayor's hand.

"Good luck. This city needs to be rid of scum like Scar and Tiphani."

Derek nodded in agreement. He turned and headed out the door, happy to have gotten what he wanted out of the meeting. Now it was time to find his kids.

As soon as Derek was out of the room, Mayor Steele picked up the phone and dialed Chief Hill.

"Hello," Chief Hill answered.

"It's Mathias. Derek Fuller was just here. I told him you would assist him in finding Scar Johnson."

"How? I don't know where he is."

"I know that. Just help with whatever you can. What I really need you to do is follow him. When he finds Scar, you need to make sure he doesn't kill him. We need Scar alive. I believe I don't have to tell you what needs to be done to Detective Fuller when he finds Scar." Without waiting for an answer, the mayor hung up the phone.

"Sneaky, sir. I like it. Use Derek to find Scar, then kill Derek and capture Scar. The city will see that you are still in control. Perhaps even better is if it could look like Scar fought back and was killed while being apprehended?" Dexter smiled at the mayor.

"Perhaps." The mayor turned to look out the window again, watching Derek walk across the plaza to his car. He hoped Derek could find Scar fast so this entire ordeal could be over. As he watched Derek drive off, he thought, *I hope this is the last time I see you alive,* Detective Fuller.

Chapter 9

Death of a Family

Halleigh's three-bedroom house sat at the end of a cul de sac in a suburb of Baltimore. She moved in because she liked the fact that there was only one way into the neighborhood. It was ideal; she would never be trapped. If anyone ever came for her, she would see them coming and could make her escape out the back and into the woods behind the house.

She loved this house. She loved that she could let Malek Jr. run around outside and not worry about him. There were no gangbangers trying to recruit her child, no hustlers on the street corners, and no shootouts. The only drive-bys were done by the mailman when he came to put mail in her mailbox. It was the complete opposite of what she grew up in, and she loved that she could let her son grow up in such a wonderfully calm environment.

On the outside, she seemed relaxed and blissful, but Halleigh had a dark secret that wouldn't go away. To her neighbors and everyone in town she seemed happy, but she wouldn't be completely at ease until she knew that Scar Johnson and Derek Fuller were dead. It was the one thing that was driving her. She couldn't be truly happy until she had exacted revenge on the two men responsible for the death of her man.

Halleigh relaxed a little when she looked out the front window and saw Dayvid's SUV pulling into the driveway. It calmed her nerves, and she felt relief whenever she saw his Escalade.

Dayvid and Halleigh had been after Scar and Derek since the day Malek was gunned down. They had secretly been following Scar and his crew from a distance, making sure that no one ever saw them. Recently Dayvid took the most risk by revealing himself and infiltrating Scar's Dirty Money Crew. This caused Halleigh to worry every day that he would be found out. Not only would her chance at revenge die, but so would Dayvid. Recently Halleigh was realizing that she had feelings for Dayvid that went beyond friendship and to lose him would devastate her. She felt they had been taking chances and tempting fate long enough. They had followed both men and plotted their deaths; now it was time to put an end to both men.

"M.J., Dayvid is here," Halleigh called out to her son, who came running.

When Dayvid opened the door, M.J. jumped right into his arms and hugged him tight. It was obvious to Halleigh that Malek Jr. loved Dayvid. He had told Halleigh a few days earlier that he wished Dayvid lived with them. This made her think that it wouldn't be a bad idea to have Dayvid move in. She had plenty of space. He could have his own room, and it would give M.J. a male figure in the house. Still, she was torn between wanting to honor Malek and wanting to explore her new feelings for Dayvid. Having him around more would give Halleigh a chance to see if she really wanted more of a relationship with Dayvid.

"Hey, little man." Dayvid tossed Malek Jr. in the air and caught him.

"Play in room!" Malek Jr. announced happily.

Dayvid looked to Halleigh to make sure it would be all right.

"You can play for fifteen minutes, and then it's time to eat dinner." Halleigh tapped Malek Jr. on his butt.

Wasting no time, Malek Jr. jumped down from Dayvid's arms and ran to his room with a big smile on his face.

"He's a trip." Dayvid laughed and followed M.J. to his room.

For the next fifteen minutes, Malek Jr. was a whirlwind of energy. He tried to play with every toy he had in his room, finally settling on playing a game of pretend football. He had Dayvid be the quarterback, and he was the wide receiver/running back. They would pretend to score touchdowns and celebrate. Then they would pretend to stand on the sidelines and watch as their defense played. Malek Jr. was in heaven.

Halleigh heard the boys having so much fun that she gave them an extra fifteen minutes to play before she called out, "Okay. Dinner is ready."

The boys came running into the kitchen. Malek Jr. was wearing his Ravens jersey and a football helmet way too big for his tiny head.

"Mama, we win football." He held his arms up in victory.

"That's great. Now sit down and eat." She smiled. For the next forty-five minutes they ate dinner. They talked, they told jokes and laughed. Everyone was having a great time. It was like they were a real family getting together at the end of a day. Halleigh felt comfortable and happy.

"Time for bed, little man," Dayvid said when dinner was over.

"You put bed?" Malek Jr. asked.

"Sure. If it's okay with your mom." He looked to Halleigh.

Halleigh smiled and gave him a nod of approval. After reading to him and waiting for him to fall asleep, Dayvid came back out to the kitchen, where Halleigh was sitting. She was facing away from Dayvid, in her own world.

"What's on your mind?" Dayvid asked.

"He really loves you." She kept her back to Dayvid. "I love him."

"That scares me. What happens if one day you never show up again?" She turned to him. After the night they just had, she wanted to walk right up and kiss him—the way a wife would kiss her husband, with passion and abandon.

"That won't happen. I'm making sure of that." Dayvid was having the same thought as Halleigh.

"How? There's no guarantee that you won't be killed. Scar could find out about us, and that would be the end of you. I don't want M.J. to have to go through that. He was too young to remember his dad getting shot, but he would be devastated to lose you." Halleigh was talking about her son's feelings for Dayvid, but she was also feeling the same way. She was not only concerned for how it would affect M.J. if Dayvid disappeared, but how it would affect her. She didn't want to admit it, but she was starting to fall in love.

"He won't find out. I promise. I'm one of his majors. He had me pick Detective Fuller up from jail and give him a warning."

"What?" Halleigh's tone instantly changed.

"I picked up Detective Fuller from jail and delivered a warning from Scar."

"Why the fuck didn't you shoot him on the spot?" Halleigh went from concerned to pissed in a split second.

"I couldn't. I'm working on something, and I have to play along with Scar for a little while longer."

"I'm getting sick of this waiting shit. You have the opportunity every day to kill Scar, but you don't do it. Now you have Detective Fuller, the man who shot Malek, in front of you, and you don't kill him. You need to man up and shoot these niggas." Halleigh was standing toe to toe with Dayvid.

"Chill. I have a plan."

"What plan? To be a pussy and don't kill these two motherfuckers?" Halleigh was letting the street come out of her. She wanted this whole thing to be over. She felt the sooner Scar and Fuller died, the sooner she could be sure that Dayvid and her son would be safe.

"Come on, Hal. Listen. I'm trying to set up a little piece of the business for us. I've been taking money from Scar, and he thinks his business is falling off. It's perfect timing. If I get blamed for Scar's death now, then we won't have anything set up for the future. I'm doing it for you and M.J. We just have to be patient."

"I'm done being patient. You tell me this all the time." She walked away from him.

"It's for us."

"What is this 'us' bullshit? There is no 'us.' It is me and my son. You are not part of that." Halleigh said the words that she hoped would hurt Dayvid and hopefully provoke him to finally kill Scar. Truthfully, she had wanted it to be "us" but was now getting confused about her true feelings.

Dayvid was hurt by that last comment. He wanted to be a part of Halleigh and M.J.'s lives forever. It was starting to feel to him that they were thinking the same thing. He was setting it up so that he could provide for them. His motivation used to be revenge, but now everything he did was motivated by how it would affect Halleigh and M.J. in the future.

"Fuck you, Halleigh. I'm trying to help you two." He glared at her.

"Well, fuck you too. We don't need your help, and if you ain't gonna kill them muthafuckas, then I will. Now, get out my house!" Halleigh had completely reverted back to her days on the street.

Dayvid was too shocked and hurt to say anything. He didn't want this argument to escalate into violence, so he just walked out of the house. The last thing he wanted to do was to leave. He was having an amazing night and didn't want it to end, but Halleigh was being disrespectful, and he couldn't stand there and take it. It didn't matter what he said; Halleigh wasn't going to listen. She was being unreasonable and wasn't appreciating what he was doing, so he was done trying to help. If she thought she could be on her own and handle her life, then let her try. He would continue setting up his little piece, but now it would all be for him and no one else. Halleigh was on her own.

Halleigh followed him to the door. "And don't come back!" She slammed the door closed. She stood with her back against the door for about a minute, until she couldn't hold her tears in any longer. She broke down and cried as she slid down to the floor.

She didn't want to kick Dayvid out, but she had let her emotions get the best of her. She was so confused. One minute she wanted to sleep with Dayvid, and the next she was fighting with him and kicking him to the curb. She sat there on the floor, feeling sorry for herself. She couldn't understand why her life continued to be a struggle. She just wanted it to be easy. She needed peace. She was sick of feeling pressure, sick of always looking over her shoulder thinking someone was after her. This evening had been so great with Dayvid and M.J., and it turned to shit in a matter of a few seconds.

Halleigh blamed Dayvid. He was holding off on killing Scar for no reason. Yeah, he said it was for them, but Halleigh didn't believe it. She had heard that same thing from Malek. He was always saying he would get out; he just had to do a little more so he could set up a future for her and their son. Look where that got him—killed. Why were the men in her life always saying it was for her? If he really wanted to do something for her, he would put an end to her struggle. He would kill Scar so she could get on with her life.

Halleigh allowed herself another minute or two for her pity party, and then she was done feeling sorry for herself. She wiped her face and picked herself up off the floor. If she wanted change in her life, she needed to be the one to make it. The only way Halleigh thought she could have peace of mind was if Scar and Derek Fuller were dead, so it was time for her to take matters into her own hands. If Dayvid couldn't do it, then she would.

Halleigh walked into her bedroom with a purpose. She went directly to her walkin closet and started going through her clothes to find the most revealing and seductive clothes she had. *If you want something done right, you've got to do it yourself,* she thought as she rummaged through her wardrobe.

When she found the perfect outfit, she tried it on. Standing in front of the mirror and admiring her body, she said to herself, "Scar Johnson, your days are numbered, motherfucker." She formed her hand into the shape of a gun, pointed it at the mirror, and mimed shooting someone. Boom!

Chapter 10

Dance of Death

It had been a few days since their fight, and Day had not seen or heard from Halleigh. He was depressed about it and couldn't stop replaying the fight over and over in his head. Even though he thought about going over there several times, his pride stopped him from doing so. She kicked him out. She was being unreasonable, so she needed to be the one to reach out to him. In the meantime, Day would continue to fuck with Scar's business and take as much money as he could. Then, when he had it all set, he would kill Scar and be set up for life—with or without Halleigh. He was trying to convince himself it would be better without her. It would be less of a headache. At the moment, he had a splitting one.

Day was sitting on the couch at Scar's place, trying to relieve the tension by rubbing his temples. He had been having stress headaches ever since the fight. He was having a hard time concentrating on anything. Not only was he stressed about Halleigh, but he was starting to second guess his strategy. Maybe Halleigh was right. Maybe he should just murk these two fools immediately. He was thinking that he might be acting too cautious, but how could infiltrating Scar's crew and basically working undercover be too cautious? He was taking a huge risk, not Halleigh. She helped out for a while, but now that he was in, she stayed out of the picture. Day was confused. He needed to sort this all out before he slipped up or his head exploded from the headaches.

The television was on, but Day had hardly been paying attention. He was supposed to be looking for any new information on Tiphani or the manhunt for Scar. It wasn't easy to get much from the television these days, as most news outlets had started to lose interest in the case. There were a few political scandals that they started focusing on. The mayor was eager to focus on them as well. It allowed him to pull focus from his poor handling of the Scar and Tiphani fiasco and point out the weaknesses of his political rivals.

Day tried to concentrate on the news, but his mind was obviously somewhere else. He had too many other things swirling around in his brain. Besides, he figured it was only a matter of time before Derek would come through with the information needed to get Scar out of Baltimore. That dude seemed desperate to get his kids back. Day didn't blame him, either. He would do the same thing for Malek Jr. Well, at least he would have, before Halleigh kicked him out.

Day watched as Chief Hill and Dexter Coram were answering some questions in front of City Hall. It was the usual political bullshit: say a lot of words without saying a goddamn thing that means anything.

Day was bored. His eyes were getting heavy, and he was about to fall asleep when Scar walked into the room. Day immediately woke up. Seeing Scar's face and his tense body language, Day sensed that Scar was not in a good mood.

"What the fuck they sayin'?" Scar tilted his head toward the television.

"Same old bullshit. A whole lot of nothin'." Day shrugged his shoulders.

Scar stood with his arms folded in front of him, watching the two men on the screen. His face was tight with anger. Day looked at him and saw him actually snarl when Chief Hill answered a question. Scar was more on edge today than he had been. He was oozing hate out of his pores.

After listening to them dance around questions, Scar was satisfied that they still had nothing on him. He quickly reached down for the remote and turned off the television.

"That fuck needs to be murked," Scar seethed.

"Who?"

"That thievin', muthafuckin' police chief," Scar said.

"You sayin' you want to kill the police chief?"

"The fuck did I just say? Yeah, I want to murk that mu'fucka."

"I thought he was on your payroll."

"You got a lotta fuckin'questions." Scar glared at Day.

"I'm just not sure if we need that kind of heat right now. Don't we already have enough comin' our way?" Day said.

"Nigga, I'm finished worrying about heat. I done killed cops before. I can kill cops again. A nigga steals from me, he needs to be murked." Scar swung his fist down like he was punching someone kneeling in front of him.

"Who stole from you?" Day got a little nervous when Scar mentioned someone stealing from him. Was Scar trying to say that he knew Day was stealing from him? Was he hinting to Day that he was going to kill him? Day immediately started trying to formulate a plan on how to fight his way out of the house.

"Chief Hill. Who the fuck you think we been talkin' about for the past five minutes?" Scar looked at Day like he was an idiot.

Day was relieved to know that Scar wasn't referring to him, but he still needed to know the details. He had to make sure not to make the same mistake and get found out. The questions he had to ask would have to be direct enough to get the answers he needed, but they also couldn't be too specific. He didn't want to alert Scar that he might be doing anything behind his back. It was going to be a tightrope walk of questioning. One false move could get him killed.

"For real? How you know that?"

"The nigga took a hun'ed-fitty Gs from me. Jacked up Sticks and made off with the shit."

"Word? When?" Something didn't seem right to Day. The only time that he knew Sticks and the chief coming into contact was at the diner. That couldn't have been when it happened, because Day had followed Sticks there and seen everything that went down.

"The other day when Sticks went to talk to him." Scar was visibly upset talking about it.

"At the diner?" Immediately Day regretted saying this. He knew that Sticks and the chief were supposed to meet, but there was no reason or way Day should have known where. Day knew about the diner because instead of going up north like he told

Scar he was doing, he stayed in Baltimore and followed Sticks. He had seen everything that went down, from when Sticks approached Chief Hill in front of City Hall to the meeting that night at the diner. If Scar thought about it, he would have realized that.

"Yep, the diner. Right in the parking lot. That cocky mu'fucka." Scar's breathing was starting to quicken and he began pacing. He was getting so agitated.

Day was in a bind. He knew Sticks' story was a lie, but he couldn't tell that to Scar. He was supposed to have been out of town when that went down. As angry as Scar was at the moment, if he found out that Day lied to him, he was liable to kill him on the spot. How could he let Scar know this was a lie without giving himself away?

"Was anyone else there?" he asked.

"Nah."

This answer sparked a lot of questions in Day's head. *Why doesn't Scar know that Flex was in the parking lot? Does Flex know that Sticks said Chief Hill robbed him? Is Flex in on it?*

"I knew I should have gone as backup," Day said. Day was trying to think of a way to make Scar figure out it was a lie. He thought back to that night for any clues. Halleigh had helped him with the surveillance that night. She was unknown to either Sticks or Chief Hill, so he figured she would be able to follow them on foot without fear of them recognizing her. He was correct. Halleigh had literally run right into Sticks. At first that made Day nervous, but then he watched as Sticks flirted with her, and he knew that she hadn't been recognized.

Day had Halleigh drive that night, and it was a good thing he did. After Halleigh went into the diner to try to hear their conversation, Day scanned the parking lot and saw Flex hiding out. Luckily he saw Flex before Flex saw him, so he was able to stay hidden.

When their meeting was over, Day watched as Chief Hill drove away. Then Sticks went into his car and handed Flex a stack of cash.

That's it! Day thought. When he saw it that night, he just assumed that Sticks was paying Flex for being his backup. That wasn't what it was, though. The money was either hush money from Sticks, or they were both in on it. The money in the trunk was probably Scar's money that was stolen—not by Chief Hill, but by Sticks.

Day had figured out who had the money. Now he just needed to find out how much Flex knew. He needed to find Flex and start asking some questions.

Day thought this was the best thing that could have happened. Day could convince Scar that Sticks was the reason the business was down. All of the money that Day had stolen from Scar could now be blamed on Sticks.

"I don't think you should take him out. Let's get a young buck to do it. Prove their loyalty," Day said.

Scar stopped pacing and looked at Day. He seemed to be searching Day's face for something. An answer? Day got a little uncomfortable as he sat there and Scar just stared at him. He couldn't tell what Scar was thinking. Maybe he'd pushed it too far and Scar was figuring out that he lied. Or was Scar starting to think that maybe Day was the one who stole the money? For the second time during this conversation, Day started to think of an escape plan. Day was on edge. He was trying to appear calm, but he didn't know if he was doing a good job at hiding his nervousness—which was making him even more nervous.

"You right. Who you think?" Scar finally broke the silence.

Day let out a sigh of relief, but quickly covered it up by fake coughing. He felt like he was starting to lose it. He had never been so unsure of himself around Scar before. He didn't know what was happening to him. One thing he knew was that he wasn't going to be able to keep feeling like this around Scar. If he did, he would eventually fuck up and end up dead. He was going to have to try to speed up his plan and take Scar out sooner than he thought.

"I like that youngin' Flex. He seem to have heart." Day composed himself and got back on track with his new plan. He could now have an excuse to meet with Flex alone.

"Yeah, I like that. He do seem to got heart," Scar said.

"A'ight, I can holla at him. You know where he at?"

"Nah. I got enough to be worryin' about than where some low level nigga be."

"I hear you. I'll find him." Day stood up to leave.

"Hold up. I need to holla at you for a minute." Scar stepped in front of Day.

This was it. Day was sure Scar was going to grill him about why the money was light. If he did, Day was prepared to put the blame on Sticks, but he would still try to keep his secret that he lied about being at the diner. Lying would be a disrespect to Scar, and in the Dirty Money Crew, that was cause for death.

"What's up?" Day stayed standing.

"Things been fucked up lately." Scar was again staring at Day.

"Word." Day was going to try to say as little as possible until he knew where Scar was going with this.

"Money been light." Scar was expressionless. "I think I know why."

Day prepared himself for what was coming next. Scar was going to bring the hammer down on him. Day's body tensed up, and his mind was going through a million different scenarios and lies all at once.

"Why?" Day balled his fists, ready to fight to the death. Scar didn't answer right away. He stood about two feet in front of Day and just shook his head slowly from side to side, holding eye contact with Day the entire time. The silence was killing Day. He had two choices: strike first and take Scar off guard, or wait and see what Scar's move would be. Day always thought of himself as a man of action, so he was going to go out swinging.

He started toward Scar.

"It's me," Scar said.

Day stopped himself before he took his first step.

"I've been unfocused about the product. This manhunt and being holed up in this dump has made me lose focus."

Day didn't say a word. He was two steps away from punching Scar in his face and possibly putting an end to his own life. He was trying to wrap his mind around how lucky he had just gotten.

Scar continued, "I need to get out of here and get my mind straight. Go talk to Derek and see what he got for us. Once I'm out of B-more, I can get the money flowing in the right direction again." He walked over to his desk and sat down.

"A'ight, boss. I'll reach out to that nigga." Day sat down.

The door opened and Sticks entered the room. The smile on his face and the bounce in his step let them know that he was in a good mood. He was wearing his usual outfit of a fitted Baltimore Orioles baseball hat, tight T-shirt, baggy jeans, and Timberland boots.

"What up, fam?" Sticks walked to the middle of the room.

"The fuck you come barging in like the drug squad for?" Scar barked.

"I got something for you." Sticks had a big smile on his face.

"Wipe that corny smile off yo' face. The only reason you should be barging into my space is because you got a million dollars for me."

"It ain't a million dollars," Sticks said.

"Then get the fuck out. My man and me are having some serious conversations." Scar motioned over to Day.

Normally this would have really pissed Sticks off, but right now he had something that he knew would make Scar happy. After Scar saw what he had, he would forget about Day.

"It looks like a million dollars. Just wait and take a look. I guarantee you'll want to love it." Sticks was loving this. He turned and left the room.

Day looked at Scar and shrugged. They didn't have to wait long for Sticks to come back in with his surprise—a woman who was following behind him.

The moment she entered the room, Day's eyes widened. It was Halleigh. She was dressed in a short mini skirt that barely covered her ass, a see-through tank top, and stripper heels. She looked like she just got off the pole.

Halleigh saw Day immediately and stopped for just a split second, but she composed herself and got on with what she was there to do. She acted like she didn't know who the fuck Day was.

"I met this chick the other night. She bad, right?" Sticks grabbed her ass.

Day flinched and almost jumped out of his seat, but he restrained himself in time so that no one noticed.

Sticks continued, "I know you heated about losing that money, and you been stressed lately, so I figured I would bring her over for you. I haven't even touched her yet. I saved her to let you have first crack, and then we can run that train."

Halleigh stood there with a seductive look on her face, not saying a word. On the inside, her stomach was doing flips. She was nervous as shit, and to make matters worse, Day was there. She wanted to run over to him and tell him to leave, to say that she could handle it from here, but she couldn't let them know that she knew him.

Earlier in the day, Halleigh had followed Sticks into a bodega and acted like it was a coincidence. She walked up behind him while he was in the back pulling a forty-ounce of Colt 45 out of the cooler.

"Ain't I seen you at the diner the other night?" she said seductively.

"Oh shit, that's right. You the fine piece that gave me the wrong digits. What up with that?" Sticks said.

"I did? You must have gotten me so worked up that I wrote the wrong number. I'm here now, though." She rubbed his arm.

That was all she needed to do to get him. They flirted for a little while longer. She told him that she was a prostitute and she worked that diner sometimes for extra cash. She convinced him that she was looking for a pimp and that maybe he could be her pimp. When Sticks mentioned he worked with Scar, Halleigh said she would fuck both for free. Let them sample the goods before they put her to work. Sticks was all the way down with that. Now they were in the room with Scar.

"Damn, you a fine piece of ass. Come here. Let me see you closer." Scar stood up and made his way around his desk. Luckily for Halleigh, Malek never brought his business home, so Scar never knew about her.

Halleigh strutted over to him like a stripper walking over to collect her dollar bill from a john. Scar grabbed her breasts and stroked her arms. "Turn around. Let me see that ass," he instructed.

This was driving Day insane. He wanted to grab Halleigh and take her out of there. The sight of Scar touching her was making him crazy with jealousy and anger. He didn't know what to do. While Scar was putting his hands all over Halleigh, Sticks came and sat on the couch next to Day.

"I heard you got jacked by the chief," Day said to Sticks.

"Yeah, fuck him. Punk mu'fucka." Sticks was non-chalant with his answer, hoping the subject would be dropped. He continued watching Halleigh grind Scar.

In order to keep from flying into a rage, Day was going to try to get Sticks to fuck his story up about getting robbed. It would keep his mind occupied and maybe keep his eyes off of what was going on between Scar and Halleigh.

Day looked over at Halleigh as she walked to the center of the room.

"Put some music on. I want to dance for you." Halleigh slowly swayed her hips and pressed her breasts together.

Scar turned his stereo on and took a seat on the couch on the other side of Day. Sticks pulled out a blunt, lit it, and passed it to Scar. The three men watched as Halleigh began to seductively strip for them. It seemed to Day that every time they made eye contact, she would glare at him with hate in her eyes.

"This bitch is fine as fuck. I can't wait to get up inside that ass." Scar took a hit off his blunt.

Day continued his questioning of Sticks, hoping that Scar would listen and hear Sticks spew some bullshit. "So, what happened? He held you up?" He looked at Sticks.

"Yeah, gun straight to my face."

"What kind of gun?"

"I don't fuckin' know. Stop askin' questions. I'm tryin' to watch this bitch dance for me." Sticks took the blunt back from Scar.

Halleigh had stripped down to just her lace thong. Scar and Sticks were getting worked up. She was doing splits and making her ass clap like a professional stripper. Day knew she had been forced into prostitution when she was younger, but now watching her dance, he thought maybe she had worked the pole at some point as well. He wanted to throw some clothes over her, pick her up, and run out of there.

Day was angry at everyone—at Sticks and Scar for putting their hands all over Halleigh's naked body, and at Halleigh for being there, dancing for them naked and allowing them to touch her. Day couldn't understand why Halleigh would be there doing this. She said she wanted Scar dead, but he didn't see how becoming one of Scar's hoes could accomplish that. Was this some sort of way to get back at Day because she was angry at him? Day started feeling like it was all his fault.

Halleigh was on her back in the middle of the room with her legs spread wide in a V shape. She closed them and spun around onto her stomach, arched her back, and got on all fours. She looked straight at Scar and licked her lips seductively.

"Come to daddy," he said.

Halleigh began slowly crawling toward Scar. Day was sick to his stomach, thinking that he was about to watch Halleigh suck Scar's dick. His whole body was taut with anger. He was desperate to try to stop it. Maybe he would kick her as she got close enough. Maybe he should just tell Scar that Sticks stole the money. He needed to figure out a way to break this thing up.

"Was anyone else in the parking lot when you got jacked?" Day asked Sticks.

"Shut up, nigga. This about to get real nasty up in here." Sticks wanted desperately to change the subject.

"Where was Flex?"

Sticks shot Day a sideways glance, thinking, *Why this nigga keep bringin' up this night? Does he know something he ain't sayin'?*

"The fuck should I know where that nigga be?" Sticks instantly got on guard. No one was supposed to know that Flex was there that night.

"It's just that you two be seemin' tight lately. I figure he would back you up. In a fightin' way, not a sex way."

"What you tryin' to say, nigga?"

Meanwhile, Halleigh had gotten up and turned her ass toward Scar. She was bending over in front of Scar, grinding her ass into his dick.

The energy in the room was frenetic. Scar was mad horny and about to fuck this chick, and Sticks and Day suddenly started beefing with each other. The music seemed to get louder and the beat seemed to quicken. Everyone was running at max energy.

Halleigh bent all the way over with her head between her knees. Scar had both his palms firmly planted on each of her ass cheeks, spreading them wide. Halleigh reached into the side of her mouth, between her gums and cheek, and pulled out a razor blade.

Sticks turned to Day to tell him to shut the fuck up. He cocked his fist to punch Day in the mouth at the same time that Halleigh spun around and swiped the razor blade at Scar's face.

Scar reacted quickly enough to avoid the razor blade. The razor's edge went sweeping an inch in front of his face.

Sticks held back his punch when he saw the commotion between Halleigh and Scar. Scar, on the other hand, didn't hold back his punch. As soon as he avoided the blade, he punched Halleigh in her jaw as hard as he could. This sent her flying across the room, and her cheek and jaw immediately started swelling.

By sheer instinct, Day instantly jumped up to protect Halleigh. He leaped across the room and landed on top of her. His intent was to cover her and protect her from any more punches.

Scar came over and tried to get at Halleigh. He was wildly throwing punches at her and threatening to kill her. Day was trying to get in the way of Scar's punches, but a few were landing. Day realized he couldn't protect her without Scar becoming suspicious. He had to make it look like he was trying to restrain her. He had to get her out of there quickly.

He picked her up off the floor and slammed her up against the wall. He held her by her throat, looked her in the eyes, and mouthed the word "Sorry" before he punched her in the stomach. She doubled over in agony.

"I'll take this bitch out of here," Day said to Scar.

"Fuck that. I want this bitch dead." Scar pulled out his gun and aimed it at Halleigh.

"Hold up, hold up." Day stepped in front of the gun. "You don't need blood on yo' hands right now. Let me take this bitch. I'll kill her and dump the body."

Scar kept his gun pointed as he thought about it. "Yeah, a'ight. Kill this bitch." He lowered his gun and gave Halleigh one last punch to the face. "Fuckin' bitch." Then he spat on her.

Sticks was just standing there doing nothing. He was sort of enjoying watching Scar beat this chick. He liked that this prostitute had enough heart to go after Scar. That was his kind of girl. Too bad she was about to die. "Sticks, you stay here, mu'fucka. How the fuck you bring some grimy bitch up in here? You gots some explaining to do. You done fucked up twice now. If I don't like what I hear, you gon' die too." He pointed his gun at Sticks.

Day wished he could stay around and watch Sticks try to squirm his way out of this one, but he needed to get Halleigh far away from there. Scar was focused on Sticks, so now was the perfect time to get ghost. He put Halleigh in a choke hold and pushed her out the door without saying a word.

Halleigh struggled to release herself from Day's hold as he shuffled her to his SUV. Not wanting to have to run around the streets of Baltimore naked, she got in the front seat of the Escalade. As soon as Day got in the driver's side, she started hitting him.

"You fucking asshole!" She was swinging wildly without any aim, mainly connecting with his arm.

"Relax." He attempted to stop her punches as he sped away.

"Why did you hit me?"

"I was protecting you. Now, stop before we crash." He was doing his best to block the uneven punches.

Halleigh realized her punches were ineffective, and she really didn't want to crash, so she stopped her attack on Dayvid.

"Thank you," he said.

Halleigh watched the world whiz by the passenger's side window. She was mad at Dayvid. She could have taken care of Scar if he hadn't gotten in the way. She'd taken a beating before at the hands of her old pimp, Manolo. It was nothing she couldn't have handled.

They rode in silence down I-95 for about twenty minutes, until Day pulled over at a rest stop. After he parked the car he turned to her.

"I'm sorry I hit you."

"I don't give a fuck. It didn't hurt anyway. You a pussy." She wouldn't face him.

Day saw that she obviously wasn't going to accept an apology, so he would try to talk some sense into her.

"What the fuck were you thinking? You could have gotten yourself killed!" He raised his voice.

"Don't act like my father. I know what I'm doing." She turned to him and matched his volume.

"You think a little bitty razor blade is going to kill him? You are fucking crazy. Let me handle it."

"I did let you handle it, and you ain't done shit. At least I'm doing something about it."

"I told you I'm working on it. Just stay out of it." They were fully screaming at each other at this point.

"Fuck you! You need my help, and now all of a sudden you want me to stay out of it? This nigga needs to die."

"I'll handle it!"

"I bet you will. What, you wanna fuck Scar? Is that it? You wanna become Scar's bitch?" she taunted.

"The fuck you talking about?"

"You know what I'm talkin' about. You coming over to my house all the time, I just danced for y'all, and now I'm sitting here butt-ass naked, and you haven't so much as looked at me or tried to push up on me. Seems to me you want to fuck Scar instead."

Day had been checking Halleigh out when she was dancing, but he was more consumed with his rage and jealousy than thinking about fucking Halleigh. He looked now at Halleigh sitting there in her thong and it got him aroused. Her body was better than he had ever envisioned it. Her breasts were still firm even without a bra, and her skin was perfectly smooth.

"You want to get fucked. Is that what this is about?" He looked directly in her eyes.

"I'm sitting here naked and you ain't doing nothing." There was a slight pause for the tension to build, and then they couldn't hold back anymore. The tension broke; they leaned toward each other and began feverishly kissing. Dayvid's hands greedily roamed over every inch of Halleigh's body. They had both been waiting for this moment for a long time. She hungrily unbuckled his belt, unzipped his pants, and reached in for his manhood. His dick was rock hard, and Halleigh couldn't wait to see it unleashed.

They slid into the back seat, and Dayvid got on top of Halleigh. She pulled his pants down and started stroking his cock. Dayvid ripped off her panties and plunged two fingers into her hole. She moaned with delight the second his fingers hit her wet pussy.

Dayvid was sucking her breasts and fingering her flower while she was stroking his hard, hot dick. She couldn't wait any longer.

"I need you inside me." She spread her legs wider as she guided his manhood to her pussy.

Dayvid slid his cock deep inside her. It felt so good to both of them. Her pussy lips wrapped tight around his dick as he rapidly stroked in and out of her.

Halleigh had not felt pleasure like this in a long time. It kind of hurt when he was all the way in, but Halleigh loved it. The more he stroked, the wetter she got. Dayvid loved how wet and tight Halleigh was. Both of them had wanted this for so long. So much sexual tension had been building toward this that they couldn't hold it any longer.

"I'm going to cum!" she screamed.

"Me too!"

Together they exploded in orgasm. Afterward, they both lay there for a while, panting, trying to catch their breath. It may not have been the longest fuck session, but it was the most intense. It was animalistic. It was complete passion that was long overdue.

They lay there looking at each other, consumed with post-sex glow. Both were in ecstasy but also shocked by what had just happened.

"Wow," Dayvid said.

"Yeah." She smiled.

"You're going to have to disappear for a while. You can't be seen anywhere."

"I know."

They kissed each other passionately.

"I'll tell Scar that I shot you and dumped your body in the bay." He softly rubbed her cheek where she had been hit by the back of his hand.

They kissed again.

"Now will you finally kill Scar?" she asked.

"Is that what this was about? You fucked me to get me to kill Scar?" Dayvid was offended.

"You're still not going to do it?"

Their bliss from a few seconds ago was now turning into another argument.

"You think just 'cause you fucked me, I'll suddenly kill Scar now? How fucking dumb you think I am?"

"What the fuck are you so scared of? I just put my ass on the line, and you too bitch-ass to do anything." She started to wriggle out from underneath him.

"You too stupid to realize what I'm trying to do."

"Fuck you. Take my ass home. I can't believe I just fucked a bitch like you." She climbed into the front seat.

"Fuck you too. You got no sense, bitch." He pulled up his pants and slid into the driver's seat. He wished he could make her walk home, but he would never do that to her. When it came to Halleigh, Dayvid had a hard time being an asshole.

Dayvid drove back to Halleigh's house without looking at her or saying a word to her. She did the same thing to him. They weren't going to see eye to eye on the situation with Scar. Dayvid wanted to tell her not to go after Scar again, but he figured there was no point in even trying, because she wouldn't listen.

He had barely stopped in Halleigh's driveway before she jumped out and ran to her front door. He rolled the window down and yelled to her as she ran, "Stay out of sight."

"Fuck you." She ran inside her house and slammed the door.

Chapter 11

Time Limit

Scar stood with his feet wide, arm extended straight out in front of him, holding his gun. Sticks was sitting on the couch, staring down the barrel of the gun. He had been telling Scar the story of how he met Halleigh, or Sincere, as she told him her name was. He recounted how he had run into her at the diner and then again at the bodega a few days later. The mention of the meeting with Chief Hill didn't help the situation. Scar was still so enraged by the thought of losing that money that he was on the verge of shooting Sticks for bringing it up again. Sticks was on thin ice, and if he didn't satisfy Scar with his story and convince him of his innocence, he was about to take his last breath.

Sticks rambled on and on. "I'm telling you. I had no idea. This bitch seemed like she was itching to get fucked. I know you been feelin' bad, so I brought her for you to cheer you up. I mean, I wanted to fuck her, but not until you had her. I mean, if she was down for a train, I was cool with that too. I'll do whatever you want. You gotta believe me. I had no idea this ho be trippin' like that." He was afraid that if and when he stopped talking, he would be shot.

When he finished with his explanation, he looked at Scar, who had been standing quietly listening to him babble. Scar said nothing. Sticks didn't know if this was a good thing or a bad thing. Was he not asking questions because he was satisfied with the story? Was he not asking questions because he was fed up and didn't believe a word? The not knowing was stressing Sticks out to the point that his eyes started to water. His heart was beating a mile a minute, and he actually started praying silently to God, something he hadn't done since he was a little boy. If ever there was a time that Sticks needed the Lord to hear him, now was the time.

Sitting there waiting for Scar to make some sort of decision and do something felt like an eternity. In actuality, it had only been about two minutes. Finally, Scar had made his decision.

"Get ready to meet your maker, mu'fucka," he snarled. Bang! Scar pulled the trigger and fired the gun. Sticks let out a scream. The bullet sped toward Sticks and landed in the wall above his head.

Sticks paused to take inventory of his body. Scar had missed; he was still alive. He looked to Scar with his eyes open wide. He was at a loss for words. He didn't know if he should thank Scar or curse him.

"Next time you fuck up, I won't miss." Scar put away his gun and left the room.

Sticks just sat there panting like he had just run a marathon. His adrenaline was so high he felt as if he might have a heart attack. His nerves were shot. He started to cry a little bit after Scar left. That was it for Sticks; he now knew he had to go out on his own. He needed to be his own boss.

Fuck Scar, he thought as he wiped the tears from his eyes. Scar and Sticks were now enemies. The next time Sticks and Scar saw each other would be when Sticks was putting a gun to Scar's head.

Dayvid sped away from Halleigh's house headed toward Baltimore. He was confused about what had just happened between them. He thought the sex had happened because there was a mutual attraction and their passion had built up so much that it had to be unleashed. The way she reacted afterward and the things she said to him, though, made him think she had other motives. She was using sex to manipulate him. This pissed him off. He had started to have feelings for Halleigh that went beyond sex, but it seemed she wasn't feeling the same way.

Day drove through the empty streets of Baltimore. It was the middle of the night, all the stores were closed, and no one was on the streets except an occasional corner boy hoping to make his last few dollars before he called it a night. Every time one of them saw Day driving up the block, they would perk up, thinking it could be the sale they were waiting for.

Day was driving around trying to clear his head. It had been an emotional few days, and he needed to put it all in perspective so he didn't do something stupid and get himself killed. Acting on his emotions right now would be a bad mistake. He needed to think rationally and stick to his plan. No matter how much pressure he was feeling, he needed to stay calm and focused.

He felt like he was close to his goal. If he could just get his contacts and connections all in place, he would have enough money to fund his own operation, and then he could take Scar out. It all seemed so fragile to him. One wrong move and it could all fall to pieces.

Halleigh was scaring him a bit. He couldn't understand why she wouldn't trust him. He had a plan that he thought was tight. She just needed to trust him and let him execute it, and then they would be taken care of. Instead, she was becoming impatient and reckless. She didn't seem to understand that she was tempting fate and knocking on death's door, putting them both in danger when she pulled stunts like the one she pulled earlier.

Day was tired. After driving around and calming himself down, he was ready to go home and sleep for the next week. He was driving down his street, thinking about his comfortable bed and about to pull up in front of his crib when his phone rang. He didn't recognize the number, so he ignored the call. The caller immediately called back. Again he ignored the call. Whoever was on the other line was persistent, because they called back instantly. Day angrily answered the phone.

"What?"

"Why you ain't answer?" It was Scar calling.

Day didn't recognize the number because Scar changed his phones like he changed his underwear. He was always trying to stay one step ahead of the law.

Quickly changing his tone, he said, "Oh, yo, I didn't know it was you. What up?"

"You do that thing?"

"Yeah, it's done. Fishes probably be eatin' well in the harbor tonight," Day said.

"Good. Fuck that bitch. Now go talk to Derek."

"Now?"

"When the fuck you think I'm talking about? Yeah, now."

"I'm mad tired, boss," Day replied.

"I don't give a fuck. I'm awake, you're awake. Go do it. If you don't, don't bother coming back here," Scar warned.

Scar was being unrealistic and demanding, but Day had no choice. He had to go. He couldn't take the chance of not being allowed back to the Dirty Money Crew. He had worked hard to establish himself solidly within the crew, and he didn't want to ruin it all because of this one little thing.

"Okay, boss. I'm on my way."

"Right choice. I'm sick of y'all fuckin' up lately. Niggas are gonna start payin' around here." Scar didn't wait for an answer. He hung up.

Day was tired, angry, and getting sick of Scar's bullshit. He wanted to get this over and done with so he could get some much needed sleep. Derek better not start playing games, because Day was not going to be in the mood.

He called Derek on his cell. Derek was not happy to be woken up.

"Fuller," Derek answered groggily. "Time to meet."

"Who is this?"

"It's Day, mu'fucka. Time to pay the piper."

"The fuck you want?" Derek was more alert now. "An update. You and me be meetin' now."

"Ah, shit. I was sleeping." Derek was stalling. He had nothing to tell them.

"I don't care."

"Now? Where?" Derek instantly started making mental notes of what he had to do before this meeting.

"The Pagoda, Patterson Park. Come alone or your kids won't see tomorrow." Day disconnected the call. Each man was coming to this meeting tired and angry.

Derek became furious and frantic. He rushed to put on clothes and make the necessary call to the officer who was assisting him.

***

Day entered the park from East Baltimore Avenue and made his way toward the pagoda. There was a stand of trees near the pagoda that provided cover for him as he waited. He scanned the area and saw no sign of Derek. He didn't have the patience for this bullshit right now. He was going to sit down against a tree and close his eyes for fifteen minutes. If Derek wasn't there when he opened them, he was leaving.

Day was in a deep sleep when he was startled awake by a sound. He jumped to his feet and pulled out his gun. Careful to stay close to the tree, he crouched and searched the area for the source of the sound. He had no idea how long he had been asleep.

The sun had just started to rise, and his eyes were having trouble adjusting to the light. Finally, Day saw Derek coming from the opposite side of the pagoda. He waited and watched to make sure that no one else had come and he was not being set up.

Satisfied that Derek was alone, Day came out from behind the tree, pointing his gun at Derek. "Put your hands away from your body."

Derek saw the gun and obeyed the command as Day approached him. He stretched his hands away from his body like he was on the cross. Day made him turn away and then patted him down. Finding no weapon, Day told him to lower his arms and put away his own gun.

"What took you so long?" Day asked.

"You woke my ass up," Derek replied.

"You do what Scar wanted you to do?"

"I talked to the mayor. He's willing to help, but it's gonna cost you," Derek lied.

"Fuck that. If you don't hurry up, it's gonna cost you."

"What's that supposed to mean?" Derek narrowed his eyes in rage.

"It means the clock be ticking on yo' kids," Day said smugly.

In a rage, Derek lunged at Day and tackled him. The two men started wrestling and punching each other. Day managed to throw Derek off of him, get to his feet, and draw his gun. Derek flipped over. Seeing the gun pointed directly at him, he remained frozen, hoping that Day wouldn't shoot.

"Back the fuck up!" Day commanded and Derek obliged. "You got one week, mu'fucka. If you don't deliver, then you gon' start seeing your kids' body parts one by one."

Day didn't dare turn his back on Derek. Keeping his gun drawn, he walked backward away from Derek, who stayed motionless on the ground, burning with anger. When he was far enough away, Day turned and quickly left the park. Derek sat there watching him and vowing that he would get revenge on Day, Scar, and anyone else who was involved in the kidnapping of his children.

Derek had enlisted the help of one of Chief Hill's officers, who had been waiting in an unmarked car outside the park. He pulled out his phone and called the officer. "The suspect is headed out the north side of the park toward East Baltimore Ave."

"Copy," the officer responded.

"Follow him, but do not engage. I will meet up with you ASAP." He hung up the phone.

Derek was going to get to Scar and save his children through Day. He didn't know how yet, but he was sure that he would figure it out. He had to; he only had a week.

Chapter 12

Confess

Day was amped after his showdown with Derek. Unaware that he was now being followed, he sped off from the park. The sun had risen and the city was waking up. People were coming out of their homes and heading off to work. All the hustlers were getting back to their corners for another day of slinging rock.

He drove through the city planning his next move. Reporting this meeting to Scar could wait. First he needed to find Flex and hear his version of the events at the diner. Day knew what he'd seen, and he didn't believe Chief Hill really stole Scar's money, but he wanted to see what Flex had to say about it.

Day stopped at home to change his clothes before finding Flex. He rushed through the front door and stripped off his clothes, heading straight to the shower. The hot water felt good streaming down his muscular back. He stood in his shower letting the water beat down on him and wash away the stress that had been piling up on his shoulders. He had been feeling pressure from everyone in his life lately. Standing there in the heat and steam, he started to let go of that pressure.

He thought back to his teenage years, his friend Malek, and the lessons Malek had taught him: how to be a man, how to take care of yourself and your business, and the most important one, how to take care of the one you love. Halleigh and Malek Jr. had been the ones that Malek loved, and Dayvid had vowed to look out for them.

Dayvid was feeling guilty about having sex with his dead friend's girl, but it just happened, and now it was done. He looked up to the heavens as the water poured down, and said a prayer to his fallen friend, asking for his forgiveness.

Day watched himself in the mirror as he dried off after his long, hot shower. He admired his cut physique and promised himself to get back to the gym and lift some weights. With everything happening in his life, he had been neglecting his normal workout routine. He needed to be in top form with everything that was about to go down. He figured there would be some hand to hand combat happening, and he couldn't afford to come out on the losing end of those battles.

Day wrapped the towel around his waist, went into his bedroom, and sat down on the edge of the bed for a second. The next thing he knew, he was lying back on the bed, closing his eyes. In an instant, he was sound asleep.

Meanwhile, the police officer who had followed him was sitting in his car out front. As he waited for Day to come out, Derek called him.

"What's the word?" Derek asked.

"Followed the suspect to a house. Suspect entered. Now I'm waiting for him to emerge," the officer replied.

"Good. Keep a close eye on him. Let me know when he's on the move."

"Copy."

Seven hours later, Day shot straight up into a sitting position. He was startled awake by a nightmare he was having in which Halleigh was being tortured. This made Day very uncomfortable. Maybe it was a sign and she was really in trouble.

He rushed to his phone and started to call her, but then hung up. Halleigh had made it perfectly clear the last time she saw him that she didn't want his help.

If that's the way she wants it, then so be it, he thought. *She doesn't think she needs my help, so she ain't getting it. Besides, it's just a dream. I'm sure it's nothing.*

Refreshed and refocused, Day got dressed quickly. He was feeling a sense of urgency, like something wasn't right, like time was running out. But running out on what? He had felt in control before, but with recent circumstances, he felt that control slipping a bit. He had to act fast. His life depended on it.

He left the house in search of Flex. There were a few places that Flex might be at this hour. The one place he didn't want him to be was at Scar's hideout. He needed Flex to himself. Day might have to let Flex know that he saw what went down, and he didn't want to take the chance of Scar hearing.

As Day drove around the hood searching for Flex, he noticed that the energy on the streets was completely different. Earlier that morning, there were only a few people on their way to work and the stores were all just opening their doors. Now every corner had a fiend copping from a corner boy, the stores were all open and lit up, and most of the windows on the apartment buildings were bright with light. Inside the apartments, the working people were settling in to watch their favorite television shows before going to sleep and then doing it all again the next day.

Day drove to the first of Flex's corners and was told by one of his crew that Flex had just been there. Unaware that he was being followed, Day drove to the corner where Flex was supposed to be.

As he pulled up, Day's SUV attracted attention. Whenever a car crept up to a corner, everyone got on alert, especially when it was a shiny black Escalade with tints. It could be a potential customer or a rival. Either you would be making money, or you would be shooting and running for your life.

Flex was talking to one of the corner boys as he eye-balled the SUV. Day rolled down his passenger's side window as he pulled up to the corner.

"Ay yo, Flex," he called out.

Not knowing who was calling him, Flex stayed where he was and cautiously looked into the SUV. His demeanor changed when he saw that it was Day. His tension lifted and he smiled.

"What up, fam?" Flex approached the SUV, reached inside, and greeted Day by slapping palms with him.

"You got time? I need to talk some business." Day didn't want to spook Flex, so he was trying to act nonchalant.

"Yeah, you know, just keeping my blocks running smooth. I always got time for business. What's up?" Flex was leaning his elbows against the car door as he spoke.

"Get in. Let's take a ride."

Flex opened the door and got inside the luxury vehicle. Noticing the leather seats and custom stereo system he said, "This is nice. I'ma buy one of these someday."

"Word? How you gonna do that?" Day tried to lead him as he pulled away from the curb.

"I got some paper saved. Just waiting for my wallet to get a little thicker."

"I hear you. That's kind of what I wanted to talk to you about." Day kept his eyes on the road as he drove.

"I'm always down to make my wallet thicker. What is it?" Flex started fiddling with the stereo.

"Nah, it ain't about making your wallet thicker. It's about the thickness of it right now."

"What you mean?" Flex looked at Day out of the corner of his eye.

"Business been dropping off as of late, but somehow you got money stashed."

Flex defended himself. "What you implying? I'm frugal, dude. Don't be spending on stupid shit."

"Okay." Day kept his eyes on the road. He purposely kept his answer short and noncommittal in order to make Flex confused and nervous.

They continued driving as the energy inside the car completely changed. Flex just stared out the passenger's window, and Day could feel the nervous energy coming off of him. It was exactly what Day had hoped for: make Flex uncomfortable and get him to confess for fear he would be killed. Now he could really start to put on the pressure.

"How long it take you to save all that?"

"I don't know." Flex kept his face turned away from Day.

"How much you got?"

"I don't know."

"I know that's a lie, but that's your business. I feel you."

"Why you so interested? I keep that shit to myself because I don't want niggas tryin' to jack me for it." Flex finally turned toward Day.

"It's not really me who's interested."

"Then who is?"

"Scar."

That caught Flex off guard. He was hoping to be on Scar's radar, but he was getting the feeling that this wasn't a good thing.

Flex argued his case. "Yo, I give Scar his cut. I ain't never skimmed off the top."

"Well, see, that's where I think you two might differ on opinion."

"Fuck that! I'd never do some grimy shit like that!" Flex was adamant.

Day had Flex right where he wanted him. For effect, he pulled the SUV over so he could turn and give Flex his full attention. They were on a deserted pier in front of a warehouse overlooking the harbor. Day had chosen such a desolate spot to scare Flex into thinking he might be killed.

Day began, "Okay, listen. Sticks been tellin' Scar that Chief Hill stuck him up and stole money from him."

"That's fucked up. So what, we gonna kill Chief Hill?"

"Sticks said it happened the night he went to talk to the chief at the diner." Day waited to see what Flex would say to this. Flex said nothing.

Day continued, "See, I think shit didn't happen that way. But here's the thing, when I asked that nigga about it, he said he gave you the money. That you was gonna hold it and he didn't know what you did with it. He said he told Scar that story about the chief to protect you."

He looked Flex dead in the eyes and asked, "So, where's the fuckin' money? If Scar find out you stole from him . . ."

Knowing the answer, Flex cut him short. "Yo, that ain't what happened. Sticks was supposed to meet with the chief and he wanted me to be lookout. . . ." Flex proceeded to tell Day what happened that night, not leaving out one detail. He was going to make sure that Day believed him, because he knew his life depended on it, and because he damn sure wasn't going to take the fall for Sticks. He was furious.

Getting Flex to confess was easier than Day had thought it would be. Day was prepared to tell Flex he had followed him and saw everything, but Flex was so shook that he gave it up without much coaxing. Now all Day had to do was to get him to tell Scar the story the way he wanted him to. He said, "If this is true, you need to let Scar know. He's already suspicious of that Chief Hill bullshit story, so you know Sticks gonna be runnin' like a bitch to Scar and change his story."

"I swear that is exactly how it went down. Sticks is a lying mu'fucka." Flex felt like he was pleading for his life.

"Then we go tell Scar before Sticks gets to him."

Still oblivious to the officer who had been following him since leaving his house earlier, Day started his SUV and pulled away, headed for Scar's hideout.

Chapter 13

The Truth Will Set You Free

The officer who was following Day was making sure to stay far enough away to remain undetected. After leaving the pier and heading up Broening Highway, the officer pulled out his cell phone and called Detective Fuller.

"Fuller." Derek answered.

"Sir, subject just left Holabird Industrial, now heading north. He has picked up another African American male. Should I keep on them?"

"Stay with them. I'll come relieve you soon."

Derek had been looking for his kids all day. Every lead he followed was a dead end, and his frustration was at its peak. He was tracking down this one last lead, and then he would give the officer a break. He had earned it, and Derek could hear in his voice that he was getting bored with his assignment. Derek knew that could only lead to one thing—the officer getting careless and losing sight of the subject.

On the ride over to see Scar, Flex started getting nervous. He was afraid that the truth wouldn't work.

"Yo, I don't know if Scar gonna like my story. Maybe we need to tell him something else."

"What?"

"I just don't think he'll believe me. Let's tell him somethin' else." Flex's nerves were making him talk fast.

"Just tell him your story."

"I'll tell him my story, but how 'bout I add somethin'? You know, make me look better."

"Nigga, you look fine from your story. Sticks the one who look like shit." Day didn't need Flex going off script now.

"Nah, I know, but how 'bout I tell him, like, I chased the chief and caught him and got some of the money back? Then I can give him what Sticks gave me. Both me and Sticks won't look so bad."

"That is some dumb-ass shit. Sticks tryin'a play you, fool. That nigga don't care 'bout you. What if Scar find out you lyin'?"

"I'm just sayin'. That way it won't look like I was tryin'a steal from him."

"Nigga, just tell him the truth and say you ain't had no idea what was goin' on. You start makin' shit up, you won't be able to keep yo' lies straight. Scar catch you slippin' with yo' lies and both of us get dead."

Flex remained quiet. He thought over the lecture Day had just given him. He was confused. He thought Sticks was cool and was having trouble believing that he would play him like that. There were still a lot of lessons that Flex needed to learn. It seemed like Day might be the one to teach him.

"You right. I'll just tell him how it really went down." They drove the rest of the way in silence.

Flex started trembling as they pulled up to Scar's hideout. Day noticed this and knew he needed to get this kid in the right frame of mind. If Flex walked in there and started fucking up his story, it would be lights out for both of them. Day was bringing Flex in front of Scar and taking responsibility for him. He was vouching for this young buck, and if Scar didn't believe him or didn't like what he was hearing, they were done. "Get yo' head on, nigga! You go in there shaking like a bitch and Scar gonna murk us both."

"I'm good. I'm good." Flex was still trembling.

"Nigga, I mean it. Stop yo quakin'." Day punched Flex in his face, connecting with his jaw. This seemed to wake Flex up and stopped him from shaking.

"You right. The truth shall set you free. Right, nigga?" Flex smiled and stepped out of the car, ready to tell his story and deal with the consequences like a man.

Day watched him walk to the entrance and said to himself, "Young buck about to become a grown-ass man."

A haze of weed smoke and a pounding bass beat from the stereo greeted them as they walked into the front room. There were women in various states of undress all over, and each girl was entertaining one of Scar's henchmen. Some were just dancing for their man; others were fully fucking them. It seemed Scar had put together a little party—or an orgy, depending on how you looked at it.

Even with all of the partying going on, Flex still couldn't really let loose. He was focused on telling Scar his story and saving his ass. Doubt crept into his mind, though, when he saw the party. Maybe this wasn't the best time to tell Scar the bad news. Maybe he should wait.

He looked at Day and gave him a look that asked, What now?

Day sensed Flex's apprehension. He didn't care about interrupting the party. He needed Scar to hear this information.

"No time like the present." Day put his hand on Flex's back and started guiding him toward Scar, who was sitting on the couch, fucking around with the finest girl in the room.

"Ay yo, Scar. Can I holla at you?" Flex said.

Scar ignored him and continued kissing the girl and caressing her smooth skin and plump, round ass. Flex just stood there watching, with Day right at his side. Day was not about to leave Flex alone now. He was so close to finally getting Scar to see Sticks for what he was; he wasn't about to let this opportunity slip by.

"Ay yo, Scar," Flex said a little louder.

Scar kissed the girl for a few more seconds then pulled away and addressed the two men. "Can't you see I'm busy? You two freaks get off watching? There's plenty of girls. Go get yourselves one and leave me the fuck alone." He started sucking the girl's bare breasts.

"I need to speak to you. It's important," Flex persisted.

"You gon' want to hear what he got to say," Day chimed in.

Realizing the two weren't going to leave him alone, Scar stopped his seduction. The girl remained sitting on his lap as Scar looked at the two men with an annoyed look on his face.

"Okay. What?"

"I think we should go somewhere a little more private and less loud," Day suggested.

"I'll make that decision. Now, what the fuck is this about?" Scar said.

"Chief Hill didn't steal your money," Flex stated plainly.

This caught Scar off guard and got his attention. He didn't want it to look like it affected him, but it did. He sat there with no expression on his face, trying to conceal his confusion. If the chief didn't steal the money, then where was it? Who had it? Scar needed answers.

"Get up," he said to the woman on his lap. As she stood, he smacked her ass and she strutted away like a model on the runway. Scar directed his attention back to the two soldiers.

"Let's go in the back room." He stood from the couch and made his way from the party, with Day and Flex following.

Scar sat at his desk as the faint sounds of the party in the next room came through the walls. Flex and Day were standing side by side in the middle of the room, facing Scar. They looked like two boys standing before the principal, about to tell on the school bully.

Scar studied their faces, looking for any sign that they were scheming. After sufficiently asserting his power and letting them know who was in control of this situation, Scar asked, "So, what is it you have to say?"

Flex began, "I've heard that Sticks is sayin' Chief Hill took money from him the night they met at the diner. That ain't the truth." He then retold his story from the beginning—everything from the start of the day, when they followed the chief in front of the courthouse, to the end of the night, when Sticks gave him the money and told him to keep it quiet. As he did with Day, he didn't leave out one detail.

Scar sat at his desk taking in every word. His facial expression remained completely neutral throughout the entire tale. "Why are you telling me this?" he asked when Flex finished his story.

Flex looked at Day with a puzzled expression. He didn't really know how to answer the question. He figured the answer was obvious—because he was trying to save his own ass and because Sticks was being a sneaky motherfucker who stole from Scar.

Scar continued, "I'm just sayin', if you hadn't told me, I woulda never known that Sticks lied to me. How you know Sticks was sayin' that story anyway—unless you were in on it?"

Scar pulled a gun from his desk and pointed it at Flex. He was heated that someone had lied and stolen from him, especially one of his own men. The story didn't add up to him, and he suspected that Flex was lying as well. Someone was going to pay for their disrespect and disloyalty.

"Whoa, hold on, boss. I told him what Sticks was sayin'." Thinking quick on his feet, Day started making up a story on the spot.

"I ran into Chief Hill and stuck my fuckin' gun in his ribs. I was gonna murk his ass for stealing from us. But when I asked him where the money was, that nigga kept sayin' he didn't steal it. The thing is, he looked so shook I thought he was 'bout to shit on his self, and I started to believe he really ain't know nothin' about that shit. I didn't wanna have a cop killing on my hands, so I let the bitch go. I figured I could always get to the chief again later if I needed to.

"So I go ask Sticks about it, and he says he really gave the money to Flex to hold on to, and he don't know what Flex did with it. He says he told you that shit about Chief Hill to protect Flex. But see, that don't really add up to me. Why would he give Flex the money instead of givin' it back to you?

"So I go ask Flex about it, and he tells me his story. I told him to come tell you." He paused for a minute. He was just making things up as he went along and talking so fast that he wasn't even really sure what he had just said. He couldn't tell from Scar's expression if he believed the story, but there was no turning back now.

"Boss, Sticks been playin' you."

"Yeah, I ain't lyin', Scar. I'm telling you the truth," Flex added.

Scar lowered his gun. "Where the fuck is my money?"

"I still got it," Flex said nervously. "I can give you what Sticks gave to me. He got the rest, like I said."

"Mu'fucka, you damn right you gon' gimme my money back." Scar stood and came out from behind his desk, still holding his gun.

"I can go get my share now, boss."

Scar approached Flex. He raised his gun and pressed it against Flex's temple. Flex stood frozen, waiting for his certain death. Day watched with wide eyes, afraid to make any move.

"Nah, nigga, you gon' bring all my money back. First you gon' get Sticks to give you his share, then you gon' murk that snake." Scar took the gun from Flex's temple and held it out to hand it to him.

Flex couldn't believe it. He felt like he was getting a second chance on his life, even though he technically didn't do anything wrong. Thankful to be alive and willing to do whatever it took to stay that way, Flex said, "Consider it already done." He took the gun from Scar and put it in his waistband.

"You gon' earn yo stripes, youngin'. If it ain't done in twenty-four hours, you best start making your funeral arrangements." Scar walked out of the room and back to the party, leaving the two standing there counting their blessings to still be alive.

Sticks was about to die at the hands of a young buck who was eager to prove himself. This couldn't have worked out any better for Day. He ratted Sticks out without having to do it himself or give away that he had seen the whole thing go down. Even though they had been fighting, his first thought was that he had to tell Halleigh his good fortune.

"You best get on that," Day said to Flex.

"Sticks about to breathe his last breath," Flex snarled.

"Let's go. Time's running out."

They walked out of the room, through the party, and out the front door.

Chapter 14

A Taste for Blood

Flex was pacing back and forth in his apartment. He was sorting out how he was going to lure Sticks into a trap. He knew the location where he wanted to meet him, an abandoned barn up in horse country, but he didn't want to tip Sticks off that something was up.

This was an important step for him and he knew it. Flex was relatively new to the game, and he had never actually killed anyone. Killing Sticks would instantly enhance his reputation on the street and solidify his position in the Dirty Money Crew. It had to be done right, and it had to be done soon.

On the ride over to his crib, Day had given Flex some suggestions on what to say to Sticks. Flex liked what Day had suggested, and he was now trying to make sure he had it all straight. Day offered to help Flex with the kill, but Flex declined, feeling that he needed to do it himself. So here he was, psyching himself up to literally and figuratively end his first life. He would be ending Sticks' life for real, and ending the life he knew before becoming a murderer. After it was done, he could never look back.

Flex snorted several bumps of coke to make sure he was in the right frame of mind for the job. Sufficiently coked up, he called Sticks.

After getting Sticks to agree to meet him, Flex jumped in his car and immediately drove north. His plan depended on the element of surprise, so he wanted to make sure he was there before Sticks.

Sitting amongst the horse stables and hay bales, Flex continued psyching himself up by doing more and more coke. He started shadow boxing and swinging a two-by-four like a bat to release some of the energy the coke had created in his body. He kept looking out the broken window for Sticks and checking the gun to make sure it was loaded. Anything to keep himself occupied. His adrenaline was maxed out. He was high as shit, and paranoia started to overtake him.

As Flex was throwing stones in the air and hitting them with the two-by-four like baseballs, the lights of a car came through the window. Flex stopped his game and peeked out the window. He recognized the car coming up to the barn as Sticks'. He pulled out the baggie of coke, did one last bump, and watched to make sure that Sticks was alone.

The car stopped, and Sticks got out of the driver's side. Flex didn't see anyone else with him, so he placed the two-by-four by the entrance and walked out front to meet Sticks.

"Ay yo, fam," he called out to Sticks as they walked toward one another to clasp hands and bump shoulders in a greeting.

"What's good?" Sticks replied. "You must be shook, nigga, havin' me come all the way out here."

"You know, I wanted to talk to you away from prying eyes. Not really trustin' Scar right now. Also wanted to show you where I'ma do Chief Hill. Make sure it's the right kind of place. You know I ain't never killed no one before."

"Word? You 'bout to lose yo murdering virginity? Damn, that's crazy. Can I watch you do it?" Sticks was amused by the information.

"I might need your help."

"Hell yeah. I'll gladly drop that mu'fuckin' chief."

"Well, yeah, I might need your help with that, but I was talking about help with Scar. This nigga be buggin'. I think he be thinkin' I stole money from him," Flex said.

"Oh shit. Why you think that?"

"Just some shit he said when he told me to murk Chief Hill." Flex was trying to be as vague as possible.

"I feel you. He definitely buggin' lately."

"I ain't sure I want to be with that nigga no more." Flex was reeling Sticks in.

This was exactly the type of shit Sticks wanted to hear. He was hoping to recruit Flex, and now it seemed as though Flex was asking to be recruited. Sticks was going to take this opportunity and start to build his army.

"For real, I been havin' problems with Scar's disrespecting ass for a while. I'm ready to step out on my own. I set some shit in motion, so Scar won't be around to disrespect us too much longer. I'm lookin' for good soldiers to come with."

"Yo, I'm down. I seen how you roll when you hit me off with that nice chunk of change at the diner." Flex put up his hand to slap Sticks' hand in a sign of solidarity.

"That's what I'm talkin' 'bout. Let's make our own money." Sticks slapped hands with Flex.

"Let's celebrate. I got some clean yayo in the barn."

"Let's do this." Sticks started walking toward the entrance to the barn, excited to have a partner in crime.

When they got to the entrance, Flex grabbed the two-by-four. Sticks saw some odd movement by Flex out of the corner of his eye, but before he could turn around, it was too late. Flex cocked the board back like he had been doing while he was waiting and swung the two-by-four as hard as he could. The impact opened a huge gash in the back of Sticks' head and sent him crumbling to the ground, unconscious.

Flex checked Sticks' pulse. He was alive, which was a good thing because Flex still needed to find out where the rest of Scar's money was. While Sticks was unconscious, Flex tied his wrists together and hung him by the rafters, his feet just barely off the ground. His arms were extended over his head, and he was hanging in the middle of the barn like a heavy bag at a boxing gym.

When Sticks finally started to regain consciousness, the first thing Flex did was punch him as hard as he could in the stomach. It knocked the wind out of Sticks, causing him to spit up blood.

"Untie me, muthafucka." Sticks spat blood at Flex.

"You tryin' to set me up, huh, nigga?" Flex balled his fist and cracked Sticks in his mouth, loosening a few of his teeth and causing more blood to flow from his mouth and down his chin.

"The fuck you talkin' about?" Sticks was trying to clear his mouth of blood, spitting it to the floor.

"You stealin' money from Scar and tellin' Day I had it." Flex picked up the two-by-four and smacked Sticks across the kneecaps. If the sound was any indication, his kneecaps had been shattered. Sticks let out an agonizing scream.

Barely able to speak because of the pain, Sticks replied, "I don't know what you talkin' about."

Flex swung the board and connected with Sticks' ribs. Another scream came roaring from Sticks. He had broken ribs now and was having trouble breathing.

Laboring to breathe, he forced words from his mouth. "Okay, stop. . . . I took money . . . from Scar . . . but I never said . . . nothin' . . . 'bout you."

"Don't lie to me, mu'fucka." Flex began laying into Sticks' body with his fists, giving him repeated body blows like a boxer hitting a heavy bag. Sticks screamed in agony with every blow.

When he was finished and tired from his workout, Flex took a step back and examined the damage he had done. Sticks hung there with his head drooped down, covered in blood, exhausted from the beating he was taking.

"Now, I know you were tryin'a set me up. Day told me. So tell me where the rest of the money at," Flex said.

Unable to lift his head, Sticks began, "Day lyin'. . . . I ain't . . . set you up. Money . . . gone."

Flex couldn't afford to beat him anymore without risking killing him, so he resisted punching Sticks. "Come on. Just tell me where the money at."

"It's . . . gone." Sticks tried lifting his head and spitting at Flex again, but he didn't have the strength and ended up spitting on himself.

"I like your heart, bro. I seriously don't want to kill you, and I won't—if you just tell me where the money is."

Sticks didn't have energy to say anything this time. He just slowly shook his head.

Flex pulled out his gun and shot Sticks in the foot. Another blood-curdling scream filled the air. Flex couldn't believe the beating this guy was enduring.

"Come on, man. Scar told me to spare your life if you just return the money. He don't want no other problems right now. He got enough on his plate with the police on his ass. Don't make me shoot your other foot."

Barely audible now, Sticks started to speak. All he said was, "My . . . basement," as blood leaked from his mouth, head, and foot.

"That wasn't so hard, was it? Now, let me untie you," Flex replied.

"Thank you," Sticks whispered.

"You dumb mu'fucka. You really think I'm gonna let you go?" Flex mocked Sticks before he pointed the gun at his temple and pulled the trigger. The shot echoed through the barn. It blew a hole right through Sticks head and sent brain matter and blood flying through the air.

Flex stared in disbelief. He had just shot and killed his first human. It was easier than he expected, and it actually gave him a rush. He pulled out his baggie of coke, took a bump, and prepared to bury Sticks.

Chapter 15

Bliss Interrupted

Dayvid drove straight to Halleigh's house. He couldn't wait to tell her the good news—Scar had ordered Flex to kill Sticks. This would open up a straight path to Scar. He would be even closer to Scar now that Sticks was gone. There was less work for them to do, and the end of their revenge plot was in sight.

As soon as he pulled in the driveway, his excitement faded. The argument they had the last time they saw each other came slamming back to his memory. Although he was excited about the news and wanted to get past their argument, he wasn't sure how she would react. He tried to tell himself that he didn't care about her and that she could go out on her own, but now, the butterflies in his stomach told him he felt more for her than he admitted.

Dayvid rang the doorbell to the house and waited anxiously. The longer he stood there, the more he had to talk himself out of turning around and leaving. He rang the doorbell a few more times and was about to walk away when he finally saw Halleigh peeking out the side window. He couldn't punk out now.

Halleigh flung the door open. "Are you crazy ringing my bell like that? You're going to wake M.J.," she scolded.

"Sorry."

Halleigh just shook her head, left the door open, and walked away. Dayvid followed her into the house and into the kitchen. Halleigh was sitting at the table when he entered.

"What do you want?" She scowled at him. Dayvid pulled up a chair.

"I didn't tell you you could sit," Halleigh snapped. Dayvid calmly stood up and pushed the chair back in. He didn't want to start out fighting, so he obeyed her command without any back talk.

"I just came by to tell you that Sticks is about to die," he said.

"Good. He deserves it." Halleigh stayed calm. Inside she was ecstatic, but she was still mad at Dayvid, so she didn't show any outward emotion. She hated the way Sticks acted toward her when she was pretending to be Sincere, like she was just some piece of meat that he owned.

"This is great news, Halleigh, and that's all you have to say? You don't want to know how or why?"

"Okay, how? Why?" she asked sarcastically.

Dayvid proceeded to tell her how it all came about. As he was telling the story, he sat down without thinking. Halleigh was so caught up that she didn't really notice. She couldn't believe how everything worked out.

"Damn, you played all them fools," she said with a smile. "So, what do we do now?"

"We go after Scar immediately. Once Sticks is dead, we make our play for Scar and blame it on Sticks. We can say that Sticks heard Scar was after him, so he acted first and ordered one of his corner boys to kill Scar."

"That is perfect." She got up from her chair.

"This is exactly what we've been waiting for." He stood with her.

Without thinking, they leaned in and passionately kissed each other. They were both caught up in the excitement of the moment. Dayvid had definitely broken down the barrier that Halleigh had put up.

"So, are we staying here or going to the bedroom?" she asked seductively.

Without saying a word, Dayvid took her by the hand and led her out of the kitchen. Unable to wait until they got to the bedroom, Dayvid had Halleigh up against the hallway wall. They feverishly groped and kissed one another, needing to fulfill their desires.

They slowly made their way down the hall, disrobing each other along the way. Once they made it to the bedroom, Halleigh lay on the bed and Dayvid got on top. They continued kissing and caressing. They rubbed their warm, naked bodies together and explored each other with their tongues and hands. Unlike last time, this time was going to last. They both wanted it to go on forever. This was love; this wasn't just a fuck.

Dayvid slowly kissed his way down Halleigh's body until his head was between her legs. He lovingly kissed and licked and teased her button until she reached an earth-shattering orgasm.

Unable to control her passion and hunger for Dayvid's penis, Halleigh grabbed his head, pulled him up from between her legs, and positioned him to enter her. She grabbed his erect penis and inserted it inside her. He obliged by slowly thrusting in and out of her glistening hole.

Consumed with each other, they were unaware that they were being watched. From the moment they got in the bedroom there had been eyes on them. Detective Derek Fuller was outside the house, looking in.

Derek had met up with the other officer after Day dropped Flex at his apartment. Derek relieved the other officer of his duty and began following Day from that point. Little did he know that if he had just met up with the officer a little earlier, he would have been led directly to Scar. Instead, he'd been following one last dead-end lead and hadn't even bothered to check in with the officer for hours. He'd missed the chance to get to his kids at Scar's safe house.

Instead, when Derek saw Day pull into Halleigh's driveway, he was thinking that maybe this was where his kids were. He parked his car around the corner from the cul de sac and waited until Day went inside. Then he got out and walked around the house, peeking into windows. He was hoping to see his kids in there, but instead, he saw Day in a bedroom with a woman. It looked to Derek like this wasn't just some booty call. The way they were having sex with one another, it looked like they were in love.

Derek watched for a little while, but he didn't want to risk getting caught by either a neighbor or by the love-birds, so he crept back into the woods surrounding the house to wait for Day to leave.

***

After hours of exploring each other's bodies inside and out, Dayvid and Halleigh lay side by side, exhausted. They were in a state of complete bliss. Both were staring up at the ceiling, trying to catch their breath. They had huge smiles plastered across their faces. Neither one had ever been so satisfied in their lives.

Finally, after several minutes of silence, Dayvid said, "I'm sorry I got you mad at me."

"It was my fault. I overreacted. I should have trusted you," she replied.

"We both overreacted. It's over now. Time to move on."

"Okay. Agreed."

They looked at each other, smiled, and kissed. "I love you, Hal," Dayvid said.

"I love you too, Dayvid." She kissed him.

They started another round of passionate lovemaking. When it was finished, Dayvid stayed on top of Halleigh. He was propped up on his elbows, face to face with her.

"Everything I do is for you and M.J. I'll always be there for both of you."

"I'll always be there for you. Let's finish our revenge on Scar and Detective Fuller and move on with our life together. Me, you, and M.J.," she said.

"I like that idea." He smiled and kissed her.

"I want to help you kill them. For my own peace."

"I know. I figured." He kissed her forehead.

"How?" she asked.

"I'm not sure yet, but we do it together."

"Like everything from now on." She smiled.

Day got off of Halleigh and sat on the edge of the bed. "What's wrong?" she asked.

"Nothing. I was just thinking about how happy I am right now." He turned to look at her.

"Me too, baby. Me too."

He got up and started putting on his clothes.

"Where are you going? You're just gonna fuck me and leave me?" she said sarcastically.

"I'm going to finish what I started. Scar's days are numbered. In fact, Scar's hours are numbered."

He leaned over and kissed Halleigh again. She got up and walked him to the front door.

Standing in front of the door, he said, “I love you.”

“I love you too. Be careful.” She kissed him and hugged him tight.

Halleigh watched from the window as he got into the truck, then she went to the kitchen to prepare a pot of mint tea. She was sitting at the table waiting for the water to boil and thinking about the amazing sex she’d just had when she heard a knock at the door. This put a smile on her face, because she knew it was Day coming back for more. Excited, she got up and went to answer the front door.

“Couldn’t get enough?” she asked.

As soon as she opened the door a crack, someone pushed it in and punched Halleigh in her face. The impact knocked her to the ground and knocked her out. Derek walked in and stood over her.

Chapter 16

Collision Course

Mayor Steele walked down the empty corridor of City Hall. It was early morning and he was the first one in the office. This was his daily routine. He would get to work early before anyone else so he could have at least an hour of calm and quiet. He would read the local and national newspapers and catch up on his paperwork. This was always his favorite part of the day, especially lately. Every day seemed to be a replay of the previous day, dealing with chaos and disaster and struggling to keep the city together. There seemed to be daily negative articles about him, and his approval rating was plummeting. Baltimore was on the verge of a revolt, and Mayor Steele was the target. He was stressed out, and it was starting to show in his face. He looked worn down and beaten.

Even though he was struggling, his personality would not let him give up. He was not about to give up his position of power, and would do anything he had to do to keep it.

As he entered his office, he felt that it was going to be a good day. He sat down behind his desk and unloaded his armful of newspapers. Not one paper had a story on the front page about him. This was the first time in a long time that had happened. The mayor felt like maybe things were starting to turn around for him.

With a deep breath in and a heavy sigh, he sat back and opened up the *Baltimore Sun*.

With his morning routine finished, he looked out the window behind his desk, sipping his coffee and watching the commuters arriving to work. When he was feeling good, he loved looking out this window. It reminded him how much he loved the city. On bad days, when he wasn't feeling so good, he hated that window. It reminded him how fickle and heartless his city could be. Today, he loved the city. Even the sun was shining on the plaza in such a way as to say it was going to be a good day. For the first time in a long time, Baltimore seemed to have a feeling of hope in the air.

Later in the day, after several meetings and a press conference, the mayor made his way back to the office with Dexter following.

"Hello, Susan," the mayor greeted.

"Hello, Mayor Steele. Your mail for the day." She handed him a stack of envelopes.

Dexter gave Susan a sleazy wink as he walked by her desk and into the mayor's office. Susan, as usual, ignored him and went about her business.

Dexter and the mayor sat and discussed some political strategy.

"Dexter, I like not having negative headlines about me splashed across the front page of every newspaper. How do we keep this up?"

"Well, sir, I think the worst is behind us. We fended them off long enough that they're getting bored with us. We'll be buried deep within their pages from now on."

"That's not good either. Now we need to get back on the front pages for positive reasons."

"Yes, sir, we do. You're right. I'll talk to our press secretary. Maybe we can do some community outreach and make it a photo op for you." Dexter wrote a few notes on the legal pad on his lap.

"I like that. Start building my image with some pictures of me with some sick kids at a hospital or something." The mayor looked off into the corner of the room, imagining how this photo op would play out.

"Yes, yes. I'll get right on that." Dexter wrote some more notes.

"What's the latest on the thorn in our side, Scar?"

"That hasn't had any changes, sir."

"Damn." The mayor was determined not to lose his good mood.

"But that is good. Nothing worse has happened, so the papers are losing interest." As usual, Dexter stayed optimistic with the mayor.

“Right. I like the positive outlook. I refuse to let this scum ruin my good mood today. Let’s start spinning our stories to the press and only accentuate the positive.”

“Yes, sir. I like this new you. Anything else?”

As his instinct had told him, the day had gone pretty smoothly for the mayor. It was a slow news day, so to speak. “You know what, Dexter? I’m feeling so good I’m going to give you the rest of the day off.”

“Thank you, sir.” Dexter smiled and got out while the getting was good.

The mayor started in on his mail. It was the usual—invitations to galas and openings, some magazines, some personal letters. As he flipped through, though, there was one envelope that caught his eye. It was a typical business-sized white envelope, but his address was handwritten, and there was no return address. The postmark was from Miami, Florida—another red flag in the mayor’s eyes. Being in politics, he knew people in the capital city of Tallahassee, but he knew no one in Miami.

Taking a letter opener out of his desk drawer, he ran it slowly under the flap, making sure not to tip the envelope. After the attacks of 9/11, some news agencies had gotten envelopes with anthrax, and now all government agencies were constantly on high alert for similar attacks. The mayor cautiously opened the letter and looked in for the telltale white powder. When he was satisfied that there was none, he removed the piece of paper inside. He unfolded it and began to read the short, handwritten note:

My condolences to you on the loss of your police chief and chief of staff. I’m coming back for you. You’re next!

The mayor got an uneasy feeling in the pit of his stomach. The note confused and troubled him. He hadn’t lost either man. In fact, Dexter had just left his office.

He spoke into the intercom on his desk. “Susan, get Chief Hill on the phone.”

His uneasiness lessened when he looked out his window and saw Dexter Coram walking across the plaza.

"Sir, Chief Hill is on the line."

"Put him through."

"Hello, Mayor. You must have read my mind. I was just going to call you." Chief Hill sounded upbeat. He was hurriedly gathering his things and preparing to leave his house.

Mayor Steele was relieved when he heard Chief Hill's voice.

"I'm on my way over to police headquarters now. We have solid intel as to the whereabouts of Scar Johnson. We are gathering troops and preparing to raid his house."

"When did this materialize?"

"Late last night, sir. I got a call from one of Scar's associates who goes by the name of Sticks. Apparently they had a falling out, so this kid gave up Scar's location."

On the way to meet Flex, Sticks had called Chief Hill with the information on where to find Scar. Sticks was confident that Flex was getting fed up with Scar's bullshit just as much as he was, so he figured now was the time to take Scar down. He took a preemptive strike and ratted Scar out to the police. Little did he know that Flex was on Scar's side and was about to kill him.

"I knew it was just a matter of time before one of these punks talked," Mayor Steele said.

"The messed up thing is that Scar is hiding in Detective Rodriguez's old house."

"The son of a bitch kills her then hides out in her house? I want this smug fucker taken down!" The mayor pounded his desk.

"It's about to happen." Chief Hill exited his house.

"Chief, you will be front and center at the press conference to announce the capture of this thug."

Chief Hill dropped his duffel bag in the trunk of the car, sat behind the steering wheel, and put the key in the ignition. "Thank you, sir. I promise—" He turned the key.

Boom!

There was a huge blast on the other end of the mayor's phone and then the line went dead.

"Chief Hill! Hello! Chief Hill, are you there? Hello!" Silence.

"Oh shit." He looked out the window to search for Dexter but didn't see him. He spoke into the intercom. "Susan, get Dexter on the phone."

After a few moments, she responded, "Sir, he's not answering. His phone keeps going straight to voice mail."

"Shit," he repeated.

It turned out not to be a good day.

Dexter was so excited to be off work early that he practically skipped across the plaza. The mayor was in a good mood and being generous, so Dexter was going to take full advantage. Not wanting to be bothered or interrupted, he turned off his cell phone. He was going to have a fun day off. Before leaving City Hall, Dexter had gone to speak to Kris, his intern. He wanted to meet Kris at a hotel.

Kris had been interning for Dexter for about six months. Their relationship started off normally, with Dexter giving Kris menial tasks like making copies, delivering memos, that sort of thing. As the internship progressed, the tasks started becoming more involved, with Dexter even asking Kris's opinion on certain subjects.

One evening, about two months into the internship, Dexter asked Kris to stay a little later to help with a bill that was being presented the next morning. They worked late into the evening, and when they finished, Dexter pulled out a bottle of vodka from his desk and poured drinks for both of them. They sat in Dexter's office drinking vodka.

It was well past midnight when the bottle was finished, and the two were thoroughly drunk. As they were calling it a night and putting on their coats, Dexter grabbed Kris and started kissing him.

Kris had never kissed a man before. He was taken aback; he didn't know what to do. He was confused, drunk, and intimidated. This was his boss kissing him, and he had never thought about sleeping with men before. He pulled away from Dexter, only to have Dexter forcefully grab him back and kiss him again. Dexter then talked Kris into sleeping with him right there in the office.

After several days of awkwardness, Dexter got Kris to sleep with him again. Kris still wasn't fully comfortable with the situation and felt pressured by Dexter, but he thought it would advance his political career, so he did it. Over time, it got easier and easier for Kris, and now they were hooking up on a regular basis.

Dexter couldn't wait to fuck. He was about to get his freak on with this twenty-year-old blond, blue-eyed intern. He had wanted a position of power just so he could use it for things like this. He wasn't a very good-looking guy, so the only way he could get people to sleep with him was to either pay or use his power. Thinking about it on the way to the hotel was getting Dexter hard.

When he arrived at the hotel, he checked in and got the room ready. He opened the mini bar, turned on the music, and positioned the camera. Dexter was into secretly filming his sexual encounters and then watching them later. He had a tiny camera that he aimed at the bed and hid in the closet.

With everything in place, he sat back on the bed and waited. Several minutes later, Kris knocked. Let the games begin. Dexter turned on the camera and answered the door.

Several hours later, after Dexter had done every degrading, kinky thing he could think of, he was preparing to leave the hotel. Kris decided to stay behind and sleep at the hotel. Since it was on Dexter, he was going to order room service and watch some movies.

Turning on his phone, Dexter saw that he had thirty-one voice mails, all seeming to be from the mayor.

"Oh Christ. Party's over," he muttered.

Completely distracted now, he went into the closet, collected his coat, and walked out of the hotel, totally forgetting about his video camera.

Listening to the messages, he walked through the parking garage to his car. They all seemed to say the same thing. It was Susan telling Dexter to call immediately.

Dexter got into his car and dialed the mayor's office, even though he should have been gone for the day. As he listened to the phone ringing on the other end, he turned the key in the ignition and *BOOM!* The car exploded into a fireball of rubber and metal, killing Dexter instantly.

Standing on the street outside of the parking garage, Cecil watched as the car went up in flames on the second level. He took out his phone and placed a call.

"It's done. Both of them are dead."

"Oh, baby. I'm gonna suck your dick so good when you get back down here. I need you. Hurry," Tiphani replied.

She hung up the phone, satisfied that her statement to the mayor was going to be heard loud and clear.

After hearing the explosion over the phone, Mayor Steele instantly went to police headquarters. By the time he arrived, the word was out that Chief Hill had been killed by a car bomb. The headquarters was in a panic. News trucks had already descended on the building, and there were officers buzzing about back and forth. Phones were ringing constantly with news outlets looking for reaction and confirmation.

He entered from the back to avoid the crush of reporters and went directly to the deputy chief's office. There were several people from every rank in the office—sergeants, detectives, lieutenants, all trying to make sense of the tragedy.

An even six feet tall with graying hair and a chocolate complexion, Deputy Chief Vince Worthe was in his early fifties and a lifelong police officer. Although he desperately wanted to be named chief of police, he had been overlooked for the position several times and was resigned to the fact that he would never make chief.

"Mr. Mayor." Vince shook his hand.

"What's the latest? Do we have any leads?"

"We're working on it. Nothing yet, sir."

The mayor handed the note to the deputy chief. "This came to me today."

Vince quickly read the note. He examined the envelope and letter and then handed it to a detective. "Get this to the lab. Fingerprints and DNA."

The detective put it into a clear plastic interdepartmental envelope and left the room, headed toward forensics.

"I was on the phone with him when the bomb exploded. He said you were gathering to raid Scar Johnson's hideout."

"We were just discussing that. We're going to need to speak with you about your conversation with Chief Hill."

"Later. There's no time now. I want this son of a bitch captured. He has terrorized this city for too long."

"We're just about to deploy."

"I want to come with you. I want to see that scumbag's face when he's captured."

Mayor Steele was swooped up in a sea of officers as they trampled through the underground garage, making their way to vans and squad cars. Someone handed the mayor a bulletproof vest and a windbreaker to wear that read police in big white letters.

Day turned to night on the ride over, and Deputy Chief Worthe filled Mayor Steele in on their plan of attack. They were going to come at him from all angles. Nothing was being left to chance. As far as they were concerned, Scar was armed and dangerous and his men would be looking to kill. The police were taking the same attitude—shoot to kill.

Mayor Steele reinforced the idea that he wanted Scar Johnson kept alive. It would be good for the city's morale if the public saw him in handcuffs. The mayor was not going to allow another bullshit trial. This time Scar would be sentenced to a life in prison.

As they turned the corner onto their destination block, Mayor Steele said, "Deputy Chief, after this is over, I will be promoting you to chief."

"Thank you, sir," he replied; then, into his walkie-talkie he said, "Okay, men. This is it. All units go."

The cars and vans sped up the block and onto the front lawn of Detective Rodriguez's house. The officers jumped out even before some of the vehicles had completely stopped. Some men ran around back. Others ran right up on the front porch with a battering ram and smashed in the front door. All had their guns drawn, ready to shoot.

"Police! Hands up! Police! Get down! Police!" They stormed the house, running from room to room, shouting at the top of their lungs.

The men who entered from the front and the men who entered from the back all converged in the middle of the house. The yelling of "All clear!" slowly died down as all the officers realized that the house was empty. There were signs that people had been there, but no one was there now.

After the commotion subsided, one of the officers called the deputy chief over his handheld radio. "All clear, sir. No sign of anyone. House is empty."

The deputy chief and the mayor walked into the house and surveyed the situation. It was true; the house was empty. It was obvious that whoever had been staying there had left in a hurry.

"Fuck!" the mayor screamed.

Scar got lucky. He didn't know they were planning a raid on his place, but he had heard about the car bombs. He figured that if you were on the police force that day, you were either dealing with the bombing of the police chief or chief of staff Coram's car. They would all be at the crime scenes or dealing with the press. There would be no one setting up or paying attention to roadblocks. Without waiting for another second, Scar gathered up his cash, guns, drugs, and the kids and hightailed it right out of Baltimore. On his way out of town, he drove right past the convoy that was heading to his hideout to bust him.

"Stupid mu'fuckas. Too late. I'm too slick," he muttered and smiled to himself.

Day was on a high. He and Halleigh had finally proclaimed their love for one another. He felt that his life was getting on track. He would have his own piece of the streets, and he would be able to provide for Halleigh and M.J. He was feeling like a real man. In less than an hour he would be rid of Scar, and his new life could start.

They had planned to ambush Scar together, but Day didn't want Halleigh in harm's way, so he decided that he would get it over with as soon as possible. As soon as he left Halleigh's house, he was on his way to kill Scar. To secure his alibi, he made sure to visit a couple of his spots along the way.

Feeling like his alibi would be solid, Day started to hype himself up. He had planned out how he would get Scar to leave the house. He would say that he finally secured a house for them to move into and that they had to move immediately.

He looked at his gun sitting in the seat beside him. Nearing Scar's neighborhood, he picked it up, made sure it was loaded, and cocked it. He wasn't going to take any chances. As he approached the street, Day noticed the block roped off and all kinds of police activity in the area. He put the gun under the seat and drove by the street slowly, craning his neck to see what was happening. As far as he could tell, there were cop cars surrounding Scar's place and officers were walking up and down the neighborhood. Day acted as if he were just passing by and continued on. His destination was directly back to Halleigh.

Just as he left the area, his phone rang.

Derek hog-tied Halleigh while she was knocked out then drove his car into her garage and dumped her in the trunk. He wasn't fucking around anymore. Following Day around seemed to be getting him nowhere closer to finding his kids. Derek was getting the feeling that maybe Day was fucking with him. He wanted to speed the process up, so when he saw Halleigh and Day together, he figured he would kidnap her to get Day to hurry the fuck up. He wanted his kids back, and if they were going to take someone he loved, then he would take someone they loved.

Heading farther out into the countryside, he ended up on an isolated dirt road way out in the woods. It was pitch black, with the only light coming from his headlights and the stars above. Satisfied that he was far away from civilization, Derek stopped his car and got out. He stood at the side of the car for a second to let his eyes adjust to the dark. The one thing that really stuck out to Derek was the stillness and quiet of the country. With eyes adjusted, he walked around to the back of the car and called Day.

“Yo,” Day answered. He didn’t recognize the number calling.

“You have fun fucking today?” “Who is this?”

“You know who this is. You have something I love, and now I have something you love.”

He opened the trunk. Halleigh was lying in there on her side, bound and gagged. When it opened and the light came on, she started to thrash and scream. It was no use.

“It’s your boyfriend Day on the phone,” Derek said to her, which caused her to thrash about even more.

Derek removed the gag from her mouth, and she immediately screamed into the phone, “Help me! I’m alone. Help M.J. He’s still home. Help—” Derek slammed the trunk shut.

Day’s heart sank in his chest. He felt just as helpless as Halleigh sounded. “Motherfucker, you better not touch her,” he screamed into the receiver.

“Threats won’t work. Just do as I say and nothing will happen to her.”

“How much you want?”

“I don’t want money, you asshole. I want my kids back.”

Day knew then that it was Detective Derek Fuller on the other end of the line.

Derek continued, “Now maybe you’ll take me seriously when I say that you need to help me get my kids back. If you don’t, you will never see—” He paused. “Funny, I don’t even know what your girl’s name is. Well, you’ll never see her again if you don’t do as I say. So, get my kids.

“I will be contacting you soon, and I better like what I hear from you. Stay close to your phone.” With that, he ended the conversation.

Day screamed at the top of his lungs and slammed on the accelerator to get to M.J. as fast as he could.

Halleigh had been screaming inside the trunk the whole time. Derek stood outside the trunk, listening to her muffled screams. He pounded on the outside of the trunk and her screaming briefly stopped. After a few seconds, the muffled screams came back. They got louder when Derek finally opened the trunk.

Halleigh’s eyes were bloodshot and tears were streaming down her face. Derek reached in to gag her mouth, and Halleigh bit his hand. He screamed in pain and pulled his hand away immediately.

"You bitch." She had bitten him hard enough to draw blood. "I was going to just gag you to shut you the fuck up, but now—" He punched her as hard as he could several times in the face until he was sure she was knocked out. He looked down at her limp, unconscious body and bloodied face.

"You better hope your man comes through or else the inside of this trunk may be the last thing you see." He stuffed the rag back in her mouth and slammed the trunk shut.

He got back into the driver's seat, started the car, and continued driving down the dirt road into darkness. He was on a collision course with Scar and Tiphani, and only one of them would come out alive.

Chapter 17

Comeback

Tiphani raced around her apartment frantically collecting her clothes and throwing them into a suitcase. As soon as she got the phone call from Cecil, she started preparing for her violent return to Baltimore. Her planning phase done, she was now in attack mode. Cecil had done exactly what she had recruited him for, making a deadly first move. Now it was time to dump him.

Yes, he fucked her good, but she could get good dick anywhere. She was done falling under the spell of a man just because he put it on her. Besides, she had come to realize that she was always wanting and curious for new dick. That would never change. Cecil's time was done.

Now she needed to get everything packed and cleaned and out of the house before he got back from Baltimore. It would be easier for everyone involved if she just disappeared. Tiphani had a funny vision of her and Cecil driving on I-95 in opposite directions, she heading north and he heading south, each unaware of the other as they passed.

With the packing finished, Tiphani began to clean the house. She put on dishwashing gloves and wrapped a bandana around her head to keep her hair from falling as she cleaned. She wasn't taking any chances. She was going to erase any trace of herself and clean every inch of the apartment. No hair, no dead skin, no fingerprint would be left behind after she was finished scrubbing. It would be like she was never there. There would be nothing for the cops to tie her to this apartment or to Cecil. She was covering all her tracks.

She went to the cabinet under the kitchen sink and took out her cleaning rags, ammonia, and bleach and started her cleaning frenzy. She was like a tornado whipping through the apartment. Nothing was left untouched in her path. She was scrubbing floors, walls, and ceilings, inside cabinets, drawers, and closets. Furniture was being moved and overturned to clean the underside. There was not an inch of space that was left untouched.

With her first pass through the apartment finished, Tiphani stood in the center of her living room. Day had turned to night. She had been cleaning for hours and hadn't even noticed. The apartment really did look like a tornado had come through. Everything was overturned and out of place. The only way that anyone could tell an actual tornado didn't come barreling through was that everything was sparkling clean.

Keeping on her cleaning attire, Tiphani went into her bedroom to retrieve her suitcase. It was filled so fully she needed to sit on top of it and mash the contents down in order to zip it closed. She dragged the heavy, hulking mass through the living room and set it down at the front door. She was going to make one quick sweep through the apartment, wiping down everything again. When she finished, she planned to be out the front door and on her way to Baltimore to exact revenge on all the hateful men in her life.

She started her quick sweep in the back bathroom and planned to make her way forward until she made it to the front door. On her hands and knees, she was wiping down the tub when she heard the front door open. She remained motionless so as not to make any noise, and slowed her breathing to listen for any sign of who it might be. Her heart pounded in her chest. She wasn't expecting anyone.

A gun would be nice to have right now, she thought. The door closed and Tiphani heard footsteps coming deeper into the living room. By the softness of the footsteps, she could tell that whoever was there was walking carefully. Tiphani's mind was racing through scenarios of who it might be and how she would escape the situation depending on the person it was.

She was trapped in the back bathroom. There was no window and nothing in there that she could use as a weapon. She thought about hiding in the cabinet under the sink, but quickly realized she wouldn't fit. She thought about trying to sneak out of the bathroom. If she could make it to her bedroom, she could jump out the window, but it was four stories high. It was almost guaranteed that she would break her leg. The hospital was not a place Tiphani wanted to be right now.

Her only option was to go out fighting with her hands. She would wait until they came closer to the bathroom and then be the one to attack first, taking them by surprise and then running out the front door to safety.

The footsteps stopped somewhere in the living room. It was dead silent in the apartment now. Tiphani could feel her heart beating in her chest. A picture of her children flashed across her mind. Was she thinking of them because she was certain this was her end, or was she thinking of them to give her strength to fight? She took it as a sign to fight. She wanted to see her kids again.

She carefully stood up from the kneeling position she had frozen in and quietly positioned herself so she could barge out of the bathroom door and start fighting the intruder. She listened. Still no sounds came from the living room. Tiphani's mind was racing as fast as her heart. Had they left and she didn't hear the door open and close? Was she hearing things? Did someone really enter her apartment?

Then she heard the footsteps slowly and carefully moving again. The intruder took a few steps and stopped again.

"Hello?" a male voice called out.

Tiphani remained silent. The voices in her head and her heartbeat were so loud she was having trouble concentrating on the sound of the voice.

"Hello? Who's there? Anyone?"

She recognized the voice that time. It was Cecil. What was he doing here so soon? He had called her from Baltimore only a few hours ago. Tiphani had to think fast.

"Cecil?" she called out.

"Yeah, it's me."

Tiphani walked guardedly into the living room. "Cecil, what are you doing here?"

"What happened to this place? Did you get robbed? It smells like bleach." Cecil looked around at the overturned furniture.

"No, I didn't get robbed," she said, exasperated. She was annoyed at herself for not moving quicker and getting out of town sooner.

"You planning on going somewhere?" Cecil motioned with his head toward the suitcase at the front door then looked at her with suspicion.

Tiphani was busted. She paused for a brief second before she could come up with something. "Not yet. How did you get home so fast?"

"You aren't happy? You told me to hurry up, so instead of driving back down, I hopped on the next plane. What the hell are you wearing?" He was referring to her bandana and gloves.

"I'm cleaning. This is what I wear when I clean." She acted offended.

"Looks more like you trashed the place. What the fuck is going on here?"

"I told you I'm cleaning."

"Cut the bullshit! Tell me what is fucking going on. I just came back from handling your business, and it look to me like you're trashing the place and getting ready to leave. Without me!" He took a threatening step toward Tiphani.

"Baby. What?" Tiphani used a cooing tone to try to soothe Cecil. "Yes, I'm getting ready to leave, but not without you. I was so excited when you called that I went in motion and started to get everything in order to leave as soon as you came back." She took a sensual step toward him.

"Why your bag look like you ready to leave right now?" Cecil wasn't that easily swayed.

"Like I said, I got excited. I got excited because you had sent the message to the mayor and because I knew you would be coming back . . ." She pressed her tits against Cecil and grabbed his ass then continued. ". . . and I could suck your dick again."

Cecil pushed her off of him. "Why does it smell like bleach? What the fuck you trying to clean that much? Did you kill someone?"

Tiphani laughed at that. "No, I didn't kill anyone." She didn't have any good excuse for cleaning with bleach and didn't see the point in lying about it, so she told him the truth. Well, sort of.

"I was making sure to get rid of any trace of either one of us ever being here. My bag was at the door because I was going to put it in the car and wait for you and stop you before you entered the apartment so you wouldn't track any of your DNA in here. Then we could head back up to Baltimore together."

Cecil took a second to absorb everything she said. It sounded convincing and seemed like it might be true. He wanted to believe her. She was fine as hell and fucked like no one he had ever met before. Plus, she had enough money for both of them to live off of for the rest of their lives.

Fuck it. It might be true, he thought.

"There's one problem with your idea," Cecil said.

"What?" Tiphani was afraid that he didn't believe her.

"When were you going to suck my dick like you promised?" Cecil smiled a devilish grin.

Tiphani smiled too because she was so relieved that he had believed her story. She got down on her knees, unbuckled his pants, and pulled out his dick. She sucked him off and swallowed every ounce of his semen when he came.

"Damn, baby, that shit felt good." Cecil buttoned his pants as Tiphani picked herself up of the floor.

"Well, you taste good, baby." Tiphani wiped her mouth and licked her fingers. "I'm going to take my suitcase to the car. Then I'll come back and do one last quick wipedown of the apartment."

"No. I'll take it to the car. You stay and clean and then come out. I don't want to get the apartment any dirtier. That is why you swallowed my jizz, isn't it?" Cecil smiled as he grabbed the suitcase and went to the car.

He wasn't about to let her leave before him. He had a feeling that if he hadn't come home when he did, she would have been ghost and he would have never seen her again. He was not about to let her out of his sight right now. Cecil wanted that money of Tiphani's and was going to make sure he got a piece of it.

Damn. I'm not going to be able to ditch him, Tiphani thought. *I guess he's coming to Baltimore with me.*

Tiphani finished wiping down the apartment and went out to the car. Cecil was sitting in the driver's seat, waiting for her. She got in the passenger's side, buckled her seatbelt, and said, "Here I come, Baltimore. You better be ready for my comeback. Let's go get me some revenge."

Cecil put his foot on the accelerator and sped off, heading north. Destination: Baltimore.

Chapter 18

Won't Back Down

Scar drove up the winding dirt driveway in the suburban hills north of Baltimore. His destination was a secluded farmhouse surrounded by one hundred acres of forest. He reached over and pulled one of his guns out of the glove compartment, laying it in his lap as his niece and nephew slept in the backseat. His GPS told him this was his destination, but that meant nothing to Scar. His trust of technology was the same as his trust in people, which was to say it was zero. If there happened to be anyone occupying this house and they saw him, he would have to blast them to protect his identity.

He rolled around the last bend and came upon the white-shingled two-story house. The headlights of his car searched over the house and revealed its emptiness. Scar relaxed a little, seeing it was the right house. He stopped the car then roused the kids and hustled them up the walkway and into their new bedroom on the second floor, where they fell right back to sleep.

Scar walked around the house after unpacking the car. He inspected every room, opening all closet doors and cabinets. This was his new safe house, and he wanted to know every inch of it. It was pretty bare bones right now. The only things occupying the place were beds for him and the kids. Until he had seen the place with his own eyes and could assess the situation, he didn't want to draw any attention by moving in a bunch of stuff and having a lot of traffic in and out. Now that he was there, he saw how secluded it was and decided there was nothing to worry about. Now he needed his shit and he needed it fast. He hated when his houses would produce echoes because there was nothing in them to absorb the sound. Wanting to get the ball rolling on filling the house, Scar called Flex.

"Ay yo," Flex answered. "Where the fuck you at?"

"On my way, boss. These country roads be fucked up. I got all turned around, but I'm on the right track now."

"You take care of your problem?" Scar asked.

"That stick been snapped in two. Broken beyond repair and buried back where it came from." Flex was proud to be able to give Scar the good news.

"Your wallet better be stuffed."

"Overflowing, boss. You ain't got to worry 'bout me. I'ma always do you right," Flex boasted.

"Good lookin', nigga. You just moved up the ladder, soldier."

"I like the sound of that."

"We gotta fill this place. There ain't shit here. Any word from Day?" Scar looked around the empty dining room.

"Nah."

"A'ight. This nigga better not be locked up. He ain't answer when I call him." He had called Day while Day was on the phone with Derek. Day wasn't about to answer the other line while he was trying to deal for Halleigh's life, so he ignored Scar's call.

Scar looked in the refrigerator for the second time, knowing damn well that it would still be empty. "I need some food, nigga. Stop off and get something for me."

"I got you."

Scar ended the call as he walked into the empty living room. He stood in front of the bay window that overlooked the tree-covered valley below. The valley started filling with light as the sun peeked over the horizon.

Scar felt a million miles from Baltimore. He needed the energy of the city. This country life was bullshit. He hated it. He had only been there for an hour, and he was already getting stir crazy.

There was no way he would be able to stay here long. He felt like he wouldn't have as much control over his operation. He was out of sight while undercover in Baltimore, but at least he was in the city and his soldiers knew it. With him being so far away, there was no guarantee that they would follow his orders. This was going to test Scar and his control over his crew.

Fuck this. This ain't right. He made a call.

"This is Fuller. Go." Derek answered his cell phone as he drove down the deserted country road.

"What's good, brother?" Scar continued looking out the window as the wildlife started to awaken to a new day.

Derek's heart sank for a second. He was caught off guard. He wasn't expecting to hear this voice on the other end of the phone.

Neither man said a word. The only sound each could hear was the other one breathing into the receiver. Their emotions were all over the place. It had been a while since they had heard each other's voices. As much as they hated one another, their family bond was making it difficult to know how to proceed with the conversation.

"How'd you get this number?" Derek asked.

"Day gave you that phone. Who the fuck you think paid for it? Think, nigga," Scar explained like he was talking to a five-year-old.

"Don't talk down to me, mu'fucka." "Chill, nigga."

"Fuck you." Derek couldn't hide his contempt for his brother. The tone for this conversation had now been set. This wasn't going to be a friendly chat.

Derek continued, "Give me my kids."

Scar smiled to himself. Instantly he knew he still had the upper hand on his brother. "What? No 'how are you, how you been'?"

"Fuck your sarcasm. I'm coming for you, and not one hair on my kids' heads better be out of place."

"Your kids are fine, and if you play along, you won't have nothing to worry about, so back up off that 'coming for you' bullshit," Scar warned.

"I'm working on getting the mayor's help." Derek realized he didn't have much to bargain with, so he backed off the threats.

"I ain't talking about that. I don't need that mu'fucka's help no more. I put Baltimore in my rearview. What I'm talking about is you and me working together like old times. Everybody wins."

"I'm not officially on the force anymore."

"But you still got connections, and we could make it so you get cleared of all charges."

"I don't need your help, and I damn sure ain't helping you. You best just get me my kids, mu'fucka." Derek forgot that Scar held all the cards and that he needed to be diplomatic in his approach.

"You makin' a mistake, brother."

"Don't call me brother. We ain't family no more. A brother would never do what you did. Family stays loyal to one another."

This hit Scar in the heart. Derek was right; he hadn't been a good brother. Was he sorry for his actions toward his brother? Yes, but there was no turning back the clock now.

"Look, what's done is done. You should think about the present and look toward the future."

"I am looking toward the future. I'm gonna continue coming for you, and I'm gonna be reunited with my kids. I won't back down."

Derek had enough of the conversation and ended the call. He had leverage on Day and would use it to find Scar and keep his kids alive, so he saw no reason to deal with Scar and his negotiations. He would find his deceitful brother and end his life.

Scar heard the silence on the other end of the phone line and returned the phone to his pocket. The sun was now completely over the horizon, and a new day was born as Scar came to the realization that the relationship with his brother was dead.

Flex entered the house with some fast food hamburgers. He handed a bag to Scar, and they both sat on the floor. Scar ate in silence as his thoughts drifted to his brother and the fact that he was going to have to be the one to kill him once and for all.

Chapter 19

From Bad to Worse

The day after Dexter and Chief Hill were killed, Mayor Steele sat slumped over his desk with his forehead resting on the desktop. He was exhausted and emotionally spent. The previous twenty-four hours had gone from being great to a complete disaster, with his emotions going up and down like a yo-yo the whole time. Now he had the task of leading the investigation into who was responsible for the bombings, keeping his city calm, and planning the funerals of two of his most trusted aides.

The door to his office opened, causing the mayor to lift his head. He had no idea how long he had been slumped over. If he had it his way, he would have stayed like that all day.

"Hello, Susan." He wiped his mouth and smoothed his hair.

"Hello, Mr. Mayor," replied his trusty secretary. "What can I do for you?"

"Your mail, sir." She placed a bundle of envelopes on his desk.

"Thank you, dear." The mayor reached for the bundle.

"You look awful, sir. Is there anything I can do?"

"You're very kind, Susan. Thank you." He gave a halfhearted smile.

"I just want to say I'm sorry. No matter my personal feelings toward someone, I would never wish death on them." She was sincere. Dexter was disgusting and creepy, but she thought death was undeserved even for him.

The mayor thanked her again then dismissed her. As she approached the door, two armed state troopers came storming in, practically knocking her to the floor. Following right behind them came the governor of Maryland, Thomas Tillingham.

At five feet four inches, Governor Tillingham was dwarfed by the two burly guards as he strode into the room. He had the swagger and attitude of a man trying to compensate for his lack of height. He was popular with the citizens of Maryland, but in political circles, he was not well liked. His rise to the governorship was contemptuous, with many people being taken advantage of and lied to every step of the way. Like so many politicians, he got into public office with the best of intentions, but when he saw how the game worked behind closed doors, with all the deals, false promises, and backstabbing going on, he quickly changed his tune. He realized he'd better start looking out for himself or he wouldn't be in politics for very long. Thus began his career as a ruthless politician who was willing to do anything to anyone who opposed him.

"Excuse you," Susan said to the state troopers then turned to the mayor. "Shall I stay, Mr. Mayor? Do you need me to call anyone?"

"No, Susan. I'm fine."

Susan composed herself and walked out of the room, glaring at the rude state troopers, who just ignored her. "Close the door, Henry," the governor instructed the bigger of the two officers as he stood in front of Mayor Steele's desk. The two politicians faced off, looking each other in the eye. It was like an old Western showdown between two cowboys, each waiting for the other to draw first. There was no love lost between these two men.

Governor Tillingham was halfway through his term and had enjoyed a high approval rating with the people of his state, but lately that rating had begun to slip and he blamed it on the mess happening in Baltimore. Most of their contact was over the phone, but Governor Tillingham thought it was time to meet face to face. He worked hard to create his image and amass his power, and he was not about to let the mismanagement of Baltimore ruin that.

"Mathias." Not breaking eye contact, the governor nodded his head slightly in a gesture of greeting.

"Thomas." The mayor mirrored the governor's movements.

Both men stayed standing. Each wanted to assume the position of power, and standing was a more powerful position. In their minds, the first to sit was weaker. “Let me begin by saying I’m sorry for the loss of two fine men,” the governor said.

“They were two of the finest and loved their city as much as anyone.” The thought of his two men made the mayor forgot about his mind games with the governor. With his mind elsewhere, he sat in his chair. The governor followed his lead and did the same. Now it was time to get to serious business.

“Now let me say, what the fuck is going on in this city?” The governor’s tone made his anger apparent.

“We have it under control,” the mayor responded with a flippant tone.

“It’s that attitude that got you into this mess and the reason I had to come down here.”

“What do you mean ‘that attitude’?” Mayor Steele squinted his eyes at the governor.

“Like maybe you aren’t taking this seriously enough.”

“Two of my staff were murdered. You don’t think I’m taking that seriously? You don’t think I’m doing everything in my power to find whoever did this?”

“See, there’s the problem. I’m not sure how much power you actually have left. Is anyone taking you seriously anymore? Your city is falling apart, crime is running rampant, and now city officials are being murdered. In fact, this isn’t the first police chief to be murdered while you were in office. Have you found the person responsible for that one yet? Seems to me that the criminals in this city have no fear or respect for you. At this point, how can you expect any part of your police force or government to have faith in any of your decisions?”

“With all due respect, fuck you. I have not lost anyone’s respect. I’ve probably gained more of it. I rode along when we went to apprehend Scar Johnson. My police force has been working so hard we found where that bastard was hiding.” The Mayor did not like getting disrespected in his own office.

“So, where is he, Mathias? Is he in custody? Why isn’t it front page news?” The governor’s words were dripping with sarcasm.

“He cleared out before we got there.”

“One step behind, as usual.” The Governor smirked and raised his eyebrows.

"Get out! Get out of my office now! I am sick of your disrespect." The mayor shot up from his chair. He was now looking down on Governor Tillingham.

If there was one thing that would set off Thomas Tillingham, it was when someone hovered over him as a form of intimidation. Growing up, he was always the smallest one in the room, so he used it as motivation. It pissed him off if someone thought him to be inferior because of his height, and he would go to great lengths to prove them wrong and embarrass them in the process. This attempt by Mathias Steele to intimidate him was about to backfire.

"Who in God's name do you think you are speaking to?" He slowly rose from his seat. "You have fucked this city up since the day you started. Your whole time in office has been marked with corruption, greed, and murder, and I, for one, am sick of it. These last two murders are the final straw. I came down here today to give you the opportunity to step down, but now seeing your attitude, I am prepared to start impeachment proceedings." He was staring daggers into Mayor Steele.

The mayor was stunned. He stood with his mouth open for a few seconds before he spoke. "You're what? You can't do that."

"I can, and I will."

"Please, Thomas, you can't. It'll ruin me."

"That's exactly the point. You'll be finished." The governor shrugged his shoulders matter-of-factly.

Mayor Steele's voice rose an octave. "Let's talk about this, please."

"There's nothing left to talk about. I've said all I have to say."

"What can I do to change your mind? Give me a chance. I promise I'll catch Scar and bring him to justice. I'll give you the credit for it if you want."

"You can't change my mind. My approval ratings have dropped ever since this shit storm started here in Baltimore. It's time for that to change—starting with getting rid of you. As far as credit is concerned, I will get credit for capturing Scar, because I am personally going to take over the case. That piece of garbage won't be polluting my state much longer."

"I'll fight it. I'll fight it and win. You can't bully me." The mayor came out from behind his desk.

"Go ahead, but I don't recommend it. You'll spend millions in legal fees, and you'll still end up losing. You'll look even worse after it's all said and done. But if you choose to fight it, I look forward to crushing you in court and in public."

Governor Tillingham was right. It would cost millions that the mayor didn't have. It would be a useless fight. The only option he had was to try to salvage his job, and if not that, then maybe he could just convince the governor to let him step down with some dignity.

"I'll pay you. How much do you want? At least let me resign on my own terms." The mayor's begging was out of control. He actually went down to his knees.

"Stop embarrassing yourself." The governor shook his head in disgust and walked out of the office with the two burly state troopers on his heels.

Mayor Steele stayed frozen on his knees. His whole world had just come crashing down on him. His political career was over. The position he worked so hard to attain was now going to be taken from him instantly. Not only would he never be a politician again, but no one would want to hire him. He would be considered toxic in the business world. Having a disgraced mayor on the payroll would hurt the bottom line, and if that caused them to lose money, then it wasn't going to happen. He would be unemployed and broke.

Mayor Steele stayed in the same position for several minutes. He was in a state of mild shock. He couldn't move even if he wanted to. He was so overwhelmed with what just occurred that his mind went empty for a little while, just so he could cope with the severity of his situation.

When he snapped out of his trance, he noticed there were tears running down his cheeks. He wiped his cheeks dry with the palms of his hands and stood up. He looked around at his office, hoping that something might give him a sign as to what he should do next. No signs jumped out at him.

He slowly walked on weak knees to his desk chair. If he had a gun, he would have shot himself right then and there. He sat at his desk, looking at his office, thinking about his situation. Scar Johnson had imposed his will on the city of Baltimore, and the mayor had done everything he could to try to stop him. This wasn't the mayor's fault; this was Scar Johnson's fault. The mayor's life was over because of one man, and that was Scar Johnson.

The mayor thought longer about his situation and blamed Derek and Tiphani Fuller as well. If Derek had found Scar like he said he would, then the mayor could have arrested him. If Tiphani wasn't such a ho and hadn't fucked Scar then helped him get acquitted, none of this would have happened.

The mayor wanted blood. If he was going down, he was bringing them down with him. He was going to get revenge on all of them, starting with Scar. He would find and kill him personally; then Tiphani and Derek would be next to die.

His mood suddenly perked up now that he sort of had a plan. He opened his briefcase and started stuffing in as many of his files as he could. When he was finished, he took one last look around his office. This was going to be his last time there. He wasn't planning on coming back. He was done being mayor of the city of Baltimore.

Fuck this ungrateful city, he thought. He had a mind to torch the office, but thought better of it.

He walked into the waiting room where Susan was sitting. She had been there since the governor had barged in. After the guard closed the door, Susan put her ear to the door and heard every word that was said between the governor and the mayor. The look in the mayor's eyes scared Susan. She was speechless as he spoke to her.

"Susan, I want to thank you for your years of loyal service to me. Take care of yourself and enjoy the rest of your life." The mayor shook her hand and walked out the door and into the next chapter of his life. He was now a civilian with nothing to lose, looking to kill for revenge.

Susan sat alone at her desk, not sure of what to do. She felt she had just seen the mayor for the last time. There was a bad feeling in her soul that a storm was brewing in Baltimore, and it was going to be violent.

Baltimore Chronicles

Volume 4

Treasure Hernandez

Chapter 1

Neighbors, who needs them?

Scar's eyes popped open. "These mu'fuckin' birds!" He had been woken up for the fifth day in a row by a flock of birds chirping outside his bedroom window.

"I hate the fuckin' country," he mumbled to himself as he wiped his eyes and lumbered out of bed. The bright morning sun was shining through the south-facing window of his bedroom. He stood and looked out that same window at the black birds cawing in the tree. "I'm putting an end to this bullshit once and for all." Still groggy from his sleep, he put on a pair of cream-colored sweat pants with a matching zip-up hoodie.

He had only been in the country house for a week, but to him it felt like a year. He hated the slow pace and solitude. There was no action, no one around, and no fun. In short, he was bored out of his mind.

The first few days at the house were not so bad. He had been occupied by all the action of moving in. Being the head of the biggest drug cartel in Baltimore had its advantages. He had some of his low-level soldiers come out to move his shit, while his top-level soldiers sat down for a meeting about how things would run. Scar told them that Flex would be representing him in the city while he was hiding out in the country.

Although Flex hadn't been with Scar's crew for very long, he showed loyalty and drive, the two things that Scar demanded. Scar noticed and rewarded Flex with a promotion. Scar felt that Flex had grown into a man—especially the way he handled killing Sticks after Scar found out that Sticks had stolen money from him. Scar had seen a definite change in Flex's demeanor after the young soldier got a taste of murder, so now, whatever

Flex said was word. If any of them had a problem with Flex, then they would have a problem with Scar.

If Day had been at the house, he would have been representing Scar, but that nigga had disappeared. At one time, Day was Scar's right hand man, but what Scar didn't know was that Day had ulterior motives. Day had infiltrated his posse and become his right hand man, all the while scheming to take down Scar's empire. Now Day was nowhere to be found. Since Scar had been in the country, he hadn't seen or heard from him. As a matter of fact, no one in his crew had. Finding out what happened to Day was one of the things on Scar's list. He just hadn't been able to investigate since his sudden escape from Baltimore.

Fully awake now, Scar went to his closet and pulled out his AK-47. He inserted a magazine full of bullets and cocked the side handle. The machine gun was loaded and waiting to inflict some serious damage. This was the last thing Scar wanted to be doing. He wanted to still be sleeping, but he'd had enough. Every morning some damn birds were interrupting his sleep, and he was sick of it.

The rest of the house was quiet as he walked out the front door into the early morning chill. He carefully and quietly walked around the house so he didn't alert the birds to his presence. They could be as loud as they wanted, and Scar hoped they would be. He figured if they remained loud, it would drown out any noise he made and it would be easier to ambush them.

"Enjoy your last chirps, you mu'fuckin' squawking crows." He raised the machine gun, propped the butt end against his shoulder, and aimed at the middle branches of the tree. A shower of bullets spit out of the gun barrel as Scar pulled the trigger. Bullet shells flew every which way and littered the ground. He sprayed the tree back and forth as the air filled with the smell of spent gunpowder. The black birds scattered in an attempt to flee as they were bombarded with bullets. Some made it out and were able to fly away. Most got caught in the line of fire.

Forced to stop shooting because the magazine was spent, Scar dropped the gun to his side. He surveyed the damage he had inflicted. There were feathers and leaves still lingering in the air, taking their sweet time floating to the ground. They would settle next to the dead birds. Smoke from the gun barrel was swirling in and around the tree branches. There were at least twenty dead birds scattered around, lying in the grass.

Scar was proud as he stood admiring his work. "Now maybe I can get some sleep." He stood on top of the hill and looked over the valley that sprawled out in front of him. There were only treetops and sky as far as he could see. It was the most isolated he had felt since escaping the heat in Baltimore to hide out in the country.

This loneliness made him long for the good old days, when he was young and he and his brother Derek were inseparable. They looked out for one another. Even though they didn't have any parents and were in an orphanage, they had each other. They were family. Scar longed for that bond again. He had it for a while, until he started fucking Derek's wife, Tiphani. That act of betrayal had pushed Derek over the edge and destroyed any familial bond they once had. Now they were sworn enemies, and Scar had no one close to him. He didn't trust anyone. He had kept everyone at arm's length while becoming the biggest player in the game. Now that he was isolated and alone, he regretted sleeping with Tiphani and betraying his brother.

He stayed there for a good hour, thinking about his past. He went over everything that had happened and all of his actions that brought him to this place. He thought back to the elation and love he felt the first time he saw his brother again after years of separation. He thought about the first time he and Tiphani hooked up, and the time his brother Derek found him in bed with Tiphani. It was bad enough that he was fucking his brother's wife, but it was worse that he was doing it in his brother's bed. That discovery sparked the feud that turned Scar's world upside down.

Before that, Derek and Scar had worked together. Scar was on the side of crime, and Derek was on the side of the law, but they worked in tandem to make extreme amounts of money and control most of the drug trade in Baltimore. With his brother working against him now, wanting revenge, Scar was forced into hiding. The entire police force was on a manhunt for Scar. All of the politicians and police officers the he had been paying off stopped taking his bribes. He was poison in the city. Without any allies in high places, he had been forced to escape from Baltimore, eventually ending up here in the middle of nowhere.

"Fuck that. What's done is done. Can't change nothin' now." He snapped back to the present and walked into the house. He wasn't about to let sentimentality get the better of him. There was a reason he was the head of the most notorious gang in Baltimore.

Scar walked in the house to find his niece sitting at the kitchen table coloring in her coloring book. His nephew was on the floor in the living room playing with his toy cars. The kids were too young to realize that they were being held as captives. Scar had originally kidnapped the children to get his brother to help him escape Baltimore. Since Derek was a former detective, Scar figured he could find out when and where the police were searching for him.

He did escape Baltimore, but it was in no way because of any help Derek provided. If Scar hadn't taken initiative and left when he did, he would have been captured. As he was driving out of Baltimore, the authorities were driving to raid his house. This pissed Scar off to no end. He was now holding the kids as punishment for Derek and to try to shake Tiphani out of hiding. Scar wanted revenge on that bitch. He was going to make her pay for betraying him and trying to set him up at the armored car ambush.

"Hi, Uncle Scar," they said in unison as he walked through the door.

"What's up, little ones? Why you up so early?" He hid the gun behind his back as best he could.

"We heard some loud bangs outside," his nephew said. He was the younger of the two children.

"It sounded like firecrackers," said Scar's niece.

"That's what it was. Firecrackers. I was tryin'a scare away the loud birds outside my window," Scar replied. "Go upstairs and change out your PJs and I'll make y'all some breakfast."

"Pancakes!" yelled his nephew.

"Pancakes." Scar smiled his crooked smile. Even though he had kidnapped the kids, they were the only things that made Scar smile these days.

The kids raced up the stairs to see who could change the fastest. Scar followed them and put his machine gun back in the closet. Since they'd been with him, he had tried to hide the guns and drugs from them. He didn't want them growing up like he did. He wanted them to keep their innocence as long as they could.

Scar started mixing together the pancake batter and warming the griddle as the kids came rumbling down the stairs. "First!" His niece crashed into the table.

"Not fair. You always win." Scar's nephew pouted.

"You'll win one day, big man. How 'bout you get the first pancake?" Scar tried to cheer him up.

Scar served breakfast as the kids occupied themselves with their own little games. They had formed a tight bond since all of the drama surrounding their family started. First, their father, Derek, had been put in jail; then their mother, Tiphani, staged her own kidnapping and disappeared. Now their uncle had kidnapped them. They had been shielded from it as much as possible, but children are like dogs; they can sense when things aren't right. Kids are smarter than adults give them credit for.

"When is Mama and Daddy coming to get us?" his nephew asked.

Scar hesitated before he answered. "Soon, little man, soon."

"Maybe we should go back to Baltimore. They might not know where we are, or they might get lost," his niece chimed in.

"I wish we could go back to Baltimore, but this is home now. I talked to your pops the other day, and he still busy. He'll get here as quick as he can," Scar lied.

"I don't like it here. I want to go back home," said his nephew.

"Me too. Me too." Scar agreed.

A somber silence fell over the table, all of them sitting with their own thoughts. The kids were thinking about their parents and wishing they were in their own house. Scar was wishing he was back on familiar ground, bangin' on the streets of Baltimore.

Scar was getting the uneasy feeling that he may be stuck in the country for a long time. If that was the case, he needed to figure out what the hell he was going to do with the kids. He didn't want to become their father. When he kidnapped them, he hadn't thought about keeping them long term. He was thinking about the present and what he needed to do at that moment. The fuck did he know about raising kids? He couldn't look to his childhood as an example. He watched his mother get beaten to death and was in and out of foster homes his whole childhood—not to mention the fact that the state separated him and his brother while they were in foster care. He already felt like he was a father figure to some of these wild-ass soldiers in his crew. He didn't need two real children to take care of and send off to school.

Usually if Scar had a problem like this, he would just kill whoever it was that was clinging to him. He was hoping to come to another solution before he had to do that to the kids.

The doorbell rang and snapped everyone out of their thoughts.

"I'll get it," said the niece.

"No. You stay here," Scar instructed with a little force behind his words.

The kids obeyed, and Scar quietly and cautiously walked to the front window. He peeked out the window so as not to attract attention from whoever was at the door.

"Who the fuck?" Scar mumbled to himself.

He quietly walked back to the kitchen and told the kids to go play out back. They obeyed and went out the back door. Scar went into a cabinet and took out a 9 mm from the top shelf. He slipped it in his waistband as he walked back to the front door. As he approached, the stranger knocked on the door.

"Who is it?" Scar stood a little back and to the side of the door in case the person started shooting or tried to kick in the door.

"Oh, hello. It's your neighbor," the stranger called back.

"Who?"

"Your neighbor, Arnold. I live just next door."

Scar looked out the window again to see if he could see anyone else. It looked to him like this dude was alone, and he for sure looked harmless. After contemplating a moment, Scar figured it was safe to open the door.

"Hello," said Arnold as the door opened to reveal Scar.

"What's up?" Scar replied to the white man wearing a wide-brimmed straw hat and overalls.

"I just came over to say hello and welcome you to our community," Arnold said. His warm smile formed his thin face into something out of a Norman Rockwell painting.

Scar was caught off guard by this unsolicited kindness. A neighbor coming over to introduce himself would never happen in the hood.

"Oh. Word. That's cool."

"I brought you some vegetables from my garden. May I come in?" Before Scar could react, Arnold had handed him a wicker basket and walked into the house. "I thought they would never sell this place. It's been vacant ever since Miss Sally passed away. Going on two years now. Oh well, guess that's the recession they are always going on about on the TV. I like what you've done with the place." Arnold slowly walked around the living room.

"Yeah, well, I was just gettin' ready to leave. So, nice meeting you." Scar was finally able to compose himself and say something.

"Oh, right. Of course. I'm so rude. I just got so excited when I saw that someone finally moved in, I had to come over. I love having neighbors. I think of them as my family. Are you here alone?"

"Yeah, it's just me." Scar looked at the door, wishing this dude would walk through it and leave.

"Oh, well, you'll have to come over for dinner. I'm just over the other side of the tree line there." He pointed to the east side of the house, where the trees were the thickest.

"Yeah, maybe."

"I get it. You're shy. Well, I won't bite. My wife and I own a small farm over there. Nothing fancy, just enough to get by. We don't need much to be happy when we have each other." Arnold smiled.

"Uh-huh." Scar awkwardly smiled back. *What the fuck is this cracker talking about?* he thought.

"You should stop by the farmers' market this weekend. I sell my vegetables there on Saturdays and Sundays. It'd be a great way to get to know everyone in the community."

"Yeah, we'll see. I really gotta be going."

"Oh, right. I forgot. I'm sorry."

Just as Arnold was starting to leave, Scar's niece and nephew came into the living room. Arnold stopped abruptly.

"Uncle Scar, there's a bunch of dead birds in the yard.

Did the fireworks kill them?" his niece said.

"Yeah, little one, that's what happened. Now, go on back outside and play. Take these vegetables to the kitchen." He handed her the basket.

"Where did you get these?"

"This nice man." Scar gestured to Arnold, who had a confused look on his face. When he realized he was being talked about, Arnold reacted like he had been thinking about something else.

"Huh? Oh, yes. Those are from my garden. Enjoy." Arnold smiled at the little girl and boy.

"Thanks." They walked off, examining the vegetables.

Scar looked at Arnold to gauge his reaction to seeing the kids. His face seemed expressionless. Scar always had trouble reading white people. They all seemed the same to him.

The kids had been on the news as missing, so Scar needed to know if Arnold had recognized them. He couldn't just outright ask him.

Scar said the first thing that popped into his head. "They came to visit and see my new place. Get out of the city for a few days."

"Sure. Right. That's what I heard this morning. Fireworks. Funny, I thought it might be gunshots or something. Oh well, I've taken up enough of your time." Arnold briskly walked out the front door.

Little did Scar know, Arnold had come over because he had heard the gunshots and he came to investigate. Arnold hated guns; they actually scared him.

Scar was shocked. He didn't know what to do. Did Arnold recognize his niece and nephew? Did he recognize Scar? Why did he seem so strange after the kids came in the house? There were too many unanswered questions for Scar's liking.

He decided he needed to stop Arnold before he alerted the cops. He pulled his gun out of his waistband and went out the front door. The second he got past the threshold, he ran right into Flex.

"Ay, yo. Where you goin' in such a rush, nigga?" Flex said.

"Kill my country-ass neighbor."

"Who? That cracker I saw just walk in them woods?"

"Yeah, him. He already in the woods? Fuck." Scar thought about chasing him, but decided it might be best not to kill him. He figured dude's wife probably knew where he was going and would come looking for him if he didn't come back. Scar would just have to be on high alert from now on.

"You want me to take care of it, boss?" Flex reached for the gun in his coat pocket.

"Nah. Leave it. We just need to be on guard. Matter of fact, get a nigga in here to install a security system. See if any mu'fuckin' police tryin'a creep up on us."

"Bet." Flex entered the house.

Scar looked toward the woods before he re-entered the house. *Damn. I thought it would be peaceful up in the country. Nigga can't get away from stress anywhere.*

Chapter 2

Powdered Courage

Security was tight at the funeral for former Chief of Staff Dexter Coram. The procession of politicians from the city and state seemed endless—not because they liked Dexter and wanted to pay their respects, but because every press outlet was there and they could get their faces on TV and their names in the papers. In fact, most of them were grossed out by Dexter and his sleazy, downlow, perverted flirting. If they didn't think they could promote their agendas, they wouldn't have been there.

Lurking just on the outskirts of the funeral was Dexter's boss, Mathias Steele. The disgraced former mayor was not invited to the funeral. Most of the city was blaming him for the death of Dexter Coram, as well as for the corruption that had riddled the city of Baltimore during his tenure as mayor. Many people in his government had been killed, including three police chiefs and most every member of the drug task force, the DES The only surviving member of the DES was Derek Fuller, who happened to be the brother of Scar Johnson, the most notorious gangster in Baltimore.

"Look at these hypocritical sons of bitches," Mathias snarled as he watched the politicians enter the church. The park across the street from the church created a nice vantage point for him to watch without being seen or recognized. "Not one of those cocksuckers is clean, and they all turned their backs on me." Mathias was enraged and mumbling to himself like a homeless person.

The minute word had gotten out that the governor was forcing Mathias to step down as mayor, no one would return his phone calls. All of his once-allies were now his enemies, and he was hell bent on making them pay for their disloyalty.

"You'll get yours, you bastards. I'll make sure of it. First I'll take out Scar Johnson, and then y'all are next." He took mental notes of every politician who entered the church.

As the crowd out in front of the church was dwindling and the funeral seemingly about to start, the biggest motorcade of them all came rolling in. From the limousine stepped Governor Thomas Tillingham. Mathias's blood boiled at the sight of the governor. He was the one man Mathias had needed to stand behind him, but the governor was the first to turn his back. Even as the mayor had struggled to keep morale high in the city, his approval rating was dropping. Residents were losing faith. When Police Chief Hill and Dexter Coram were blown up separately on the same day, the city was suddenly on a witch hunt, and Mathias was the target. When the governor came in, he could have backed Mathias and calmed the cries for his resignation, but instead the governor forced him out of office. It was politics as usual. In the end, no one had any loyalty.

Mathias watched the governor shake a few hands and make his presence known before entering the church. The hoopla died down and calm descended upon the street. The only people left were the press and State Police keeping an eye on the surrounding area. Calming himself down, Mathias sat on a bench and read the newspaper he had bought on his way to the funeral.

His calm didn't last for long. The headline that he had been avoiding since he bought the paper brought his anger right back. It read: HOW MUCH DID HE STEELE? The article was full of speculation about Mathias and his time as mayor. Mathias was furious about the things being said about him in the article. He was being blamed for the crime on the streets and for allowing Scar free reign over the poorest neighborhoods while protecting the rich sections. The article blamed him for starting a class war and turning his back on the neediest citizens. They also hinted that he may have actually been working with Scar.

The thing that really upset Mathias the most was the part of the article that said the governor had come in and rescued Baltimore. Officially the deputy mayor was in charge, but everyone in politics knew that Governor Tillingham had taken control and was cleaning up the corruption left behind by Mathias Steele.

Mathias felt like the article made him look incompetent as it blamed him for all of the city's problems.

Mathias was in denial and blamed Scar for the problems in the city. "I'm gonna clear my name and show these fuckers who's really responsible for this shit."

Mathias closed the newspaper and turned his eyes to the front of the church. After an hour of sitting there and obsessing over the article, he watched the people file out at the end of the funeral service. Governor Tillingham appeared at the top of the steps and the media swarmed. The governor held court like a king among his peasants. Mathias seethed on the inside.

As the governor was speaking to the press, he looked across the street into the park. Without missing a beat, he whispered into the ear of one of his staff, who then whispered into the ear of one of the police officers guarding him. The next thing Mathias knew, there was an officer standing right next to him.

"Sir, I am going to have to ask you to leave," the officer said to Mathias.

"This is a public park. I think I'll stay," Mathias calmly replied without looking at him.

"Sir, I don't want to ask you again. You need to leave this area. It's for security purposes," he said a little more forcefully.

"I am no threat, and you can't make me leave a public space. Now I'm asking you to leave," Mathias replied, keeping his eyes locked on Governor Tillingham.

The governor was watching the whole thing transpire while he kept answering questions from the press.

The officer quietly spoke into the microphone attached to the sleeve of his suit, then awaited the reply from his superior. "Copy," the officer answered.

"Sir, if you do not cooperate, I will have no choice but to use force to remove you."

"Fuck you." Mathias lost his cool. "Do you know who I am? I'm the mayor of Baltimore. You take orders from me." Mathias was staring at his reflection in the cop's sunglasses.

The officer grabbed Mathias by the arm with one hand, while his other hand was on his weapon. He picked Mathias up off the bench and began shoving him away from the church.

"If you don't leave now, I'll arrest you."

"Fuck you. I'm the mayor!"

"No, sir, you were the mayor. Now you are no one." The cop pushed Mathias to the ground.

Mathias was humiliated and wanted to jump up and fight. He thought better of it when he looked up at the officer standing over him with his weapon drawn.

"You'll regret this." Mathias stood up covered in dirt and walked away steaming mad.

It was now a tie between Scar and the governor at the top of Mathias's most hated list. As he walked away, Mathias vowed to himself to give a little payback to the governor for his disrespect.

Mathias walked into East Baltimore with one thing on his mind. He needed to buy a gun. He didn't know how to go about buying one, but he figured he had a good chance of buying it in the hood. As mayor, he spent no time in these neighborhoods. This was all new territory to him. He felt like an exposed target walking these streets. His designer suit and tie made him stick out like a sore thumb.

He tried to appear calm as he proceeded down Eastern Avenue. His eyes were darting back and forth; his body was tense, like he was waiting for an attack at any minute.

A young boy about thirteen years old jumped out of a doorway and blocked Mathias from going any farther. "The fuck you doin' around here, nigga?" the boy asked.

"I'm looking to purchase something," Mathias said.

"You got money, I got what you need. I can make you feel good."

"I'm not here to buy drugs."

"The fuck you need then?"

"Young man, I doubt you can help me. I need to speak with someone older. Perhaps you have an older brother?" Mathias asked.

The young banger looked at Mathias with disgust and confusion on his face. They stood staring at each other, the boy trying to figure this dude out, and Mathias not knowing what to do or how these negotiations were supposed to happen.

"Yeah, a'ight. I can introduce you to my brother. He inside. Follow me."

They walked toward the boarded up house they had been standing in front of. The boy walked up the three steps to the front door and pushed the plywood board back so they could enter. As soon as Mathias was inside the doorway, the young boy spun around and caught him with a fist to his jaw, sending Mathias slamming into the wall.

"Mu'fucka, who you think you is? I got what you need." The boy stood in front of Mathias, pointing a gun at him.

Mathias was stunned.

"Now, what you need, nigga?"

"I–I need a gun," Mathias stammered. His heart was racing. Never before had he been in a situation where his life could end at any second. He had been sheltered his whole life. He was now getting a taste of what the streets were really like.

"Shit. Why you think I can't get that for you?"

"I don't know. I've never bought a gun before."

"You a cop?" the kid asked.

"No."

"You look like a cop. I hate cops. I have no problem shooting cops."

"I'm not, I'm not. I swear." Mathias was trembling. The boy stood there studying Mathias. He wasn't nervous at all, because he had been on the streets since he was nine. He'd lost any fear he had years ago.

"Open yo' shirt."

"What?"

"Open yo' shirt. I wanna see if you wired."

"What?"

The boy reached out and ripped open Mathias's shirt, exposing his bare chest. "A'ight, you ain't wired. Step into my home." The boy pushed Mathias deeper inside the house and followed behind, keeping his gun aimed at Mathias's back.

The house was dark and cold. There was no furniture except for a television, a dirty mattress on the floor, and an old torn-up couch in the living room. The boy pushed Mathias down onto the couch. Mathias was beginning to think his life was going to end in this god-forsaken place.

The boy pulled a pen cap out of his pocket, along with a baggie full of cocaine, and tossed both to Mathias. "Yo, before we go any further, you need to take a bump from that baggie."

Mathias caught the baggie and pen cap. "I don't know what that means."

"Nigga, snort some cocaine from the bag so I know you legit. Scoop it out with the pen cap and snort it."

"I'm not here to buy drugs."

"Mu'fucka, if you don't snort some shit right now, you gonna die." He raised the gun and aimed it a Mathias's head.

"Okay, okay." Mathias opened the bag, scooped out a huge bump, and snorted it up his left nostril. He immediately felt a burning, then a numbing sensation in his nostril. To him it felt like the cocaine shot straight through his skull, directly into his brain. His eyes widened and his heart started racing. He felt great.

"Wow!" Mathias smiled, which made the boy smile as well.

"Now I know you legit. You want a gun? You wanna be a gangbanger, Grandpa?"

"Yeah, I need a gun." The cocaine was making Mathias clench his jaw.

"A'ight. I can get you a gun. But you ain't just buying a gun from me. I'm a businessman, and my business is cocaine. You need to buy some shit from me so my bosses can see I'm hustlin' out here."

"Oh, definitely. Whatever you need." Mathias's leg was twitching rapid fire.

"How much money you got?"

"I have a thousand dollars. Is that enough?"

The boy didn't say anything. He just stared at Mathias. This was much more than the boy was going to ask for. He was trying to hide his shock and excitement.

"Damn. That's all you have? Usually I wouldn't do this, but I like you, so I'll sell you a gun, that bag, and bullets for a thousand. You gettin' a good deal. Normally it would be at least fifteen hun'ed."

"Thanks. I appreciate it." Thoughts were racing through Mathias's mind a mile a minute. He reached in his pocket and handed the boy the stack of cash.

"Bullets not included." The boy emptied the clip of his gun and handed it to Mathias.

"Oh, sure. Yeah, of course." Mathias put the gun in his pocket. Now that their transaction was complete, both of them couldn't wait to leave. The boy wanted to jet before this dude realized he got suckered. Mathias wanted to leave because the cocaine had him so high he needed to get outside and walk.

"You need more coke, you come see me. I got rock, too, if you need it," the boy said.

"Yeah, yeah, okay." Mathias walked out as fast as he could.

Once on the street, Mathias was so high he didn't realize that he speed-walked all the way back to his nice, safe section of Baltimore. The cocaine had him flying high and feeling like he could conquer the world. He was positive that he would destroy Scar and Governor Tillingham now that he had a gun. He felt invincible, and he couldn't wait to get home to do another bump of coke.

Chapter 3

Hotel Love

The lobby of the downtown Baltimore hotel was empty as Cecil entered through the front door. He wasn't surprised, since it was the middle of the night. He saw only one person, a little Asian man swinging a buffing machine back and forth over the marble floor.

I don't know why motherfuckers don't be robbin' hotels more often. Ain't no one here to stop you. I might have to take this place down myself, he thought.

He made his way through the massive lobby to the front desk. Sitting atop the counter was a silver bell like Cecil had seen in the movies.

This shit is crazy. Not even a person at the front desk. I should just rob this place now and stay somewhere else.

He pushed the button to ring the bell. There was some rustling in the office to the left behind the desk. After a short delay, a young white guy in his early twenties came out of the office. His eyes were bloodshot and his hair was disheveled. Cecil figured the kid had been asleep in the office.

"Hello, sir. How can I help you?" the clerk said.

"I need a room."

"All right." The clerk typed something on the keyboard and read the computer screen in front of him. "Do you have a reservation?"

"No, I don't. I didn't think I would need one." Cecil joked, "And by the looks of your empty lobby, don't look like I need one."

Either the clerk didn't get the joke or he ignored it. "Okay, sir. No problem. I would be glad to assist you." He typed a few more things into the computer. "Will you be needing one or two beds?"

"One."

"We have a nice deluxe room with a king size bed."

"That sounds fine."

"I'll just need some information from you. First and last name, please."

Cecil was a little caught off guard by the question. He paused for a second. He knew enough not to give his real name. "Chuck Bell."

"Okay, Mr. Bell. Your mailing address?"

"Ah, well, that's a problem." Cecil paused and the clerk looked up from the computer screen. "See, my wife and I are moving here to Baltimore, and we don't have a place to live yet. I just got a job. I had to leave Atlanta to move here."

He was lying, of course. He had come from Florida to Baltimore with Tiphani Fuller, his girlfriend. She had told him a sob story about how three men—Scar Johnson, Derek Fuller, and Mayor Mathias Steele—had ruined her life and taken advantage of her. She was seeking revenge against these three men and had convinced Cecil to help her kill them.

According to Tiphani, Scar was a vicious criminal who tried to have her killed after she presided over his case. Instead of protecting her, the mayor had Tiphani arrested for corruption, which Tiphani said was based on lies and rumors; and Derek was trying to keep Tiphani away from her children. For these actions, Tiphani decided they all needed to die, and Cecil was so blinded by the good head she gave him that he was willing to do anything for her.

Little did Cecil know that she had chosen him when she read his rap sheet while he was in prison. She saw that he was a decorated soldier with extensive combat experience. He was smart and dangerous, the perfect man for Tiphani's scheme. That was why she started visiting him in jail and developed a relationship that continued after he was released.

The clerk blankly looked at Cecil. Cecil had no idea what the kid was thinking, and it made him a little nervous. He quickly calmed down, telling himself there was no reason to worry. Tiphani was the only one who knew anything about his involvement in the recent murders in Baltimore, and she was an accomplice, so she sure as hell wasn't going to speak up. Cecil had made sure that a few weeks ago, when he came up from Florida for the first time, no one had seen him blow up the cars of Police Chief Hill and Chief of Staff Dexter Coram. Those murders were the first wave in Tiphani's retaliation, and they had brought about the firing of Mayor Steele. Now Tiphani and Cecil were here together to finish the job.

"Congratulations on your job, sir," the clerk said. "It's not a problem if you don't have an address. Your work address will be fine."

Damn. I can't tell him my job is to kill three dudes, Cecil thought.

"Ah, just put down City Hall as my workplace." It was the first place that came to Cecil's mind.

"Excellent, sir. You're here to get Baltimore back on the right track. Lots of changes going on over there at City Hall. Personally I thought Mayor Steele was horrible. I'm glad to see he's out of there." The clerk entered the address of City Hall without even needing to ask.

"Yeah, he made a real mess of this city. Unfortunate that the police chief and his chief of staff were murdered."

"Yes, it was. I hope they find the son of a bitch that did it. Excuse my language, sir. I just get angry when I think of innocent people losing their lives."

"It's all right. I like your passion. I hope they find him too." Cecil smiled. He found it funny that this kid had no clue he was speaking to the killer himself.

"Now, the last little part of business. I need a credit card from you."

"I'll be paying cash." Cecil started to take out a stack of bills from his pocket.

"That's fine, sir, but we still need a credit card for incidentals."

"I can pay cash for whatever that is," Cecil said.

"We need a credit card in case of damage to the room, and items from the mini-bar."

"I don't have my wallet. Just take the cash and I can get you the credit card tomorrow."

"I'm sorry," the clerk said. "That's not possible."

The clerk was starting to get on Cecil's nerves. Cecil didn't want to have to kill the kid, but if he started to feel like he was making too much of an impression on the kid and the clerk would remember him, then Cecil wouldn't hesitate to murder the little shit.

Cecil calmed himself down. "Okay, I understand," he said.

"Thank you. I'll be glad to give you a room once you have your credit card, Mr. Bell," the clerk responded.

Cecil walked away boiling on the inside. He had wanted to stay at a "no-tell motel," but Tiphani insisted on staying at a 5-star hotel. Ever since he had met her in Florida, Tiphani had been a bit too reckless for Cecil's liking. She was supposed to be hiding out down there, but she would often go out without any sort of disguise and spend large amounts of money on frivolous things. This type of thing was exactly what he wanted to avoid.

Cecil walked outside to the car, where Tiphani was waiting. He got back into the driver's seat.

"So? We checked in?" she asked.

"No, the little fucker needed a credit card and wouldn't let it slide. I told you we needed to go to one of them hourly joints. They don't be asking all sorts of questions like this bougie-ass place." Cecil put the keys in the ignition to drive off.

"Hold on. We ain't goin' to no sleazy hooker hotel. Do I gotta do everything?" Tiphani pulled the visor down, checked herself in the mirror, applied lipstick, and straightened her wig. "Give me the cash. I'll be back with a room key."

Cecil handed her the cash, and she stepped out of the car and strutted into the hotel. She was sick of all these trifling men in her life letting her down. It always seemed like she had to do everything. Every man she came into contact with tried to play her, and now she was going to play them. It was her time. These men could all go to hell, and she was going to be the one to send them there.

Just as Cecil did, Tiphani rang the bell that sat on top of the front desk. The young clerk appeared a moment later.

"May I help you?" the clerk began.

"Hello. My husband was just in here, and there seems to be a misunderstanding."

"You must be Mrs. Bell." The clerk smiled.

"Ah, yes, yes, I'm Mrs. Bell." Tiphani quickly realized that Cecil must have given a fake name.

"Welcome. As I explained to your husband, our policy is that we need a credit card to reserve a room."

"But we would like to pay cash. We hate those damn extra fees the credit cards charge."

"I hear you. Those interest rates will kill you. These days you got to save any way you can."

"I'm glad we cleared that up. So, how much is the room? We'll pay for the whole week up front." Tiphani went into her purse to get the cash.

"Oh, no. You misunderstand me. You can pay cash at the end of your stay. We need a credit card at the beginning to safeguard against anyone running out on the bill and to cover any extra charges that may occur."

"I can assure you we won't run out on no bill. We're not some ghetto couple," she said.

"Yes, I understand your husband works for City Hall."

Tiphani was taken aback for a second. *What the fuck this nigga been telling this boy?* she thought. Then, just as fast, she got amused by the irony and humor in the fact that Cecil said he worked for City Hall, since he had already killed the chief of staff and was back again to kill the former mayor.

"Yes, he does. We are very excited to be here with all of the changes. Any idea what happened to Mayor Steele?"

"No, ma'am. The news is saying he walked out of his office and hasn't been heard from since. Good riddance, I say. He was the worst."

Tiphani giggled. "Yes, he was." She was hoping that their mutual dislike for Mathias Steele would make the clerk bend the rules and let them stay without giving a credit card.

The clerk smiled at Tiphani. "I like you guys. So many times guests come in here and are so rude when I tell them they need a credit card."

"I like you too. You're cute. I promise we won't ruin your room."

"I know you won't, but I still need a card. If it was up to me, I'd let you stay, but it's not. I'm trying to put myself through college with this job. I don't need to be getting fired right now." He shrugged his shoulders.

"That is so commendable that you are putting yourself through college. I did the same thing."

"So you understand."

"I do. Do you know what I did to put myself through college"—she looked at his nametag—"Evan?" She said his name seductively. She was done trying to get what she wanted through normal means. She was going to plan B. She was going to get what she wanted from a man the easiest way she knew how. Tiphani found that men were always willing to barter when sex was involved.

"No, ma'am, I don't." He was a little uncomfortable all of a sudden.

"Well, let's just say that if I can show you, I can promise you would be satisfied."

"Ma'am?"

"Is there anyone back there with you?" Tiphani asked, looking toward the office.

"No."

She leaned over the desk and whispered in his ear. "Then let me come back there. I want to taste you."

Evan's dick sprang to attention. He stood there frozen, unable to move. He had spent many late nights fantasizing that a guest would come down and offer herself to him. Now that it was happening, he didn't know how to react.

"Come on, baby. Open the door." Tiphani seductively massaged her breasts.

Evan swallowed hard. His heart was beating fast. He went around and opened up the door to the back office. Tiphani came around and followed Evan into the office. "Now, I'll give you what you want, and I promise it will be the best you have ever had. You need to promise to give me what I want."

"Mrs. Bell, I can't. I'll lose my job."

Tiphani reached down, undid his belt, and unzipped his pants. Evan sucked in a deep breath of air. His legs began to tremble; he was so excited and nervous.

Tiphani got on her knees and pulled out his dick. She was excited as well. She thought of white boys' dicks as a treat, like a kind of dessert. She always thought that white boys were juicy and loved their taste. She was pleased with the size when she unleashed his manhood and began kissing the head.

"Now"—she gave a little kiss—"how about"—another kiss—"you let me"—another kiss—"pay cash?" Another kiss, then she looked into Evan's eyes before swallowing his entire dick in one gulp.

"Ahhh. Okay!" Evan groaned.

Tiphani began sliding her mouth up and down on his shaft. Evan tilted his head back and closed his eyes in ecstasy. He couldn't believe what was happening.

Tiphani stroked and sucked his dick furiously. She was loving the taste of this young college white boy. "Mmmmmm. I love this dick," she moaned as she continued stroking his shaft with her left hand and playing with her clit with the right. She then started sucking on his balls. This drove Evan over the edge.

"Oh God. That is good. Oh shit." He looked down to watch Tiphani work.

He grabbed her head and forced his dick into her mouth again. She took it with ease as he began fucking her face. He gave her mouth full strokes, and her saliva acted as lubrication. He had never had a woman be able to swallow his whole dick.

He got so turned on watching his cock pump in and out of her face that he couldn't take it anymore. He pulled out and shot his load all over her face, just like he had seen in the many pornos he watched late at night at work.

He stood there panting and smiling as he watched Tiphani wipe cum from her cheeks and lips. "Mm-mmm." She licked her fingers.

"Holy shit. I feel like I was in a porno. That was amazing." He put his dick back in his pants and zipped up.

Tiphani got back to her feet. "So, will I be staying in your hotel?" She smirked.

"I'll see what I can do." Evan smirked back.

A short while later, Tiphani walked back outside to the car. She knocked on the driver's side window, startling Cecil awake. He jumped, wiped his eyes, and opened the window.

"Room sixteen-oh-four. Bring the bags up." She handed him a room key and walked back into the hotel.

She went back to the desk one more time and rang the bell. Evan appeared, still looking a little flustered.

"Hey." He had a huge smile on his face when he saw Tiphani.

"Here's a little extra for your college fund." She winked, handed him five hundred dollars, and walked to the elevators. Evan stood there shocked and in love as he watched her get in the elevator.

Tiphani was in the shower when Cecil entered the room. She finished washing up, dried off, and hopped in bed, where Cecil was already under the covers, watching television.

"What did you do to get this room?" he asked.

"Something you couldn't, obviously." She pulled the blanket up to her neck.

"What would that be?"

"I charmed him and helped him relieve some stress."

"What's that supposed to mean?"

"Exactly what it sounds like. I got down on his level and told him how I put myself through college."

"How did you do that?"

"I fucked dudes for cash." She turned her back on Cecil.

"Baby, that is so sexy." He nestled up behind her and pressed his dick into her ass cheeks.

"I'm not fucking you right now," she said.

"Come on, baby. That story made me horny." His dick started to get hard as he rubbed it on her ass.

"I want to sleep. Tomorrow we start our hunt for the three dead men." She was using the nickname they had come up with for Scar, Derek, and Mathias.

"Come on." He reached around and started playing with Tiphani's pussy.

It turned her on. Cecil's fingers made her realize she didn't get off when she sucked Evan, and her pussy needed some attention. She started to breathe heavier and opened her legs a bit for easier access.

"I promise tomorrow I will hit the streets hard looking for them mu'fuckas," Cecil whispered in her ear.

Without saying anything, Tiphani guided Cecil's dick inside her, and he started fucking her from behind.

Chapter 4

Fight for My Life

"Let me the fuck out of here!" Halleigh screamed at the top of her lungs. Her muscles ached, her throat hurt, and her eyes were stinging from crying. She was locked in a small room with a single mattress. There was a tiny bathroom attached with a sink and toilet. She had no idea how she had gotten there. The last thing she remembered before waking up was being in the trunk of a car.

Former detective Derek Fuller had kidnapped Halleigh because he was desperate to get his kids back from Scar. He knew that Halleigh's boyfriend, Day, worked for Scar. Derek kidnapped Halleigh and told Day that if he wanted her back, he would have to get Derek's kids from Scar. So far it wasn't working. Day claimed he didn't even know where Scar went after he escaped from the city. Derek didn't give a shit what Day said; he was going to hold Halleigh until he got his kids back.

Because of the lack of windows in the room, Halleigh had no concept of time and no idea how long she had been there. To Halleigh, it felt like an eternity. She was slowly beginning to lose her will to live. Her life was a constant struggle, and she was tired of the fight. She felt like she was never able to catch a break. Whenever she felt like she was on the right track, someone would come along and put an end to her peaceful feeling. This time, that person was Derek Fuller.

The lock on the door unlatched. The loud thud startled Halleigh and made her jump. She was definitely on edge. Derek Fuller violently pushed the door open and entered.

"The fuck you screaming for again?" he said.

"Fuck you!" she spat.

"I told you no one can hear you and I don't give a fuck."

Halleigh had nothing to say to that. She stared at Derek, wishing he would die. She felt powerless. She was unable to do anything and started to cry.

"Goddamn." Derek walked out and locked the door behind him.

Halleigh collapsed on top of the mattress, sobbing. She wished her life would end. Lying there she thought back on her life—raped as a young girl, forced into prostitution, her first true love murdered. She realized that she was never in control of any of it. She was always a victim; someone else always dictated what path her life would take. Then she started to think about her little boy, the love of her life, the only one that mattered to her. She saw his smiling face, she heard his laugh. The vision strengthened her and stopped her sobbing. Halleigh didn't want her son raised without his mother. She needed to protect him and teach him how to be strong.

How can I teach my boy to be strong if I can't show him a good example and be strong myself? she thought. She resolved right there to stop being a victim, to start taking matters into her own hands and dictate how her life would go from that point on. She was doing it for her son. Malek Jr. was going to be a survivor, and Halleigh was going to teach him how.

Sitting up, she tried to come up with a plan to escape. She took a mental inventory of the room. The only thing there was the mattress she was currently sitting on and a fluorescent light recessed into the ceiling. In the bathroom was a bar of soap, a toothbrush, and toothpaste. She saw nothing that could help her. The only way out she saw was going to be to fight. If she could take Derek by surprise, she might have a chance to stun him long enough to escape.

Halleigh went to the door and stood in different positions around it, seeing which one might be the most advantageous for her attack. None seemed particularly good. She looked around the room once more. Pretending to be asleep when he came in was out of the question. She figured being in a prone position would put her at a disadvantage and weaken her. There didn't seem to be any good place in the room to take Derek by surprise.

Halleigh then had the thought that she would hide in the bathroom. When he entered, she would wait until he was in front of the bathroom door, and then rush out and attack him, possibly hitting him with the door and knocking him out. This was her best chance, she thought.

Halleigh waited in the bathroom for what seemed like an eternity. While sitting on the toilet, she thought about her son—his laugh, his smile, how he must be missing his mama. This gave her more motivation and energy for her attack.

Being confined in such a small space was making her antsy. Her nerves were making her rock back and forth, continuously sit up and then right back down, and pacing for two steps back and forth. She thought about screaming to get him down there faster but decided against it. She wanted him relaxed to catch him off guard. If she screamed, he would be coming down already on edge and looking for trouble.

Derek unlocked the door and entered holding a paper plate with a peanut butter and jelly sandwich. Halleigh held her breath when she heard the door open. Her heart was in her throat and her mouth went instantly dry. Now that the time had arrived for her to fight, she wasn't sure she could go through with it.

"Hey," Derek called out.

Halleigh didn't answer. She just stared at the door. Derek stepped farther into the room. "Halleigh? I brought you food."

Again, no answer from Halleigh.

"You in the bathroom?" Derek walked toward the bathroom door.

Halleigh listened to his footsteps getting closer to the door. This was it, time for her to decide if she was going through with it. She stood up from the toilet and quietly placed her hand on the door handle. One half of her wanted to just open the door and take the food, and the other half was ready to fight. She was struggling with her emotions and was afraid to make a decision.

"Stop fuckin' around. You in there?" He raised his voice as he directed it toward the bathroom. He was standing directly in front of the bathroom door.

Decision time. Halleigh turned the knob and opened the door with all the force she could muster. "Aghhhhh!" She screamed, slamming the door into Derek and knocking him back. The sandwich went flying to the floor.

Halleigh rushed out and jumped on top of Derek, raining punches down on him. Continuing to scream to keep her adrenaline up, she landed punches wherever she could and with as much force as possible.

Derek covered his face and tried to avoid the windmill of punches being thrown at him. After his initial shock was over, Derek realized that her punches weren't doing any harm. In one swift movement, he grabbed Halleigh's arms and flung her off of him, sending her crashing into the wall. She crumbled to the floor in a heap.

Derek immediately pounced on top of her and subdued her. He pinned her down on the floor, making it impossible for her to move. She struggled to get free, but his weight was too much for her. After several seconds of fighting to break free she gave up, but before she did, she spit in his face. It was the only thing she could do to feel as though she still had some power and to let him know how she felt about him.

"Fuck you, bitch. I ought to beat your ass," he said.

"Fuck you, motherfucker." She attempted to wriggle free.

"The fuck you thinkin'?"

"The fuck you think I'm thinkin'?" she shot back.

"You're a dumb ass tryin' to come at me like that." He laughed.

Her face was tight with anger and embarrassment. "Just get up off me."

"Nah. I kind of like being on top of you." Derek smirked and moved his hips in a sexual manner.

Halleigh was disgusted. She was mad at herself for trying to overpower Derek. She was mad for not thinking of a better way to escape.

"Fine. Stay on top of me. Do whatever you want to do," she said in a monotone and turned her head.

"Shit, I don't want to do anything to you when you say it so unsexy. I'm not a rapist."

"No, you're just a kidnapper."

Derek had a mind to slap the bitch. "If I let you up, don't try any bullshit. I'll knock you the fuck out. Got it?"

"Whatever. I don't need to be bit more than once to know it hurts. Just let me up."

Derek jumped to his feet and put some distance between them. He made sure to land standing between the door and Halleigh, in case she had any ideas of trying to run out. She slowly stood as she straightened her clothes and hair.

"Thank you," she said, trying to regain her composure.

"What the hell?"

"I'm being held against my will. What do you think?" she said sarcastically.

Halleigh was wishing he would just leave. She had some planning to do. She was going to escape from captivity and find her son.

"Don't get sassy, bitch. It'll get you nowhere," he warned. "It's a shame you had to get stupid today. I was going to let you upstairs to take a shower."

"Big deal." She flicked her wrist.

"I was looking forward to watching you wash that fine little body of yours." He looked her up and down.

"Your loss, not mine." She shrugged her shoulders. She was trying to act cool. Her insides were doing back flips, and she didn't want him to know how scared and angry she was.

"I would say your loss. I might have even joined you in that shower. Now you'll just have to eat alone." He gestured with his head to the sandwich on the floor.

"Nothing to drink?"

"Water from the tap, bitch."

His phone vibrated in his pocket. He took it out and looked at the caller ID. "It's your knight in shining armor," he said to Halleigh.

"Dayvid?" Her mood perked up.

"Maybe he's ready to do right by you."

He answered the call, "Speak." He walked out and locked the door behind him.

"Dayvid!" Halleigh screamed, hoping that Dayvid would hear her. She ran to the door and put her ear to it, hoping to hear their conversation, but Derek was already out of range.

She let out a deep sigh and went straight to the bathroom. She was a ball of nerves. Now that Derek was gone, she couldn't hold her emotions back. Knowing that Dayvid was on the phone put her over the edge. The second she was in the bathroom, she leaned over and grabbed the sink with both hands and broke down crying.

Now she had even more incentive to break free. Before she was determined for her son, but the way she felt when she knew Dayvid was on the phone told her she needed to do it for him as well. She was in love with the man and wanted to be his wife. She wanted him to be her son's father. She wanted to give him a child.

These feelings for Dayvid had only recently begun to stir in Halleigh. When she met Dayvid, she was dating Malek and Dayvid was his protégé. After Malek was killed, Halleigh and Dayvid started spending more time together. During this time, their feelings for one another had blossomed.

"Get it together." She looked up above the sink out of habit to see her reflection, but there was no mirror.

Derek had removed it so she couldn't use the glass as a weapon.

"Damnit," she mumbled to herself.

Halleigh wiped the tears from her face and resolved to fight some more. She stood in the bathroom thinking of a way, any way, to escape. She wracked her brain, but nothing was coming. The only thing she could do was replay her last failed attempt over and over.

"Think, Halleigh, think." Her eyes searched the tiny bathroom. "I need a weapon." Her eyes continued to dart back and forth. They landed on her toothbrush.

"Holy shit. The toothbrush. People make shanks out of those in prisons." She snatched the toothbrush off the sink and frantically searched her "cell" for a surface to sharpen the toothbrush handle. She had a renewed burst of hope and energy.

That burst didn't last very long as she realized there weren't really any good surfaces for her to sharpen the toothbrush. The linoleum in the bathroom, the carpeting in the main room, and the dry wall in both were lousy as sharpening tools.

Fuck it, she thought and started to vigorously rub the toothbrush on the carpet, praying to God that her new plan for escape would work.

Chapter 5

The Hunt with Some Extra Baggage

"Speak," Derek answered the phone.

"We need to meet," Dayvid said. On the other end of the line he heard a muffled female voice calling his name.

"Halleigh!" he screamed, hoping she would hear him.

"No use screaming, nigga. She ain't gonna hear you."

"Let me speak to her. You better not do nothin' to her," Dayvid warned.

"I'm not doin' nothin' to her that she don't want," Derek taunted.

"I'll kill you, nigga."

"Come on, stop the bullshit." Derek chuckled.

"I swear to God, nigga." Dayvid was furious.

"You just do what you need to do and she'll be fine. But hurry up. I think she's startin' to feel me." Derek couldn't help giving Dayvid shit.

"Fuck you!" Dayvid screamed at the top of his lungs. His screaming startled Malek Jr., who had been sleeping in the backseat of Dayvid's car. "Dayvid?" Malek wiped his eyes.

Dayid removed the phone from his ear and covered the mouthpiece so Derek couldn't hear. "Hey, little man," he whispered. "Everything fine. Go back to sleep."

"You screamed," Malek Jr. said. Dayvid put the phone back to his ear.

"Who the fuck you talkin' to?" Derek asked. "None of yo' business."

"Is that D.J.?" Derek thought he might have heard his son in the background.

Dayvid realized from the urgency in Derek's voice that he could use this to his advantage. "It was no one." Dayvid made sure it sounded like he was trying to cover up that it was D.J.

"Let me speak to him." Derek sounded desperate. "D.J.!" he screamed.

"No use screaming, nigga. He ain't gonna hear you." Dayvid repeated Derek's words exactly.

"Fuck you!" Derek yelled.

"Looks like the tables have turned, nigga." Dayvid laughed.

Derek was livid. He wanted to strangle Dayvid. It killed him that he felt powerless to protect his children and that he had no idea where they were.

"Listen to me and listen good. If there is any harm to my children, if you have my kids and haven't given them to me, I will kill your woman right now."

Dayvid had a decision to make. Should he call Derek's bluff and continue making him think he had his kids, or should he tell the truth and buy some time? Dayvid looked at M.J., who was looking out the window, quietly singing to himself. Dayvid couldn't risk losing Halleigh. He would never forgive himself if he was responsible for M.J. growing up without his mother. He also wasn't sure if he was capable of raising M.J. on his own. It had only been a week and he was already having trouble taking care of him.

"Relax, nigga. It ain't yo' kid. I promise. But let me tell you, if you do any harm to Halleigh, I will find yo' kids and dead them little shits. You hear me?"

Derek had no choice but to believe him. "Okay, okay. Just get me my kids." He hung up.

"I'm hungry," Malek Jr. announced from the back seat.

"A'ight, little man. We'll get you some food in a minute."

"Nooo, I'm hungry now. Nuggets."

"Chill! We have to buy them shits first." Dayvid immediately felt bad for snapping at Malek. He turned to look at Malek and apologize. Malek was just staring at him with a scared and shocked look on his face. Dayvid couldn't have felt any worse. He was on edge. Taking care of a child and figuring out his next move was becoming a problem.

"I'm sorry. Let's get some nuggets." Dayvid pulled out into traffic, heading for the nearest fast food joint.

Dayvid drove along not really paying attention to where he was going. He was thinking about how he was going to get Derek's kids away from Scar. Hell, the first thing he needed to do was find Scar. It had been a week and Dayvid had not spoken to or seen Scar. As soon as Dayvid saw that Scar's house had been raided, he called Scar, but Scar didn't answer. Dayvid had no idea if Scar had been picked up or just threw his phone away. He spent all week at Halleigh's house watching the news for any information on Scar. Nothing was said about an arrest, so he figured Scar must have gotten out before the raid.

Dayvid figured he'd give one more attempt to reach Scar on his phone, though he didn't have much hope that he would. Dayvid dialed the number. He was right; the phone was not in service. He wasn't surprised. When he saw the raid, the first thing Dayvid had done was throw his own phone away.

After a week away from the streets, he had no idea what was going on. He figured things had quieted down enough that he could come back out from hiding at Halleigh's. He needed to find Scar, somehow convince him to let Derek's kids go, and save Halleigh. He had a feeling that time was starting to run out on Derek's patience. He figured Derek was searching for Scar as well, and if Derek found him first, that would spell the end for Halleigh. Dayvid had to act fast.

Dayvid headed toward his old corner. He would start his search there, trying to get information on what the hell was happening, and hopefully find out about Scar. He rolled through the hood and saw some familiar faces, but it seemed different to him. He couldn't tell if it really was different, or if the week away from the grind had made him see things in a new light.

Some of the young soldiers out there hustling saw his car as he pulled up to his old corner. They thought he was a customer and started strolling to his car.

"Is this nuggets?" Malek asked.

"Oh, no, little man. Soon. I just need to talk to my friends for a second." Dayvid had completely forgotten that Malek was in the car.

The corner boy walked up and nodded his head. "What's good?" he asked.

"You tell me. Been out for a minute," Day responded. "Oh shit. I didn't recognize your ride. What's crackin', Day? It's been a second. Where you been?" He reached out and they bumped fists.

"Layin' low after I seen Scar's joint get raided. You heard from that nigga?"

"Nah. Rumors and shit, but ain't nothin' definite."

The corner boy shrugged his shoulders. "Word. You got any paper for me?"

"Nah, B. Flex come by earlier and collect."

"Yeah? Where he at? I need to connect with that nigga," Dayvid asked.

"I'on't know. He don't be sayin' much. Did ask about you, though."

"What's he askin'?"

"Nothin'. Same shit. 'You seen Day?' That kinda shit. I told him no. You want me to say somethin' to him if I see him?" the boy asked.

"Let him know I stopped by. Tell him to holla at me." Dayvid wrote his number on a piece of paper and handed it to the boy.

"Bet." The boy took the paper, they slapped palms, and he walked back to his spot on the corner.

Dayvid drove off wishing he had been able to get more information from the kid. He wasn't surprised that Flex wasn't saying much. He suspected that Scar had ordered everyone to be tight-lipped right now. After the death of the police chief a week earlier, the cops were knocking down doors all over Baltimore. The less anyone knew about Scar, the safer he would be.

Dayvid needed to find Scar. What was his next move? Flex would know where Scar was. His plan was to drive around to all the spots he thought Flex might be. Even if Flex wasn't there, Dayvid would leave word that he was back on the block.

He was focused now. He made a mental list of all the spots he needed to hit. His mood was high. He turned the car stereo on and stepped on the gas, his sights set on his first stop.

"My tummy hurts," Malek Jr. said.

Dayvid didn't respond. He couldn't hear him over the music.

"My tummy hurts. I'm hungry," Malek said a little louder.

Dayvid heard him this time. "What?"

"My tummy hurts. Nuggets." Malek pointed to the fast food joint they were passing.

"Shit," Dayvid mumbled. He had forgotten again that M.J was in the car. "Okay. Let's get nuggets." Malek smiled as Dayvid turned the car around. *Goddamn, this kid is going to get in my way. How the fuck I'm gonna deal with him?* Dayvid thought as he pulled into the parking lot of the restaurant. He loved Malek, but the kid was pissing him off at that moment. He needed to find the kid's mother, but he couldn't do it if the kid was always looking to eat or complaining about being bored. How could Dayvid take care of his business and the kid at the same time? He needed to figure it out soon or Halleigh might be dead.

Chapter 6

Typical Country Morning

Scar walked downstairs after a long, restful night of sleep. No birds waking him up this morning. He smiled and said to himself, "Guess them birds got the hint."

Usually he was the first one awake in the house, but he had slept so long that his niece and nephew were already in the kitchen eating breakfast.

"How'd y'all get that cereal?" he asked.

"I climbed up and got it," said his eight-year-old niece, Talisa.

"You crazy." Scar smiled. He was feeling good from being so well rested. It's amazing what one good night's sleep can do for a person. The day before, Scar was ready to take his chances, leave his country house, and go back to Baltimore. Now he was chillin'.

No need to rush back to the bullshit hustle. I can just chill here, outta the limelight for a minute, and make my money from a distance, he thought.

He sat down and poured himself a bowl of cereal. They all sat in silence, each in their own thoughts. Scar looked out the window at the sun beaming between the trees. Maybe he could get used to this country living. He had never taken the time to look at trees or nature while he was living in the city. He was starting to enjoy the slower pace.

The silence was broken by D.J. "Uncle Scar, it's boring here."

"Play with yo' toys," Scar answered.

"They're no fun."

"Yeah, I'm bored here too. When is Mama and Daddy coming back?" Talisa chimed in.

"Soon," Scar lied.

"We want to go home," Talisa said.

"You ain't," Scar snapped.

The children were startled by his abrupt answer. Scar instantly felt bad seeing the shock, confusion, and sadness on their faces. He changed his tone immediately.

"How 'bout Flex take you to the store? Buy you what you want," he said smoothly.

The children didn't answer. They just shrugged their shoulders in agreement. The rest of their meal was finished in silence.

Scar understood the children's feelings. It was slow in the country, especially since they couldn't really travel around. Scar couldn't leave his property, so when Flex wasn't there, that meant the kids had to stay there as well.

"We're finished. May we be excused?" Talisa asked.

"Yeah, go on." Scar stayed staring out the window as the children scurried to their room.

Scar was starting to really love his niece and nephew, but he didn't want to be dealing with them all the time. He had his own shit to deal with, and he didn't want to have to handle their bullshit as well. Scar needed to figure out a way to end all of this mess soon so he could figure out what to do with these kids. He had a feeling that these kids would be without parents by the time all was said and done.

Scar felt it was inevitable that he was going to have to kill his brother. As far as Tiphani was concerned, he wasn't sure if he would ever see her again. She may have skipped the country after news of their affair broke and her career as a judge was destroyed. If he did see her again, he would be killing her too. Thinking about his brother and his ex-lover made him seethe.

Scar picked up his phone. "Yo, when you stoppin' here?" he asked Flex.

"On my way. Be there in like forty-five." Flex merged onto the highway.

"I need to blow off some steam. Pick up that ho Charisma on your way."

"A'ight. Gonna take me longer to be there, though."

"Just do it. I need to bust a nut all over that bitch. Get my head straight. You feel me?"

"Word, I feel you." Flex hung up and exited at the next off-ramp.

Scar cleared the table and turned on the television. The news about his manhunt had slowly been decreasing. Scar knew this meant nothing. He had gotten word from some of his soldiers that they were still looking for him just as hard, even if the news wasn't picking it up. He flipped through the channels, never really staying on one station for very long. His mind was distracted with thoughts of his brother. He was hoping he wouldn't have to kill him, but he knew that the moment he kidnapped Derek's kids, he had crossed a line and it was all-out war.

A few hours passed with Scar wandering around the house and the children playing in their room or in the backyard. This seemed to be the routine they were falling into.

"We're hungry." Talisa came through the back door.

Scar was getting fed up with having to deal with the kids' neediness. He wanted to say "Get it yourself." Instead, he asked them what they wanted.

"Spaghetti." D.J. followed his sister into the house. Scar held his tongue and just sighed as he went to the kitchen to start cooking. He would take the opportunity to make something for himself as well. He hadn't realized how hungry he was until the children said something. As he was pouring water into a pot, Flex came striding through the front door.

"Ay, yo," Flex called out.

The children went running to greet him. These days, anything different to break up the monotony of the day would excite them.

"We going to the store," D.J. said to Flex.

"Great," Flex said, not really paying attention to the little boy.

"Who are you?" Talisa asked the woman in skintight jeans, high heels, and a form-fitting top.

"My name's Charisma, dear. What's yours?" Charisma bent down to shake Talisa's hand.

"Talisa. You want to play with my dolls?"

"Not now, dear. How 'bout later?"

"I'll get some new ones at the store for us." Talisa stared at Charisma with adoration. She hadn't been around a female in a long time.

Flex and Charisma walked into the kitchen, where Scar had already dumped the water from the pot into the sink.

"Brought you some presents." Flex smiled and emptied a duffel bag full of cash onto the kitchen table. "Business startin'a pick up again."

"Okay, okay. My day is startin' to look up." Scar rubbed his hands together. He picked up some of the bills to see what denomination they were. Looked like mostly fifties and hundreds to Scar. He put the money back in the pile. "What's good, ma? Come here and give yo' man some love," Scar said to Charisma. She seductively walked over to Scar, wrapped her arms around his neck, and began kissing him. Scar grabbed her ass as they kissed and grinded their pelvises into one another. Scar's dick was standing at attention. He broke their embrace.

"Get yo' ass upstairs and be ready for me," he said to her.

She composed herself, straightened her hair, and walked out of the room without saying a word.

"While I take care of my business upstairs, take them kids to the store and buy them whatever they want. They buggin' me with their whining and shit, sayin' they bored." Scar reached into the pile of cash and handed a fistful of bills to Flex. "This should cover it. If not, fuck 'em. Oh, get 'em some food too." He handed him a hundred dollar bill from the pile.

"D.J, Talisa, let's go," Flex called out.

The kids came running into the kitchen ready to head out the door. The minute Flex walked through the door, they had been prepared to leave. They couldn't wait to get out of the house. Flex gathered them up and followed them out the front door.

Scar quickly got to his bedroom, where Charisma was already making herself comfortable on the bed.

"Your kids is cute," Charisma said.

"They my niece and nephew. Why you ain't naked yet?" Scar asked.

"It's more fun when you take my clothes off for me," she purred.

"A'ight." Scar approached the bed, his smile broken up by the namesake scar that disfigured his face. He eased her back and lay on top of her. They started right where they had left off in the kitchen, grinding their pelvises and passionately kissing. Scar removed her top to reveal perfect, firm breasts, and started sucking her nipples.

"Mmmm. Yeah, Daddy," she cooed. She reached down to unleash his manhood.

She stroked his erection. "Oh, Daddy, I want to give you your own baby. Fill me up. I'll be your baby mama."

Scar jerked back from her. "The fuck you just say?"

"Nothin'. I don't know. I was just talkin' dirty." She tried to kiss him.

"Like hell you was talkin' dirty."

"Baby, come on. Make my pussy hurt. I need it." She reached down for his dick.

"You tryin'a trap a nigga'? I oughta beat yo' ass for thinkin' that shit." Scar was getting progressively angrier.

Just as he was about to haul off and hit Charisma to knock some sense into the bitch, there was a knock at the front door.

"Who the fuck?" Scar jumped to his feet and grabbed a gun from under his bed. As quietly as possible, he walked downstairs to the front door. There was another knock on the door, and then the doorbell rang. Scar cocked his gun. He couldn't think of who could be at his door.

Goddamn, we need to get a security system up in here. Scar walked to the window in order to catch a glimpse of the motherfucker who was knocking on his door. As he peeked out the window, he looked directly into the eyes of his neighbor. Arnold waved when he saw Scar looking out the window.

"Hello, neighbor," Arnold called out.

Fuck. He saw me. Why this white mu'fucka keep bothering me?

Scar begrudgingly opened the front door. "You need something?" he asked.

"Oh, no. Just stopping over to say hello. Cooking up some oxtails later. Trying something new to expand my palette. Wanted to invite you and the kids over for a little feast."

"No. Can't make it."

"Oh, come on. It'll be fun. A little getting to know your neighbors session."

“Don’t think the kids like oxtail.”

“No worries. I can make them some grilled cheese sandwiches or whatever they prefer.”

“Maybe another night.”

“Oh, nonsense. I won’t take no for an answer. Let’s say seven o’clock?”

“Um . . .” Scar didn’t trust this cat. He wasn’t buying this neighborly crap. There was some other reason this dude kept coming around. But just in case this dude was legit, Scar played it cool.

“Great,” Arnold said, not even waiting for an answer. “Seven o’clock. Say, before I get out of your hair, do you mind if I use your commode?”

“What?”

“Your bathroom. Do you mind if I use it? I don’t think I’ll be able to hold it in until I get through the woods to my home. Weak bladder.” In an attempt to make a joke, Arnold made a grimacing facial expression.

Scar sighed in exasperation. “Fine. Make it fast.” He stepped aside to let Arnold in.

“It’s around the corner.” Scar pointed in the direction of the bathroom.

Scar anxiously waited at the front door for Arnold to do his business.

Charisma came down from the bedroom. “Come back to bed, Daddy,” she said seductively.

“Get yo’ ass back upstairs,” Scar snarled.

“I’m lonely, Daddy.” She pouted and batted her eyes. “I’ll be right up.”

Satisfied, she obediently turned and went back upstairs. Arnold came from around the corner.

“Was that your daughter?” he asked Scar.

“What?”

“Was that your daughter?” Arnold repeated.

“No. She ain’t my daughter.” Scar looked at Arnold like he was stupid.

“Oh. I heard her call you Daddy. I just assumed.”

“She a friend.”

“Well, invite her tonight. The more the merrier.” Arnold smiled.

Scar had no idea what to make of this crazy white dude. Was he for real? Were people in the country all this friendly, or was this dude playing an angle?

"Well, I'm off. The vegetables need tending. Got some real beauties to sell tomorrow at the farmers' market." Arnold walked toward the front door.

As he got about halfway to the door, he stopped and turned to Scar. "By the way, you might not want to leave so much cash laying around your house."

"What you say?" Scar was instantly on guard.

"I happened to see the money on your kitchen table. You should put that into a bank. I'll talk to my brother Erik. He's a manager at the savings bank in town. He's a good guy. He'll set you up."

"I don't think so." Scar reached behind him for his gun.

Just as Scar put his hand on the handle of the gun, Flex came barreling through the front door.

"Yo, Scar!" Flex yelled out, thinking that Scar would be in a distant part of the house. He stopped dead in his tracks when he saw Scar and Arnold standing directly in front of him.

"Oh shit. I thought you'd be upstairs." Flex was holding a brick of cocaine.

Arnold saw the cocaine in his hand and started sweating. He realized at that moment that he was in trouble. The piles of cash, the cocaine . . . These men are drug dealers!

Scar pulled out his gun and smacked Arnold in the head, knocking him out cold.

"The fuck you doing back?" Scar yelled at Flex.

"I forgot I had this brick in the trunk. I didn't want to be driving around all day with this shit. You know people around here be gettin' pulled over for driving while black," Flex said.

"Goddamn. Now what we do with this nosey mu'fucka?"

"We got to dispose of him," Flex said matter-of-factly.

"Shit. Help me tie him up." Scar shook his head slowly. Flex went out to his car and got some rope from the trunk. They proceeded to gag and tie Arnold up, and then they put him in the basement.

"Take them kids to do their shit then come back here. We take care of this snooping nigga later tonight."

Flex went out the front door, and Scar went upstairs to pound some pussy, while Arnold lay in the basement unconscious.

Chapter 7

My Own Private Crack Den

The cocaine had run out, and former mayor Mathias Steele was fiending for another bump. He had spent the last two days snorting coke, watching television, and pacing around his house. He had wanted to hatch a plan to exact revenge on Scar, the governor, and anyone else he felt had wronged him, but this didn't happen. His mind was scattered and racing in a coke-fueled frenzy. He couldn't keep focused on one thought long enough to follow it through. Whenever he would begin thinking about a plan, he would soon find his thoughts drifting back to cocaine.

Mathias had given up any hope of ever working in politics again. No one was taking his phone calls. He was an outsider now. All of his old government friends were ignoring him. He had lost his identity, his personality; he had lost the career he had worked so hard to build and wanted for so long. The only thing he wanted now was for the people responsible for his downfall to hurt as much as he did. Before he was going to make that happen, though, he needed more cocaine.

He wiped his index finger across the glass top of his coffee table, where he had been cutting his coke. Mathias was in luck. There was residue left on the table, and he swiftly rubbed it on his gums. With a renewed sense of energy, he put the gun in his coat pocket and stepped out the door. Mathias squinted and shielded his face as the bright sunlight hit his eyes like a lightning bolt.

"Damn." He went back inside for his sunglasses. With his eyes now protected, he was able to comfortably function outside. He rushed to his car and drove the Cadillac to his new favorite spot, the dope house where he was becoming a regular. On the ride over, he couldn't decide on the music he was in the mood for, and switched between radio stations at hyper speed. He stopped on a news station that was replaying a speech by Governor Tillingham on the state of the city. Mathias couldn't concentrate because he was so angry hearing the governor's voice. He heard bits and pieces of the speech as he weaved in and out of traffic.

"Corrupt former mayor . . . asleep at the wheel . . . useless police force . . ." were a few of the quotes he heard that sent him into a simmering rage.

He pulled up in front of the house and scanned the area to make sure no one was watching him or had followed him. The cocaine was making him extra paranoid. No one had any reason to be following him. No one even cared about him anymore.

Satisfied that he wasn't being followed, he made his way to the house. He was getting anxious knowing that just beyond the door, he was going to get his hands on some coke. For Mathias, it couldn't happen fast enough.

He gave three quick knocks on the door. His palms were sweating. He wiped them on his pants. The door opened slightly, and he heard a man's voice.

"What you need?"

"An eight ball." Mathias wiped his forehead with his palm.

The door opened to allow Mathias entry into the dark house. There were three men sitting around the living room in a haze of marijuana smoke. They were all staring at Mathias as he walked in. Mathias looked out of place next to the three men, all wearing the typical urban outfit—fitted baseball hat, oversized T-shirt, jeans hanging low on their hips, and brand new Nikes. Mathias, on the other hand, was wearing a blazer, a button-down shirt, slacks, and loafers. He might not be a politician anymore, but he still dressed the part.

"Gentlemen." Mathias nodded to the men. They said nothing.

"You need a ball?" asked the man who had let Mathias in.

Mathias jumped as the man spoke. He was definitely on edge and had forgotten the other man was in the room when he saw the three others.

"Yes." Mathias cleared his throat and swallowed.

The man went into another room and came back holding an eight ball of cocaine. Mathias's eyes widened when he saw it. He pulled out his cash and exchanged it for the coke.

"Look, do you mind if I try it out before I leave?" Mathias asked.

"Feel free, my nigga."

"Thank you. I didn't get your name."

"It's Best, 'cause I got the best shit in town." He laughed.

"Thank you, Best." Mathias sat on the sofa, stuck his car key into the bag, scooped out a mini pile of coke, and snorted it.

"Ah, that's nice." Mathias fell back into the sofa with a smile on his face.

"Told you I got the best shit."

"Yes, you do."

The three other men had turned their attention to the NBA game on the television.

"Hey, Best, let me ask you something." Mathias snorted another bump.

"What's good?"

"If I'm looking for Scar Johnson, do you know where I could find him?" He scooped another bump and snorted it.

"Nah, dude. He ain't been nowhere to be seen." Best lit up a blunt, feeling relaxed. With the way this dude was snorting coke, there was no way he was a cop. "I might know somebody who know where he is, though." He exhaled a big cloud of smoke.

"Oh yeah? Who?" The excitement in Mathias's voice was obvious.

"How much it worth to you?"

"That depends." Mathias was sensing he was about to get into a negotiation. This excited him. Besides all of the power, negotiating was his favorite part of being mayor. And he was good at it.

"Depends on what?" Best took a drag of the blunt.

"How close is this person to Scar?"

"Only like his right hand man."

"Well then, that could be worth something. If it was true." Mathias was grinding his jaw he was getting so high.

"Oh, it's true, my nigga. Belie'dat."

"I'll tell you what. I'll give you a thousand dollars if you tell me who it is."

"Bet. Let me see the money."

Mathias chuckled. "Hold on, young buck. I'll give you half now, and if you introduce me to him, I'll give you the other half." Mathias pulled out five hundred dollars from his pocket.

"A'ight." Best grabbed the money. "Dude's name is Flex. He come by to collect his cash, but it always be at different times. Never the same day or time, so I can't tell you when to come back."

"What does he look like?"

"He mad diesel. He always working out at the gym. He a young cat, too. Most times he wearin' a Ravens cap on his head."

"Well, you let me know when he comes around and I'll give you the other half." Mathias got up to leave and handed Best a slip of paper with his number written on it.

When Mathias got to his car, he didn't start it. He sat in the passenger's seat, going over the information he had just received. It wasn't much, but it was enough to probably be able to identify Flex when he came by to collect. Mathias planned to stay in his car and stake out the house until Flex showed, then follow him to Scar.

He took out his coke, looked around, and then his paranoia kicked in again. He felt too exposed, sitting there in his car. He started to get uncomfortable and started fidgeting. He did a bump and quickly put the coke away. This plan wasn't going to work.

Mathias got out of the car and went back up to the house. Same as before, he gave three quick knocks on the door.

"You forget somethin', nigga?" Best asked.

"I'll give you a thousand dollars right now if you let me stay here and wait for Flex."

"I don't know, nigga. You lookin' like five-o might scare my customers."

Mathias showed Best the cash.

"A'ight. But you gotta stay in the back room the whole time. I don't want to see your tight ass in the front room at all."

"Just keep me supplied with coke and I'll stay in whatever room you like." Mathias clenched his jaw.

Best opened the door, took the money, and showed Mathias to his room. There was a small bed, a television, and a nightstand in the room.

The drugs were obviously affecting Mathias's ability to negotiate, but he didn't care. He talked himself into thinking he'd won the negotiation. As long as he was high, Mathias felt like a winner.

"Comfy," Mathias said sarcastically. He sat down on the bed, placed his coke on the nightstand, and prepared to wait for his meeting with Flex.

Chapter 8

Chance Meeting

Tiphani slowly slid the key card into the slot on the door. The lock disengaged, and she quietly opened the door to her hotel room. She tiptoed to the bathroom, gently closed the bathroom door behind her, and turned on the light. She looked at herself in the mirror, pleased that she had gotten in once again without waking Cecil. Visions of the sex session she'd just had with the front desk clerk, Evan, flashed in her mind as she splashed warm water on her face.

For the past three days, she had gone to the lobby in the middle of the night to pay for their room and get some dick from the young clerk. She told herself that she was fucking the clerk so they could keep their room without any hassle. That might have been part of it, but she was really enjoying teaching the young man how to satisfy her. It was like an artist with a block of clay. She could mold him into whatever she wanted. She was making him into her perfect fuck machine. When her revenge on everyone was complete, she planned on keeping her new little toy around. Yes, she would have other men, but Evan would always be her boy on the side—until she got bored or he got too old for her liking. Then she would drop his ass and tell him to kick rocks.

Tiphani took off the wig she was wearing to help mask her identity and placed it on the counter. She smoothed out her natural hair and smiled at her reflection in the mirror. She was pleased with herself. She had found a man to help her exact revenge on her enemies, and as an extra bonus, she could fuck the hotel desk clerk whenever she wanted.

Standing there staring at her face in the mirror, Tiphani thought about her children. She hadn't thought of them in a while. As she was inspecting her features, she thought about her daughter, Talisa, and how much the little girl was starting to resemble her. She wondered where they were and if they were safe. Her post-sex euphoria was now replaced with sadness and guilt.

Ever since she fled to Florida, she hadn't thought too much about her children. The longer she was separated from them, the less she thought of them. She was actually enjoying the fact that she didn't have to worry about them and take care of them. This realization caused Tiphani to feel a huge sense of guilt. She was torn between wanting to be a good mother and wanting to make herself happy. If she was being truthful to herself, she was happier when they weren't around. When she pictured her future, the kids were never part of her visions. Tiphani was confused about her feelings. She didn't want to abandon her kids, but she felt happier alone.

"They would be better off without me," she said to her reflection. "I need to make sure they're safe, and then I can disappear. It's better for them." Her eyes started to tear up.

Cecil opened the bathroom door and startled Tiphani. She flinched and grabbed at her heart when the door opened.

"Who you talkin' to, baby?" Cecil asked.

"No one. Myself." Tiphani splashed water on her face again, trying to hide her annoyance that Cecil had interrupted her time in the bathroom.

"You ain't goin' crazy, are you?" Cecil smiled at his attempted joke.

Tiphani rolled her eyes as she wiped her face with a washcloth.

"You look good, ma." Cecil bit his bottom lip.

"Ugh. Get outta here with that tired-ass, corny line." Tiphani sat down to pee, not caring that he was in the room. "And why you bite your bottom lip? That shit is so played and not sexy." She wasn't trying to hide her annoyance anymore.

Cecil got angry at Tiphani's salty attitude. He knew that she had just sneaked into the hotel room and he was trying to look past it. In fact, he knew she had been doing it for the past three days. He had a mind to slap some sense into this bitch for her disrespect, but he restrained himself. He was well aware that Tiphani had offshore bank accounts with stacks of money, and he wanted a piece of it. He was going to play it right with her and get his share when the time was right. So, for now, he would have to play it cool, even though he was starting to become leery of her.

"Why you up so early?" he asked.

"I had to pee." With a look of What are you, stupid? on her face, she pointed to herself sitting on the toilet.

Her lie angered Cecil. He knew damn well that she had been out, and he was doing everything in his power to remain calm, but he was unsuccessful.

"I heard you sneak in a few minutes ago." He looked straight into her eyes, challenging her to answer.

For a second, Tiphani was caught off guard, but she quickly recovered. Without missing a beat, she answered. "Oh, I went downstairs to pay our bill. Evan's being cool and taking care of it so no one asks questions. I just need to make sure I keep paying."

"Really? Evan's being cool." He mimicked her words.

"Yes, really."

"It takes two hours to pay a hotel bill? You think I'm stupid? Are you fuckin' him?" Cecil couldn't hide his anger or his jealousy.

Tiphani laughed, not because she thought it was funny, but because of nerves. She was stalling to think of an answer.

"I'm not fucking him. We talk. He wants to go to law school and has lots of questions for me. Evan's a sweet kid."

"For the last three days he's been asking you about law school?"

Tiphani was in a groove. There wasn't a question Cecil could ask that would rattle her. "No. We talk about other stuff. I'm tryin' to stay on his good side and not cause any suspicion. I'm not tryin' to get caught."

Cecil didn't have anything to say to that. He looked at Tiphani and tried to read her face, to see if there were any signs of her lying. He never could read her very well, and he'd definitely never really trusted her.

Cecil had been suspicious of Tiphani ever since they left Florida. He'd come back from his first trip to Baltimore only to find her packing up all her shit. He'd just committed murder for her, and it looked like she was ready to leave him high and dry. Being a sucker for her sex skills, he'd ended up believing the story she told. She said she'd been cleaning the house of both of their fingerprints before they jetted from Florida. The more time they spent together, though, the more he realized he was probably being played for a fool. However, he'd come too far to get rid of her just yet. He deserved to get paid for the work he'd already put in, and the only way he could do that would be to get access to her offshore money. He would just have to keep on doing what he was doing and keep one eye on Tiphani at all times.

Tiphani felt uneasy as Cecil examined her. To break his thought process, Tiphani used the one weapon she always used with men. The one thing that she knew men were weakest for.

"Baby, you know you the only one I want to fuck. I can't get enough of your dick." This wasn't totally untruthful. She couldn't get enough of Cecil's dick, but she also couldn't get enough of most men's dicks. She was insatiable when it came to sex.

Tiphani got on her knees in front of Cecil and slowly pulled down his sweats. Cecil's manhood instantly sprang to attention. "Mmmmm." Tiphani moaned as she wrapped her hand around it.

Cecil grabbed the sides of Tiphani's head and she started to work on his erection. As usual, Cecil instantly forgot about his suspicions as he watched Tiphani do her thing.

Tiphani finished Cecil off with her head game, then climbed into bed and ordered room service. Cecil followed.

"We need to get our shit in gear. I'm done relaxin' in this room doin' nothin' but orderin' room service, watching movies, and fuckin'. It's time to hunt down our prey," Tiphani said.

"Just say the word. We eat, then we go." Cecil stretched out on the bed.

"No. I'm not going. You're going. I can't take no chances of being recognized in the streets." Tiphani needed some time away from Cecil.

"Just wear your wig like you been doin' when you go to the lobby."

"Fool, that's in the middle of the night and only one person is seeing me. Besides, one stupid wig ain't gonna fool no one in the streets."

Cecil sprang up from his prone position to a sitting position and got in Tiphani's face. "Bitch, don't you call me a fool. You will regret it."

Tiphani sucked her teeth. "Please. I dare you." She calmly got out of bed to create some distance between them. She was nervous, but she wasn't going to let Cecil see that.

"Don't test me." Cecil wanted to smack the shit out of her. He was getting sick of Tiphani's attitude, but the thought of all her money kept him in line once again.

Tiphani ignored him as she went and opened the curtains, letting in the morning sun. She looked out over the Inner Harbor.

Cecil went to the bathroom and started the shower. The hot water and steam calmed him down. He figured getting out and driving around would do him good, take his mind off his growing doubts about Tiphani's loyalty.

"I'll start the hunt." He walked out of the bathroom and started putting on his clothes.

Tiphani was eating an omelet off the room service tray. "Thanks, baby." She smiled. "I've written down addresses of spots that I could remember where Scar frequented. You could start there." Tiphani gestured to a piece of paper on the service tray.

Cecil picked up the paper along with a strip of bacon. He ate the bacon as he read over the list. "There's only three addresses on here."

"That's all I could remember."

"It should be enough to start with." Cecil shrugged his shoulders.

"Before you start, buy some throwaway phones so you can update me on what you find. I don't want you calling the hotel directly." She handed him a hundred dollar bill.

Cecil took the bill and one more piece of bacon and then walked out the door.

***

Cecil was cruising the streets of Baltimore, getting accustomed to the geography of the city. He had dropped the cell phone off with Tiphani and gone straight out on the hunt. It felt good to be out on his own. After being released from prison in Florida, he had spent almost all of his time with Tiphani. The only time he was away from her was when he came up to Baltimore by himself to murder the police chief and Dexter Coram.

He had stopped off at the first address on Tiphani's list, but the house was vacant. Now he was just driving and taking in the sights of Baltimore. He noticed a lot of hustlers on the streets. He thought about questioning them about their knowledge of Scar, but figured it would be a waste of his time. If they were on the streets, they probably never had any contact with the boss of the operation. Scar wouldn't waste his time with the street hustlers. Cecil thought his best bet was to find the mid-level hustler, one who had met Scar but didn't have total loyalty to him. Someone who thought he could run the operation better.

Cecil pulled up in front of the second house on the list. It was a small, red brick, one-story home. He checked his 9 mm to make sure it was ready for action. He wasn't going to trust these grimy-ass Baltimore cats for shit.

Cecil knocked on the door. He heard some rustling on the other side and felt as though someone was looking at him from somewhere. He looked around and saw a set of eyes peeking out from one of the windows. The eyes disappeared, and Cecil heard some muffled voices.

"Who is it?"

"I'm looking for someone."

"He ain't here."

"I'm also looking for something."

"We don't got it."

"You don't got any weed?"

"You a cop?"

"No, sir."

The door opened slowly and Cecil was allowed entry. "I like that, a nigga referrin' to me as 'sir.' That got a nice ring to it. Sir." The young dealer smiled and smoothed the air in front of his face with the palms of his hands like he was looking at his name on a billboard in Times Square.

Cecil took in his surroundings immediately—two stoned dudes on the couch and two dudes at the door standing on either side of him. He was outmanned for sure, but he figured the two on the couch would be easy to take out. Their reflexes would be slow due to how stoned they were. The two surrounding Cecil might be another story. As a soldier in the Army, Cecil had been highly trained in hand to hand combat, but these two looked like they could scrap. They could be a problem.

Let's try and get out of here with no problems, Cecil thought.

"What you say you need?" said the dealer who opened the door.

"I'm looking for the chronic. I heard you might be able to oblige a nigga."

"You heard right, partna." The dealer walked deeper into the room. "How much you need?"

"Let's start with a quarter, and if I like what I see, well, let's say I could be lookin' for some serious weight."

"You sure you ain't a cop? That shit sounds like a cop talkin'. Tryin' some entrapment bullshit on a nigga." He looked at Cecil out of the corner of his eye.

"I can assure you I am no cop. In fact, I'll buy a bag then sit down and smoke a blunt with y'all." Cecil thought this would be a good opportunity to put the men's fears to rest. With their defenses down, he figured he would have an easier time of getting information out of them. He also wanted to get a little buzz on.

"A'ight, a'ight. I like that. You a smooth cat." He went into the kitchen. When he came back, he tossed three different bags on the coffee table for Cecil to choose from. "They all weighed out. Take yo' pick."

Cecil inspected the bags and chose the greenest, hairiest-looking buds.

"Let's get high." Cecil opened the bag, sat on the couch, and rolled a blunt. He lit it, filling his lungs with smoke when he inhaled and relaxed into the couch.

"I didn't catch your name." He exhaled and passed the blunt to the young dealer.

"Best." He took the blunt and inhaled the thick, pungent smoke.

"Two-tone." Cecil told him his nickname. He reached for the blunt. "This some serious shit, my man. We ain't get shit this good in the joint, for sure." Cecil inhaled another lungful.

"Where was you locked up? Jessup? Hagerstown?"

"Nah. Nowhere 'round here. Down south. Florida. I'm up here on some business." Cecil passed the blunt.

"Word. You a businessman?" Best took a hit off the blunt.

"You could say that. I'm looking for a few dudes. One you may know. Scar Johnson."

Best choked on the smoke and coughed it out. "You the second nigga be comin' around here askin' about Scar. That nigga Scar got ghost a minute back. Nobody heard nothin' 'bout him."

Cecil cocked his head. "Who's the other dude lookin' for Scar?"

"Some rich-ass fiend. Tell you what. For the right price, I'll point you in that nigga's direction." Best arched his eyebrows.

Cecil needed to know who his competition was and why he was looking for Scar. He went into his pocket, pulled out cash, and counted out five hundred dollars he had stolen from Tiphani.

"This do you right?" He handed Best the cash.

"This'll do just fine." Best nodded his head and pointed to the back room. "Go talk to him. He be fiendin' out in the back."

"Anyone back there with him?"

"Nah. Just that sad-ass nigga by his self."

Cecil felt like he got played. He wanted to beat Best's ass, but he couldn't fault the dude for tryin' to make an extra buck. He probably would have done the same thing if he were in Best's position. So, instead of fighting to get his money back, he let it slide and made his way to the back room.

Before opening the door, he positioned his gun to easily draw and readied himself for a fight. He swung the door open and sprang into the room with the agility of a cat.

"What the fuck?" Mathias jumped away from the door and fumbled for his gun, dropping it to the ground.

Cecil saw the gun and immediately drew his and pointed it at Mathias. "Hold up, nigga," Cecil warned Mathias and picked up the stray gun.

Mathias was glistening from the sweat that covered his body. He was so wet he looked like he had just stepped out of the shower. He stood there shaking and jittery, with his hands help up in surrender. "Okay, okay. Take what you want."

"You lookin' for Scar?" Cecil grabbed Mathias's gun.

"Yes. Are you Flex?"

"Why you lookin' for him?"

"I need to speak with him. That's all." Mathias didn't know the mystery man pointing the gun, and he wasn't about to give up any information that wasn't needed.

"Why you waiting here? He supposed to be here?" Cecil asked.

"Best told me that Flex would know where Scar was."

"Who's Flex?"

"One of Scar's men. You're not Flex?"

"No. When is Flex supposed to be here?"

"I don't know. I was just going to wait for him." Mathias couldn't hold his arms up anymore. He relaxed them and they dropped to his sides.

"Put yo' hands back up! What's so important you need to speak to him?"

Mathias followed Cecil's orders, but this time, instead of raising them all the way up, he rested his hands on the top of his head. "You work for Scar?"

"If I worked for him, would I be looking for him?" Cecil looked at Mathias like he was an idiot.

"True." Mathias nodded in agreement. "Why are you looking for that snake?" He was thinking that since this guy was looking for Scar as well, perhaps they could work together.

"It sound like you ain't much of a fan of that nigga," Cecil said.

"I'm not. And by the looks of it, you aren't either." The energy in the room was beginning to relax. The conversation between the men was becoming more casual.

"That's right. What you after him for?"

"Can I lower my hands, please?" Mathias raised his eyebrows in a pleading way.

"If you try any stupid shit, I will put a bullet in yo' ass." Cecil kept his gun trained on Mathias.

Mathias slowly lowered his arms to his sides. "Ah, much more comfortable and civilized." He smiled and shook his arms to get the blood flowing back to them. "To answer your question, I'm looking for payback from Mr. Scar Johnson. That's why I am waiting."

"Payback for what?" Cecil asked.

"He ruined my career, and I plan on ruining him." Cecil didn't say anything. He just stared at Mathias, trying to figure him out. He couldn't imagine what career this dude was talking about. He didn't look like a drug dealer, so Scar probably didn't move in on his turf. If anything, he looked like a sweaty-ass drug fiend.

The longer Cecil looked at him without saying anything, the more uncomfortable Mathias was getting. The more he looked at Mathias, the more Cecil felt like he knew this dude from somewhere.

"And you? You haven't told me why you want to see him." Mathias awkwardly broke the silence.

"Hold up. What career you in?" Cecil was trying to place where he recognized this dude from.

"Let's just say I was in a political office."

Cecil's eyes went wide. "Ooohhh shit! That's right. I knew it. You the grimey-ass mayor. I'm lookin' for you too. You look mad different, though. I didn't know you was some fiend. All sweaty and jumpy. No wonder you was corrupt. Your ass was needin' a fix." Cecil laughed.

Mathias ignored all of the insults being hurled at him. "Why are you looking for me?"

"I'm gonna kill you."

Mathias almost shit himself when he heard those words. His muscles locked up and he stood frozen. He wanted a line of coke.

"Wh–wh–why?" he stuttered.

"You see, like Scar ruined your career, you ruined my woman's career, and I promised to get revenge for her." Cecil cocked his gun.

"Wait, wait, wait, wait." Mathias put his hands up in front of his body like he was going to block the bullet. "I'm sure we can come to some agreement. Are you positive I'm the one who wronged your woman? I'll make it up to you—to her. Who is your woman?" Mathias was talking a mile a minute, saying anything that came to mind in order to stall for time.

Cecil cut him off. "Nigga, I know you the one I been lookin' for. You done fucked with my woman. She had a good ole job as a judge, and now she on the run."

"I promise, please, I'll do whatever it—Wait, did you say she was a judge?" Mathias stopped his babbling when Cecil's words actually registered.

"You have trouble hearing? Yeah, that's what I said, nigga."

Mathias started laughing uncontrollably, to the point of being almost psychotic. Cecil swore he could see Mathias's eyes glaze over with crazy. There was now a decision for Cecil to make: Put this crazy motherfucker down, or get some information out of him. He chose the latter.

Cecil side-kicked the laughing Mathias in his stomach. "Stop yo' fuckin' crazy-ass laughing."

Mathias doubled over from the blow, clutching his stomach at the point of impact. Although in pain, he continued to laugh. "Your 'woman' wouldn't happen to be Tiphani Fuller, would she?" Mathias stayed hunched over.

"Don't matter who my woman is. You fucked with her, and now you gon' pay."

"Go ahead, kill me. You're with that black widow, she's gonna eat you up and spit you out. Your fate will be worse than mine." Mathias cackled a demonic laugh.

"Don't tempt me, old man."

"Do you even know anything about her?" Mathias unfolded himself and looked directly into Cecil's mismatched eyes, one hazel and one brown. It was Cecil's trademark, the reason his nickname was Two-Tone. "She's a manipulator, a user. She'll get what she needs from you and then leave your ass high and dry."

Mathias's tone made Cecil listen. It was the tone of someone who was speaking from experience, not someone who was begging for his life.

Cecil flashed back to the day he caught Tiphani trying to leave him in Florida. *I should have trusted my instincts then. I knew that bitch was grimy, but I let her talk me out of it,* he thought.

Mathias continued. "Do you even know what happened? I didn't run her off. She fucked with the wrong people and had to go into hiding so she didn't get killed."

"You were the one who tried to kill her," Cecil said, repeating part of the story Tiphani had told him.

Mathias let out one short burst of laughter. "Is that what she told you? I have known Tiphani a long time. She is a very driven woman and will do whatever it takes to get what she wants. She also has an insatiable appetite for sex, which helps her get what she wants. Men will do anything for her once they get a taste of her. Me included.

"I was fucking her for a while and she made me think I was special. Turns out she was making most of the men in City Hall feel special. Once I found that out I stopped it, but by then it was too late. She had gotten exactly what she wanted. She held it over my head, and in order to keep her from telling the world, I was forced to promote her and give her whatever she wanted."

"Sounds to me like you just got played. I won't let that shit happen to me." Cecil replied, although he wasn't feeling as confident as he sounded.

"You have already been played, my friend. You're out trying to clean up her mess. You know why she wants me dead? Because I was forced to have her arrested. You know why she wants Scar dead? So he doesn't kill her first.

"Look, Scar isn't a saint, and I want him dead as well, but that's for personal reasons. Tiphani is just mad because Scar played her. She started fucking him, and she fell in love. He used her and her judicial power to get himself acquitted. When things went bad for them, they went very bad, and now both of them are out for blood. But I can assure you that Tiphani Fuller is by no means an innocent victim.

"If you don't believe me, there are plenty of newspaper articles written about it. In fact, there's a video tape of Tiphani and Scar having sex. Feel free to look it all up."

Cecil was livid. This was exactly the opposite of what Tiphani had told him. She had painted herself as a victim, a sort of damsel in distress. Everything the mayor had just said made sirens go off in his head. His suspicions about Tiphani were stronger than ever. He was definitely going to do some research, but he was almost sure he was going to find out that Mathias was telling the truth.

This bitch thinks she can play me? She's sadly mistaken, Cecil thought.

"They say don't kill the messenger, but in this case, my brother, you about to die." Cecil smiled wickedly.

As his finger tightened around the trigger, the door to the room opened and hit him in the back, causing him to stumble forward and misfire. The bullet whizzed past Mathias's head and lodged into the wall behind him. In a split second, Mathias reacted and ran forward, knocking into Cecil and Best, who had entered the room. The impact of Mathias barreling into them sent all three tumbling to the floor.

The gun that Cecil had taken from Mathias landed right in front of Mathias's face. He quickly picked it up hopped to his feet and ran for the door. Cecil took aim and fired at Mathias. The bullet landed in the doorframe. Mathias made it through the door just in the nick of time.

Cecil jumped up in pursuit, knocking Best back to the ground as he frantically ran by him. Mathias haphazardly pointed his gun behind him and let off two shots as he ran out the front door. This stopped Cecil momentarily and gave Mathias a chance to separate from the melee. Lucky for Mathias, the three dudes who had been in the living room were nowhere in sight. They either hid when they heard gunshots, or had left before any of it started.

By the time Cecil made it to the front door, Mathias was nowhere in sight. There was no telling which way he had run.

Best came running up behind Cecil. "Yo, let him go. I don't need nothin' attractin' attention to my place."

"Fuck!" Cecil screamed as he scanned the empty street.

"Let's talk inside," Best said to Cecil. "You right. Let's go inside."

When Best turned to enter the house, Cecil shot him point blank through the back of the head. No witnesses. That's how Cecil liked to keep it. The three dudes that saw him before would get theirs later.

Chapter 9

Common Ground

Sweat was dripping from Halleigh's forehead. She had been vigorously rubbing the toothbrush handle against the carpet for hours. She stopped and inspected her progress as she wiped the sweat away with her forearm. Unfortunately, the fibers on the carpet weren't doing much to alter the shape of the handle. If anything, the back and forth motion of the rubbing had started to wear away the carpet and create a hole. The plastic on the toothbrush had barely been affected. Definitely not enough to satisfy Halleigh, especially with the amount of effort she had been exerting.

Halleigh sat and caught her breath for a moment as she tried to keep herself from getting discouraged. She kept her mind focused on her son, the main reason for her escape.

Sitting on the floor with her back against the wall, Halleigh's eyes randomly roamed the room. She was stuck. It was her prison. No way out except through the locked door. She had to start thinking like a prisoner. She had to fight for her life, and as she'd learned earlier, she wouldn't be able to overpower Derek; she just wasn't strong enough. The only weapon she had was a toothbrush, but at the rate that was going, it wouldn't be sharp enough to use for days, possibly weeks. Her situation was looking bleak.

The fluorescent light in the ceiling flickered and caught her attention. She was in a trance, staring at the tubed bulb when it hit her. She could use the light bulb as a weapon. She could swing it like a baseball bat at Derek. When it broke, she could use the broken glass to cut him and then flee. She contemplated breaking the bulb first and just using the glass, but was afraid Derek would hear it smash, thus defeating the "taken by surprise" tactic she was going for.

Halleigh reached up, stretching her arm as high as it would go, but was unable to reach the plastic covering. She thought for a moment then dragged the mattress and box spring across the carpet, placing it just underneath the light. Standing on her toes on top of the mattress she was able to extend and reach the cover. She removed the cover, exposing the fluorescent light. The bulb was too warm to touch, and she quickly pulled her hands away. The switch for the light was on the other side of the door. Even if she were able to turn it off, it would be a while before it would be cool enough to touch.

Halleigh heard movement upstairs. Derek was heading toward the stairs to the basement. She quickly took off her shirt, using it like an oven mitt as she turned the bulb and pulled it down. With the bulb in hand, she jumped down from the mattress and ran to the door just as Derek was opening it.

She swung the long bulb like a baseball player swinging at a fastball. It connected with Derek's left arm and exploded with a loud pop. Derek instinctively tried to shield his face from the attack. Halleigh leaped at Derek, attempting to stab him with the broken piece of glass left in her hand, but he was too quick. His training on the police force prepared him for such attacks, and he easily blocked her advances.

In one fluid move, Derek knocked the weapon out of Halleigh's hand, spun her around, and forced her onto the bed face down. Halleigh struggled to break away from Derek, but he had her hands firmly secured behind her and his weight was too heavy for her to move. "Calm the fuck down!" Derek commanded as Halleigh continued her fight. She was like a wild dog that wasn't about to be tamed—teeth bared, foaming at the mouth and growling.

Derek had enough. He cocked his fist and punched her in the back of the head. The force of the blow knocked her out instantly.

Halleigh was disoriented as she slowly opened her eyes. It took her a moment to figure out where she was and remember how she had gotten there. She replayed the attack on Derek in her mind. The last thing she remembered was lying face down on the bed, hands behind her, with Derek on top. She was still face down, but when she tried to touch the pain stemming from the back of her head, she was unable to move her hands.

Shit. I'm handcuffed. Halleigh unsuccessfully tried to free her hands from behind her back.

"Welcome back." Derek was cleaning up the broken glass strewn about the basement.

"Let me go." Halleigh squirmed on the bed, trying to flip herself over.

"That ain't happenin'. Just relax."

"Fuck you."

"Listen, bitch. I could do some serious damage to you, to the point of killing your ass. So, if I was you, I'd shut the fuck up and just chill." He roughly flipped Halleigh onto her back and straddled her.

Halleigh looked into Derek's eyes with hate.

"Now look at this. I'm on top of a fine piece of ass and she don't have a shirt on." Derek traced a finger around Halleigh's upper body.

Halleigh remained silent. She clenched her jaw and braced herself for whatever was to come. From her days as a prostitute, she was able to mentally separate herself from a situation. She would just let Derek do whatever he wanted to do.

"What's the matter? You got nothing to say? You've been naughty and need to be taught a lesson, but if you're a good girl, maybe I'll let you go." Derek rubbed Halleigh's breasts over her bra. Halleigh still said nothing. Derek could see that she had checked out.

"Seriously, what the fuck is your problem? One minute you're attacking me every time I come down here, and now you're lyin' here like a rag doll. Bitch, I'm about to rape you. You should be fighting for your life." Halleigh's eyes welled up and a single tear fell slowly past her temple into her hair.

"Goddamn, snap the fuck out of it. Speak." Derek slapped her across the face.

"What do you want me to say?" Halleigh's voice was just above a whisper. Tears were steadily streaming from her eyes now.

Derek didn't know what he wanted her to say. He was just pissed that she seemed disgusted by him. A small part of him wanted her to be attracted to him. He didn't want to rape her. Yeah, he wanted to fuck her, but he would never force himself on her. He was just playing mind games with her, showing her who was boss.

"Just stop being stupid and attacking me. I'll always win," Derek said.

"I'll never stop fighting for my son." Halleigh wouldn't look at Derek.

"You got kids?" Derek swung himself off of Halleigh and stood up.

"Just a son. He's the most important thing in my life. So, do what you want to me." Halleigh slowly turned her head to look directly at Derek. "But I will tell you this: I will never stop fighting for him. He needs his mama, and I will not let him down. Not like my mother did to me."

Derek couldn't bear to make eye contact with Halleigh. Her words hit him directly in the heart. He felt the same way about his children. He would do anything for them and would stop at nothing to protect them. He was feeling guilty because he was unable to come to their rescue. He was letting them down.

"What's his name?" he asked.

"Malek Jr. He's named after his father. I feel like I'm letting him down." The tears began again.

"I know what you mean."

"You have a son?" she asked.

"And a daughter. I would do anything for them. Including kidnapping. That's why you're here."

"Why me? I didn't do anything to your kids."

"You didn't, but Scar did. You're here so that your man will hurry the fuck up and help me find my kids."

"Day has nothing to do with that. Let me go. I'll find them for you. I'll help Day and we'll get them back."

Halleigh's speech was rapid as she pleaded.

"I can't do that."

"Yes, you can. Our kids need us. I promise to find them. Just let me go. From a mother to a father, I promise. Please." Halleigh was sitting up. Hope was running through her body. She was going to appeal to the father in Derek. This was her chance.

"No!" Derek yelled.

"Please." There was desperation in her voice.

There was a long silence. Neither one said anything as they thought about their children, each feeling helpless. Each was determined to be there for their children any way possible.

"I'm sorry." Halleigh decided to change tactics.

"Just stop trying to overpower me, all right?"

"I'm sorry your kids got kidnapped. I understand your hurt. I would do the same thing if I was you."

"Thanks."

"It kind of turns me on, seeing a man fight for his family, doing whatever he has to to protect them. So many punks out there that wouldn't do anything. Takes a real man." She gave him a seductive look.

"The fuck you doing?" Derek asked.

"Nothin'. I'm just tellin' you like it is. It's makin' me a little horny."

"Stop the bullshit."

"Seriously, Daddy, take these cuffs off and I'll make all the hurt go away. I want you to take your anger out on my pussy."

"Yeah? You want Daddy to fill you up?"

Derek approached Halleigh slowly. Suddenly, she couldn't believe she hadn't played the sex card right from the beginning. Men were so stupid, always thinking with their dicks.

"Yeah, Daddy. Fill me up," she said, mentally preparing herself to pounce as soon as Derek uncuffed her.

Derek was standing right in front of Halleigh with a big grin on his face. "You think I'm stupid?" He punched Halleigh in her face as hard as he could, knocking her out cold for the second time.

Chapter 10

Truth Kills

Cecil exited the library on the warpath. He had gone on the library computers and read article after article about Tiphani and her affair with Scar. There was even a clip of the press conference the mayor had given where they played a blurred-out version of the video of Scar and Tiphani fucking. If there was one thing that Cecil couldn't stand, it was being manipulated. He figured himself to be pretty straightforward and he expected the same from others; so when someone was untruthful and trying to manipulate him, he took it personally. He felt it was his duty to teach the untrustworthy person a lesson, and that was what he was about to do to Tiphani. He would teach her not to fuck with people's emotions.

Driving back to the hotel, Cecil had a death grip on the steering wheel. His body was tense with anger as he thought about Tiphani. He was running through ways in his head to torture her, make her regret ever trying to play him. He would bring her to the brink of death, make her think he was going to kill her, and then back off at the last second as she begged for her life. Cecil still wanted her money, and killing her would lose him access to all of her offshore bank accounts. He might be angry and want revenge, but he wasn't stupid when it came to money. He knew where to get it, and he wasn't about to cut off his supply line.

By the time Cecil made it back to the hotel and parked the car, his emotions were a mixture of anger and excitement. He was looking forward to the torture and beating he was about to inflict on Tiphani. Torture may be against the law, but that didn't stop the military from teaching Cecil the intricacies of torturing information out of the enemy. There was a fine line between torture and interrogation, and Cecil was one of the best at walking that line. He was now looking forward to stepping over the line into torture territory. He always found it fun trying to find exactly the right technique that would put the enemy over the edge and make them spill all their secrets. Watching the enemy squeal in pain always brought a smile to his face.

Cecil walked through the lobby with focus and determination. He made a direct line to the elevators and pushed the button for his floor. His mind was occupied with torture techniques. He was running through the file cabinet of techniques in his head, contemplating which one to start with. Start slow and build to the climax was always Cecil's way.

The elevator doors opened. Cecil, still focused, walked out, turned right and headed down the hallway. He was on autopilot right now, his mind filled with visions of things to come.

He slid the key card into the slot and pushed the door to open. His shoulder met the door with a thud. The door didn't budge. He tried the card a second time. Again, the door didn't move. The third attempt yielded the same results. This time Cecil noticed that the red light came on, indicating the door was locked. He pounded on the door.

"Tiphani. Open the door." He waited for a response. Nothing. He pounded again. He listened for any movement on the other side of the door, but only heard silence. He stood there taking deep breaths, trying to calm himself.

Where is this bitch? He looked around the hallway, trying to figure out his next move. Did he go to the lobby and wait for her? Did he go drive around Baltimore so no one would get a look at him in the lobby? Tiphani was sure to get a good beating over this.

Cecil stepped back from the door and contemplated either kicking it or tampering with the locking mechanism. As he stared at it, he finally realized he was standing in front of the wrong door. He was standing in front of 1504; they were staying one floor up in 1604. Cecil hadn't been paying attention when the elevator doors opened. He had been in his own world and automatically stepped off, assuming it was his floor. Angered at his mistake, he kicked the door.

He started back down the hall, and as he was about to turn the corner, he heard the bell announcing the arrival of the elevator. Instead of running to catch the door, he slowed his pace when he heard a familiar female laugh. It sounded like Tiphani's laugh, and she was getting off the elevator. This confused Cecil. Did she make the same mistake as he did and get off on the wrong floor?

Cecil stopped in his tracks and waited to catch her off guard as she came around the corner. Standing there, Cecil heard a male voice as well.

Who the hell is that? Instead of the voices coming in his direction, they trailed off toward the other side of the hotel. He swiftly and quietly followed, rushing past the elevators and peeking his head around the other corner. He saw a man and a woman, their arms and legs intertwined, tripping over each other as they kissed and laughed their way down the hall. There they were all over each other.

It took all of Cecil's discipline not attack them. Tiphani and the front desk clerk were obviously about to go fuck. With his head just poking from around the corner, he watched them pause in front of a door at the end of the hall. Evan used a key card and opened the door. He stepped aside, let Tiphani enter first, and smacked her on her ass as she strutted past him. This prompted a little squeal of delight from Tiphani.

Once the door was shut behind them, Cecil softly walked up to the door and listened. It was quiet at first. He could hear muffled voices, but couldn't make out what they were saying. After a minute or two, Cecil heard Tiphani's familiar moans. Cecil imagined Evan's face between her legs. It took all of his strength not to pound on the door. His entire body was tense with rage. His suspicions had been right: Tiphani was fucking the young hotel worker.

If she thought she could lie to him and play him, she was wrong. All of the information he had learned recently about Tiphani—and now to catch her out in a blatant lie and fucking another dude—had Cecil about to blow a gasket. He had had enough. He started to walk away, but not before hearing the sound of flesh slapping against flesh and the loud screams of ecstasy from Tiphani.

Cecil violently poked the elevator button with as much force as he could muster. He needed to take his aggression out on something or someone, and the button was the first thing in his way. The doors opened to an empty elevator car, and Cecil pushed 16 on the panel with the same intensity as before.

With the focus of a surgeon, Cecil entered his room, went directly to the closet, and pulled out his duffel bag. Almost robotic in his demeanor and actions, he placed the duffel on the bed and checked the contents. Satisfied, he slung the duffel over his shoulder and left the room.

He exited the elevator in the lobby and focused his sights on the exit. He kept his eyes fixed on the front doors and made a direct line to them. Nothing was going to distract Cecil from his mission. He walked through the front doors and straight to the car.

Forty-five minutes later, Cecil was back in the hotel room. Tiphani was sprawled out on the bed. She was propped up against the headboard, watching the television.

"Hey, baby." He went directly into the bathroom. "I missed you," Tiphani called out.

"I bet you did," he replied.

Cecil came out of the bathroom holding his duffel bag.

"I don't remember you leaving with your duffel," Tiphani said.

"I didn't. I came back to get it. You weren't here." Cecil turned off the television. "Where were you?"

Tiphani started rummaging through the minibar. "I needed to get out. I walked down to the water. You needed your bag. That must mean you found something."

Cecil couldn't believe how easy it was for Tiphani to lie. He wondered if she had thought about her alibi beforehand, or if she just came up with it. "I didn't find anything. No one knows shit. Why didn't you wear your wig if you were going outside?" he asked.

Tiphani touched her hair. "Oh. You're right. I forgot to put it on. I hope no one recognized me." She gave a quick, nervous laugh.

Cecil was in awe at how easily her lies came to her. She wasn't about to get tripped up by his questioning. "Yeah, I hope no one recognized you."

"When are you going back out to look for those evil motherfuckers?" She poured herself a glass of wine from the minibar.

"I'm not. Like I said, no one knows anything. The trail is cold." Cecil turned on the television again.

"What?" She turned to him.

"Did I stutter? I'm not going back out there."

"I thought you wanted to help. These men ruined me. They deserve to pay for that." Her eyes started to well with tears.

Cecil ignored her fake-ass tears. He knew she was making herself tear up for effect. "Speaking of paying, if you want any of these grimy-ass B-more cats to talk, you gonna have to pay up."

"Is that what this is about? You want money?"

"The money ain't just for me. Hustlers wanna see cash before they're gonna talk. I'm sure they know where Scar is. They're just not speakin' for free. Besides, I already took care and murked two of your problems, so a little paper my way wouldn't hurt."

"I thought you loved me. This was just about money?" Tiphani downed the glass of wine in one gulp. "You know I love you." She crawled onto the bed and pulled Cecil down on top of her. She was going to use the one thing in her arsenal that she always used. She was going to let her pussy do the convincing.

Tiphani ripped Cecil's shirt off of him and shoved her hand straight down his pants. Despite knowing that Tiphani was a liar and a cheater, he still wanted to fuck her. Cecil used all of his aggression to fuck her as hard as he could.

After an aggressive and at times violent bout of sex, they lay panting next to one another on the bed.

"I know you don't want to, but you're gonna have to pay. Those cats out there want money. We pay, we find Scar," Cecil said.

"You're right. I want that motherfucker dead." Blinded by her obsession for revenge against Scar, Tiphani easily agreed. She jumped out of bed and went to her purse. She took out a small notebook, flipped through the pages, and stopped when she found what she was looking for.

She picked up the phone, dialed a number, waited a few seconds, then punched in some numbers that she read off the page in the notebook. After a few more seconds she said, "Yes. I would like to transfer fifty thousand dollars. Yes. Same bank. Thank you." She hung up the phone and threw the notebook back into her purse. "I'm taking a shower. You got my hair all knotted up." She looked at herself in the mirror. "Then I'm going out to pay whoever tells me where to find Scar."

"You sure I was the one that knotted your hair up? Some of that cash better be for me," Cecil said as she entered the bathroom.

As soon as Cecil heard the shower going, he jumped up from the bed and went to Tiphani's purse. This was a bit of good fortune for Cecil. She usually didn't let her purse out of her sight, even when she went to the bathroom.

Cecil quickly flipped through the notebook. He stopped and smiled when he found it. It was the numerical code to one of Tiphani's offshore accounts. He ripped the page out and stuffed it in his front pocket.

Meanwhile, Tiphani was in the shower trying to figure out what Cecil's last comment meant. Did Cecil know she had been fucking Evan? Tiphani convinced herself that there was no way he could have known that. She chalked it up to Cecil being a jerk.

Tiphani was mad that Cecil was not going to be helping her without getting paid, but she figured he was still her best bet. She calmed herself down and decided to pay Cecil. It would speed up the process of finding and killing Scar and Mathias. It was little to pay to get what she wanted. Plus, she figured she could get the money back from Cecil later on. She was confident that all she needed to do was fuck him and he would eventually do whatever she wanted.

After drying off, she came out to see Cecil still in the same position on the bed, watching television.

"I'll go get your money. You deserve it for being so strong and brave. I just need you around me, baby. I can't get enough of your fine self." She was obviously trying to butter him up.

"A'ight, baby. You know I don't like asking for money. Hurry back so I can put a hurting on that pussy." He leaned over and smacked her ass. She cooed and began to dress.

"Where are the keys, baby?" she asked.

Cecil reached in his pocket and threw the car key to Tiphani. She caught them in one hand and started for the door.

"Don't forget your wig. Can't have anyone recognize you and ruin it all." Cecil smiled.

"Oooh, you're right. I keep forgetting that shit." She lifted the wig off the dresser and adjusted it on her head. Satisfied with her appearance, she leaned in and gave Cecil a romantic kiss good-bye.

"Can't wait to taste you when I get back," she whispered in his ear.

"Hurry back," he replied.

Once she exited the room, Cecil turned off the television and then lay back with his hands behind his head, staring at the wall like he was thinking—or waiting. He took in the silence of the room. He was calm. Less than five minutes later, a huge explosion occurred outside. It shook the building. Cecil simply smiled, got off the bed, gathered his belongings, and calmly left the room.

When he got into the lobby, it was chaos. People were everywhere, running in all directions, screaming into their phones. Cecil walked coolly through the chaos and right out the front door. He glanced in the direction of the parking lot, the center of the chaos. He could a see large cloud of black smoke with a fire at its center. It was exactly what he'd expected to see, the aftermath of the type of car bomb he had planted in his car.

Tiphani had taken the car more willingly than he had expected. *I guess she won't be coming back anytime soon.* Cecil smiled to himself and kept walking into the heart of Baltimore.

Chapter 11

Good News, Change of Heart

Derek turned on the ignition and quickly reversed his car out of the driveway, causing the wheels to screech as the rubber fought for traction. The episode with Halleigh had Derek at his breaking point. He hoped she was dead. How dare she think she could play him? He was sick and tired of women thinking they could use sex to manipulate him. Tiphani had played him for years, and he would never allow that to happen again.

Good riddance, Halleigh. Hope you enjoy your grave, you conniving little bitch. You and Tiphani will make great friends in hell.

He was done waiting around for Day. He was going to take back control and take matters into his own hands. This cat and mouse game with Day needed to end. It was time for Derek to start his shock and awe campaign on the streets of Baltimore. His children had waited long enough; it was time for Daddy to rescue them.

Derek made the hour-long trip into Baltimore in a little over thirty-five minutes. He was passing every other car on the road, not caring if he was pulled over for speeding. He cruised into Baltimore and began his slow and methodical route around the city. He was going to hit all the hot corners and shake some things up.

At the first corner, a kid about thirteen years old saw Derek get out of his car and immediately ran the opposite direction.

Damn, I still have that cop look to me, Derek thought. The next corner, he took a different approach. He stayed in the car and acted like he was copping. The young buck who obviously controlled the block sauntered over to the car.

"What's good?" the kid asked, leaning into the driver's side window.

"I'm looking for something," Derek answered.

"I got what you need."

"You know where Scar Johnson is?"

The kid backed up from the car. "Nigga! You think I'm a snitch? Kick rocks, mu'fucka." He walked back to his corner and stared at Derek with a scowl on his face.

Derek thought about getting out and kicking the kid's ass, but the three other kids standing next to him were probably strapped. He wisely chose to move on.

His approach to the next corner had to be different. He wasn't getting the results he wanted. He was impatient and didn't have time to draw this whole thing out.

Derek parked his car around the corner from his next destination. He walked around the block and made eye contact with the kid running the corner, mimicking what he had seen done many times while on a stakeout. The kid took the bait and approached Derek.

"You good?" the kid asked.

"I'm looking, but I think there's eyes on us. Follow me." Derek kept walking past the kid as he said this.

The kid looked around to see where they were being watched from then followed Derek around the corner and into a building. As soon as both of them were through the front door of the building, Derek spun around and slammed the kid against the wall.

"Yo, what the fuck!" The kid struggled to get away from Derek's grip.

"Shut your mouth." Derek put a gun to the kid's head. A look of fear swept over the kid's face and he stopped struggling. "Take whatever you want. Money in my pocket, drugs is in my sock."

"I'm not robbin' you. I need some information from you," Derek said.

"I don't know shit," the kid pleaded.

"Where is Scar?"

"I told you I don't know. I ain't never seen that dude."

"Don't lie to me, motherfucker. Where is he hiding?"

Derek pressed the gun into the kid's temple.

"I swear I ain't lyin'. His man Flex be handlin' the re-up."

"Motherfucker, tell me what I want to know." Derek shoved

the gun in his mouth. "If you don't tell me in ten seconds, I will blow your head off. One . . ."

Tears fell from the kid's eyes as he struggled to break free. He was trying to scream, but the barrel of the gun was muffling the sound. Derek reached ten and removed the barrel of the gun from his mouth. The kid instantly started pleading.

"Please don't shoot. I swear I don't know nothin'. Please."

Derek looked into the kid's eyes to try to read his thoughts. He figured if the kid did know something, he wouldn't be punking out so easily. He was just some young teenage wannabe about to get swallowed up by the streets.

Derek put the gun to the kid's temple, stared into his eyes, and kneed him in the balls. The force of Derek's knee to his groin made the kid double over in pain. As soon as he leaned over, Derek slammed the butt end of the gun to the back of his head, opening a huge gash and knocking him to the ground.

Derek needed to come up with a different approach if he was going to get any answers. He got back into his car and slammed the door shut.

"Fuck!" he shouted. He sat there trying to calm himself. He needed his head clear so he could come up with a better plan. His mind wandered to Day and how useless he had been. If only Day had been able to get him some information faster, he wouldn't be out on the streets beating teenagers, and he would have his children.

It suddenly occurred to him that he knew where Day would probably be. He started the car and made his way to Halleigh's house. On his way there, he thought back to the last time he was at the house and how he had surprised Halleigh then kidnapped her. He would stick to the same strategy with Day. He would hide in the woods and wait for his victim.

When he arrived, he was pleased to see Day's truck in the driveway. He considered taking him by surprise while he was inside, but decided to wait. If he went up to the front door as he had done with Halleigh, there were too many windows that Day could look out. He would have a better chance of sneaking up behind Day as he made his way to the truck. So Derek went to the woods, to the same spot where he had waited the first time. He had a clear view of the front door, so no one was coming in our leaving without Derek seeing it.

Derek started getting hungry and impatient after waiting in the woods for two hours. He was starting to question whether Day was even in the house. He made a deal with himself that he would give it another hour then come back the next day.

Twenty minutes into his last hour, Derek saw signs of life coming from the house. The garage door opened up and Day out walked. Derek perked up and forgot about his hunger. He readied his gun and moved into position for the ambush.

Day stepped back into the garage, which gave Derek the opportunity to move even closer. He was crouching on the side of the house behind some bushes, ready to pounce as soon as Day came out again. His body was like a compressed spring ready to unleash.

Derek started to jump up when he saw movement, but immediately pulled back when he realized it wasn't Day. Instead, a little boy came bopping out. Derek retreated behind the bush.

"Yo, M.J. Wait up. Stay by the car," Day said from inside the garage. M.J. obeyed and waited by the passenger's side.

Derek watched as Day followed behind and pressed the button to close the garage door. Day then opened the back door of the truck and put M.J. into his car seat.

"When is Mommy coming home?" M.J. asked.

"Soon, little man. Soon. I promise," Day answered. Derek saw sadness in M.J.'s face. He thought about his own kids and how they must be feeling. He felt guilty for keeping Halleigh separated from her son. Like Derek, she would do anything for her child.

He was conflicted now. On one hand, he could use Halleigh to get his own children back—although that approach was taking a lot longer than he had expected. On the other hand, he was keeping a mother from her child.

His guilt won out. He decided not to ambush Day. The kid was an innocent bystander; he didn't deserve to see any violence. Derek figured he would have just as much success hunting down Scar on his own.

He sneaked back to his car and drove back to his place in the country.

Derek was feeling helpless and useless as he thought of his children on the drive back. They were somewhere out in the world with that monster, Scar. He couldn't believe that his own flesh and blood had turned on him so severely. It was beyond Derek's comprehension to think that one brother could be so different from the other. His once-deep love for his brother had turned into an even deeper hate.

To try to think of something else and not end up killing himself for feeling so useless, he turned on the radio. Derek's thoughts were still swirling, and he was unable to fully focus on the radio. Soon, though, he found himself listening carefully when the DJ came on with a breaking news story.

Disgraced former judge Tiphani Fuller has been found dead. Police believe she was the target of a car bomb explosion in Baltimore this afternoon. Miss Fuller is the third government figure to be killed by a car bomb within the last few months. All government agencies have been put on high alert. . . .

Derek stopped listening after that. He was stunned. He didn't know how to feel about it. At one time, Tiphani had been the love of his life. He was going to grow old with her. They were going to watch their grandkids together. He had been devastated when he found out that she was fucking his brother. It was the start to this whole mess that he was now in.

He thought back to everything that had happened. This thing had gotten out of control. There had been too much death and mayhem, and now it needed to end. Derek was tired of fighting. He just wanted his children back and to keep them safe.

He chuckled to himself as he thought about it. He couldn't believe that he actually felt a little sad at hearing of Tiphani's death. His emotions were definitely mixed. Part of him was sad; the other thought she finally got what she deserved.

The only thing good that came from that woman was my children. Derek made a deal with himself: from that point on, he would never think about that woman ever again.

Getting back to the house, Derek started feeling more in control. He felt that he now had a better handle on how he would find his children. Instead of relying on Day, he would take matters into his own hands, and he would come up with a better plan than the ones he'd tried today. If you want something done right, you have to do it yourself.

He went directly to the basement. He wasn't sure if Halleigh was dead from his last punch, but in case she was alive, he wasn't taking any chances. He cautiously opened the door. History was not going to repeat itself and have Halleigh sneak-attack him again.

To his surprise, when he opened the door, he found Halleigh sitting on the bed, her hands still handcuffed behind her back. She looked like hell. Her face was swollen and bruised from the punches Derek had landed. Her hair was a mess, and her eyes were bloodshot.

"You got up." He entered.

"Fuck you," she spat.

"Thanks for not attacking me when I came in."

"I would have killed you if my hands weren't cuffed." Halleigh was done with etiquette. She had taken too much abuse, and her hopes for escape were fading.

Derek approached her carefully. He could see the wildness and uncertainty in her eyes.

"Back the fuck away from me," Halleigh warned.

"I'm not gonna touch you. Turn around. I'm taking your cuffs off." He held his hands up so she could see the key.

She contemplated whether to trust him. She was his prisoner; she figured she had no other choice. Reluctantly, she turned to give him a clear view and easier access to the cuffs.

She held her breath as he inserted the key and unlocked the cuffs. They easily slipped off her wrists and Derek threw them on the bed. Halleigh's breathing relaxed a bit as she rubbed the sore spots of her wrists where the cuffs had dug in.

She was a bit confused by Derek's attitude. His demeanor seemed different. He was less on edge and seemed almost at peace.

Derek started to walk back toward the door without saying a word. As soon as he turned his back, Halleigh reached under the mattress and pulled out the sharpened toothbrush. While Derek was away, she'd tried to sharpen the toothbrush on the metal of the handcuffs. Not being able to see what she was doing made it a difficult task, and she did the best she could. It was an uneven job, and she would have liked it to be sharper, but it would have to do.

She jumped up and lunged at Derek. With all of her strength, she tried to plunge the toothbrush into his neck. At the last second, he moved out of the way, and she jammed it into his shoulder instead.

Derek screamed out in pain as he flipped her over his shoulder and onto the floor. Halleigh had the wind knocked out of her, and as she writhed in pain, Derek pounced on top of her.

They were in a familiar position, Derek on top of Halleigh, pinning her down. Halleigh looked into Derek's eyes and saw evil. He reached back and pulled the toothbrush out of his shoulder. Blood immediately came oozing out of the wound. He raised the toothbrush over his head, and with all the rage and force in his body, he brought it down, directed at Halleigh's head.

Halleigh closed her eyes and braced herself for the certain death about to overtake her. She heard a loud thud in her ear. She waited to feel the pain of the toothbrush entering her face, but she felt nothing. The only sound in the room was Derek's heavy breathing.

Halleigh opened her eyes and saw him still over her, wild-eyed and panting. He had slammed the toothbrush into the floor right next to Halleigh's left ear. His hand was still wrapped around the handle, and the toothbrush was stuck into the carpet.

"Why the fuck you keep attacking me? I was going to let you free." He pulled the toothbrush out of the carpet and got off Halleigh.

She was speechless. She had been certain that she was about to die. Unsure of what was happening, she stayed on the ground. She didn't want to provoke Derek into another attack.

Halleigh watched as Derek walked to the door. He stood there and stared at Halleigh like he was waiting for her to do something. She didn't know what he expected, so she stayed put.

"Go! Get the fuck out of here. You're free. This thing has gone on long enough. It's between Scar and me." He motioned for her to go through the door.

Halleigh slowly got up, unsure if Derek was telling the truth or fucking with her emotions. She hesitantly walked past Derek. Walking up the stairs, she was still nervous, half expecting some surprise attack at the top of the staircase. She got to the top and was relieved when nothing happened. Her body began to relax.

Derek kept his distance as he followed her up the stairs, so as not to spook her. She found her way to the front door of the house.

"Wait," Derek said.

She stopped, thinking that was the moment when he told her he was lying. She felt defeated.

"You need some clothes." He went to the bedroom and came back with a sweatshirt and sweatpants.

"Thank you." She took the clothes and put them on. They were too big for her small frame, but she tightened them as much as possible.

"Go back to your son and tell him you love him." Derek smiled weakly. Sadness swept over him.

"I will. You do the same." She walked out the door not having a clue how to get back to her house. She didn't care. She was seeing the sky for the first time in a long time. She was free.

Derek watched her run down the long driveway until she was around the bend and out of sight. He was feeling melancholic. There was a bad feeling in the pit of his stomach.

This is not going to end well, he thought as he went to tend to the wound in his shoulder.

Chapter 12

Stay Away From the House

Talisa and D.J. came barreling through the front door with toys filling their arms. They ran directly to the living room, dumped their toys on the floor, and energetically ripped into them. Flex followed, looking exhausted. The kids had him running all over the toy store. He was afraid of what Scar would do if anything happened to them, so he had been extra cautious, not letting them out of his sight.

"Ay yo, Scar," Flex called out.

Scar came lumbering down the stairs when he heard the ruckus the kids were causing.

"Look at my new dolls." Talisa presented them to Scar.

"That's nice." Scar brushed her off.

"Where is Charisma? She said she would play with me," Talisa asked.

"Charisma, get your ass down here!" Scar yelled up the stairs.

Charisma quickly came down like an obedient dog.

"I got new dolls. Look. You want to play?" Talisa asked Charisma.

"Play with the kids," Scar ordered.

"Sure, I'll play with you, honey." She pursed her lips at Scar and sat on the floor to play with the toys.

"Speak to me in the kitchen," Scar said to Flex.

They both moved to the kitchen and sat across from each other at the table. The pile of cash was between them, still covering the tabletop.

"What we gonna do about the white boy?" Scar asked.

"We got to get rid of his ass," Flex said matter-of-factly.

"Goddamn." Scar shook his head in disbelief. "Why this fool had to be so nosey? I came out here to lay low and not attract any problems. Then this mu'fucka come snoopin' around."

"Maybe that fool is dead already. I'll go look." Flex got up to go to the basement.

Arnold started writhing around the moment he saw Flex. He strained against the ropes tied around his wrists and ankles. The chair he was sitting in was bucking back and forth. He was unable to speak or scream because of the gag stuffed in his mouth.

"Calm down, nigga. Ain't no sense in you actin' all crazy. Your snooping ass ain't escapin'." Flex stood in front of Arnold and smiled. He enjoyed watching the struggle.

Flex slapped Arnold across the face, which stunned him and stopped his struggle instantly. Arnold just stared at Flex in shock. The slap knocked him back into reality. He realized it would be better to relax and cooperate than to fight.

He had no idea how long he had been down in the basement. If only he could speak to them, he could tell them he wouldn't tattle on them. He would tell them that it was their business, not his, and they could use drugs if they wanted. Arnold wanted to tell them that he had smoked a little marijuana when he was a teenager. He figured it would show them he understood and passed no judgment against them. He wanted to assure them that he would not turn them in. If only they would take the gag out of his mouth, he figured he could make things right and be back home.

The doorbell rang as the two men stared at each other.

"Keep quiet." Flex went upstairs to check things out. He stuck his head out the basement door. "Yo, Scar. Who the fuck is that?" he whispered.

Scar cautiously peeked through the window. Standing at the front door was a woman in overalls, her brown hair in a bun on top of her head and a worried look on her face.

"It's some white bitch," Scar whispered back. She rang the bell again.

"Ignore her," Flex said.

"Nah. I'll get rid of her." Scar went to answer the door.

Flex retreated behind the basement door, but kept it opened just a crack, so he could hear what was being said.

"Can I help you?" Scar greeted the woman.

"Hello, I'm Betsy, your neighbor. Arnold is my husband." She smiled weakly.

"So what?" Scar answered rudely.

"Well, I came home this morning from the post office and Arnold wasn't there."

"What that got to do with me?" Scar was trying to be as rude as possible so she would get the hint and leave.

"I thought he might be out in the fields, but after a few hours I started to get worried. I went out there, but I couldn't find him. I called all of our friends, and no one has seen or heard from him."

"He probably ran out on y'all."

"No. His car is still in the garage, and I don't find you're comment funny. Have you seen him today?"

"He ain't been over here, if that's what you're askin'." Betsy looked into Scar's eyes. She had a bad feeling about this man. It wasn't just the scar on his face that frightened Betsy; it was something behind his eyes. There was a danger lurking in this man. There was no reason for him to be so rude to her. She was worried about her husband and just wanted to find him. She wasn't expecting such attitude from her new neighbor, especially after her husband had gone out of his way to welcome him to the town.

Flex crept back down the stairs.

He pulled a gun on Arnold. "It's your bitch. She snoopin' around askin' questions about you."

Arnold began struggling wildly and trying to scream. He was hoping to make enough noise so Betsy could hear him.

"You best stop with that shit," Flex seethed through clenched teeth.

Arnold ignored his warning and continued trying to alert Betsy.

Flex cocked the gun and pointed it at Arnold's head. "I'm warning you, nigga. If you don't stop, I will go up there and murk your bitch."

Arnold stopped flailing and his scream turned to a whimper. Flex quietly sneaked back up the stairs. He peeked through the crack in the door. Scar was standing at the door, holding his gun behind his back. His finger was on the trigger, ready to shoot.

"I'm starting to get very worried. This isn't like him to disappear. Are you sure he hasn't been over here?"

"I told you I ain't seen him. How many times I have to say it?"

"I'm sorry to worry about my husband and think that you might be able to help," she said sarcastically. "You have made it very clear that I am bothering you. I know this is asking a lot from you, but if you see him, tell him to come home immediately." Betsy turned and went back toward her house. She was furious at Scar for his rudeness. Never had she ever experienced someone so cold. She sensed there was something going on at that house. She did not trust her new neighbor. Little did she know how close she had come to her husband—and to death.

Scar closed the door behind her. Arnold heard the door close and he started his screaming again.

"I told you to shut the fuck up!" Flex screamed down to Arnold.

Scar opened the basement door. "What the fuck you screamin' about?"

"This mu'fucka won't stop squirming and screaming like a bitch."

Scar was heated from the confrontation with Betsy. He didn't need no white bitch snooping around like her nosey-ass husband.

"Let's take care of this fool then take out his old lady. Get him ready to take outside," Scar said.

Arnold went crazy. His eyes were bloodshot and tears were streaming down his face. His throat was getting raw from his attempted screaming. The ropes were cutting into his wrists and ankles and causing them to bleed. Arnold didn't feel any pain at this moment. The only thing on his mind was getting free and saving his beloved wife.

Flex tried to subdue Arnold and release him from the chair. He attempted to untie Arnold's left hand and hold it still. As soon as his wrist was free, Arnold wrestled it away from Flex and removed the gag from his mouth.

"Please, please. This is a misunderstanding." He was holding off Flex and keeping the gag away from him. "I won't tell, I promise. I just wanted you to feel welcome."

Flex flipped the chair and Arnold onto his side. This temporarily halted Arnold's speech, but he quickly started up again.

"Let me go. I'm a simple farmer. I don't know anything. I'll leave you alone."

Flex wrestled the gag from Arnold. "Shut yo' mouth." Before Flex could stuff the gag back in Arnold's mouth, Arnold screamed, "Help!" He screamed so loud that he strained his vocal cords, but to Arnold it felt like he had ripped them.

Scar ran up the stairs. "Yo, Charisma, take them kids upstairs," he yelled.

"Uncle Scar, we're not tired. We want to keep playing," Talisa called back from the living room.

"If you don't go upstairs, I will put a serious beating on your ass," he threatened.

The kids could hear a different tone in their uncle's voice. He meant what he was saying, and the kids obeyed at once. Charisma followed right behind, not wanting to get in the path of a raging Scar.

By the time Scar got back downstairs, Flex had Arnold restrained and lying on the ground. Fear was all over Arnold's face. He never thought he would be in a situation like this. He was a simple man who lived in the country because of the quiet life it afforded him.

He loved his wife and his life, and he never harmed anyone. Never would he have imagined dealing with monsters like Scar and Flex. Their evil was too much for Arnold to comprehend.

"Pick him up. Take him out back," Scar instructed. Arnold fought back as best he could, but he was running out of strength. His muscles were feeling heavy and unresponsive. Flex tried picking him up, but Arnold wouldn't stay still and was making it too difficult. Flex punched Arnold several times in the face until Arnold was unconscious.

Scar and Flex picked him up and carried him deep into the woods behind the house. Along the way, Arnold had woken up, but he was still so dazed he wasn't able to do anything. He tried to pay attention to where he was and how long they had travelled, but it was useless. His brain was too hazy to figure anything out.

"A'ight." Scar stopped walking and let Arnold go. Flex did the same.

Arnold landed with a thud on a bed of pine needles. He looked up from the ground and could see that tall pine trees surrounded them. He knew exactly what part of the forest he was in. This was Arnold's favorite place to stroll by himself.

He watched as Scar and Flex hovered over him. They were discussing something, but he couldn't hear what they were saying. Everything was muffled, like he was wearing earplugs. He was having trouble focusing his eyes. It would all become blurry when someone moved. The punches to his face must have dislodged a nerve in his eyes.

Scar looked down at Arnold. "Damn, this sorry fool. You think he really was being nice?"

"I don't know. Either way he a dumb mu'fucka. He should have just kept to his self," Flex answered.

"You right. This shit is the real world. It ain't no TV show from the fifties. Not everybody be wanting their neighbors all up in they business." Scar looked down and studied Arnold's swollen and bruised face.

Arnold looked at Scar and pleaded with his eyes. His body ached and his head was throbbing. Scar's face was blank. Arnold could see that anything he did now to survive was useless. He didn't want the last thing he saw to be the face of a monster, so he moved his gaze to the trees. Arnold loved the land and always felt at peace surrounded by these trees. He was now looking to the trees for comfort in his final minutes.

"Wrong place at the wrong time," Scar said to Arnold.

Two shots rang out and echoed through the forest. Arnold lay motionless, with two bullet holes through his head. The blood poured out of the holes and seeped into the earth. Scar and Flex stood in silence as they examined the corpse. After a few moments, Flex broke the silence.

"Oh shit. You almost blew that mu'fucka's head clean off."

"Go get some shovels. We need to bury the body," Scar instructed.

"For real? Some bear will probably eat him if we just leave his ass."

"Just do what I say."

"A'ight," Flex begrudgingly agreed.

Flex left Scar there and started the trek back to the house. He didn't see the point in burying the body. It was just some stupid white boy who the animals would tear to shreds. No one would find him before he was ripped up and unidentifiable. Burying him was more work than they needed to be doing.

Flex was getting sick of having to take orders from Scar. There were a lot of things that Flex would do differently. To Flex, not only would they be different, but they would be better. Flex would ride with Scar for a little while longer, but it would soon be time to branch out on his own.

Before he could go out alone, he would need to figure out an escape plan. He still had loyalty to Scar and wanted to avoid the usual murdering of the king to take his throne. He wanted to find a way for both of them to split the kingdom evenly.

While Flex navigated his way out of the woods and contemplated his future, his phone started ringing.

"What's good?" he answered.

"What the fuck? I been calling your ass like crazy and your phone be off," said the young corner boy.

"Nah. I'm out in the middle of nowhere. Reception is shit. What's so urgent you keep calling?" Flex asked.

"This cat Day be around here asking about you. Say for me to give you his number if I see you. You want me to murk that dude?" The corner boy was hoping the answer would be yes. He saw this as an opportunity to gain some street cred. He would have done it already, but he wanted to make sure that was what Flex wanted. He saw Flex as his way to move up, and he would do anything Flex wanted.

"When was this?" Flex stopped walking.

"Yo, a few hours ago. I been trying you ever since. This ain't the first time this nigga be around here. First time, I ignored his ass and threw his number out. What you want me to do?"

"You keep his number this time?"

"I got it."

"Text me that shit. Sit tight and don't do nothin' right now."

"A'ight." The corner boy hung up.

Flex received the text as he was making his way back to Scar and the dead body. Scar was sitting next to Arnold on the ground, looking up at the sky when Flex came back.

"Where the fuckin' shovels?" Scar asked.

"Change of plans. Day surfaced, and he lookin' for us."

"What?" Scar stood up.

"Got a call from my boy. He gave me Day's number. Says Day been stopping by, asking questions. What you wanna do?"

"Call that disappearing mu'fucka," Scar said. Flex dialed the number.

"Where the fuck you been, nigga?" Flex started right in when Day answered.

"Flex?"

"Who the fuck you think this is?"

"Yo, I'm glad I finally found you. Shit's been crazy,"

Day said.

"Like I asked, where the fuck you been?"

"I heard they raided Scar's place. I ain't know what was goin' on, so I went underground. Once I figured it was safe I came out, and I been looking for you ever since. You ain't easy to find. Niggas went deep into the shadows."

"I been right out in the open," Flex told him. "Fuck them pig mu'fuckas. They can't touch me."

"Where you at? I need to get some work in."

"Hold up, nigga. You disappear and you think you can just come back like that? I got to run it by Scar." Flex looked over to Scar. Scar nodded his head.

"Come on, man," Day asked. "My pockets be light since all this shit went south."

"It ain't go south for me. I don't let nothin' affect my paper," Flex bragged. "I'ma text you where to meet. You best be here pronto, nigga."

"Tell me where to go. I'm leaving now."

"And don't be thinkin' of comin' here with anyone other than your own self." Flex ended the call.

"What you think?" Scar asked Flex.

"You know I never trusted that nigga." Flex frowned.

"Let's see what he got to say for his self. We'll bury this fool later." Scar started back toward the house.

Betsy was standing at her kitchen sink washing dishes when she heard two loud blasts echo through the woods. Her nerves were on edge, and the sound startled her. The plate that was in her hand shattered when it hit the floor. With hands shaking, she made her way to the living room and picked up the phone. She dialed the phone and waited for an answer on the other end.

"Yes, this is Betsy over on Shunpike Road. Can I speak with Officer Maki, please?" She waited for the officer to transfer her call.

"Hello, Betsy," Officer Maki answered.

"Hello, Adam. I need your help. Arnold is missing, and I think my new neighbors have something to do with it."

"What do you mean?"

"Well, I haven't seen Arnold, so I went to our new neighbor, and he acted very strange. I didn't get a good feeling from him. There was an evil to him. I think I just heard two gunshots in the woods, and I'm terrified that it . . ." Her voice trailed off and her eyes filled with tears. She couldn't bear to bring herself to say the words she was thinking.

"Betsy, it's all right. I'm sure Arnold is fine," Officer Maki assured her. "He'll show up. But I'll go over and check things out. Can you give me a description of your neighbor?"

"Yes. He is a large black man, and he has this unsightly scar that disfigures his face." She sniffled and dabbed at the tears in her eyes.

"Betsy, did you say he has a scar on his face?" There was concern in his voice.

"Yes."

"Do not go near that house again. Do you hear me? Stay away from that man." Officer Maki's tone had changed from reassuring to alarmed in an instant. There had been a statewide bulletin sent out with Scar's picture on it. If Officer Adam Maki was right, the state's most wanted man was hiding out in his little town.

Chapter 13

Crack Effort

Mathias crept out from behind the dumpster after the anonymous car drove by. He put his gun back in his pocket and looked up and down the block before continuing on his way to the dope house. He had become increasingly more paranoid after his run-in with Cecil. Everything was starting to frighten him. He saw danger in every car that passed and every person who looked his way. It didn't help that he had graduated from snorting cocaine to smoking crack. He had convinced himself that it calmed his nerves, but it only made him jumpier and more agitated.

He hated to have to go outside. The only time he left his house was to buy more crack, which was becoming more and more frequent. He was dipping into his savings to feed his habit. He had all but given up on looking for new employment. All of his old allies were now enemies to him. No one would take his call. He had even applied to a local fast food restaurant, but they could see "crack fiend" all over his face and wouldn't even interview him.

Mathias's eyes darted from side to side as he scurried down the street. The quicker he got to the house, the sooner he could be back home safe and sound. He would have preferred to drive, but he had traded his car to his previous dealer for three months of free crack. Their deal ended almost immediately, when the dealer got pulled over, got into a shootout with the cops, and was killed.

He made it to the building and knocked. A set of eyes peeked through a slot in the door.

"What?" the person behind the door barked.

"I need weight," Mathias answered.

The door opened halfway, and Mathias slipped through. There was another man standing there, who led Mathias down a dark hallway to the back room. There sat a fat man behind a table. He was surrounded by another three dudes, all holding automatic weapons.

"Speak," the fat man said.

"I need four eights of rock." Mathias was on edge. The three men with the weapons were making him nervous.

The fat man pulled a shoebox out from under the table. He removed four eight balls of crack and placed them on the table.

"There you go, big man."

Mathias pulled out the money and laid it on the table. The fat man counted it.

"All good. Take yo' shit and get the fuck out."

Mathias obeyed. He quickly took the bags stuffed them in his pocket and hightailed it out of the house. Once outside, he rushed to find a place to take a hit. He was all worked up and needed a hit to make his mind right.

He found an alley and ducked in, then sat behind a dumpster and prepared the pipe. The first hit went into his lungs, and Mathias was flying high. He sat there with his eyes closed, enjoying the ride. Then he felt a kick to his ribs. He opened his eyes to see a skinny little teenager standing over him.

"Give me your shit, crackhead." The boy kicked Mathias again.

Mathias scrambled to get away from the boy. The boy kicked him again. Mathias was trapped between a wall and the dumpster. He had nowhere to run.

"I said give me yo' shit or I'll kill you." Another kick to the head.

Mathias got lightheaded. He fumbled in his pockets. The boy backed up, thinking Mathias was going to give him the crack. Instead of the crack, Mathias pulled out his gun and blindly shot at the boy. The shot hit the boy directly in the chest, bringing him crumbling to the ground.

Mathias jumped to his feet. His eyes were wide with fear and surprise. He had never shot anyone. He watched the blood drain out of the boy's chest, staining his white T-shirt red. The boy was making gurgling sounds as he struggled to breathe.

Out of panic, Mathias ran as fast and as far as he could go. When he could no longer run, he slowed to a walk but kept on moving. He needed to create as much distance between the shooting victim and himself.

Unable to go any farther, Mathias found some shelter in a small park near City Hall. He was panting and sweating. He found a corner of the park and sat under a tree that would do well to hide him from prying eyes while he smoked his rock. He wiped the sweat from his brow and packed his pipe.

The anticipation of the high made Mathias forget about the incident he had just run from. He torched the rock and inhaled deeply. The smoke penetrated his lungs, and the chemicals entered his blood stream and shot straight to his brain. He felt the rush of the crack surge through his body. He took another hit, then another.

Mathias couldn't stop himself. He kept hitting the pipe, smoking the rock, and then repacking for another round. He finally took a break, but only because he was jittery, uncomfortable, and mumbling to himself. He was sitting under the tree, scratching all of the itchiness throughout his body. He had burned through an eight ball in under an hour.

"Keep it moving, buddy." The policeman standing over Mathias startled him and made him jump. The former mayor hadn't tended to his hygiene in a while. His clothes were tattered, his skin was dirty, and his beard was overgrown. The officer, not really paying much attention, didn't recognize Mathias.

"What?"

"You gotta move. Can't stay here," the officer replied.

"This is a public park. I can sit wherever I want," Mathias countered.

"Not today you can't. Get up."

"I know the laws. You can't kick me out of here."

"Yes, I can and I am."

"Well, I'm staying, and there's nothing you can do."

"I'm warning you. If you don't stand up now and vacate the park, I will arrest you." The officer unlatched his handcuffs from his belt.

Mathias contemplated standing his ground and continuing to argue, but saw that he was pushing his luck. If he got arrested, he would be frisked, and then he'd be without his beloved crack. He definitely didn't want that to happen. Mathias begrudgingly obeyed the officer.

Before walking away, Mathias took note of the officer's name. "Bullshit beat cop. I'll get him fired when I'm back in power," he mumbled as he skulked away.

"What did you say?" the officer called to Mathias.

"Nothing," Mathias shot back and kept on moving. Mathias was still mumbling to himself about his run in with the officer as he walked into a crowd of reporters and citizens gathering in front of a podium at the entrance to the small park.

"What's this?" Mathias vigorously scratched his neck.

"The governor is going to give a speech." Disgusted by Mathias, the photographer eased away from him.

Mathias's body tensed up and his heart began to race. This was the reason he was being kicked out of the park.

It's not enough for him to ruin my career and force me out of office. Now he has to humiliate me by kicking me out of the park. Mathias was exaggerating everything in his mind. The governor had no idea Mathias was anywhere near the park. The copious amounts of crack were starting to affect Mathias's common sense.

The anger coursing through his body caused Mathias to become even more fidgety. He couldn't stand still. The man who had destroyed his life and backstabbed him was going to be in front of him at any moment. Should he leave, or should he stay? He couldn't decide what to do. This could be his chance to humiliate the governor in public and get his position back. But how could he do it? His mind was unclear and unfocused, which was making him more and more agitated.

Mathias looked up to see the governor's motorcade pull up across the street. A rush of excitement came from the crowd as the reporters saw the governor exiting his car. Before he knew it, Mathias was pulling out his gun and running across the street.

"You ruined my life, you backstabbing piece of shit." Mathias started shooting with the precision of a blind man. The bullets were flying in every direction.

Screaming and shouting could be heard as the crowd scattered. Like a well-choreographed dance, police officers jumped on top of Governor Tillingham to shield him; others covered members of his cabinet, and the rest surged toward Mathias. Making it farther than one would think, Mathias emptied his gun of bullets before being violently tackled to the pavement.

"Drop the weapon!"

"Get the fuck off of me!" he shouted

"Stay down! Arms behind your back! Don't move!"

Officers were shouting at him from every direction.

"Leave me alone! I order you! Do you know who I am? That man is a criminal." Mathias struggled against the weight of three cops. They had pried the gun away from him and cuffed his hands behind his back. They were going out of their way to handle Mathias as roughly as possible, pressing his face into the pavement as they frisked him.

"A fucking crazy crackhead." One of the officers pulled out the crack from Mathias's pocket.

"That's not mine."

The cops jerked Mathias up and shoved him into a black Suburban with the darkest tint on the windows. They all piled in and sped off in a caravan of police cars and SUVs, lights and sirens at full strength.

"Enjoy the view out the window now, crackhead. It will be the last time you ever see the outside world. Your life is over."

Chapter 14

Not So Welcome Back

Day pulled up in front of the house after the long drive into the country.

"You need to behave when we go inside," he said to M.J., who was quietly sitting in the back.

M.J. just nodded. He was becoming more emotionally cutoff the longer he was separated from Halleigh. His bright and cheery personality was becoming introverted. Day noticed it, but he couldn't do anything to prevent it. He was busy dealing with the stress of finding Derek's kids so he could reunite M.J. with his mother.

They were deep in the country. Crickets, owls, and peepers all sang their songs and came together in a symphony only heard at night in the country. Day took M.J. out of the backseat. They both stood next to the car surveying the house. Day was looking for any signs of an ambush. He knew that Flex had it out for him, and because of the tone of their phone call, Day had a feeling that Flex might act up. He saw nothing suspicious. M.J. sat in awe at the size of the house.

Day and M.J. guardedly walked hand in hand toward the front door. From the side of the house, Flex came sneaking up next to them. He pounced on Day and put him in a chokehold. Day managed to stay on his feet as he fought against the attack, but Flex had him beat.

"You finally come out of hiding, punk ass?"

"Yo, chill," Day said through choked breaths.

M.J. was paralyzed with fear. He stared at the clash with eyes wide open.

The struggle continued. “Stop,” M.J. said softly.

The two men kept scuffling.

“Stop,” he said louder and hit Flex on his thigh.

The tiny tap on the leg caught Flex’s attention. He spun to see what had hit him.

“What? You brought a kid to help you fight? Ha!”

Flex chuckled as he released Day.

Day bent over and rubbed his neck, taking time to catch his breath.

“What’s up, little man? What’s your name?” Flex approached M.J.

“Leave . . . him . . . alone.” Day’s breathing was labored.

“What the hell you bringin’ a kid for? Thought I told you to show up alone.”

“I . . . had to.”

“Get yo’ ass inside,” Flex barked.

Day entered the house with M.J, following. They stood just on the other side of the door and waited for Flex. Before Flex could dole out any more punishment or orders, Scar came from another room.

“Well, well, well. Look who came out of hiding.” Scar carefully eyed Day as he walked up to the trio.

“Yeah, and he brought some protection along with him.” Flex laughed at his own joke.

Day ignored Flex. “What’s up, Scar? It’s been a minute.”

“You damn right it’s been a minute. Who the hell is half pint over here?” He gestured to M.J. with a head nod.

“Yo, he my son. I had to bring him. It’s a long story.”

“I got loads of time, nigga. Enlighten me.”

Day was caught off guard. He wasn’t ready to have to explain who M.J. was and why he was there.

“Oh, ah, well, you see, okay, you want to know. . . .” Day had no idea what to say.

“Spit it out, nigga.” Flex shoved Day in the shoulder. Scar just stared blankly at Day. It made Day feel uncomfortable, like Scar could see right through him. “Like I said, he’s my son. My baby mama, me and her don’t really have much communication. Well, I found out she got hooked on the pipe and my little man here was being neglected. So . . . you see, I found this out right around the time I was lookin' for a place for you. That's why I was a little off about securing that spot I was tellin' you about."

Scar just stared at him like he was waiting for him to continue. Day continued to make up a story.

"I had secured that spot for you, and I was heading to let you know. That's when I drove by your place and that shit was swarming with all sorts of FBI, DEA—"

Scar interrupted. "You don't gotta tell me who all was there. I know." He leaned against the wall and glared at Day. "I've heard enough of your babbling anyway. Now I'm gonna ask questions, and I want answers. First, where the fuck you been?"

"I went deep underground. Seeing all of that shit, my first thought was that you got picked up. I was plannin' on staying real low until I heard otherwise."

Flex and Scar exchanged a look.

"You heard otherwise? That's why you out looking for me?" Scar asked.

"I didn't hear nothin' about you."

"Where were you 'deep underground'?"

"I was at the place I had found for you," Day continued to lie.

"When I'm gonna see this place?"

"Whenever you want."

"How about right now?"

Day was about to lose it. If Scar took him up on his offer, he was fucked. It would be the end of Day if he couldn't take Scar to a house.

Day was scrambling his brain to come up with a plan to get out of this mess when M.J. took off running into the living room.

"M.J." Day called out.

M.J. ignored him and kept on heading to the next room. Day started to chase him, but Scar stopped him. "Don't worry about that. We got business to attend to." Scar put a hand on Day's chest.

Day's knees got weak. "He shouldn't be runnin' around. I'll get 'im."

"He's fine. He probably saw toys in there. Let the big boys stay in here."

Hearing the word "toys," Day figured that Derek's kids were close by. He attempted to change the subject right away.

"Yo, you got any work for me? I need to get back on the grind."

"Don't get ahead of yaself. You don't just come waltzing yo' ass back in and expect to be welcomed with open arms. You still got some questions to answer."

"A'ight. Ask away." Day acted like he was standing strong, but inside he wasn't so confident.

"First off, why the fuck we ain't never heard of no kid before?" Scar asked.

"You know I don't like to mix business with my personal life. I don't want him growing up in the game. I want little man to have a better life."

Scar slowly shook his head as he surveyed Day. "A'ight. Why the fuck it take you so long to come and find us?"

"I told you. I wanted to make sure the heat died down. I had no idea if y'all had gotten picked up."

"How'd you find out we didn't?" Flex asked.

"When I didn't hear nothing about it on the TV, I went out on the street and started asking niggas if they seen y'all." Day didn't look at Flex. He kept speaking to Scar.

"How we know you ain't got picked up and the feds got you doing their dirty work?" Flex said to Day then turned to Scar. "This nigga is lyin', Scar. I can feel it. He got pinched and now he workin' to put us behind bars." Flex had always been jealous of the tight relationship that Day and Scar once had. He didn't want Day coming back in and taking his place.

"You fool-ass nigga, if I was workin' for the feds or anybody, they'd be here right now." Day cut his eyes at Flex.

"You wearin' a wire then."

"Come check me." Day put his arms out to the side. With the quickness of a cat, Flex moved in and roughly handled Day.

"Easy, nigga, before I have to beat yo' ass," Day warned.

"Fuck you. I'm checkin' for a wire, you snitch-ass bitch." Flex ripped Day's shirt open to look for the wire. The fight started immediately. Day grabbed Flex, and the two men started to wrestle. They knocked over a side table as they fell to the floor with a loud thud. Punches were landed as they fought for leverage. Day got an upper hand and started punching Flex in his face.

"Cut the bullshit!" Scar grabbed Day and easily tossed him off of Flex. Day slammed into the hallway wall as Flex struggled to his feet.

"Uncle Scar!" Talisa heard the noise and came running with her younger brother. "What is that noise?"

"It's nothing."

"Who is that?" Talisa pointed at M.J., who had silently peeked his head into the room.

"He came to play with you. His name is Malek," Day chimed in right away. His nervousness turned to excitement when he saw Derek's two kids. He was so close to his goal. Now all he needed to do was get out of there alive and call Derek.

Talisa and D.J. walked over to Malek as the adults all watched.

"Do you like trucks?" D.J. asked.

"Uh-huh." Malek nodded.

"Let's play," Talisa said. She walked into the living room with the two boys following her.

Once the children were out of sight, Scar punched Day in his stomach, knocking the wind out of him and bringing him to his knees.

"What the fuck?" Day huffed.

"That was for disappearing, nigga. While your bitch ass was hiding and dealing with yo' kid, we was tryin' to keep this business runnin'. You lucky that's all I did."

"Yeah, nigga. It was up to me, yo' ass be dead by now." Flex was standing behind Scar.

Day caught his breath and stood upright. "Look, I told you what happened. Obviously I ain't wearing no wire." He gestured to his bare chest, which had been exposed when Flex ripped open his shirt. "I'm here now and I need some work. Let's cut the bullshit."

"Nigga, you don't tell us what to do." Flex puffed his chest out.

"You think I'm gonna just give you your old spot back?" Scar asked.

As Day was about to answer, D.J. came into the room and cut him off. "We're hungry."

"Get the fuck outta here!" Scar yelled at the little boy. D.J's fear froze him. He stood staring at his uncle with watery eyes as wide as saucers. His lips started to tremble, and he started to cry as loud as only a child can.

"Damn, man. You don't gotta be like that. The kid's just hungry," Day said.

Scar snapped his head around to Day. He was obviously angry. His face was tense, and he was staring at Day like he wanted to kill him.

"Mu'fucka, you so concerned about them kids, you can take 'em. Yeah, matter of fact, that's your first job back with the organization. Take them kids until I say you finished."

Day couldn't believe his good fortune. He couldn't have dreamed it to work out any better. Instead of telling Derek where to find his children, he could now hand deliver them, reuniting with Halleigh that much sooner.

"Fine, if that's what you want. I'm willing to do whatever it takes to get back in." Initially he was going to protest, thinking that would be what Scar expected. Instead, he agreed so he could speed it up and get out of there.

"Yo, can I speak to you?" Flex said to Scar.

"Speak."

"Not in front of this shady mu'fucka." Flex gave a challenging stare to Day.

Scar gestured with a head nod for Flex to follow him to the adjoining room.

The two men spoke in hushed tones.

"We need to take care of that thing in the woods. Let's make Day dig the ditch," Flex said.

"Nah. I don't want that nigga knowing nothin' 'bout nothin' right now. Somethin' ain't right with that nigga."

"That's what I been sayin'," Flex agreed. "I don't trust that nigga."

"He gonna take them kids out my hair so we can take care of that mess out back. Then when he come back, we take care of his ass for good."

Flex couldn't hide his excitement. "Finally. I been thinkin' that nigga need to get murked for a minute."

"Get ready to be diggin' two graves tonight, son."

"No doubt. I'll dig that mu'fucka's grave myself." Flex was smiling from ear to ear.

Even though he wanted to take the kids and leave, Day waited patiently for the two men to return. He didn't want to stir up any more suspicion, so he was going to let them dictate how this meeting would go.

"All good?" Day asked as the two men returned from their private meeting.

"As long as you take them kids out my hair, yeah, it's all good."

"Like I said, whatever you need me to do, boss."

"Good. Take them kids and come back tomorrow night."

Day gathered up the kids as fast as he could. They were having fun playing together, so they were somewhat resistant to the idea of leaving. When Day bribed them with a trip to Dave and Buster's, they were quick to jump in the car.

"Sayonara, mu'fucka. Enjoy your last day on the planet." Scar stood in the window and watched as Day drove away with the kids.

Once out of sight of the house, Day called Derek. "I know where your kids are," he said.

"Tell me."

"They in the backseat of my car."

"Let me speak to them." Derek's heart was beating fast.

"Let me speak to Halleigh," Day countered.

Derek didn't want to tell him that he had released her. "Trust me, she's safe."

"Trust me. I got your kids. Meet me in two hours." Day gave Derek the address of Halleigh's house and hung up the phone.

"Shit," Derek said to himself. He was now regretting letting Halleigh free. For all he knew, she could have made it home by now. If Day got home to see Halleigh, Derek's chances of rescuing his children could be in jeopardy.

Derek grabbed his gun, jumped in his car, and sped toward a hopeful reunion with his children. He had no idea what he was going to do once he met with Day, but he was prepared to do whatever it took to keep his children safe.

Chapter 15

Painful Reunion

Derek arrived at Halleigh's house well within the two-hour timeframe Dayvid had given him. He parked in his usual spot around the corner and out of sight of the house. He proceeded to his hiding place in the woods and began his wait for Dayvid—and hopefully his children.

As he sat there in the cover of the trees, he thought about his strategy. How could he stall Day and reclaim his children? His bargaining chip was Halleigh, and he had let her go. Now he had nothing. He didn't know what he was going to do. His strategy was going to be to wait, see what Day did, then react. He sat in nervous anticipation as he carefully watched the house.

This could be the end of a long nightmare, he thought as he leaned up against a tree trunk. He vowed to himself that when he got his children back, he would get as far away from Baltimore as possible. He was tired of living his life always searching for retribution. He was going to devote his life to his children and raising them to be trustworthy, responsible adults.

The sound of the garage door opening and Day pulling in pulled Derek from his thoughts. He watched the garage door slowly close as he stood and positioned his gun in his waistband for easy retrieval. He took a deep breath and prepared himself for the showdown.

He pulled out his cell phone and redialed the number Day had called him from.

"Welcome home," Derek said after Day had answered. He could hear the children in the background, talking to one another. "Now, bring my kids outside."

"The fuck make you think you callin' the shots, nigga?" Day drew his gun while he peeked out the window, looking for Derek. "Let me speak to Halleigh."

"You don't speak to her until I see my children."

"Let me see you. Come to the front of the driveway." Derek followed orders and came out from the corner of the house. He stood at the end of the driveway and raised his arms like Jesus on the cross. He knew he was taking a chance and that Day could shoot him, but he gambled, thinking that Day wouldn't do anything until he saw Halleigh.

Derek put his phone to his ear. "You satisfied?"

"Where is she?"

"Come outside." Derek hung up.

Day was hesitant. He didn't have a good feeling about this situation. Not seeing Halleigh had him concerned. He was starting to think that Derek might be playing him. Before going outside, he ushered the children upstairs into Malek's room.

"Y'all stay up here and play. If you good, we can go to the toy store later."

The children's eyes lit up and smiles stretched across their faces. They were already thinking about the toys they would buy. There was no way they were going to ruin their chance to get new toys.

Day looked out all of the windows of the house to make sure there was no ambush about to happen. He slowly opened the door and walked onto the front lawn. When Derek saw Day, he slowly walked toward him.

"That's far enough," Day said, keeping a safe distance between himself and Derek.

The two men were now face to face, each man at opposite ends of the yard, like an old Western showdown at high noon. The question was, who would be the first to flinch?

"This has gone on long enough. Let's end this now. Bring my kids outside."

"Nigga, you think it's that easy? You ain't gettin' shit until I see Halleigh," Day said.

"I guess we have a standoff then, because I'm not bringing Halleigh until I see my kids."

"Let me speak to her." "No," Derek answered.

Day was becoming frustrated. He was getting the feeling that Halleigh was dead. Why else won't he let me speak to her? Day thought.

"Look, let me speak to her and this can all be over," Day said.

"She doesn't have a phone."

"Then let me see her. Take me to her."

"If you give me my kids, then I'll tell you where she is."

The situation was becoming heated. With each passing second, both men were becoming increasingly more agitated. Derek didn't know how much longer he could hold Day off, and Day was losing hope that Halleigh was alive. Something needed to give. This game couldn't go on any longer. It was just a matter of who would make the first move.

Derek felt like he was running out of time. He thought Day would figure it out sooner or later, so he needed to make things happen. His children needed him and he needed them. He started walking toward the front door. "Stay put, nigga. I'm warning you." Day positioned himself between Derek and the door. Derek hesitated for a second then resumed his march. "Stop, mu'fucka."

Derek didn't listen. He felt his only shot was to call Day's bluff and fight his way through the door. Derek took two more steps, and Day reached in his waistband for his gun. Derek saw this movement and did the same. Shots came firing out of both guns as each man attempted to dodge the flying bullets.

It was seconds of chaos, then complete silence. Both men lay still on the grass; each had been hit. Derek felt a sharp pain in his right shoulder. He reached over with his left hand and winced in pain as he touched the hole where the bullet had pierced him.

With a bullet lodged in his shoulder, picking himself up off the grass was difficult. He had minimal use of his right arm. Keeping an eye on Day the entire time, he got up and cautiously walked over to check on Day, who hadn't moved yet.

Blood had saturated Day's shirt. His mouth hung open, with a small bloodstream trickling out of it and down his cheek. It appeared to Derek that he had hit Day in the abdomen and chest.

Derek shook his head. He hadn't wanted it to end like this. He just wanted peace. He didn't want to kill anyone. Derek regretted lying to Day. He regretted getting caught up in his brother's crimes. If he had told the truth to Day, maybe this wouldn't have turned out like this.

As he was bending down to pick up Day's gun and check his pulse, a car came speeding down the street.

Derek swiveled around and pointed both guns at the oncoming car. The car screeched to a halt in front of the house and the passenger's side door flung open. Derek kept his guns aimed, his right shoulder burning in pain.

Halleigh jumped out and ran to Derek. As she got closer, she realized that Day was on the ground, covered in blood.

Seeing Derek with a gun, the guy driving the car sped off before Halleigh had barely exited the car. He didn't even wait for her to close the door. He just reached over while he sped off and closed it himself. He had some warrants out and wasn't about to get caught up in whatever bullshit was happening. He had just picked Halleigh up while she was hitchhiking, hoping that for his good deed she would let him get a little piece.

"What did you do?" she screamed.

Derek lowered his gun. "It's not what you think."

Halleigh dropped to her knees beside Day. She grabbed his shoulders and started shaking him. "Wake up! Dayvid! Wake up! It's me! It's Halleigh!" Tears were streaming down her face. This was not the reunion she had been envisioning. She was supposed to come and surprise Day then profess her love for him. They were supposed to make passionate love, get married, and live happily ever after.

She cradled his face in both hands, and through her sobs she spoke to him. "I love you. You can't leave me. Do not leave me. You hear?"

Day's body was limp. He wasn't responding to Halleigh's pleas. Derek stood there not knowing what to do. He wanted to help Halleigh and ease her pain, but he was the one responsible for her pain. He felt ashamed and useless.

With her hands covered in blood, Halleigh jumped up and started hitting Derek in the chest as hard as she could. She was a wild beast attacking her prey.

"What have you done? What have you done?" she screamed over and over as she continued to pound on Derek's chest. He feebly tried to protect himself from her blows, but felt that he deserved the punishment he was getting.

She continued throwing punches until she had spent all of her energy and could barely lift her arms. Her arms hurt from punching, her head hurt from crying, and her heart hurt from all the pain she had gone through in her life. She wanted to end it all right there. She had lost all hope. She saw no reason to keep on living. Life was too hard and only filled with disappointment.

"I can't do this anymore," she sobbed. "It's too much. It's too hard." She reached for Derek's gun.

"Whoa." He pulled the gun away. "What are you talking about? What about your son? You need to stay strong for him."

"Why?" Halleigh asked. "It's no use. He's just going to learn that life is one big 'fuck you' then you die."

"Don't say that. You're a fighter. When I kidnapped you, did you give up? No. Why? Because you were fighting for your son so you could be there for him and give him the stable and safe life you never had."

Halleigh wiped tears from her face. Derek's words had broken through to her, but she still wasn't convinced that she shouldn't just end it all.

"I don't even know where Malek is. I give up." Her body was tired and weak. She stared at her feet as her head hung down.

"He's in the house. He needs you."

Halleigh looked up. Hearing that Malek was so close gave her a sudden burst of energy and excitement. "He is?" Her hopelessness instantly turned to hope. Without thinking, she ran to the house. She took the stairs two at a time. She couldn't get to her son fast enough. She burst through the door and saw Malek and two other children huddled in the corner.

"Mama!" Malek jumped up and ran to her. Halleigh scooped him up in her arms and squeezed her little boy as tightly as she could. She planted kisses all over his face and head.

"Daddy!" D.J. and Talisa yelled in unison. Derek had come running up behind Halleigh. He dropped to his knees when he saw his children, and they came crashing into him. It was the family reunion Derek had been dreaming about. He started crying the second he saw his two beautiful children.

"Mama. Why are you bleeding?"

In her haste, Halleigh had forgotten that her hands were covered in blood.

"You too, Daddy." Talisa pointed at her father's chest.

"Ah, we were trying to help a man that was hurt. We're all right. We'll get cleaned up later." Derek deflected the question. "Halleigh, can I speak to you?"

She didn't want to let go of Malek, but she relented and met Derek in the hallway just outside of Malek's room.

"I'm getting far away from Baltimore. I suggest you do the same."

"Where am I supposed to go? I can't go back to Flint." Halleigh had left the memories and hardship of Flint behind and had nothing to go back to. She figured it would be a dead end going back to the city where all of her heartbreak had started. She wanted a new life, and going back to Flint would be a step in the wrong direction.

"Do you have any family anywhere? Out west? Down south?"

"I think I have a cousin in Little Rock."

"Then go there."

Halleigh thought about it for a minute. "Okay. I'll pack up and head out tomorrow."

"No. You have to get out of here now. It's too dangerous for you in Baltimore. The police will be here asking questions. You have to go right now. No time to waste." It took no time for Halleigh to realize that Derek was right. She needed to get as far away from Baltimore as she could.

"Malek, come here, baby." He came running. "Tell your friends good-bye. We're going to visit cousins in Little Rock."

Usually Malek would put up a fight before leaving his friends, but since he hadn't seen his mama in so long, he was eager to spend time with her. He clung to his mother's leg and said his good-byes.

"Take him through the garage. He doesn't need to see out front," Derek whispered to Halleigh.

Halleigh picked up Malek and ran down the stairs into the garage. A few seconds later she came rushing back into the house.

"I need the keys to the truck."

They quickly searched the house and couldn't find them.

"They must be on Day. I'll get them. You wait in the truck," Derek said.

Outside, Derek knelt down and went to reach in Day's pocket. As he put his hand inside the front pocket, Day grabbed Derek's ankle. Derek jumped back and fell onto his ass. "What the . . . ?"

"Shoot me," Day said barely above a whisper.

"You're alive?" Derek was in shock.

"Shoot me." Day barely had enough strength to turn his head to face Derek.

Derek ignored him and went back to rummaging through his pockets. He found the keys and ran back into the house.

"Here. Now, go. Don't look at the front yard when you back up. Just go. You don't need to see that again." Halleigh took the keys. She started the truck and backed out of the garage. Even though she desperately wanted to look one last time, she followed Derek's directions and averted her eyes from the body lying on the lawn.

Day heard the garage door open and struggled to move enough to see his truck backing out. As the truck reversed out of the driveway, he could see Halleigh through the windshield.

"Halleigh," he called out breathlessly. She wasn't going to hear his whisper.

He tried again to summon the breath to make his voice loud enough for her to hear. The bullet had punctured his lung, making it too difficult for him to gain any force behind his words. "Halleigh. Wait," he whispered as his head fell back and he stared up into the sky.

Derek waited until Halleigh was out of sight then went back out to Day. Day was lying there with his eyes closed. When he sensed someone standing over him, he slowly opened them.

"Kill me," he whispered when he saw Derek. He was in excruciating pain and was barely able to breathe. "Please."

"I'm not killing anyone. There has been enough murder already."

Day struggled to get his words out. "Please. Put me out of my misery. I have nothing left."

"I won't shoot you. No doubt the police are on their way. You can decide your fate before they get here."

"I'm begging."

Derek walked away, but stopped after a few steps. "I won't kill you, but you can decide what to do before anyone gets here." Derek dropped one of the guns on the ground and proceeded back into the house.

He gathered his children and ushered them out the back door, through the woods, and to his car. He buckled them in and drove away from the curb, happy to have his children back where they belonged.

"Who likes the beach?"

"Me!" Both children raised their hands.

"Who wants to live on the beach?"

"Me!" They raised their hands again and waved them wildly.

"Good, because we're moving to California."

Day stared at the gun a few feet from him. He summoned up the strength to roll over onto his stomach. After taking a few seconds to recover from the exertion and the pain, he began crawling on his stomach toward the gun. It was taking every ounce of strength and will for him to crawl. With every inch he moved, he was leaving a trail of blood behind him.

Unable to crawl any farther, he collapsed. He stretched out his arm to the gun. His fingertips were millimeters from touching it. With one last burst of energy, he lunged and grabbed the gun. In agonizing pain, he rolled over onto his back. He took the gun in both hands and placed the barrel in his mouth.

Day heard sirens in the distance. He closed his eyes and said a prayer. He thought about Halleigh and M.J. one last time. The sirens were getting closer. Day finished his prayer, thought to himself, *I love you, Halleigh,* and pulled the trigger. The gun dropped onto his chest. Day was gone.

The EMT didn't even bother trying to resuscitate him. With his face blown off, it was obvious to them that Day was dead. They loaded him into the back of the ambulance and quietly pulled away from the house as detectives began knocking on doors to question neighbors about what they'd seen.

Chapter 16

Sneak Attack

The sun still hadn't risen in the east as Flex patted the dirt with the back of the shovel to flatten it out. It was the final patch of dirt to be smoothed over the makeshift grave they had dug. He and Scar had been in the woods all night, burying Arnold.

Even though both men were out there, Flex had done most of the work. Needless to say, this did not sit well with Flex, but he kept his mouth shut and just kept digging. He had a good mind to whack the shit out of Scar with his shovel every time Scar would take a break and make Flex keep on digging.

"That should do it," Flex said.

"You stupid? Cover that shit with leaves 'n sticks 'n shit," Scar said in a condescending tone.

"We in the middle of nowhere. No one's gonna see this." Flex gave Scar a dose of his own attitude.

"You a dumb mu'fucka, you know that? That snoopy-ass wife come out here and see fresh dug earth, you don't think she gonna start digging?"

"I shoulda had her ass out here digging tonight. Woulda had this shit done a lot sooner. Sure she woulda helped more than your ass did."

"What the fuck you just say?" Scar made a move toward Flex. He stepped on the grave, and his foot sank into the dirt up to his ankle. "Fuck. Now I got dirt all in my shoe." He stopped his attack as he got distracted and pulled his foot free.

Flex started laughing when Scar pulled his dirt-covered foot from the ground. "Oh shit. That's funny." He pointed.

"Mu'fucka, you best watch what you say," Scar warned as he took off his boot and shook out the dirt.

"You right. I'm tired. It's been a long night. That shit was wrong." Flex's words said he apologized, but inside he was still telling Scar to fuck off.

"Damn right it was wrong. You eat because of me. I'll take that away just as easy as I gave it to you. I may be layin' my head in the country, but I still run B-more," Scar said.

Flex paused for a second, stared at Scar, then said, "You right." Flex started spreading leaves over the grave. As he did this, he thought, *You may run B-more now, but your time is coming to an end. It's time for a new regime, a new king.*

The two men walked back to the house in silence. Each man had a feeling that something was not right. The stress of their situation was tearing them apart. There was a power struggle beginning, and neither one was going to give in. Scar wasn't going to let some young upstart try to muscle his way into his seat, and Flex wasn't going to allow an old has-been to continue to keep him down.

They walked side by side so they could keep an eye on each other. Each man thought that if the other got behind him, it would surely mean a shovel to the back of the head.

"Leave the shovel outside," Scar instructed as they reached the house.

"A'ight. We still gotta clean up the basement."

"Nah. You take Charisma home and get some rest. I'll take care of the blood downstairs."

"You sure?" Flex was confused. He thought for sure that Scar would make him go directly down to the basement and clean up Arnold's blood.

"I'm sure. I'll take care of it. You did good work tonight. Get some rest and we can start fresh tomorrow." Scar just wanted Flex out of his sight for a while. He thought that maybe the fact that they had been up for so long was the reason they were getting on each other's nerves.

"A'ight," Flex answered. "Yo, Charisma. Get yo' ass up. We leavin'," he yelled up the stairs. After waiting a few seconds and not hearing anything moving upstairs, he ascended the steps.

Charisma was still asleep when Flex entered the room. He shook her to wake her from her slumber. "Let's go."

She rubbed her eyes and stretched her body to work out the kinks. "What you want?"

"It's time to leave."

"Good. I'm g'tting bored out here."

Flex and Charisma walked downstairs together. They were both in a hurry to get back to the city. Charisma wanted to get back to hang with her girls, and Flex needed to start lining up soldiers.

"Yo, we out." Flex walked past Scar without even stopping.

Scar said nothing in return. He stayed silent as he sat at the kitchen table with the pile of money in front of him.

Flex pulled out of the driveway as fast as he could. He needed to get back to his crib, lay his head, and get some shuteye. The sun was just peeking over the horizon as he and Charisma drove the winding country roads.

Not even a mile from Scar's house, as Flex steered the car around a long, lazy curve, flashing blue and red lights came from the opposite direction. The police caravan came speeding around the corner. There was every variety of cop car Flex could imagine: vans, SUVs, cruisers, unmarked cars. Flex was certain that it wasn't just local cops, either. The unmarked cars looked too new and nice to be some smalltown cop cars. Those were federal cars, most likely DEA, FBI, or both. Flex had a good idea where they were heading.

After the cars were around the corner, Flex took out his cell phone. Just as he was about to push the button to call Scar and warn him, he had a change of heart. He stopped himself from making the call and put the phone back in his pocket.

Fuck him. Nigga can fend for his self.

"What was that?" Charisma asked.

"Mind yo' business."

They drove the rest of the way to Baltimore in silence.

Scar was still sitting at the kitchen table when he heard a car come speeding up his driveway.

What this dumb mu'fucka forget now? He trippin' if he think I'm givin' him any more cash.

He looked over to the window next to the front door and saw the flashing lights shining through. "Fuck!" He jumped up and ran up to his bedroom, taking the stairs two at a time. He dove under his bed and grabbed his AK-47, then went to his closet and pulled out the fake wall in the back. Behind the wall was an armory of weapons: shotguns, Uzis, handguns, and enough bullets for a war. He armed himself with every weapon he could handle.

Running to the second floor window that overlooked the front door, Scar began loading his weapons. When he looked out the window, he saw dozens of officers exiting their cars and fanning out on his property.

Four officers crouching down with their guns drawn started toward the front door. Before they had a chance to get there, Scar let his AK sing. The window shattered as the bullets pierced the glass and made their way directly to the four officers. Scar easily took the men out. They were down before they knew what was going on.

Scar's gunfire triggered a reaction from the dozens of other officers. They opened fire on the house with abandon. Bullets smashed out windows, lodged into the side of the house, and sent splinters of wood flying in all directions. Scar hit the ground as soon as the officers opened fire.

When the melee quieted down, Scar jumped up and returned fire, causing the officers to take cover. As he was firing out the front window, he heard the back door get smashed in. He ran to the top of the stairs, and as soon as he saw an officer, he opened fire again.

He drained his AK of its bullets and threw it off to the side. He grabbed his shotgun and began blasting down the stairs. After emptying the shotgun, he ran back to the front window and opened up with his Uzi.

"You mu'fuckas ain't no match for me!" he screamed down to the officers as the bullets sprayed wildly.

As he spewed bullets all over the front yard, a flash bomb came crashing through the window behind Scar. It detonated before Scar could throw it back. It stunned Scar and sent him crashing to the ground. Directly following the flash bomb, a smoke bomb hit the floor and filled the room with smoke.

Scar gained his composure and, through the smoke, started randomly firing at the door to the room. He emptied the clip and started reloading.

As soon as there was a lull in his gunfire, officers stormed into the room. They pounced on top of Scar like a football team diving for a fumble. There was a pile of bodies on top of Scar. Arms and legs were flailing as all the officers either reached for Scar's guns or tried to get their shots in.

"Get the fuck off me!" Scar roared.

"Stay down. Don't move!" Several of the officers were yelling.

Scar ignored their warnings and continued to fight. They were gouging his eyes, punching his kidneys, and bending back his fingers, but Scar still tried to scurry away. He fought a valiant fight, but the number of officers was too overwhelming for him.

The officers subdued Scar and cuffed his wrists and ankles.

"Scar Johnson, you are under arrest."

"Y'all ain't got nothin' on me."

"We have enough evidence to put you away for life. I'm sure once we go through this place, we will find even more crimes we can charge you with."

Scar immediately thought about the blood in the basement that he hadn't cleaned up. *Fuck!*

As the officer read him his Miranda rights and went through the list of charges, Scar stopped listening. He just sat on the floor in the middle of the room, staring out the back window. He was caught, and he didn't have Tiphani to bail him out this time. He thought about his brother, Derek, and his mother, and all the foster homes he had been through.

As he reminisced, a black bird flew onto the windowsill. Scar and the bird stared at one another. Scar's only thought was: *Mu'fuckin' birds! I hate the fuckin' country.*

Chapter 17

Fall from Grace

The gavel came down with a thud. Mathias Steele sat there in shock. He had just been sentenced to life without parole for the attempted murder of the governor. How had he fallen so far so fast? It seemed like yesterday to him that he ruled Baltimore. He had every criminal paying him off, he had all the other politicians scared, and he could do whatever he pleased. Now he was headed to a maximum security prison.

"What now?" Mathias asked his attorney.

"They take you to prison. I'm sorry. We will fight this."

"I'm going to a white collar prison, right?"

The attorney shook his head. "I tried, but unfortunately you made a lot of enemies, and no one was willing to cut you a break. You're going to max. General population." His tone was sympathetic.

The court officers came to handcuff Mathias and lead him back to the bowels of the courthouse. They began the process of transporting him to his new home behind bars.

Mathias was forcing down the shitty food in the chow hall. He had been in the prison for a day and was miserable. He was fiending to get high, his body ached and itched all over, and his cellie was a huge Mexican dude who snored all night. It was his worst nightmare come true.

As he stared into the slop on his plate, three big, bald dudes surrounded him. The biggest of the bunch sat to his left.

"You new in here."

Mathias didn't look up from his plate and refused to say anything.

"You the mayor who a crackhead now, right?"

Mathias remained quiet. The big dude discreetly punched him in the ribs so the CO wouldn't see. "I asked you a question."

Mathias grimaced "Yes. That's me."

"Was that so hard? I'm Blade."

"Nice to meet you," Mathias begrudgingly answered but still wouldn't look at the man.

"You need anything in here, I'm your man."

This finally caught Mathias's interest, and he turned to look at the hulking six foot six monster of a man. "You get me high?"

"You gonna suck my dick?"

"What?"

"You wanna get high, you gonna have to suck my dick," Blade said.

"Fuck that." Mathias went back to eating.

"Nigga, you will be suckin' my dick. Believe that. Watch yo' back." Blade took another shot at Mathias's ribs as he got up from the table. The three men strode through the chow hall with confidence. They were obviously feared men in this prison.

Mathias was walking through the common room back to his cell. Even though he was now one of them, he still had his air of superiority and felt he was better than the rest of the convicts. He had no desire to hang with any of the common criminals he was surrounded by. He preferred to spend his time alone in his cell.

One of the men who had surrounded him earlier got up from a bench across the room and started toward him. The dude had his right hand cupped around a shank. Mathias saw this and turned in the opposite direction. The man picked up his pace and Mathias did the same. Mathias headed back toward the chow hall. As he turned a corner, he ran into a CO.

"Where are you going?" the CO asked. "To my cell."

The prisoner chasing Mathias saw him speaking with the guard and stopped his pursuit. He covered the shank and turned on his heels in the opposite direction.

"Wrong way, prisoner. This is the chow hall."

"I'm sorry, sir. This is my first day here. I'm all turned around."

"I'll take you there. That inmate looked like he wanted a piece of you."

Mathias was relieved to get an escort back to his cell. Little did he know that it was probably the worst decision he could have made. As he walked through the prison with the guard, all the other inmates saw him. He was immediately labeled as a friend of the guards and a snitch. He made enemies on the inside that he didn't even know he had.

That night, he got the beating of his life. Around two in the morning, his cell door opened. Blade had bribed the guards. He wanted to show Mathias who was boss. A dozen inmates were standing outside his cell, waiting for their chance to beat on the snitch.

Mathias was barely able to open his eyes before the first blow connected to his face. Growing up privileged, Mathias had never been in a fistfight. He had no idea what to do to defend himself, so most of the inmates were getting clean shots. They were relentless, and with Blade's encouragement, it made the inmates even more violent. Punch after punch connected with Mathias's body. Whenever he covered one part of his body, the inmates would focus on another. After a while, Mathias just passed out, yet the inmates still continued their attack. They were like a pack of wolves attacking a carcass. When it was all said and done, Mathias was beaten to within an inch of his life. He spent the next month in the infirmary.

After they found the blood in the basement at Scar's hideout, the authorities scanned the surrounding area and found the makeshift grave where Arnold was buried. Betsy was relieved to have found her husband's body to be able to give him a proper burial. It was a beautiful ceremony for a kind, warmhearted, caring man that left this earth much too soon.

Now Betsy sat in the front row of the courthouse as the verdict was read. She wanted to be there when they put the man responsible for her husband's death behind bars.

"On the charge of first degree murder, we, the jury, find the defendant guilty."

A buzz went through the courtroom. Betsy wept openly and hugged the prosecutor. There were other charges being read, but Betsy didn't listen. The murder charge was the only one she was interested in.

Even though she felt some satisfaction that Scar would be going away for life, she wasn't comforted. She would always have a hole in her heart. She would never get her husband back.

"I hope you rot in hell!" She jumped up from the court bench as Scar was being led out. He didn't even turn. He kept shuffling along with the court officers.

The judge banged his gavel. "Order!"

The attorney grabbed Betsy's shoulders to calm her down. He escorted her out the front and away from Scar.

After being processed and admitted, Scar walked through the common room with his prison-issued items. Inmates stopped what they were doing and watched as the famous Scar Johnson walked by. Each one was sizing him up, scheming to be the first one to take him down and make a name for himself.

When Scar got to his cell, there was a skinny little dude lying on the bottom bunk. Scar stood in the doorway and stared at the dude.

"Oh, hey. You my new cellie?" the effeminate man said.

"Get the fuck up. You on my cot, punk," Scar said menacingly.

"Uh-uh. This my bunk. You're on top."

Scar dropped his things and grabbed the dude out of the bunk. "Mu'fuckin' faggot. I said this my bunk." He pushed the dude out the cell door.

"You done fucked up." The effeminate man ran away.

Scar stripped the bed of the guy's sheets and put on his own sheets. Satisfied that he had asserted his dominance over his cellie, he lay down on the bed.

About fifteen minutes later, Blade entered Scar's cell with two men behind him. They picked Scar up off the bunk and went to town. They threw him to the ground and began the beating. Kicks were slamming into every part of Scar's body.

Scar was taken by surprise, but he put up a good fight. He grabbed one dude's foot and pulled him to the ground. He struggled to get on top of the inmate and started slamming his fist into the guy's face.

It didn't last long, as the other two pulled Scar off their friend. They pinned Scar down and focused all their anger on his head. Fists and feet rained down. Scar got in a couple more good shots, but in the end the three hulking men overpowered him. Scar was in a fetal position on the floor, covering up as best he could as they kicked him like a soccer ball.

"Don't ever call my bitch a faggot. You respect my bitch. Yo' ass sleeps on the top bunk," Blade commanded as he gave Scar one last kick to the ribs and walked out.

Scar's cellie came prancing in. "I told you, you fucked up." He stripped the bottom bunk of Scar's sheets and threw them on top of Scar. "And you can make my bunk up for me." Then he pranced back out of the cell.

Five minutes later, Scar had picked himself off of the floor and was sitting on the toilet. He was wiping blood from his mouth when Mathias appeared at his cell.

"Looks like you got a nice welcome. You deserve it," Mathias said.

"Fuck you." Scar snapped his head up to see who was mocking him. He was shocked to see the former mayor of Baltimore standing in his cell. It was even more shocking that he was wearing prison-issued clothing.

"The fuck you in for?" Scar asked.

"I tried to kill the governor."

"Oh shit. You a killer now," Scar mocked. He looked at Mathias and saw all the bruises and scars on his face. "Looks like you got worked over pretty good yo'self."

"I did. That's why I'm standing here right now."

"If you don't get out my face, I'll work yo' ass over too."

"Hold up. We need each other in here."

"The fuck you mean?" Scar spit blood through his legs and into the toilet.

These two men had been adversaries, battling for control of Baltimore. Scar had wanted this man dead and vice versa. Now Mathias was proposing they work together. Scar didn't trust Mathias's intentions.

"After I got worked over, I was in the infirmary for a while. I made some friends up there. I can get my hands on any painkiller I want." Mathias raised his eyebrows.

"I don't fuck with that shit."

"You aren't hearing me. You are a marked man in here. Everyone is going to take their shot at the big, bad Scar Johnson. If we work together, I could hold some of my clients off for a while."

"I don't need yo' protection," Scar said.

"No, you don't, but I need yours. I will cut you in on my business if you take out that bastard Blade. He's the one that just kicked your ass and the one responsible for landing me in the sick bay. I want that motherfucker dead. You take him out, you become head nigga, and we could run this place—you, the muscle, and me, the supplier. We split it fifty-fifty."

Scar thought about the proposal for a second. He couldn't believe how far they had fallen. They were once kings of Baltimore, and now they were fighting for their existence in a federal pen. He was surprised at the turn of events in his life.

"Fuck it. I'm in here for life. Might as well." Scar stood and shook Mathias's hand. "Now, let's get to planning. I wanna be runnin' this joint by the end of the week."

Chapter 18

Different Faces, Same Old Story

Cecil sat in the driver's seat of his sedan, staring intently at the front door of the bank in downtown Baltimore. He watched customers and employees walking in and out during a typical workday afternoon. The guard stood at the front door, oblivious to Cecil's peering eyes. He was too busy daydreaming about relaxing and fishing on his new boat when his retirement began in two months.

Cecil was getting anxious. He had been sitting there too long. His plan was to get in and out; it had already been forty-five minutes. Something needed to happen. The inactivity was making him uneasy.

Just as he was preparing to get out of the car and go into the bank, Cecil saw the manager go up to the guard, say something, and point to Cecil's car. Cecil stayed put, but he discreetly reached for his gun and placed it on the seat between his legs. He didn't like that they were aware of him. He was supposed to remain anonymous during this scam, and to protect his identity, he was willing to do whatever it took.

The guard and the manager looked at the car and then walked away from the door. Cecil thought about driving away, but he decided to stay put and wait out the situation.

The manager came back into view and opened the front door so the guard could walk through. A young woman dressed in business attire and carrying a large duffel bag followed the guard. The guard stopped just outside the door, surveyed the situation, and then escorted the woman toward Cecil's car. Cecil watched all of this transpiring and cocked his gun as the guard got closer to his vehicle.

The guard stopped at Cecil's car and, same as before, he surveyed the surrounding area. The woman he was escorting walked up to the rear passenger's door and opened it. Like a longshoreman throwing a sack of potatoes, she heaved the duffel bag into the back seat and slammed the door shut.

Cecil had a fleeting thought to throw the car into gear and speed off. Before he was able to turn on the car and do that, the woman opened the passenger's side door and got in the car.

"Got it, baby." She smiled.

"What's with the guard?"

"They wanted to escort me. Said it made them more comfortable." She shrugged her shoulders.

The guard tapped on the window. The woman opened the window.

"You take care—and be careful with all of that." The guard motioned with his head toward the backseat.

"We will," responded Cecil. He pressed the button to make the window close then started the car and drove away from the curb, leaving the guard to watch them drive down the street.

"What took so long?" Cecil asked.

"They insisted on counting it all out. It took a while. That's a lot of money," she answered.

"I started to think you dipped out the back door."

"Babe, you know I would never do that to you," the woman said.

Cecil had met the woman one day when he went into a coffee shop to grab some lunch. She had commented on how attractive Cecil's mismatched eyes were. Her comment sparked a conversation, and Cecil persuaded her to take a break and sit with him. He learned her name was Brooke and she was working her way through college at the coffee shop.

"How old are you, Brooke?" Cecil had asked as he sipped his coffee.

"I'm twenty-one," she said with the pride of someone who'd recently turned that pivotal age.

"What are you studying?"

"I want to be a teacher, but I don't know if I'll make it."

"What do you mean?"

"This job doesn't exactly make me rich. I'm behind on my tuition and may have to drop out."

Cecil and Brooke had continued to talk until her break was over. They exchanged phone numbers and planned to meet later that evening.

Cecil had left the coffee shop with a little bounce in his step. He felt that fate had intervened and he had met the perfect woman for his plan. He needed a woman to help him retrieve Tiphani's money from her offshore accounts. Brooke seemed to fit everything he was looking for—smart, respectable-looking, in need of money, and just gullible enough to not question him.

They had met that night and slept together, and then continued to sleep together every night for the next week. One night, while they lay in bed, Cecil proposed his idea to Brooke. She would call the bank overseas, he would provide her with all the information she needed, and then she would go to the bank and retrieve the cash. "Easy," he'd said. He would, of course, pay for her tuition and spending money.

Brooke hadn't thought twice about it. She trusted Cecil, and the thought of having her tuition paid made the decision even easier.

"What now?" Brooke asked as they drove down the highway with the bag of money.

"I don't know. Let's take a road trip."

"Okay, but I need to go home and get some clothes," Brooke said excitedly.

"We have five million in cash in the back seat. We can buy you whatever you need."

"That sounds better." She smiled from ear to ear. Cecil wasn't planning on taking a road trip. He was planning on leaving and never coming back. He had been in Baltimore too long. He hated the city and wanted to leave as soon as possible. To Cecil, it felt like the Wild West. He wasn't without sin, but he expected a certain amount of loyalty from people and he saw none in Baltimore. Everyone was all about themselves—except Brooke.

About an hour into the trip, Cecil pulled into a rest area with a visitors' center. There was one car in the parking lot, presumably owned by the person who worked at the visitors' center.

"What are we doing?" asked Brooke. "Need to stretch my legs."

"Okay. I need to pee anyway." She unfastened her seatbelt and exited the car. Cecil did the same and made sure to bring his gun. He followed Brooke as she walked to the bathroom in the back of the building.

Cecil now had a decision to make. He hated leaving witnesses who'd had any contact with him, but he liked Brooke. She was a sweet girl who wasn't trying to harm anyone.

Does she live or does she die? Cecil pulled out his gun and hid it behind his back as he closed the gap between them. Brooke heard footsteps coming up behind her as she reached the bathroom door. She quickly turned around.

"Babe, what are you doing?" She was relieved that the footsteps belonged to Cecil.

"Making sure you're safe."

"Thanks. I'm fine." She leaned in and gave him a peck on the cheek. "Can you go inside the visitors' center and see if they have any snacks?"

Cecil discreetly put the gun back in his waistband. "Of course."

They parted ways.

Brooke walked back to the car after she finished up in the bathroom. She was in a good mood. The stress she felt from school and work had disappeared for the first time in a long time. She was excited about the impromptu road trip. She didn't care where they went; she was just happy to be getting away for a while.

When she turned the corner and faced the parking lot, she stopped dead in her tracks. She was confused by what she saw—or actually, what she didn't see. Cecil's car had disappeared. She ran to the visitors' center to alert Cecil that his car was stolen. She frantically pushed through the door and ran to the first person she saw, the little old man sitting behind the desk.

"Where is my boyfriend?" she blurted out with wild eyes.

"Haven't seen him. In fact, I haven't seen anyone in about an hour. I'm about to close up."

"Tall black guy, one hazel eye, one brown. He didn't come in here?"

"Nope."

Brooke ran back outside and ran around the parking lot. She searched in every direction, but she saw nothing. Stopping in the middle of the parking lot, she slowly turned in a circle. She didn't understand what was happening. Where was Cecil? Where was his car?

The sun had set, and the parking lot lit up as the lights flickered on overhead. Brooke looked at the empty parking space where the car had been parked. This time, she noticed something on the ground. As she approached the object, she saw that it was the duffel bag that held the money. On top of the bag was a slip of paper with her name scribbled on it.

She was hoping it was a note from Cecil, some sort of explanation, but her hopes were dashed when she picked up the paper and saw the rest was blank. The bag wasn't full, but there were several stacks of cash left inside. Brooke counted the stacks. It was two hundred thousand dollars.

The little old man came from the visitors' center. "Did you find him?" he called across the lot. Brooke quickly stuffed the stack she was holding back into the bag.

"No. He left me."

The man came closer. "I'm sorry. I can give you a ride to the bus or train if you want."

"That would be great. Thank you."

Cecil was well on his way down the highway. When Brooke had turned around at the visitors' center and Cecil looked into her innocent eyes, he couldn't bring himself to kill her. He liked Brooke and wanted her to keep her innocence for as long as she could. That was why he decided to leave her. He didn't want her getting mixed up in his shady life, and he figured he was better off alone. He left her enough money to pay for her tuition, plus she wouldn't have to work for the rest of her time in school.

Cecil watched the road in front of him. There was no looking back. He was on to the next city, destination unknown.

***

In another slightly different visitors' center, a young corner boy sat slumped in a chair. He had a scowl on his face and on his head sat a Ravens cap. He tugged at his baggy jeans as he waited for the man he was visiting.

The door at the end of the long row of visiting booths opened up, and the boy sat up straighter. He kept the scowl, though. Scar sauntered into the room.

The guards directed Scar to the booth where the boy was sitting. Scar sat across from the boy and picked up the phone so he could hear his visitor on the other side of the plexiglass. The boy did the same.

Scar's face was bruised and swollen. It looked to the boy like he had been freshly beaten. In fact, he had. Scar's plan to take over the jail was not going according to plan. Blade had a stronghold on the prison, and Scar's reputation on the outside didn't help him at all on the inside. He had pissed off a lot of people when he was ruling the streets, and it was now coming back to haunt him. At the rate it was going, Scar would either be someone's bitch by the end of the month, or he would be dead. He certainly wouldn't be running the joint.

"Nigga, you ain't Flex." The beatings hadn't lessened Scars attitude any.

"Nah, I ain't. Flex sent me in his place."

Scar had gotten in touch with Flex in hopes that he would be able to get some help to him on the inside.

"This some bullshit. I ain't dealin' with no corner boy. Tell that nigga I only deal with him."

"I don't think so. Flex sent me to tell you that he runnin' shit now. Your time is over. Rot in hell, mu'fucka." The boy hung up the phone and walked out of the room, leaving Scar screaming at the top of his lungs and pounding on the plexiglass until the guards restrained him.

Flex listened intently as the boy recounted the story. When he finished, Flex peeled off five hundred dollars from the knot in his pocket and handed it to the boy.

"You done good, Slam," Flex told him. "Now, let's bounce. I got a meeting. You driving." He tossed the keys to his Suburban to Slam.

The boy hid his excitement. He'd just received five hundred dollars, and now he was going to get to drive Flex around. At thirteen years old, he had never seen so much money or had so much responsibility. He and his friends had been stealing cars to go joyriding since he was ten, so driving was nothing new to him. The excitement came from the fact that he was making something of himself, making his own money and chauffeuring the notorious Flex.

Slam pulled into the abandoned warehouse and parked the car in the center of the cavernous structure. Flex and his crew stepped out of the truck. A few minutes later, a caravan of black sedans and Suburbans with tinted windows came rolling into the warehouse. Flex and his crew stood and watched the theatrics of all the cars fanning out and coming to a synchronized stop.

After the cars had taken their places, a stretch limousine pulled in and stopped right next to Flex. Flex did nothing. He wasn't nervous, and even if he was, he wasn't about to show it. The back passenger's window rolled down.

"Get in," instructed the man in the car.

Flex took a briefcase from one of his crew and got into the limousine. Inside sat the new mayor of Baltimore. Mayor Richard Malenchek had taken over after a special election was scheduled. He won in a landslide victory, with the help of Governor Tillingham. There were rumors that the election was fixed, but there was no definitive proof.

"How are you?" the mayor asked. "Good, good."

"Do you have something for me?" The mayor looked down at the briefcase and raised his eyebrows.

Flex passed the briefcase to Mayor Malenchek, who placed it on his lap and flipped open the latches. He ran his hand over the cash inside.

"Like we agreed?"

"Six hundred Gs," Flex answered.

"Well, good luck to you on your business venture this year. I will make sure that my administration does not interfere for the next twelve months."

"See you in a year," Flex said.

Flex and the mayor shook hands to seal their deal.

"I think this is the start of a lucrative business deal for both of us." The mayor gave a wicked smile.

Flex exited the limousine. He stood with his crew and watched the caravan drive away from the warehouse. With the mayor in his pocket for the next year, Flex was now free to take over the drug trade in Baltimore without any repercussions or backlash.

The faces may have changed, but the corruption in Baltimore would always stay the same.